‖‖‖ ‖ ‖‖‖‖‖‖ ‖ ‖‖‖ ‖‖‖‖‖‖‖‖‖‖ ‖‖ ‖‖‖

W9-CLW-268

The Machines

MUSKELLUNGE: American nuclear fast attack submarine ca. 1978

JOSHUA L. CHAMBERLAIN: American nuclear dry deck shelter submarine (converted from SSBN to SEALs-special operations support)

ANTYEY III / HAZAEL: Russian / Syrian nuclear missile ("Oscar II+") submarine.

Running Deep

A Novel of Submarines, SEALs, and Souls

About the Author

Robert Evan Stevens is a former nuclear submariner and international business executive. An Annapolis graduate, he served on nuclear fast attack submarines and on nuclear fleet ballistic missile ("boomer") submarines. After leaving the Navy, he entered private business, serving as vice president and board of directors member for major international technical services firms.

The novel *Running Deep* is his first work of fiction. The story is based on his experiences as a submariner, as well as on his more recent business involvement with nations of the former Soviet bloc. Mr. Stevens is the author of numerous technical and business publications dealing primarily with applications of nuclear, subsurface utility engineering, and mission support technologies.

He currently is working on a sequel to *Running Deep*. Entitled *Great Was the Fall of It,* the new novel will continue the theme of intrigue and danger emerging from the fragile politics of the collapsed Soviet empire. As in the earlier work, the book will explore not only modern technologies and their impact on geopolitics, but also deeper truths revealed in the souls of characters caught up in extraordinary events.

Bob Stevens graduated from the US Naval Academy in 1965, from the Navy Nuclear Power Training Program/Submarine School in 1967, and from the University of Pennsylvania Wharton School of Business Advanced Executive Management program in 1985. He is a Registered Professional Engineer (P.E.) in five states, and a member of the Academy of Fellows of the Society of American Military Engineers. He received the Society's *President's Medal* in 1997, in part for founding and co-chairing its International Action Committee.

Bob and his wife Susan are active in applying Evangelism Explosion ("EE") training in nursing homes in their community. They call their outreach "EE-GEM" (Gospel to the Elderly Ministry). Bob and Susan have four sons. The older three Stevens boys are Naval Academy graduates currently serving on active duty around the world; the youngest attends Messiah College in Grantham, Pennsylvania.

Back cover black-and-white photograph is from the author's private collection (**USS PUFFER SSN652**, broaching following test of emergency blow). *NOTE: the author, then a US Navy lieutenant, was serving aboard PUFFER as Engineering Officer of the Watch during the operation when this photo was taken.*

All other cover photographs are courtesy of the United States Navy.

Running Deep

A Novel of
Submarines, SEALs, and Souls

Robert Evan Stevens

Winning the Battle Series
BOOK ONE

ANCHORHOUSE PUBLISHING COMPANY
Crofton, Maryland

Running Deep

A Novel of Submarines, SEALs, and Souls

Published by:
Anchorhouse Publishing Company
P.O. Box 3361
Crofton, MD 21114

Winning the Battle
Series - BOOK ONE

All rights reserved. No part of this book may be reproduced or transmitted in any form or by any means, electronic or mechanical, including photocopying, recording or by any information storage and retrieval system, without written permission from the author, except for the inclusion of brief quotations in a review.

Copyright © 2002
Printed in the United States of America

This book is a work of fiction. All characters, with the exception of persons such as VADM Hyman G. Rickover, Saddam Hussein, Hafez al-Assad, Mikhail Gorbachev, Boris Yeltsin, and Vladimir Putin (who are mentioned in the context of the story to enhance realism) are fictitious. Any resemblance of the fictional characters to actual persons, living or dead, is purely coincidental.

All quotations from scripture are from the King James Version.

Publisher's Cataloging-in-Publication
(Provided by Quality Books, Inc.)

Stevens, Robert Evan.
    Running deep : a novel of submarines, SEALs, and souls / Robert Evan Stevens. -- 1 st ed.
    p. cm. -- (Winning the battle series)
    LCCN 2001093042
    ISBN 0-9712254-9-4

    1. Nuclear submarines--Fiction. 2. International relations--Fiction. 3. United States--Politics and government--Fiction. 4. Russia (Federation)--Politics and government--Fiction. 5. Nuclear weapons--Fiction. 6. Terrorism--Religious aspects--Islam. I. Title.

PS3569.T4522R86 2001   813'.6
           QBI01-700906

Foreword

Dr. D. James Kennedy

Who could be more qualified to write a novel about submarines than a graduate of the United States Naval Academy who served aboard nuclear submarines? Who would be expected to handle the subject of international intrigue more than a former businessman who has had dealings with the government of the former USSR? And who better prepared to write a book than a professional journalist?

Robert Evan Stevens brings together in *Running Deep* this combined background of technical knowledge, political know-how, and masterful story-telling. From the very opening paragraph of Chapter One, he has the reader caught up in almost terrifying suspense, local color, and fascinating character portrayal that make turning to the next page seem almost compulsory.

Of course I'm not going to give the story away, but the setting is in the Syrian region of influence and the "news peg" revolves around a terrorist attack near Tel Hazor, Israel, that results in hostage-taking which includes Americans.

With the extremely facile touch of an experienced writer, Stevens is able to switch the reader from scene-to-scene and from sub-plot to sub-plot as he weaves a complex account of the adventures of a British archaeologist, a beautiful Syrian girl, an American tourist, a Russian engineer, and a Christian pastor.

I am particularly thrilled with the denouement toward which all of these components of the drama sweep the reader. It has to do with the presentation of the Gospel of Jesus Christ by the protagonist - a presentation which has the deepest personal meaning to me as a minister of that Gospel, and as Founder and President of Evangelism Explosion International. For the dialogue employed by the author is patterned precisely after the EE Outline which has been carried around the world to every nation over the past forty years.

What excites me - and, I believe, will excite every reader of this book - is the knowledge that Robert Evan Stevens is himself a former EE trainee who currently uses the method in ministering to elderly residents in an on-going Nursing Home Ministry.

Here is a man of great accomplishments in his military and business careers who has a wonderful testimony to share - and who has the abundant talent of creative writing which enables him to express that testimony persuasively, convincingly, and effectively. That, to me, is exciting!

I believe this novel is destined to become a bestseller. Its author has found that *Running Deep* has meaning not only to submariners, but to all people who have accepted the Gospel. He makes the point, by including the EE Outline in his narrative as a vital part of the flow of his story, that presenting the Gospel ought to be a vital part of the flow of our lives.

D. James Kennedy, PhD, is Senior Minister,

Coral Ridge Presbyterian Church;

Chancellor, Knox Theological Seminary;

Founder and President, Evangelism Explosion International;

and President and Speaker, Coral Ridge Ministries,

Television and Radio.

Contents

(Illustrations in Italics)

The People:

THE RUSSIANS

Vladimir Drednev -"The New Russian Salesman," he rocketed to the top along with Yeltsin, then Putin, and the rest. Now, in a new Russian regime, he has claimed the title of Minister of Defense. But he bows to no one...except, perhaps, the almighty dollar.

Admiral Sergei Leonovich Glutsin - Famous as the "Father of the Giant Submarines" in the old Soviet Navy, he agonizes over the crumbling of his once-mighty submarine fleet. But he has a plan to re-fortify the budget of his armada...

Dr. Kaspar Ivanov – He is thought to be the leader of a program to bring power plants to Russia's old allies in Syria. In reality, he is one of the few guardians of a terrible secret. How many will have to die before the secret is revealed?

Dr. Andrei Khalinko – He is director of Project *Titus*, hidden from the world above by the enormous caverns at Khokskya. But the world above was changing – and so was the mission of Project *Titus*.

Tatyana Patinova - She was Rypkin's close professional associate. They toiled at the secret, underground submarine construction site in Siberia's Khokskya. Others thought their relationship was more than professional. Does she dare to hope the same?

Viktor Rypkin - A young Russian engineer, he was involved in the proudest project of his career: the massive, secret new submarine, *Antyey III*. But now is he to be a pawn in his country's grab for Arab cash? He feels betrayed by his country and by the one girl he had ever loved. Who would be the next to betray him?

Captain First Rank Yuri Yevshenko – He was in command of the world's newest, most fearsome tactical missile submarine. But he has become merely a hired hand under the rule of the ship's new owners.

THE SYRIANS

Colonel Adib Bildad – He is the dreaded chief of Mutanabbi's special Security Forces. His brutality is feared even by his own people. American hostages come to know him as "Colonel Boots."

Jadeel Dovni - Viktor Rypkin, the Russian engineer, is enthralled by her beauty and by her mental capacity. She is introduced as Rypkin's interpreter on a new Russian-Syrian power plant project. But Viktor begins to suspect that she – and the project – may be more than they seem.

Walid El Zophar – Russian Admiral Glutsin detests him as a "Syrian snake." But Drednev knows that El Zophar is a valuable coach who has the ear of the right people within the new, aggressive Arab leadership circles.

Dr. Mustafa Mutanabbi – He is the brilliance behind the emergence of Syria as the aggressive new "Point of the Spear" of the Arab world. How far into the abyss of terror will his burning passions take him...and the rest of the world?

Shafiq Talas – Multi-lingual, multi-talented, he is one of El Zophar's ace agent-associates. His specialty is collecting nuclear materials.

Hazael Zabadi – He is the figurehead who has emerged as ruler of the new regime in Syria. He is embraced by the region's militant Arabs as their chief. But it is Hazael's nephew, Mustafa Mutanabbi who pushes the buttons.

THE BRITISH

Professor Archibald Pender-Cudlipp – He is an English archaeologist, toiling in the Syrian desert among his beloved ancient pots and bones. But he refuses to mind his own business. Will it cost him his darling wife? His project? His life?

THE AMERICANS

The "author" – He is a self-professed "stumbling journalist." A lead from an old classmate directs him to a major story. And the story runs far deeper than the headlines it generates.

Admiral Robert Copper – The three-star was a friend of Bill Winning from back in the old days. Now his former shipmate needs big-time help. How far can the admiral go to risk disobedience to his boss...the President of the United States?

Lieutenant Eric Lindahl - He leads an elite unit of Navy SEALs into a desperate mission. Trying to rescue hostages may be a daunting enough challenge, but what he faces beyond that has never been done in the chronicles of warfare.

Brett Nelson, Rob Petrocelli, John Scott – Together with their boss, Eric Lindahl, they comprise the Gold Unit of the Navy's SEAL Team Six. What they do is so sensitive that only the Secretary of Defense, or the President, himself, can order them into battle.

Pastor Gary Tarr – The pastor from the Winnings' church back home in Massachusetts, he preaches a Redeemer that was willing to *give His life a ransom for many.* Now, as one of the Hazor Hostages, will the preacher be willing to lay down his own life for his friends?

Steve Whitney - The "author" learns from this elderly man that *the effectual fervent prayer of a righteous man availeth much.*

Bill Winning - A former submariner, now a businessman, he is taken as one of the Hazor Hostages. Will America abandon him for fear of involvement in "another desert war?"

Susan Winning – She is a dedicated wife and mom, not one to take "no" for an answer when it comes to getting help for her missing husband. She gives life to the proverb: *Favour is deceitful, and beauty is vain: but a woman that feareth the LORD, she shall be praised.*

Introduction

THERE IS MUCH I CANNOT TELL. The government has, rightly I think, restricted some details from public revelation for reasons of national security. Obviously, there are still aspects of this episode that have yet to be resolved. But, there is also much that now can be told, and must be told.

It is that unique aspect, the untold story about the "Hazor Hostages" incident, that I want to relate. You have no doubt heard and seen the news of William Winning, a victim of last year's terrorist attack on the tour bus near Tel Hazor, Israel. You may be aware of the connection between the hostages and the terrifying rumor about the sale by the Russians to Syria of a new version of a top of the line *Oscar* class (*Kursk*-type) nuclear submarine. While particulars of these matters are discussed in this book, the story goes far deeper than missile-firing nuclear submarines.

Mr. Winning is in adamant agreement with the government that national security interests must be protected. He has, of course, cooperated fully with authorities in limiting his public interviews to security-cleared statements. But he is also determined that the full story be presented to the American people. He is not at all satisfied that media coverage to date has been balanced and comprehensive. It is for this reason that he contacted me to tell the story.

Bill Winning and I are not strangers. We were classmates at the Naval Academy at Annapolis. But our paths separated after graduation: he was picked up for the nuclear submarine program as one of Admiral Hyman G. Rickover's chosen; I went in to the destroyer fleet, and later to a (somewhat stumbling) career in journalism. I did not see Bill again until I recognized his face, familiar even with the graying and wrinkling of a quarter century, pictured as one of the Hazor Hostages early last year. Since then, of course, we have all seen him again and again in those countless interviews following his rescue.

It was another of our Annapolis brethren, Admiral Robert Copper, who suggested to Bill that he contact me to write this story. Admiral Copper has been a key figure in the Hazor Hostages situation. He currently is engaged in the ongoing Syrian

Oscar submarine affair. Bob Copper was four years ahead of Bill and me at the Naval Academy, and we did not know him well then. But Bill Winning's first tour at sea was as a shipmate of Bob Copper on the old nuclear attack submarine USS *Muskellunge*, back in the 1970s. It was this connection that established a friendship between Copper and Winning that was such an important part of the hostage story.

I had only known Admiral Copper from having interviewed him for articles that I had written for a Washington-area newspaper. While the admiral declined to be interviewed directly for this book, he did refer me to Captain Chip Depew, his chief of staff. Captain Depew was an enormous help in obtaining access to other U.S. Navy Sources (and to assure no breach in national security integrity). Chip also enabled me to gain access to declassified transcripts of recent testimony of Syrian agents.

Admiral Copper did agree to read the book's manuscript, and graciously offered that "it is about time this story gets told."

When Bill Winning called me to talk about the project, he wanted to introduce me to others of his colleagues whose story fills these pages. I have spent some of the most extraordinary hours of my life listening, often until late in the night, to the remarkable tale related by these men.

Talking to Bill Winning's wife, Susan, and her father, Dr. Steve Whitney, also has been a particularly rewarding experience. For those among us who may have discounted fervent prayer as "merely a crutch for the weak," these two will make you think again.

I have, wherever possible, based the dialogue and circumstances of this book directly on the words and accounts taken in interviews of principal participants. Some material is, obviously, based on conjecture, but I have attempted in such cases to adhere to facts or observations drawn from primary sources.

What follows is the account of an exceptional incident in modern history, one that is still unfolding. But, more important, at least to its central characters, is the story that until now has not been printed. It is the story of people, and not just the submariners, who have learned what it means to be running deep.

Chapter One

Tragedy at Jaris

Late September
The Village of Q'adi, in Northwestern Syria

T HE PROFESSOR AWOKE WITH A START. It was the voice again! The first time he heard it, he had dismissed it, assuming it was just someone in the next room-stall, whispering, perhaps talking in his sleep. In the darkness, and without his glasses, he could not make out the time from his wrist watch, but he reckoned it was around 3:00 am. He slept fully dressed, his wallet and keys in his pocket. He had removed his glasses and placed them carefully inside one of his boots, which he had tucked under his cot. This was not the kind of hotel where one takes any chances.

Calling this hovel a "hotel" was taking great liberties with the word. It was a shed, really, with stalls separated by curtains placed along the long central corridor. Each stall contained a straw-stuffed mattress on a cot and a rickety little wooden table upon which was placed a crude ceramic bowl. The only running water was a spigot on the end of a pipe that stood about one meter off the ground just outside the door at the far end of the hallway. About twelve paces beyond the water spigot was a latrine, a "two-holer."

Always before, Dr. Archibald Pender-Cudlipp had slept at Naamani's. Only slightly more commodious, to be sure, hardly a hotel by European standards, but at least Naamani's had rooms with walls, and real, wooden doors that could be shut and properly locked. Unfortunately, Naamani's was also more than four times the expense of this pigsty called "Faud's," the only other public accommodation in the little village.

Professor Pender-Cudlipp's budget had been cut, and he was being forced to take extraordinary measures to keep his little archaeology project alive. Staying at Faud's was certainly an extraordinary measure.

The professor placed his head back down on the cot, his rolled-up jacket serving as a pillow. He lay on his side, pulling the ragged wool blanket back up over his shoulders. He closed his eyes, but did not sleep. He waited. He listened. He heard a loud snore down the hall. Nothing more.

It had been a long day: a five-hour journey from Pender-Cudlipp's archaeological excavation site at the Wadi El-Jari, including a long delay at the Syrian army checkpoint at Jabal ad Farabi. He had endured a frustrating afternoon of trying to find necessary medicines and supplies, and then haggling for decent prices. He knew that the next day would be another long one. He would have to get to the Message Center early to send a message back to the University of London, his primary sponsor for the Jaris Project. Just before leaving Q'adi, he would obtain as much fresh provision, meat, fruits and vegetables as his old Ford Bronco could carry. Then it would be another grueling trip, over the Farabi Badlands of northern Syria to the Jaris Project site, perhaps another tedious confrontation with the Syrian checkpoint guards. His wife, Shari, was not well, and he was eager to return to camp with some of the medications that might ease her pain. Dear Shari. The professor began to drift again toward sleep...

No voice this time, but a noise, just a bit of a sound of ruffling cloth, made its way, ever so slightly, into the mind of the almost-asleep professor. Then another noise, a gravelly, sliding sound. And it was nearby. It almost sounded as if it were coming from directly below his cot. Archibald Pender-Cudlipp did not move, but his eyes opened wide, his ears seeking clues.

A second set of noises, more of the slight, scratching, sliding sounds, came, but this time from further toward the foot of the cot.

Earlier, before he had turned in for the night, Pender-Cudlipp had pulled the curtain that served as his "door," and had latched it with a safety pin. It was dark; only a slight trace of light, from the single bulb that lit the entire central corridor, penetrated into the professor's stall. Only a slight trace of light, but it was just enough.

A hand, large and covered with dark hair, reached up from below the cot, directly before Pender-Cudlipp's bulging eyes. The professor froze, momentarily, in incredulity and fright. Slowly, the hand moved closer to the professor's chin. Then the silence was shattered.

A small, dark figure erupted out from under the cot. His head was shrouded with a burnoose; a cloth covered his nose and mouth. He grabbed frantically for Pender-Cudlipp's chin with his left hand. His right hand, gripping a tiny dagger, emerged from under a dark shawl.

Just as the intruder made his move, Pender-Cudlipp was ready with a counter-attack. He exploded from the bed, both hands bringing his blanket up in a furious flurry. Shouting with a savage growl, Archibald pulled the blanket down over the intruder's head and arms. The professor pushed his stunned attacker as hard as he could, across the room. The little man stumbled into the front "door"-curtain, lost his balance and crashed to the floor, getting entangled in the curtain as he fell.

Behind him, Archibald Pender-Cudlipp saw the other intruder rush toward him. The professor grabbed for the ceramic bowl on the table next to him, and swung at the shrouded head of the second man. The man ducked, and Pender-Cudlipp missed his head, but directed a strong blow along the back of one of his shoulders. The attacker fell face down, near where the professor's boots lay at the head of the cot.

Pender-Cudlipp spun around to prepare for another attack from the first assassin, but that one had scrambled to his feet, and was racing down the hall toward the back entrance. The second attacker had regained his footing and lunged past the professor, out into the hall, close on the heels of his partner.

Before he had a chance to feel relieved for having survived the attempt on his life and wallet, Dr. Pender-Cudlipp noticed something that made his blood boil. As the second attacker made his escape, barging through the rear door of the hotel-shed, the professor noticed that the thief had made away with his boots and - worse - his glasses!

Pender-Cudlipp's vision was bad, and getting worse. How could he continue the archaeological work at Jaris without his glasses? And this was the only remaining unbroken pair he had. It would take months to replace them, and how could he fit that into his budget?

"Come back here, you scum!" Archibald shouted at the top of his voice, in perfect Arabic. "You break those glasses, I break your worthless neck!" He ran out of the door and into the Q'adi night after the two thieves.

He heard their footsteps racing down an alley off to his right. He sprinted down the alley, in a seething rage. But it was a futile chase, and he knew it. All he could accomplish now was to get lost in the darkness of this filthy slum, this section of the village that they called Das-Q'adi. And that would merely give his attackers a second chance to slit his throat and to finish their task of filching his wallet.

Pender-Cudlipp returned to the back door of the hotel, walking in his stocking feet, still fuming with anger. A small group of hotel clients had gathered near the door, and others peeked from behind their stall curtains, curious about the ruckus. They had seen this big Englishman many times before, knew he was one of the archaeologists that occasionally graced their desert looking for pots and bones. They knew he was in the village every week, usually staying overnight. They knew he spent much money and that he spent it carefully; he normally bargained with skill.

"What is all this? What have you done?" The hotel proprietor, clad in his ragged nightwear, had emerged from his room, near the front of the shed.

"Looks as though you have a problem with your blasted curtains, Faud. Better get someone in here to fix it." The professor mumbled in English through gritted teeth as he shoved past the obese old Syrian and out the front door into the street. He knew that the office of the local police prefect was only two blocks down the street.

A sergeant was on duty. It was 3:22 am, it had been a quiet evening, and the sergeant dozed at his desk. He jerked to attention as the professor burst into the office, without so much as a knock on the door. To the sergeant, Pender-Cudlipp looked agitated. Worse, he looked furious, and he wore no shoes.

"Professor Archie!" Sergeant Butros fumbled for an appropriate greeting. "You are up early this morning!" Staring down at Pender-Cudlipp's stocking feet, he queried, "Er...uh... have you misplaced your boots?"

"Butros," fumed the professor, "I had plenty of help 'misplacing' my boots. Two of your cronies from Das-Q'adi tried to slit my throat just a few minutes ago, while you were in here sound asleep. Prefect Shishakly will not be pleased that his sergeant sleeps while guests in his city are assaulted less than two blocks away. They didn't get my throat and they didn't get my wallet, but they jolly well did get my boots. And, Butros, my glasses were in my boots."

Butros reached over to a pile of papers that were in a basket to his right. "All right, all right, Professor. We cannot watch all the bandits from Das-Q'adi at the same time. Here is a complaint form. Have a seat. Please relax. Fill this out, give me all the details, and I'll get somebody on it first thing in the morning."

Pender-Cudlipp's voice grew in volume along with his anger. "Sergeant Butros, I can't see your stinking forms without my glasses, and *this* is the 'first thing in the morning.' I suggest you get off your duff, and get over to Das-Q'adi and," the professor lowered his voice and spoke in slow, deliberate Arabic, *"find my boots and find my glasses, and find the swine that tried to slit my throat!"*

Archibald Pender-Cudlipp walked barefoot down the hard-packed dirt street from the prefect's office to the Message Center, four blocks away, in the center of the market area of Q'adi. It was nearly 7:30 am, well past dawn. He and Sergeant Butros had been totally unsuccessful in finding anyone who would admit to having seen Professor Archie's attackers or his boots. Pender-Cudlipp began to realize the futility of his search. And time was running short. Now he had to get a message off to London. The university expected a weekly report on progress at the digs, and, unfortunately, there had been precious little progress to report in recent weeks

Mostly, the lack of progress was London's fault. They had cut back his budget so drastically that he had been forced to dismiss two Syrian locals from his team. One other local, one of the most experienced of the lot, had quit in disgust. That left Archie with a staff of only six, including Shari and himself. Hardly enough to keep up the pace that his benefactors at the university would expect. If it were not for the small grant he had received from the Americans at the Smithsonian, his work at Wadi El-Jari would probably have died.

It was this work to which Professor Archibald Pender-Cudlipp had come to devote his life. Ten years before, he had been living a most comfortable life. An assistant professor of Middle Eastern archaeology at the University of London, he had been able to make frequent jaunts to Syria, Jordan, Turkey and Israel. It was enough to keep his interest fresh and his knowledge up-to-date. He had mastered the Arabic language and felt generally at home in Arab culture, although he had never stayed long in the area at any one time. But, he knew this was not true archaeology. He was studying only what others had found. A restless urge had grown in him to make a dent of his own in the unfolding of knowledge of the region's incredible history.

At about that same time, he had met a most exceptional girl. Shari al-Kuwatly was the daughter of a wealthy Damascus merchant. She had been sent to London to go to college and, so her father had wished, to learn the ways of the West. Her father dearly loved his bright-eyed little girl, and was well aware that her prospects for a happy life were much greater in London than they would be in her native land.

But, her passion was for this land. Not for the nation of Syria, nor its government, nor even its people, but for the land itself. To her, the deserts and wadis, the mountains and the seashore, the extremes of wet and dry, cold and hot: these were what she loved. From the time she was a little girl, she had taken her greatest joy from visits to the country, poking about the ruins of old forts, immersed in ancient stones and shards.

Shari had enrolled in Pender-Cudlipp's class at the university, and had dominated it with her knowledge of, and delight in, the untapped wealth of archaeological resources of her land. She had also begun to capture the affection of the professor. Up to then a confirmed bachelor, Professor Archie had never before met a woman with the same zeal for esoteric adventure and the same sense of the deep, deep significance of digging into the past. They were married in London shortly after Shari received her degree from the university.

Shari had suggested an idea that had immediately appealed to Professor Pender-Cudlipp. As a girl, she had visited several archaeological sites near the ancient city of Antioch, in what is now southern Turkey. Antioch had been a powerful metropolis during the days of the Hellenistic Empire established by Alexander the Great. In the Christian era, it had become an early center of the new Church. The Bible records that it was in Antioch that followers of "the Way" were first called "Christians." Several small, but thriving communities had grown up around Antioch, including one about 70 kilometers to the south, in the territory of modern-day Syria, a little village known to ancient historians by its Latin name, *Jaris*. Shari related the legend of Jaris to the fascinated professor.

The Jaris of two thousand years ago had been a prosperous little community, occupying an oasis in the otherwise barren region north of the Farabus mountain range. Today the mountains are known in Arabic as the Jabal ad Farabi, and the region is almost entirely barren. But, two millennia ago there was considerable trade that passed through Jaris from Jerusalem and Damascus in the south to the great city of Antioch, only two days by camel caravan from Jaris. Much of the Jaris Valley was cultivated, and it produced a fine variety of grapes, as well as a highly sought-after fabric woven from the wool of the hardy stock of sheep bred there.

Christians began coming down to Jaris from Antioch after having been taught by some remarkable preachers named Saul, Barnabas and John Mark. They settled in Jaris and told the people there about what they called, in their native Greek language, the *euangelion*, the "good news." These evangelists succeeded, in very short order, in converting nearly the entire population of the little community.

But world history was in the process of taking an ugly turn. Nero had found his gory way to the throne of the Roman Empire; persecution of the Christians in Rome was about to enter a holocaust stage. Things were not much better for the followers of Jesus in the east. Persecution had spread nearly everywhere, and did not fail to reach even the relatively remote village of Jaris. Arrests, imprisonment, and execution of the Jaris Christians became common. As in Rome, the occupants resisted bravely, and had constructed a system of "catacombs," underground hideouts, that also served as graves for the martyrs.

No one knows exactly what happened, but on a dreadful day about the year 65 AD, a company of Roman soldiers, evidently accompanied by local militia troops, swooped down on Jaris, killing every man, woman and child in the village. All the supposedly secret catacombs in the area were entered and scourged. And, that little town, once prosperous and fertile, simply ceased to exist. It was so completely annihilated that little memory remained even of its existence.

But Shari knew where it was, and was convinced that an archaeology dig in the region, now called the Wadi El Jari, could result in major and valuable finds. Her father had agreed to help finance an initial excursion, and the university had also been enthusiastic about the project, agreeing to support it with a budget and with staffing help.

Project Jaris had begun six years before, full of the excitement of new discovery. Several important discoveries had indeed been made, and had been sent back to London for study and display. But then Shari's father died, and the executors of his estate, Shari's brothers, had little sympathy for the venture. Meanwhile, too, the university had succumbed to the worldwide recession and found it necessary to cut archaeology projects' budgets across the board. At that time also, the Syrian government had fallen into the jingoistic hands of Hazael Zabadi, full scale war with Israel seemed imminent, and Archibald and Shari found themselves struggling to keep the project, and themselves, alive.

Now, this matter of sending messages, which he did every week, had become Professor Archie's lifeblood. He had to keep the interest level of his benefactors high. But, to do this, he had to produce results. And, to get results, he had to have more support in terms of money, workers, and equipment.

Archibald had drafted messages, neatly printed on bits of notepaper, to two of his sponsor agencies. He handed the first of these messages to the Syrian Army official censor, Captain Fatnabbi, who was on duty at the Message Center in Q'adi:

TO: DR. J.W.L. MCQUAID
    PROFESSOR, DEPT OF MIDDLE EASTERN
      ARCHAEOLOGY
    UNIVERSITY OF LONDON
    LONDON 75, ENGLAND, U.K.

NO SUCCESS SO FAR IN SECTORS BD 80 TO 85.
THREE LOCALS RESIGNED AFTER LAST CUTS IN
BUDGET. REQUEST SEND TWO ADDITIONAL
VOLUNTEERS WITH OWN FINANCIAL SUPPORT.
REQUEST PROFESSOR MCGREGOR EXPEDITE
SENDING TOSHIBA LAPTOP WITH SUPPLY OF
DISKS. SECTORS AP TO AR 65 LOOK PROMISING
AS BURIAL SITE CIRCA 65 AD.

> DR. A.A. PENDER-CUDLIPP
> Q'ADI
> AL-JUMHURIA AL-ARABIA AL- SURIA
> 655JAS/841QAF (OUTCODE)

Captain Fatnabbi read the message carefully. His English was incomplete. "What is this 'T-O-S-H-I-B-A   L-A-P-T-O-P,' Professor? It is furniture, or automobile?"

"No, Captain. It is a small computer. It is operated by a battery and it fits on your lap." Pender-Cudlipp explained tolerantly, in his fluent Arabic. It did not pay to lose patience with the censors. And Archibald knew Captain Fatnabbi well. Fatnabbi did not possess great patience. "I need it," explained the professor, "for recording data of the items I have found at the Wadi El Jari. The disks are like phonograph records that record the data."

"You are not finding success in your exploration, I see," said the captain as he studied the professor's face.

"We have found many important artifacts, Captain," said Pender-Cudlipp. "But I was hopeful that this particular sector would turn up more than it has, so far." Archibald handed over to the captain the second message, which was similar to the first:

TO: DR. SAMUEL G. GROVER
DIRECTOR OF FIELD OPERATIONS
SMITHSONIAN INSTITUTION
900 JEFFERSON DRIVE
WASHINGTON, D.C. 20560
U.S.A.

NO SUCCESS SO FAR IN SECTORS BD 80 TO 85.
AGREE WITH YOU ABOUT PROSPECTS FOR
GRAVES AT SECTORS AP TO AR 65. HAVING
STAFFING PROBLEMS, REQUEST ANY SELF-
SUPPORTING VOLUNTEERS YOU MAY BE
ABLE TO SEND.
>   DR. A.A. PENDER-CUDLIPP
>   Q'ADI
>   AL-JUMHURIA AL-ARABIA AL- SURIA

655JAS/841QAF (OUTCODE)

Fatnabbi read the second note, studying it carefully. He then handed both notes over to the transmitter operator, who typed the messages in to the machine and sent them on their electronic way. The message contents were recorded in the Message Center Log and the original notes were returned to Pender-Cudlipp. He paid his fee to the clerk and departed.

Now it was time for other business, and to get back to Shari as quickly as possible. Archibald stepped, barefoot, out of the little shack that served as the Message Center. The sharp stones in the street cut at the soles of his feet and rekindled the anger that had burned in him at the audacity of those Das-Q'adi bandits, to steal his boots and his glasses. To Archibald, that was nearly as despicable as the attempt to slit his throat.

Now he had to hurry to get to the produce bazaar. This was Friday, the one day of the week that fresh produce could be had in the village. It was this day that the farmers, what few there were in the region, brought their meager crops to town. They set up their flimsy wooden booths at about 8:00 in the morning; most of the worthwhile produce would be sold out by noon. Of course, other merchants also took advantage of the Friday Morning Market to hawk their huge variety of wares. For about four hours every Friday morning, the little village of Q'adi came to life. Just as was Archibald Pender-Cudlipp's custom, nearly everyone in the region headed for Q'adi on Friday. It had been this way for centuries.

Adding to Archibald's anxiety was that he knew he must return quickly to the Wadi. Shari's physical condition had rapidly deteriorated over the past three weeks, and recently she had been in considerable pain. He had obtained some medicine for her from an old physician who lived in the village; one of Archie's few friends in town. Doctor Al-Afaz, who had known Shari's father, had advised Archie to bring her with him on his next visit, despite how she might protest. Shari would undoubtedly continue to refuse: she hated Q'adi and was much happier at the dig site. At least Archie could, perhaps, ease her pain with the medicine. And Shari would be expecting him to return this afternoon.

The professor tried to hurry through the bazaar, but the quality of the produce this week seemed exceptionally poor and he had to take his time to be careful to get his money's worth. There was no organization to the arrangement of the booths. It was not uncommon to see meat vendors set up shop directly adjacent to a manure monger's filthy stand. It was never the same from week to week; it was strictly first-come-first-served as far as the positioning of the merchants. Huge swarms of flies competed with ragged customers for the fresh goods, and the clamor and stench of the bazaar would have nauseated any stranger to the scene. This was not a place for tourists.

As Pender-Cudlipp rummaged through the bazaar picking out what he could of decent fresh produce, his eye fell on an astonishing sight: his boots! Unmistakably, certainly, his boots!

"Scum!" Pender-Cudlipp muttered to himself in Arabic. "What utter gall. It has been less than six hours since those swine stole my boots, and now they are already back on the market!" The booth's merchant hovered nearby, haggling with a local youth over the purchase of an American-made pocket knife. But the merchant also kept an eye on the Englishman: a prospective customer?

Archie strolled past the boots, pretending to be casually inspecting everything on the table. The price of the boots, marked on a little card tucked in the laces, was preposterous. Even after haggling it would be absurd. And for him to shell out his precious, limited funds in any amount for his own boots was equally absurd. And, to think that Butros, or anyone in the prefect's office, would take his side in this matter was just as unthinkable.

Archibald removed his old Meerschaum pipe from his breast

pocket. He took a pouch of tobacco from the same pocket and filled the pipe as he slowly, calmly walked away from the boots toward an open area nearby. He took a match from his hip pocket and struck it, lighting the pipe. As he walked past a refuse container located at the end of the merchant's booth, he flipped the match, still lit, in the container. He then walked slowly back toward his boots, looking indifferently in the other direction.

The refuse container was full of paper and a straw-like packing material. In less than ten seconds, it was a roaring inferno. The canvas top to the merchant's tent soon became engulfed in flame, and complete chaos broke out in the Q'adi Bazaar. People rushed with blankets, and then cups of water, then buckets. Police whistles pierced the smoky air. Frightened shouts of "*FIRE! FIRE!*" stirred the Friday-morning crowd into a mob.

Archibald Pender-Cudlipp casually strolled along with the escaping mob. He stopped only to back into a quiet corner to squat on a wooden box and pull on his newly re-acquired boots. To his great delight, in the toe of his left boot he found, perfectly intact, his precious glasses.

At just that moment, Sergeant Butros rushed past, bucking the flow of the throng, trying to get to the scene of the fire. He stopped at the sight of the big, bespectacled Englishman, with the lit pipe and the big smile, putting on his boots.

"Pender-Cudlipp! What is happening here?" Butros gasped. "Ah! I see you have discovered your boots. And your glasses. Your fortune is good! Obviously better than Sami's!" He indicated the hapless merchant who was beating out the last sputtering flames that smoldered in his refuse container. "People should be much more careful with lighted matches, should they not, Professor?"

"They should, indeed, Butros!" Archibald smiled tightly as he picked up his bag of fresh vegetables and fruits and headed for his vehicle.

––––––––

Professor Archibald Pender-Cudlipp pressed hard on the accelerator of his ancient Ford Bronco. It had been a welcome gift from an American benefactor, and had seen many thousands of miles of Syrian dust, but never before at this pace. The professor bounced violently in his seat as he sped along the rugged trail leading north out of Q'adi. Archie had not expected such a miserable delay in the village. Now, all his attention was focused on Shari and on getting back to camp as quickly as possible. He pushed his vehicle to the limit. He hoped the shock absorbers, axles, and wheel bearings could stand the punishment.

According to the map, the direct-line distance between Q'adi and the professor's dig at Wadi el-Jari was thirty-five kilometers. The road that connected them was nearly three times that distance: ninety-seven kilometers of winding, rocky road that often was more of a mountain trail than a road. It normally took the professor about four hours to make the trip, and that was only when he was not held up en route by a rockslide or by the Syrian army. This latter factor had recently become especially troublesome. Since the Assad government had fallen to the even more militaristic Hazael Zabadi and his henchmen, the army checkpoints had become more frequent, and the soldiers' attitudes more belligerent. Occasionally these checkpoint stops had cost the professor an hour or more. They also frequently cost a crate of oranges, a loaf of fresh bread, or a box of cigars: *baksheesh*, small "payment" for the soldiers' trouble. Often the detainment time could be reduced if the *baksheesh* was attractive enough to the guard. Pender-Cudlipp fervently hoped that he would not run into such a delay this particular morning. Shari could not stand much more of a wait.

The professor was making good time. He knew this road well. Focusing intently on the mission at hand, he was setting, by his reckoning, a new personal record for the trip. At this rate he would be able to reach the crest of Jabal ad Farabi in about two and one half hours, a full half-hour under his normal time. From the crest, it was only one more hour to his camp, at normal speed. Unless...

The road ahead of Pender-Cudlipp took a sharp turn to the right, around a steep hillside. Having rounded the corner, Archibald could see, far down the road, at the base of the valley, a flurry of activity. Unwelcome to Pender-Cudlipp's eye, the activity included one of the security checkpoints he so dreaded.

Not that he had anything to hide, but he knew that this would mean a delay. Pender-Cudlipp slowed the vehicle, muttering curses in English and Arabic at this misfortune.

As the Bronco pulled up to the guard station at the bottom of the valley, Pender-Cudlipp could see that new, peculiar construction work was underway in the area. A culvert-bridge now spanned the little wadi, and a bulldozer had carved a rough road up the far mountainside. Construction equipment was in place, busily preparing the site for some sort of building. The professor could see several flatbed trailers loaded with pre-fabricated concrete slabs, rolls of corrugated metal, and wire fencing. A small guardhouse had been nearly completed, constructed of concrete block masonry at the point where the new road turned off from the old, main road.

The Bronco rolled to a stop. Two soldiers emerged from the new guardhouse. One of the soldiers, a corporal, carried an AK-47 semi-automatic rifle. The other was a man whom Pender-Cudlipp knew all too well. It was Colonel Adib Bildad. The professor had met the colonel before, about two months previously. Bildad had led a group of security agents on an "inspection" of the dig site at Wadi El-Jari. They were evidently looking for information about a young American archaeology student that had worked at the dig during the previous summer. Archie learned later from one of the soldiers in Q'adi that this man Bildad was, in fact, a top security agent. He was reported to be very well connected to high levels within the Zabadi government. The professor was surprised, and not very pleased, to see him here.

The armed soldier signaled for Archie to get out of his vehicle. The professor was forced to place his hands on top of the vehicle while the soldier pat-searched him.

Colonel Bildad said, in his threatening voice, "Professor Pender-Cudlipp, you have picked a most inopportune time to come our way. Certainly you will not object if we look through your things."

Pender-Cudlipp suffered the indignity of the search with a wry grin. He craned his neck around to look at Bildad. "Your guy has a bigger gun than I have. How can I object?"

"How true." Bildad took Pender-Cudlipp's wallet and his visa case that were handed to him by the guard. He began to rummage through the papers. "Come with me, Dr. Pender-Cudlipp. I have a few questions to ask you."

The two men went inside the still-unfinished guardhouse, to

get out of the bright late-morning sun. The guard took a seat outside in the shade of the building.

Bildad began asking questions, many of them redundant from their earlier meeting. Many of the questions were about the young American archaeologist. "We have reason to believe," Bildad explained at length, "that this student was, in fact, an Israeli agent. You understand, of course, why we are so curious about him."

Bildad went on to ask many other questions. He asked about Project Jaris. He asked about the budget cutbacks from the University of London, and he asked numerous questions about the workers at the site. Pender-Cudlipp again and again attempted to interrupt the flow of Bildad's questioning to explain to the colonel about Shari's condition, and how urgent it was for her to receive her medication. Bildad simply disregarded the professor's appeals.

After nearly an hour, Bildad finally paused in his barrage of questions. The colonel walked to the door of the guardhouse, leaned out, and ordered the guard to unload the Bronco to search for contraband. Pender-Cudlipp objected strenuously, but the colonel ignored him.

Bildad took his seat again and continued his questioning. He asked the professor about his opinions on various matters. He asked questions about Israel, about Syria and about the new Syrian president, Hazael Zabadi. He asked questions about the position that Archie's own country, the United Kingdom, would take in a conflict between Israel and Syria. Pender-Cudlipp knew all the right answers, but he wondered if his insincerity showed through to the colonel.

More time passed. As Archie thought of his ailing wife suffering in the unusually high noonday heat, he became more impatient. "Excuse me, Colonel. My wife is waiting for me now at the project site. As I have told you, she is quite ill. It is essential that I get to her quickly with medication that can relieve her suffering. I have nothing that is contraband. I have no knowledge that can help you. But if you have more questions for me, will you please come with me to the camp? I will be glad to answer every question as we travel. I will then give you a ride back here, after I have given my wife her medicine. But, I beg you, please let me proceed."

Archie glanced out the door, and noticed that his Bronco had been completely unloaded by the guard. Its contents, boxes of fruit, bags of vegetables, cans, and bottles of every kind of provision were scattered all about the vehicle.

"Possibly your guards are thirsty?" said Pender-Cudlipp as he rose, attempting to leave.

Bildad did not restrain the professor, but followed him out toward the Bronco. He walked over to a crate of fresh oranges and tapped it with his boot. The guard smiled, picked up the crate, and carted it off toward the guardhouse.

"You may proceed," said Bildad, "but I tell you, *do...not... leave...the...roadway* before you get to the Wadi. I tell you again, Professor, do not leave the roadway. *It would be fatal.*"

The professor raced the car recklessly over the rugged terrain. Now, instead of playing games to see whether he could break his speed record for the trip, he was trying to make up for lost time. By now it was mid-afternoon and the relentless sun scorched the landscape. It was abnormally hot, even for this time of the year. He knew that Shari, without her medicine, would be suffering intensely in this heat.

Finally, Professor Pender-Cudlipp reached the turn to the road that ran along the steep, narrow chasm known as the Wadi El-Jari. He had only about twenty minutes more to travel.

Ahead, along the road, the professor thought he could see something moving toward him. A goat? Some other animal?

As he got closer, Pender-Cudlipp could see that it was no animal, but a man, a man running - in this heat! The professor soon recognized the lean form and dark features of Khalil Hinnawi, the professor's oldest and most-trusted Syrian worker from the digs. The man was running at full speed down the center of the road, frantically waving his hands at the approaching professor. Archie skidded to a stop, unfastened his seat belt, and bolted out of the door of the Bronco. He ran forward to meet the delirious Khalil Hinnawi.

"What is it, what is it, Hinnawi?"

The Syrian fell, nearly exhausted, into Pender-Cudlipp's arms. "It is Mrs. Pender-Cudlipp, Professor! She is dead! She is ...."

Khalil Hinnawi broke into uncontrollable sobs.

Pender-Cudlipp helped the Syrian toward the Bronco.

"Calm yourself. Calm yourself, Hinnawi." Pender-Cudlipp opened the passenger-side door and helped the man in. "Here, let me get you some water!" He reached back into the rear of the vehicle and pulled forth a large container of water, unscrewed the top, and handed it to his associate. "What are you saying? You are delirious! What are you saying, Hinnawi?"

Khalil Hinnawi took a long draught of the water, then set the container at his feet. Slumped over, he broke once again into tears. "She is dead, Professor."

Pender-Cudlipp stood silent for a moment. He looked up toward the blistering sun, and pounded his fist on the roof of his vehicle. No tears came, but he pounded his fist until it was worn bloody.

Chapter Two

<u>Test Depth</u>

December
Southeast Expressway, outside Boston

BILL WINNING CRANKED UP THE HEAT A NOTCH. Winter's going to hit hard this year, he thought. The old van was not very comfortable in cold weather. Bill usually drove the newer Neon for his commute to his office in Boston, but Susan had taken the little car when she left earlier this morning. She had gone over to Cambridge where she had been invited to be part of a television program.

"The *Gregg Bentley Show*," muttered Bill, to himself. "I'd really love to see this!" He knew that Bentley had built his reputation, and the popularity of his call-in show, by expertly, brutally, ripping his interview "guests" to shreds. Bill was against her doing this. He had warned Susan not to let herself in for the punishing treatment he knew she would receive. But if there ever was a match for Bentley, it was Bill's wife Susan. This was especially true when the subject of the debate was dear to her heart, and most especially when she was told she "couldn't handle it." There was no talking her out of it.

Bill had wanted to be there, if only to console her afterward. But they agreed it was more important for him to get to the office today to clean up matters there. He was a vice president at a small engineering company in the city, and he took his responsibilities seriously. He and Susan planned to begin a long-awaited vacation trip the next day. He wanted no loose ends to hang over him while he was away.

Winning turned off the radio. No point in listening to the traffic report. He was stuck in dead slow on the so-called "expressway" and had no alternate route, anyway. Listening to the news didn't perk up things: Economy slumping. Threat of war worsening between the Syrians and the Israelis. Budget battles in Congress.

He had seen a program the night before about Congress's cutting military budgets. His old friend and shipmate, Bob Copper, now a three-star in the Pentagon, was one of the panelists. "Did a pretty good job, too, for a nuke," chuckled Winning to himself.

Bill's thoughts began to roll back to that time, more than twenty years before, when he was a nuke, too, riding the boats as a nuclear submariner. He remembered those days when he and his shipmates were the stalwart first line in the death-struggle with the old Soviet Union…back when he first met Bob Copper.

As he crawled forward in the Boston rush hour traffic, his mind returned once again to an episode from his youth, an event that often emerged in his mind at idle moments…and also in his nightmares:

April 1978
North Atlantic Ocean
Aboard nuclear attack submarine *USS Muskellunge*

For Lieutenant (Junior Grade) Angus William Winning II, it was time to begin running deep.

The submarine's 1MC general announcing circuit crackled throughout the ship.

"Now, this is the captain." The voice of the commanding officer burst out of the speakers. "We will be taking the ship down for her initial dive to test depth. We will be going down in increments of 250 feet to one thousand feet, then in increments of 100 feet the rest of the way. Now, all hands man test dive stations."

Young Bill Winning had been waiting for this announcement from his normal steaming duty station in the tiny enclosed area called "Maneuvering," located in the ship's engine room. The announcement was Bill's signal to make way down to the engine room bilges, his assigned test dive station. No hurry, it would take only a few seconds to climb down into the bilge area with a flashlight where he was to inspect for leaks as they went deep. Having reported aboard *USS Muskellunge* only the prior weekend,

Bill was the junior officer aboard. Inspecting the bilges for leaks was about all the responsibility they were willing to hand him.

Winning tried to appear calm as he settled his half-drained coffee mug into its plastisolled holder near the Reactor Plant Control Panel. He had to force himself to make every move slowly to avoid betraying the tension that was mounting inside him.

Bill Winning had just completed nearly six years of education and training. Four years at the Naval Academy at Annapolis had been a breeze, compared to what followed: six months at the Navy Nuclear Power School at Vallejo, California; six months of nuclear reactor prototype training at West Milton, New York; six more months at the Navy's Submarine School at New London, Connecticut.

But this was different. This was the real thing. During all his training he had simply never considered the reality of what he was being trained to do. He would be riding inside this metal tube they called a submarine to what they termed "test depth": the submarine's maximum permissible operating depth. Now he was part of the *test* to see if this tube could stand this *depth*. If they were so sure she could do it, why did they call it *test*? That this was a brand-new submarine, among the first of a new class of nuclear fast attack boats, merely added to Winning's anxiety.

Lt. (J.G.) Winning was astonished at how cool everyone else was. Was he the only one who felt the sweat beginning to trickle down his back? He was the newest member of the crew, to be sure, but was he the only one who never before had been to test depth on a new, first-of-its-kind submarine? Many of these guys weren't even Navy; some were civilian shipyard workers that had to ride the ship on her sea trials. They were all going about their business as if it was just another day at the factory.

One thing he did know: he could not, absolutely could not, reveal this sudden grip of anxiety to anyone else on the ship. And Bill Winning was a pretty good actor. So, he flashed his best Elvis-smile as he stood up and grabbed the flashlight from its place next to the coffee cup. He gave the flashlight a flip.

"Well, I'd better mosey on down to the lower forty." He forced his voice to its lowest obtainable octave.

"Hey, Mr. Winning! Before you go below, give me a hand."

Chief Swensen poked his immense, cherubic head around the corner of the narrow door that led into Maneuvering. Swensen's huge torso followed. In one hand was a large ball of twine; the other held a Navy-issue pocket knife. Swensen looked over at Winning's boss, the engineering officer, Lieutenant Bob Copper. Copper sat in the corner of Maneuvering at the little stool that was the throne of the duty Engineering Officer of the Watch. Lieutenant (J.G.) Winning was on duty as Copper's trainee.

Chief Swensen and Lieutenant Copper shared a brief chuckle. Neither winked, but they might as well have.

"Go ahead, Bill," said Lieutenant Copper, shaking his head, still smiling. "Bear a hand for the Chief. Then hustle on below so we can report test dive stations manned."

Chief Swensen handed the ball of twine to Winning, but kept the bitter end. Swensen awkwardly maneuvered his bulk over an I.M.O. ("I Move Oil") hydraulic pump just aft of Maneuvering and reached up to attach the twine to a small bracket that was welded to a beam on the starboard bulkhead.

"Pretty nimble for a big guy, Chief," said Winning. He smiled as he lied. Bill felt he was doing a decent job of sounding loose. "What's the story on the twine?"

"Little trick I learned when I was on *Thresher*." Chief Swensen took the ball of twine from Winning, and began to unroll it as he clambered over toward the other side of the engine room. At the ship's centerline, he stopped, took some metal washers out of the pocket of his "poopysuit" overalls, and tied them to the twine. Then he continued on to the port bulkhead, where another bracket was fastened just over one of the ship's oxygen generator units.

"We'll pull this tight," said the chief, "then, when we get to test depth, we'll see how far it droops. Then we can use a little high school geometry to see how much compression the hull takes back here."

Swensen went back to the center aisle of the engine room, climbed up on the railings between the two Ship's Service Turbine Generators and made a pencil mark on a vertical brace near the stretched twine.

"This'll be just as accurate," said the chief, "and about a million dollars cheaper than all that fancy laser-theodolite junk those forward pukes are using up in Control." Chief Swensen rarely had anything good to say about anyone, not nuclear trained, that worked forward of the engineering spaces.

"I didn't know you were on *Thresher*, Chief." Winning winced a little as he mentioned the name of that ill-fated boat. *Thresher* had sunk, with all hands aboard, fifteen years before.

"Yep," said Swenson. "I was on *Thresher* for a couple of years, just after I got out of Nuke School. Got transferred off just two months before she went down. Had a lot of good friends went down with her. You see the pictures, Mr. Winning?"

"They showed us some of the pictures in Sub School," said the junior grade lieutenant. "I hear they cleaned them up, though, to get rid of the real gory stuff. I hear some of the pictures showed bodies and heads and arms and legs. Not very pretty." Winning's voice stayed cool, but a shudder raced down his spine. Swensen was looking the other way, so the chief could not see, at least visually, the impact this turn of the conversation was having on the green j.g.

Believe it or not, I was on *Scorpion*, too" Chief Swensen mentioned another nuclear fast attack submarine that had met catastrophe, this one in 1968. "Only temporary duty; I left her about a year before she went down. Hey - Mr. Winning - in case you ain't noticed, this submarining business is no day at the beach. Boats go down. Good men go down with 'em."

The chief finished climbing down from the railing that had supported his bulk, barely, while he had made his pencil mark. "And if you're lucky enough to stay off the bottom," continued Chief Swensen, "you get to stay at sea about 300 days a year for 30 years. You got a family - forget 'em. But I don't mind tellin' you, if us American submariners ain't willing to pay the price, you can bet the Russkies will, and they'll bury us, as they say"

Chief Swensen's face broke into a huge Nordic smile. If he had a white beard, he'd make a great Hallmark Card Santa Claus, thought Winning. The wrinkles around his eyes attested to a face accustomed to smiles and laughter. This in spite of the demands and sacrifices of the life he and his fellow submariners had chosen.

"OK, we're set with the twine," said the chief as he dusted his hands. "After we get to test depth, I'll holler at you to help me make this measurement."

It was a promise that would not be kept.

Swensen stuck the ball of twine, the knife and his pencil back in his poopysuit pockets. "Time for you to go below, Sir," he said.

Winning grinned along with the chief at the irony, so familiar to anyone who ever served in the armed forces: the punk kid officer fresh out of school versus the seasoned non-com, old enough to be his father, calling him "Sir." It put pressure on both of them. Both of them knew how to handle it.

Winning lifted the small deckplate grating hatch, just outside the door to Maneuvering, and began to climb down toward the bilges. Before going below, he glanced through the door to see Lieutenant Copper still sitting at the desk, going over some log readings.

Copper looked up. "You get the Chief squared away, Bill?"

"The other way around, Bob," said Winning as he shut the hatch over his head, disappearing into the lower level of the engine room.

———

USS Muskellunge was running slowly at Periscope Depth, shallow enough for one of her periscopes to penetrate the surface, before she began to make her initial descent to test depth. As was the prevailing operational practice at the time, when she went deep, she would increase to flank (high) speed, so as to be able to use her fairwater and stern planes to try to help keep her up should she suffer a flooding problem. Of course, should her stern planes fail in full dive, that high speed would spell disaster. But, among the many lessons learned in the tragic sinking of the *Thresher*, flooding while deep is the more likely, and therefore more fearful, casualty. And submariners want every advantage they can get.

Muskellunge's skipper was Commander Laurence Falston. He had been one of the team of engineers that, over the years since the *Thresher* incident, had developed hundreds of innovations to make submarines safer (and, of equal importance to the submariner, quieter). This was Falston's first command, and it was proving difficult for him.

Falston was a brilliant engineer. He had been hand picked for the nuclear program by Admiral Rickover, himself, when Falston was still a nuclear engineering major in the ROTC program at Penn State. Falston had taught at the Nuclear Power School for three years. He had served several shipboard tours, but most of that was with submarines in the shipyards, not at sea. Maybe that was why he had been passed over for promotion to the rank of captain on his first shot in the promotion zone. Whatever, this was Falston's opportunity to make it big as commanding officer of a deployed submarine. First, however, he had to get this ship commissioned. This first dive to test depth was an important step in that process.

———

Lieutenant (J.G.) Winning worked his way aft along a grating that led back to the main condensers. Even though Bill was of only average height, he had to stoop considerably to avoid banging his head on the maze of pipes, valves and cable trays that ran just under the main engine room deck. He came to another small trap door that led down to the bilges. He had to squeeze through it, crawl down, and then aft a little more. This brought him to the main seawater intakes and their giant, hydraulically operated isolation valves. Here the clearance was only about 3 to 4 feet, so it was a matter of crawling on his hands and knees. It was particularly hard on the knees. Winning began to think of a way to improvise, to jury-rig a set of knee pads as soon as he could get the opportunity.

The sore knees were only part of the discomfort of this job. The engine room was nearly unbearably hot. On *Muskellunge*, as with all American nuclear powered submarines, the forward spaces were comfortably air conditioned, but the engine room was not. The only portion of the engine room that approached any form of comfort was the Maneuvering area. Maneuvering was cordoned off by curtains and force-fed with air conditioning blowers that tried, usually in vain, to keep up with the heat load being generated by the two ship's service turbine generators, the main propulsion engines and literally hundreds of other pieces of machinery contained in the cramped confines at the rear end of the submarine.

The high temperatures in *Muskellunge's* engine room were especially intense because Commander Falston had talked the Bureau into using an experimental insulation that would help reduce the size and weight of the equipment mounted on the platform known as the engine room "bedplate." The weight and space reduction allowed the use of a revolutionary new design of sound isolation mounts. These "Muskie Sound Isolation Mounts" were much like giant shock absorbers that suspended the entire upper level engine room and most of its equipment. The result was a huge reduction in the sound that would be transmitted through the hull into the water for unfriendly sonar-ears to hear. But for the poor non-qual j.g. who had to crawl, hands and knees, through the bilges in temperatures approaching 140 degrees Fahrenheit, it was quite a price to pay.

At Submarine School, Winning had heard much about this new, improved Muskie Sound Isolation Mounts development. He had also heard much about the man who had pushed to be the first commanding officer to deploy the Muskie Mounts, Commander "Liquid Larry" Falston, his new skipper. Falston's reputation for booze was as widespread as his reputation for pushing submarine technology to new limits. Winning had first met the CO the previous Sunday, as the new j.g. reported aboard and presented his orders. Falston had spent that Saturday night - and evidently much of Sunday morning - out in town on a binge, and he reeked, even though by the time Winning met him it was nearly six in the evening. Liquid Larry's conversation was coherent, but Winning found him to be just short of revolting. Now, however, they were at sea, and Winning had a job to do.

———

The ship proceeded down, as promised, in 250-foot increments. At each increment, Winning crawled around the lower level engine room, making his rounds. He then worked his way up to the hatch outside maneuvering, and poked his head out. He reported to the throttleman just inside the door, a second class petty officer who manned the sound-powered phones.

"Completed lower level engine room rounds at 750 feet, no leaks, conditions normal," said Winning, as though he knew what was "normal," having been at sea for only three days.

The throttleman received reports from the others that were making inspections of other areas of the engine room, and then relayed the report to the control center, located in the operations compartment near the forward part of the ship.

"Control, Maneuvering. Engine room inspected at 750 feet. No leaks, conditions normal."

"Maneuvering, Control, aye." The junior officer who acted as communications coordinator in Control triggered his sound-powered phone and responded. He made a grease pencil check next to "engine room" on a plastic sheet held on a clipboard. Turning to the duty Officer of the Deck (OOD), he announced, "Engine room reports no leaks, conditions normal, Sir."

"Aye." Lieutenant Commander Sal Rizzuto acknowledged the report. Rizzuto was the OOD, at his station at the periscope stand.

The periscope stand is elevated about 18 inches above the main deck in the operations compartment. It is surrounded by a stainless steel rail, and is lit by special spotlights, rigged red at night for better night vision. The periscope stand looks much like a little stage. And so it is, a stage, with the actors' lines carefully rehearsed.

Only, sometimes the actors are called on to ad-lib...for life or death.

Just behind the OOD, seated on a pivoted stool, was the ship's captain. Liquid Larry Falston was watching his fairwater planesman. It was the planesman's job to hold ordered depth while at the same time to steer the ordered course.

"You wanted to see me, Captain?" Commander Dave O'Leary, the executive officer, entered Control. The "XO," the ship's second in command, had been in the sonar shack since the dive started, listening to *Muskellunge*'s engine noises as she went deep. The new design of Muskie Sound Isolation Mounts was working well. Even at flank speed, the engine noise projected through the hull into the water was remarkably low.

"Yeah, XO," said Falston, "why don't you take over here and keep an eye on Rizzuto while I stroll back aft to square things away back there. I want to take a look at that main shaft seal when we get to 1000 feet." Falston swung down from his stool and headed aft.

————

Back in the engine room, after his 750-foot report, Lieutenant (J.G.) Winning climbed all the way out of his hole, fashioned knee pads out of a couple of pads of graph paper and some rubber bands, and went back below.

The ship continued on down, now proceeding in hundred foot increments. During his rounds at 1200 feet, Winning caught the sound of the captain talking, with considerable intensity and volume, to Bob Copper.

"Lieutenant Copper," screamed Liquid Larry, "I don't care how much experience you and the chief have with shaft seals, I want that packing torqued down tighter. *Now torque it down!*"

"Aye-aye, Captain," responded Copper. His rather cheerful demeanor was neither fawning nor angry. Winning, unseen from his vantage point in the bilges, about ten feet below them, reflected that Copper must have learned his lessons well as a plebe at the Naval Academy. A "Cheery Aye-Aye" is an indispensable commodity for a plebe - and evidently also for an engineer officer.

The inspection rounds were getting rather routine by now, and the "kneepads" made it a little less painful. But the heat and humidity, and the tension of going deep were wearing out the young officer. Ventilation outlets, located at some of the stops on his tour, blew some relatively cool air in his face and provided some relief. He lingered at these stops.

The most comfortable spot was immediately beside the big main seawater isolation valves. Here the cool seawater entered the submarine to make the short journey to the ship's main condensers, and thence back out of the ship. This system is much like the radiator and water cooling system in the engine of an automobile. Without water flowing in the radiator and the rest of the cooling system, the automobile shuts down. Similarly, without the main seawater system, a submarine shuts down, fast.

But that was not what Winning was thinking as he sat for a moment, his back propped against the main seawater system's bare metal piping. What he appreciated most about it was that it was C-O-L-D ! The water entering the system at this depth in this particular spot in the Atlantic was about 33 degrees Fahrenheit. This made it great for turbine-cycle efficiency, and, more important to Winning, it provided some blessed relief from the cruel engine room heat...

THRONGGGGGGGG...SKREEEEEEEEEE...WHOOOOOOOSH!!!

The noise was deafening to Winning's ears, driving out all conscious thought. All his muscles reacted at once as though in complete spasm. A piercing pain ran down his back, followed by another painful jolt, this one to his forehead. A mixture of blood, and water and hot water vapor surrounded him, clogged his eyes, blinded him.

There was more to this dreadful noise than its amplitude to wrench Winning's gut and to drive reason from his mind: it was accompanied by a low, rumbling vibration and followed by a banshee's scream. The vibration was more than audible. He could feel it as surged like a giant sine wave forward toward the submarine's bow, then aft, then forward again. The banshee-shriek gave way to the more horrible gushing sound of water-flow.

————

It is said that at the instant of death, or at a moment of extreme trauma, one's life passes before one's eyes. For Angus William Winning, this was not precisely the case. For him, in the few milliseconds that immediately followed the onset of the *Muskellunge* Incident, his thoughts raced to an almost forgotten scene, another incident, which had taken place almost two years previously:

For Bill Winning, in his mind's eye, he was again enjoying a lovely spring afternoon in Annapolis. He had accepted the invitation of one of his midshipman buddies to attend a Saturday picnic on the shores of the Severn River. A preacher named Steve Whitney, from a Christian discipleship group called the "Navigators," was the picnic's sponsor.

At Midshipman Winning's side was one of the loveliest girls he had ever met. Tall and slender, with dark golden hair and brilliant blue eyes, Susan Whitney was the pastor's daughter.

Bill Winning, more to make conversation to "impress" Susan than because he had any particular conviction about, or interest in, religion, prodded the Reverend Mr. Whitney about the Bible. Winning chided the Bible as "a collection of myths," not really in tune, as Bill said he saw it, with all of today's body of scientific knowledge and advanced civilization.

Susan Whitney had been standing close to Bill much of that afternoon, up to that time seemingly enjoying his company and laughing at his playful conversation. But, as Bill jokingly scoffed at the Bible, Susan changed her countenance as though he had slapped her in the face.

"You jerk!" she had shouted, pulling back from him in disgust. "Doesn't your brain go any deeper than that?" Her face glowing with anger, she seemed about to say more, but her dad cut her short.

"Back off, Susan!" The Reverend Mr. Whitney spoke sternly to his daughter. "He's raising a legitimate point." Then he turned to a slightly stunned Midshipman Bill Winning, and smiled. "Look, Bill, I understand your point, because I used to think that way, too. But let me ask you a question. You criticize the Bible. Have you ever read it?"

"Well, sure...I...parts of it." Winning stammered. But the more he attempted to explain what he thought he knew, the more he proved his ignorance.

He had, nonetheless, enjoyed a nice chat with Susan's father that afternoon. They had talked about the Bible, and about many things. It was interesting, and Steve Whitney really seemed like a nice fellow, but Bill's mind was not primarily on the preacher or on the conversation. Mostly his thoughts were centered on the preacher's daughter, that beautiful girl who had been so lovely and so cheerful and then had turned so cold to him. She really believed this Bible stuff!

———

Now, more than two years later, he was in a far different world. As pain coursed through Winning's body and as his legs and arms raced wildly to flee the lower level engine room of the *USS Muskellunge*, one last thought ended his reverie, words that he had not pondered until this very instant. In this fleeting moment in the bowels of a submarine engine room gone berserk, Winning could see the letters on the pages of Steve Whitney's well-worn Bible:

"And as it is appointed unto man once to die, but after this, the judgement..."

"GOD!" Winning screamed in agony, "WHAT DO I HAVE TO DO..."

Tears poured down his face from the pain, from the outrageous noise, from terror, and, mostly, from regret.

———

At that first startling blast of noise and pain, Winning had jolted upright, his forehead banging into the angle iron that formed an edge of a cable tray.

It had taken Winning less than three seconds to burst through the tiny bilge hatch, scramble to the main engine room deck hatch and crash it open, and to shout, at the top of his lungs: "FLOODING IN THE ENGINE ROOM"!

He then collapsed, his legs still dangling through the hatch. As he had ripped through the upper level hatch, a corner of the metal grating had opened a large gash along the back of his shoulder. A pulsing flow of blood began to pour down his back. The blood mixed with the steaming water that saturated the back of his poopysuit. Blood, red-brown and sticky, gushed from the cut in his head, and soaked his hair.

Standing less than four feet away, at the entrance to Maneuvering, Commander Laurence Falston had reacted with bewilderment to the initial noise that was still ringing and "whooshing" with incredible volume. But now, as the hatch flew open, and this mass of blood, steam and water screamed of flooding, Falston's eyes bulged out, his mouth flew open. He had been through hundreds of flooding drills, and he had been to dozens of first aid lectures and practice sessions, but he had never heard anything quite like this. He had never seen someone so bloody as this apparition from the lower level engine room. He leaped into Maneuvering, grabbing the 1MC microphone.

"FLOODING IN THE ENGINE ROOM ! FLOODING IN THE ENGINE ROOM!"

Falston's voice screamed, cracked, choked, "This is the Captain! "SOUND THE COLLISION ALARM! EMERGENCY BLOW THE AFTER GROUP! EMERGENCY BLOW THE AFTER GROUP!

The initial noise had started as a loud, low frequency rumbling noise, then had progressed to a high-pitched shriek that sounded as if it were metal rubbing against metal. Then had come the most fearsome noise of all, the WHOOSH! of pressurized water or steam. All this had come in a sequence that took about seventy-five hundredths of a second. Now, an even louder noise filled the tiny engine room: a piercing POP! and the scream of high pressure air being blown from the banks of emergency blow canisters into the ballast tanks. Then, almost as an afterthought, the collision alarm, a screeching, warbling siren, was barely perceptible above the cacophony.

The ship shuddered, the feeling resembling that of an old pickup doing 65 miles an hour over a set of railroad tracks. She began to nose down, gently at first, but then in a lurch she pitched down rapidly to almost thirty degrees "down bubble."

At that point, things began to come loose, literally. Above the din of the screaming high pressure air and the collision alarm, and above the continuing WHOOSH! of steam and water, came the sound of clanking and banging of equipment and gear accelerating forward against bulkheads and machinery. Professionals had rigged this ship for sea, but this was, after all, a relatively green pre-commissioning crew, and rarely had anyone seen pitch angles more than about fifteen degrees. The ship was also full of test gear, in various states of seaworthiness, placed by the shipyard workers.

Three of the civilian workers had been standing between the ship's service turbine generators just aft of Maneuvering, along with Chief Swensen. Two of them immediately hit the deck, screaming in utter terror, as the ship began to nose down. The other, a test engineer named La Plante, stumbled and began to lunge backward, trying in vain to gain his footing. Chief Swensen stepped out into the passageway to break La Plante's fall, grappling him with both arms.

But Swensen lost his balance also, as the ship continued to pitch downward, and the two of them stumbled backward, awkwardly. The terrified test engineer was wrapped firmly in the arms of the huge chief machinist's mate as they tripped, backward, still facing aft, past the slumped-over Lieutenant (J.G.) Winning, and the stunned Commander Falston. Falston watched, dumbfounded, as he held on to the side of the door to Maneuvering, the 1MC mike at his side, his mouth agape, his eyes bulging.

At the forward end of the engine room, the two men slammed backward into the bulkhead. Chief Swensen hit first, his bulk hitting with a fearsome "THUD!" As he hit, his head turned slightly and snapped back against a protruding brass nozzle fixture. The nozzle penetrated his skull just above his right ear. Blood began to ooze out of the side of Chief Swensen's head, poured down his right shoulder and on to the head of La Plante. The shipyard worker, still cradled in Chief Swensen's arms, merely sat there, eyes tightly shut.

The captain, now dazed, confused and sickened by the blood, knew one thing. He had to act. He had remembered this: emergency blow was what would get you to the top the quickest. BUT HE HAD TO STOP THE FLOODING!!

"SHUT... MAIN... SEAWATER... ISOLATION... VALVES!" He choked, his voice quavering as he yelled over to Lieutenant Copper in Maneuvering, where the valve activation switches were located. Commander Falston now had one other thought: he was a dead man.

"WAIT! WAIT! *NOT SEA WATER*"!! Lieutenant (J.G.) Winning raised his throbbing, blood-soaked head. He looked directly at Bob Copper, who was about to reach for the isolation valve activation switches. Winning used up all his remaining strength to make himself heard above the din, and then slumped back over in a heap, his legs still dangling through the deck hatch.

"Captain! He's right! That's steam, not seawater! This is an INTERNAL break! We're NOT FLOODING!" Copper's voice boomed through Maneuvering. Copper was a large man, with a voice to match. His voice and his command presence had helped him pave many paths as one of the few African-American officers serving at that time in the nuclear submarine Navy. Now, that voice and that commanding presence saved the ship.

Copper disregarded Falston's order to close the main seawater isolation valves. He keyed the nearby 27 MC speakerphone. It connected him to the Control Room. "Conn, Maneuvering. We DO NOT have flooding in the Engine Room. I say again NO FLOODING IN ENGINE ROOM! We've got an internal break. Get this down-bubble off the boat before we lose the reactor. Suggest you blow the forward group, secure the after group blow!"

"Maneuvering, Conn, Aye!"

Before the last transmission had been sent, another round of POP-SCREAM! noises rose throughout the boat. The ship shuddered again, this time even more violently. The ship's angle held steady at about forty-two degrees down bubble, then began to recede.

Commander Falston stood, gripping the maneuvering room door, his eyes staring at Chief Swensen's motionless form. Falston's mouth was still open, and foam had formed around the edges of his tightly drawn lips. He tried to speak, but no words came.

Lieutenant Copper keyed the 27MC mike again. "Conn, Maneuvering. Get the corpsman back here quick! We've got a couple of guys hurt real bad. Also, XO, you'd better get back here, too. Commander Falston needs some help."

"Maneuvering, Conn. You got it!"

Bob Copper went into action. He made his way out past the trembling Falston, grabbed the Engine Room Supervisor, a first class machinist's mate, and yelled instructions into his ear. The sailor scurried off toward the port side of the engine room, toward the ship's fresh water distilling plant. Copper climbed back over to Maneuvering and barked orders to the throttleman and to the reactor operator. Soon the WHOOSH-noise subsided.

Lieutenant Copper went back out into the passageway outside Maneuvering. He stooped down on his knees to where Bill Winning lay, half in and half out of the deck hatch. A second class electrician's mate named Zylkowski had slid down alongside the bloody young officer. Zylkowski had ripped open the top of his poopysuit, had torn off his tee shirt, and was pressing the shirt against Winning's forehead to try to stop the bleeding. Copper helped Zylkowski pull Winning's legs up through the hatch, stretching him out along the passageway. To each of Winning's knees was fastened, by several tightly stretched rubber bands, absurd graph-paper kneepads, soaked with blood.

Further forward, two other sailors slid down to where Chief Swensen and the shipyard worker had slammed into the forward bulkhead. Copper left Winning in the hands of Zylkowski, and crawled down to join the sailors as they tended to Swensen, who was motionless, wide-eyed, dead. The shipyard worker, La Plante, was screaming, shaking uncontrollably from horror, still in the bear-hug of Swensen's corpse.

Commander Falston slouched down to a sitting position. Still grasping the 1MC mike with one hand and the edge of the door to Maneuvering with the other, he tilted his head back, closed his eyes and began to sob.

The Navy's official report of the *Muskellunge* Incident contained volumes of recommendations, affecting both operations policy and ship design.

The new design of Muskie Sound Isolation Mounts had been very effective from a ship noise-reduction standpoint, but had failed in one important aspect. The hull of *Muskellunge* compressed as the ship began going deep, as expected. But, as the hull compressed, the large amount of "play," deflection in the isolation mount shock absorbers, allowed the bedplate to come in contact with the hull. This so jarred the entire bedplate that several of the mounts broke away, and the bedplate settled, noisily, two inches onto the hull-mounted frame.

This settling of the bedplate was, in itself, only an insignificant problem, easy to correct.

But the shipyard had mistakenly welded, directly to the hull, a hose fitting that ran to the port side fresh water distilling plant. When the bedplate, and the machinery mounted on it, dropped suddenly as the bedplate mounts broke, it caused the hose connection to shear loose, at a location in the lower level engine room near where Bill Winning was making his rounds. The water at this point in the distilling plant system was under pressure at just over 215 degrees Fahrenheit. So, it was boiling water, suddenly spewed from the distilling plant that had made such a fearful racket and scalded the back of the young officer when the incident began.

Commander Laurence Falston was immediately relieved of command. Even before the investigation was complete, he had submitted his resignation from the Navy. It was promptly accepted.

Lieutenant Robert Copper, the Engineering Officer of the Watch, was commended in the Navy's report for having had the presence of mind to recognize, even amid the noise and confusion of the moment, that the ship was not flooding. Had he shut the main seawater isolation valves as ordered by Commander Falston, the reactor would have shut down, and main propulsion would have been lost. It is possible that, with the resultant loss of the effect of fairwater and stern planes in controlling ship's angle and depth, the ship may have joined her sisters *Thresher* and *Scorpion* at the bottom of the Atlantic.

Lieutenant Commander Salvatore Rizzuto, the OOD, also received glowing commendation in the official report. From his stage up in Control, he was able to use the ship's speed, together with the fairwater and stern planes, along with skillful venting and blowing of the ship's ballast tanks, to bring *Muskellunge* under control.

The incident report noted numerous injuries: eleven shipyard workers and eight members of the ship's crew were hospitalized with broken bones, concussions, and cuts, primarily from falling equipment and debris during the angle excursion.

There was one fatality: Senior Chief Machinist's Mate Elwood Lief Swensen.

The press took little note of the incident. Back in Swensen's hometown of Fergus Falls, Minnesota, the local paper showed his portrait photo and a Navy press-release column commending his heroism in saving a shipyard worker, at the cost of his own life.

The editorial page in the same paper devoted about twice as much space to an article by a local pundit decrying the military imperialism of the U.S.A., "...sending our sons to death to support the greed of the Military Industrial Complex." The article would have disgusted Senior Chief Swensen.

Disgust was precisely the effect the article had on at least three of those who were in Fergus Falls to attend the Chief's memorial service: a shipyard test engineer named La Plante; a tall, black Navy lieutenant named Copper; and a bandaged-up young Navy lieutenant (junior grade) named Winning.

For Bill Winning, this incident marked a turning point. Although Commander Falston's preliminary report was particularly critical of the young officer, the final, official Incident Report only mildly chastised Winning for having made a report of flooding that turned out to be incorrect.

But, Winning had earned the lifelong respect of another officer, one whose career would receive a huge boost from his performance in the *Muskellunge* Incident, Lieutenant Bob Copper.

Copper's report was ebullient in its praise for Winning. Despite Winning's inexperience, despite the extraordinary confusion and noise, despite painful injuries and being nearly unconscious, Bill had managed to decipher the mistake of his first report of flooding. Lieutenant (J.G.) Winning had mustered the strength to call Copper's attention to the key to the techno-puzzle: *it was not seawater.* Yes, Copper had shown extraordinary expertise in keeping *Muskellunge's* power plant on the line. True, Sal Rizzuto had shown great skill in controlling the ship's depth. But Copper knew in his heart that it was Bill Winning who had saved his career, even, possibly, his life.

For Winning, there was something more. In that moment when he was, for all he knew, at the end of his life, he had come up short. Yes, his engineer's mind had functioned well and had enabled him to figure things out in this emergency. But his heart had failed him. *"...it is appointed unto man once to die, but after this, the judgement."* The Reverend Steve Whitney's Bible had it underlined in red.

Bill had not understood much of what Steve had said that day, months before, at that picnic. But, whatever he had said, it was from this book called the Bible. And Susan Whitney was right. He, Bill Winning, was a jerk. He had been quick to laugh at the things in this book, but he had never read it. He would try to contact that lovely girl again. And, he was determined to find a copy of the Bible and study it, cover to cover.

Bill Winning had begun to learn something about running deep.

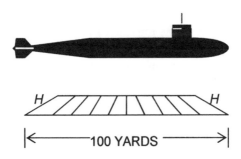

|←————100 YARDS————→|

SCALE ILLUSTRATION
(Approximate)

USS *MUSKELLUNGE*

American Nuclear Attack Submarine
(ca. 1978)
Modified "Sturgeon" Class SSN
Displacement: 4,250 tons (surfaced)
4,960 tons (submerged)
Length: 302.2 ft.
Beam: 31.8 ft.

Chapter Three

Comrades

December
Moscow

A DMIRAL SERGEI GLUTSIN was not accustomed to waiting. Back in the days when there was a Soviet Union and a mighty Soviet Navy, a driver and car had been at his disposal to whisk him about the great city whenever he was on official business. In those glorious years that he had served as Admiral-in-Charge of the Soviet Pacific Fleet, the car had, in fact, been a nicely appointed limousine. In addition to a mere driver, Admiral Glutsin was, on such visits, accompanied by his aide, a senior *kapitan vtorogo ranga*, and at least one "security representative," assigned from the KGB.

But here he was, on what could well be his most important visit of all, no aide, no driver, no car. Michail Gorbachev and his accursed *Perestroika* had seen to that. Admiral Sergei Leonovich Glutsin was waiting for a bus. A bus! It was early December, cold, drizzly-wet and windy.

At least, mused Glutsin, the weather here in Moscow is real. He was dressed for it: a heavy wool civilian suit under an old Army-issue fur-lined parka.

He had detested Havana during his many visits there. Havana's steamy swelter was good only for insects and sugar cane, certainly not for men, not for Russians. And Damascus was worse. Admiral Glutsin had just returned from ten days in that horrible place, where the insects were more obnoxious than Havana's, and the Syrians didn't even have the redeeming virtue of sugar cane rum.

But the Syrians did have friends with money - evidently lots of it.

Glutsin was second in line at the corner bus stop, behind a young woman dressed in a shabby wool jacket. The woman carried a cloth bag containing what looked like books. She was, probably, a student. A small, broken-ribbed umbrella drooped down over the young woman's head. She was trying to keep the books dry under her coat. She was not succeeding.

A group of about a dozen people huddled around a little fire smoldering in an old, rusted petroleum drum about fifty meters from the corner. The people were in such ragged garb that Glutsin could not tell, for most of them, whether they were men or women, old or young. The only thing certain: they were miserable. One of the men/women cuddled a tiny infant, wrapped in an old, rain-saturated blanket as near as possible to the warmth of the sputtering flame. In the West, passers-by would have looked on in astonishment at the plight of these homeless souls. This scene was not merely that of a few vagrants collected at a steam-pipe manhole. This was a scene of misery on a massive scale: whole families wandering the streets in search of bits of edible garbage or of fuel for barrel-fires. In the West, the scene would have evoked pity, perhaps, or disgust, or compassion or anger. But in Moscow it had become so commonplace, even in this relatively "good" section of the city, that few even took notice.

Glutsin noticed, but he had seen so much more misery than this that he, too, was growing almost numb to such scenes. He had seen good men, sailors, even officers from his own command, shaken from the service as his impoverished country scaled back division after division of the old Soviet Navy. He had watched his own men and their families suddenly driven from shut-down bases out into the civilian world, where no jobs, often no homes, and little food could be found.

Admiral Glutsin had fought the cutbacks. He had done whatever he could do on a personal basis to help these men find work, find shelter. But too often his men, these men he had led so proudly, these men who could probably have conquered the world, were left utterly without hope. The reports of alcohol, deserted families, homelessness and suicide among his former comrades reached his desk almost daily. Glutsin might have grown numb to the plight of the Moscow homeless, but when he considered his own sailors, it fueled a rage within him that ate at him like a cancer.

And the ships! Those magnificent machines that could have humbled even the Americans. Truly the glory of the Soviet Union, they could have, at the push of a button...

But now, many of these masterpieces of technology lay rusting at the sides of barely-tended piers. The Ministry could not even manage the resources to keep them in proper mothballs. And, when they tried to operate, they reaped the whirlwind of disrepair and lack of training. The shame and tragedy of the sinking of the submarine *Kursk* was only the most obvious manifestation of the failure that had descended on his beloved navy.

Glutsin, however, had conceived an idea. He had control of great machines. There were those with much money who would buy them. He would sell them!

The bus approached the corner, full to the doors with unsmiling, thoroughly soaked Muscovites. The student pushed her way aboard, followed by Glutsin, who thrust a shoulder into the young woman's back, pushing to make enough space to get into the stairwell of the bus. The driver had to try twice to shut the door before the crowd had jostled itself enough to make room for the two new riders. No one spoke as the bus pulled away.

Glutsin stood in the stairwell of the bus, staring out the grimy window of the door as the bus trundled down a broad avenue. Along nearly every block was more evidence to the admiral's weary eye of neglect, decay, hopelessness. He had to struggle against an inclination to sentimentality. What promise there had been!

He knew full well that for many along these streets, little had changed. Even at the height of the Soviet Great Power days, the power and "greatness" was for a select few who had learned to play the game - and Sergei Glutsin had learned to play well. Most of these denizens of the street had to struggle then, as they struggled today, for a place to stay, a bite to eat. But in those days, now seemingly so long ago, there had been a sense of direction, a sense of control. Glutsin's jaw clenched tight. "I must get it back." He muttered aloud through gritted teeth.

———————

Vladimir Drednev was a tall man, thin and athletic, appearing considerably younger than his fifty-seven years. His suit was of the latest Italian fashion, his hair carefully styled, his skin tanned from a recent holiday at the seaside. As a youngster, he had risen rapidly through the ranks of the Soviet Army. His political talent and devotion to the Party had become evident to the High Command when he was a junior officer acting as an "advisor" in Southeast Asia in the '60s. This led to other sensitive assignments, and recognition of other, rare skills. Drednev soon became particularly well regarded for his adeptness in negotiating arms sales to client states around the world.

More importantly, back in 1991 during the ill-fated "coup" attempt, he had demonstrated the wisdom, not to mention courage, to stand with Boris Yeltsin. He had organized a cadre of "loyal" troops, even had arranged a tank for Yeltsin to use as a platform from which to address the world. The tank-podium had been, in fact, Drednev's idea. Now, long after the departure of Yeltsin, long after the demise of Putin, he had continued his own climb to power. Vladimir Drednev was now the Russian Minister of Defense. It was rumored that his power in the new government was second only to that of President Starazhnikoff himself.

Drednev stood alone at a large oval table, sipping coffee from a finely crafted china teacup. He read from the editorial page of *The Washington Post*. Drednev relished observing the irony of America's slide into socialism, while his own country, the "New Russia," struggled so doggedly, and so vainly, to master the mysteries of capitalism.

Admiral Glutsin appeared at the open doorway, knocked twice, paused briefly, and walked in. Drednev did not look up from his newspaper.

"Good morning, Mr. Minister." The Admiral had to be careful to use the correct form of address for his new superior. Long gone with the statues of Lenin and Stalin was the familiar, one-size-fits-all address: "comrade." Glutsin, not in uniform, did not salute, but he stood at attention near the doorway.

Drednev placed his coffee cup neatly in its saucer, as he finished reading George Will's latest jewel of wisdom. He then flipped the newspaper onto the table, turned to the admiral, and smiled broadly.

"Sergei Leonovich, welcome home!" Minister Drednev walked over to Admiral Glutsin, extended his hand, shook it vigorously and clasped him warmly on the shoulder. He led Glutsin back to the table and offered him a chair. "Sit down, sit down. You have had a long journey. And a successful one?" The smile disappeared abruptly.

"We shall see, Mr. Minister," said Glutsin. His steel-gray eyes looked directly into the tanned face of Minister Drednev as the admiral took a chair and sat. Glutsin continued, "Are we to wait for others to join us at this meeting?"

"No, Admiral," responded Drednev. "No one else knows of our 'enterprise.' I mean no one. And I believe it is wise to keep it that way for the present time. Let us put a credible plan together before we begin to expand the circle of knowledge. You must certainly understand this. Now tell me of your journey to Damascus."

Admiral Glutsin nodded. "Well, for one thing, you were absolutely right about this Walid El Zophar. He roars like a lion, but I do not believe the jungle trembles at his roar. He is a nobody. He is in a position to buy nothing! I feel that I have just wasted ten days in the most miserable city in the world. Have you ever been in Damascus, Mr. Minister?"

"Many times," said Minister Drednev. He sat on the edge of his conference table, looking down at Admiral Glutsin. Drednev took a cigarette from a pack of Marlboros and lit it as he spoke. He made no offer of the pack to the admiral. Drednev continued, "I agree with you that Damascus is a decidedly unpleasant city. But you came to me with a product in need of a client, and it is in Damascus that we shall find that client. Of course, I also agree that Walid El Zophar has a considerably exaggerated opinion of his own place in life. I had told you to expect that. But I disagree when you say he is a nobody. Are you familiar, Sergei, with the Wharton Business School?"

"The Wharton Business School?" repeated Glutsin. He struggled with the strange English-sounding words. Glutsin spoke no English. In fact, the sound of these English words fell on his ears as fingernails scraping against a chalkboard.

"No, Mr. Minister, I am not familiar with this thing," Glutsin answered. The thought crossed the mind of the crusty admiral that his new boss, the slick Vladimir Drednev, was cut from the same bolt of cloth as the Syrian snake, Walid El Zophar. Evidently the world was destined to be run by such men. For a fleeting moment,

Glutsin regretted bringing Minister Drednev in on his scheme. But Drednev was right: he did need a buyer, and Glutsin had no idea where to start. Besides, Drednev was in the admiral's chain-of-command. Where else was he to turn?

Drednev explained, "When I was stationed in the U.S. in the early 1980's, after I left active duty, I spent two weeks in Philadelphia at a marketing seminar conducted by the University of Pennsylvania. Their business school, called the Wharton Business School, is considered one of the best in the capitalist world. I learned many fascinating things in this program."

Drednev, still drawing from his cigarette, reached across the table to a china coffee pot and refilled his cup as he spoke. After replacing the pot, Drednev had an afterthought. "Oh. Would you care for some coffee, Sergei?"

"Thank you, no, Mr. Minister," responded Glutsin. "I had plenty of tea earlier this morning." The admiral thought, but did not say, "...while you were probably still asleep."

"Well," Drednev continued, "one of the professors I met at the Wharton Business School was a Dr. Frank Levine. He introduced me to a concept which I have found most valuable in making sales." Drednev paused. "You do understand that is what we are, do you not? We are salesmen making what may be one of the most important sales in history. It is possibly the most significant sale since Napoleon sold half a continent to the American President Jefferson."

"Yes, Mr. Minister," grunted Sergei Glutsin, "this sale can be significant to a great many people." The admiral noticed that modesty was not a prominent characteristic of his new superior, the Minister of Defense.

"Yes," Drednev proceeded with his lecture, "and to make sales, we need to understand who is buying. I mean, specifically which individual. And we need to know why he buys. Dr. Levine called this 'knowing the buying influences.'" Drednev again used the English term, leaving Glutsin to wonder at its translation. "You see, there are three buying influences. First, there is the 'user buyer.'"

Admiral Glutsin shifted uncomfortably in his chair, but Drednev continued, "You see, the user-buyer is the person who will use whatever it is you are selling. If you are selling aircraft, for example, the user-buyer is possibly the test pilot that checks it out, approves it. He usually is not the one with the money, but you must have him on your side to make the sale. Then you have the top dog. The man who controls the money. Dr. Levine called him the 'economic-buyer.' It is his signature that authorizes payment, executes the contract. For little sales, like shoes and potatoes, the user-buyer and the economic-buyer are usually the same person. But, for very big sales - 'big ticket,' as the Americans say - the two are usually separate individuals. For our enterprise, Admiral Glutsin, we are talking very, very big ticket. We need to know who is the user-buyer and who is the economic-buyer. You see?" Drednev stopped, waiting for a response from his pupil.

Glutsin again stirred in his chair. He did not see. "I do not have such command of your English terms, Mr. Minister," said Glutsin. "I must ponder a moment. I do not see how we are to know who makes these decisions, and why they make them. But, you said this Dr. Levine described three factors. You have described only two."

"Aha!" exclaimed Drednev. He jumped up from the table and patted Glutsin on the shoulder. His pupil had passed. "You do see! The third factor, the third so-called buying influence is what Dr. Levine called a 'coach'." Here Drednev used the Russian word.

Glutsin nodded, appreciatively.

Drednev walked toward the entrance of his large, ornate conference room and closed the door. He then stopped at the antique china cupboard near the door and removed a cup and saucer. Returning to the table, he smiled at Glutsin, "You must have some coffee, Sergei Leonovich. It is American *Maxwell House*. I think you will enjoy." Drednev poured.

"Walid El Zophar is a boor," Drednev went on. He spoke in low tones, no longer the excited professor, but now the international salesman. "El Zophar grossly exaggerates his power and influence. But he has something that is, for us, at this stage of our enterprise, vital. He has contacts. He is our 'coach'."

Drednev paused, looked for a long moment into the eyes of Admiral Glutsin, then continued, "I have used him before. He proved to be very valuable for a sale of tanks and artillery pieces that I made to Syria in 1988. A couple of years later he was instrumental in coaching a sale of aircraft when Hafez Assad was still in power. This sale was especially germane to our enterprise because it involved cooperative funding from a variety of Arab financial sources."

Drednev sipped delicately from his cup of coffee. He proceeded, "But this idea you have presented, Sergei, dwarfs these others. And, I must say, I am impressed with your vision. You realize, of course, that your scheme will completely change the balance of power in the Middle East. If Saddam Hussein had your *Antyey III* submarine and its missiles during his little escapade a decade ago, Israel by now would have ceased to exist. Not to mention Saudi Arabia, Kuwait and Iran. You do understand this?"

"Of course I understand this, Mr. Minister," said Glutsin. Although the admiral might be out of his element in discussing capitalist marketing tactics, he needed no lecture in military strategy. "But the Syrians are not the Iraqis, and Hazael Zabadi is certainly no madman as was Saddam Hussein. Ever since Hazael took over in Syria, he has had remarkable success in consolidating Arab opinion." Glutsin was somewhat relieved to be on familiar discussion-turf.

The admiral continued, "And, as I have mentioned to you before, sir, I believe that this - this 'enterprise,' as you call it - will work to our advantage in some very important ways. As I..."

"Yes, yes," Drednev interrupted, "you explained it very eloquently when we first met, Sergei. Indeed, it is true that we desperately need the money. And I agree in principle with your plan to apply the money to refurbish our shipbuilding and repair industries. An ideal way to carve a *niche* for ourselves in the world marketplace, I must say."

Glutsin exploded, "An ideal way to provide work, a LIVELIHOOD FOR MY PEOPLE...our people...Mr. Minister!" Glutsin's hand had clenched into a fist as he spoke. He thrust his fist toward the table, stopping just short of its polished surface. His hand spread as it gently touched down. Glutsin took a deep breath, struggling to maintain composure before his superior.

Glutsin continued, speaking slowly, deliberately, "I am sick...TO TEARS" Glutsin's eyes moistened. "I am sick of seeing my people, my crews, my officers, my electricians - and their families - going hungry. And I am sick of seeing my ships rusting.

We are the best in the world, Mr. Minister, at building these ships. And these ships are the best in the world."

"And the *Antyey III* is, no doubt, the best of the lot, Sergei," said Minister Drednev. He spoke slowly, consolingly, the tone of his voice matching that of Admiral Glutsin. Both of Drednev's hands spread out on the table, near Glutsin's, as he leaned forward to make his point emphatic. "The most capable submarine ever conceived for the kind of warfare we face. It would have been unthinkable only a very few years ago to have even considered placing such a weapon in the hands of others."

The Russian Minister of Defense did not exaggerate. *Antyey III* was a hyper-secret project being conducted in a protected enclave, called Khokskya, north of the Russian navy base at Magadan on the Sea of Okhotsk in northeast Russia. *Antyey III* was a modification of the dreaded cruise missile-firing submarines known to Western observers as the *Oscar* class. It was believed in the West that the first of the original *Oscars* had been launched in 1980 at Severodvinsk. Only slightly smaller than the mammoth *Typhoon* class that had gained renown in American bookstores and movie theaters as the fictitious *Red October*, the *Oscars* were even more grotesque in appearance because of a shorter, squared-off profile. The ill-fated *Kursk* was an *Oscar*-class submarine.

The *Oscars* were as deadly as they were massive and ugly. While the *Typhoon*'s mission was to stalemate the American strategic nuclear threat with its Inter-Continental Ballistic Missile capability, the *Oscars* were intended for launching shorter-range ship-to-shore missiles. The earlier *Oscar* class submarines were capable of carrying twenty-four "Shipwreck" missiles (the Western name for the Mach 1.6 SS-N-19 cruise missile) tipped with nuclear warheads.

The usefulness of the giant ICBM's was vastly diminished in the new Post-Cold War era, but the *Oscar*'s ability to launch multiple ship-to-shore stealth missiles while submerged and virtually undetectable, could be of enormous impact in a limited land engagement. The further modifications made on the *Antyey III* made her even more effective for limited warfare applications. Frighteningly more effective.

The secrecy of the *Antyey III* program was a vital factor,

particularly from the perspective of the Glutsin/Drednev "enterprise." Indeed, the development of the program had been one of the most zealously guarded secrets of past Soviet-Russian regimes. Gorbachev, Yeltsin, and Putin had realized that the game was up as far as the Soviets' ability to keep pace with American technological development. They knew that, simply as a matter of economics, they could not afford to continue the high-tech arms race. And, they knew that, before long, they would have to submit to strict controls and inspections as part of nuclear arms limitation agreements with the Americans. So, the idea of a medium-technology weapon like *Antyey III* appealed to them: It was less expensive, it could well slip through the disarmament inspection "net," and it could be a powerful ace up their sleeve in any limited conflict, abroad or at home.

There was nothing "medium" about the submarine itself. *Antyey III* was, as boasted by Minister Drednev and Admiral Glutsin, one of the finest submarines ever built, certainly the best of the behemoths produced by the Soviet Union. She incorporated the very latest in sound-dampening technology, and was fitted with the latest improvements in "Cluster Guard" anechoic tiles. She was powered by two pressurized water nuclear reactors, with an improved capability to run on natural convection reactor coolant flow. This meant she could operate at higher power levels than her predecessors without running the relatively noisy reactor coolant pumps.

But the ingenious development of *Antyey III* was her weapons system. Her predecessor's fearsome missile tubes had been modified to accommodate the simple, inexpensive, and deadly "Katapaltes" system. Instead of the giant "Shipwreck" missiles with their complex, and extremely expensive, support systems, the Katapaltes system made up for lack of sophistication with sheer volume. *Antyey III* was capable of carrying ninety-six of the stubby Katapaltes missiles. The missiles were certainly capable of being fitted with nuclear warheads, but even with non-nuclear biological, chemical or conventional explosive warheads, this was an awesome weapons system. A single ship like the *Antyey III* could turn the tide of battle for nearly any scenario short of all-out strategic war between superpowers. This ship was the equivalent of a fleet of submersible, stealth battleships.

Minister Drednev leaned back in his chair, a slight smile announcing a change in mood. "Sergei, my friend, a few years ago, you would have been shot for suggesting such a plan," said Drednev. "But today, we fight a different war - against a different enemy." He took a long, last drag from his cigarette and snubbed it in an ashtray.

Drednev continued, "Tell me, did our friend Walid introduce you to a man named Mutanabbi, a Dr. Mustafa Mutanabbi?"

"Yes," answered the admiral. He relaxed his posture, and took a sip from his coffee cup. Glutsin regretted having let his emotions become so transparent. "Dr. Mutanabbi was presented to me as an important official of the Syrian military. I am not certain of his title, but he is a very young man - too young to have any real authority. I must say, however, he does seem to be a most intelligent young man. My meeting with him was, in fact, the one bright spot in an otherwise dismal trip. You know this man Mutanabbi?"

"Indeed, I do know him," said Drednev. "Mutanabbi is the nephew of President Hazael Zabadi. He is the son of Hazael's sister. I met him here in Moscow in 1983. He was attending the university. He is, as you observed, very bright. He is, more to the point, also very lucky. When Syria's government was overthrown last year, and Hazael Zabadi took over, Mustafa Mutanabbi's stock went up enormously. He has inordinate power for one so young."

"Perhaps," said Admiral Glutsin, "but I was most disappointed that Walid could not seem to arrange for me to see General Zaim, himself. Zaim is the head of the Syrian military. He is the one with whom I should be conferring about matters of this significance."

"No, no, Sergei," Minister Drednev corrected the admiral. "You are incorrect. Hazael Zabadi kept Zaim around after the coup only because Hazael needed the loyalty of Zaim's troops. Zaim is loved by his men. He would be at home charging headlong into a desert battle astride a noble stallion. But he is not the man to whom Hazael will look to make the decision about the purchase of a tactical-missile-firing nuclear submarine. Hazael will be obligating funds to us that are more than four times his current total annual military budget. For advice on this deal, he needs brains, not bravado. He will look to Mutanabbi. I tell you, Sergei, Mustafa

Mutanabbi is, for us, the *user-buyer*. It is your job to sell him. Now tell me of your conversation with our *user-buyer*."

Admiral Glutsin slid his chair closer to the table, sipped again from his cup of coffee, and began to recount his dialogue with Mustafa Mutanabbi. The two men had hit it off well, the intense young Syrian intellectual and the seasoned, equally intense Russian admiral. For one thing, Mutanabbi spoke fluent Russian, so there was no need for an interpreter. There had been only the two men present in the Damascus hotel room, so the conversation had proceeded with comparative candor. It had been a long conversation and it had covered many important points.

Minister Drednev allowed Admiral Glutsin to ramble on, stopping him only occasionally to understand a point, or to encourage embellishment of a detail.

"You say," said Drednev, "he seemed to like your idea of a 'buddy system' to operate the submarine, matching up a group of Syrian officers for each of the 'Operations Consultants' we will provide?" Drednev snubbed out yet another Marlboro and reached into his pocket for the next. He offered the pack to Glutsin.

"No thank you, Mr. Minister." Glutsin refused the cigarette, "but I will have some more coffee." Glutsin reached over to the pot and poured. "Yes, Mutanabbi liked the 'buddy system' concept, but he was adamant about maintaining command and control in the hands of a Syrian. I almost got the impression that he, himself, might want to come aboard *Antyey III* as her Syrian skipper. At the time I thought he might be joking."

"Do not think it a joke, Admiral Glutsin," said Drednev. "In fact, I think that to encourage him in this - this fantasy - might well enhance our sales prospects. But, go on."

"Well," Glutsin continued, "he seemed to be willing to accept our general terms regarding the nature of the weapons to be carried aboard and of the maintenance and material management provisions. He did not like our price. But, I did not believe him to be a decision-maker in any event, so I did not indicate that we had any inclination to haggle."

"We will end up having to haggle, Admiral," said Drednev. "It is part of the unalterable constitution of the Middle East. But I will take care of that with the *economic-buyer* at the appropriate time."

"Hazael Zabadi?" asked Glutsin.

"Hazael Zabadi," nodded Drednev. "I will deal with him. But it is your mission to seal the enthusiasm of our *user-buyer*, Mustafa Mutanabbi."

Drednev paused a moment, then continued, "I should also tell you this, Admiral, about Mustafa Mutanabbi. I explained to you that his mother is President Zabadi's sister, and that is certainly important. But what is also important to know is that his father was a top man in the Syrian army during the 1967 war with Israel. He was captured by an Israeli commando unit and died in captivity under what were, I understand, rather horrible circumstances. Mustafa Mutanabbi was only a small child at the time, but his little mind and heart were filled with hatred for the Israelis. I have heard that this hatred has never abated. As his mind and heart have grown, so has his hatred. He is a brilliant young man, but he is possessed by the strongest of passions. We should not let our emotions rule our actions, should we, Admiral Glutsin?"

"No, Mr. Minister, we should not." Admiral Sergei Glutsin could take a hint.

Drednev tapped his fingers lightly on the table, as a gavel announcing that the meeting was now adjourned. He stood, and Admiral Glutsin stood as well.

"There is one more thing, Admiral," said Drednev. He looked down at his older, shorter, stouter colleague. "You and I, we are very different people. But to make this plan succeed - and it is a brilliant plan - it will take your skills as well as mine. We are what the Americans call a 'joint venture.' It will take both of us to make it work."

Minister Drednev ushered Admiral Glutsin to the door. "I have made plans for you to return to your favorite city in a few weeks, just after the first of the year." said Drednev. "I want you to meet again with Mustafa Mutanabbi. He is rather busy these days, but El Zophar has got him to set aside some time in January for you. You have done well Sergei. Your plan is moving ahead faster than I, at first, thought it might. But Mustafa Mutanabbi is a key. He might not be able to make the deal we seek, but he can certainly kill it. You must continue to take good care of our user buyer, eh?"

———————

Glutsin's mind raced as he wandered toward the cloakroom at the far end of the hallway, away from the now-closed door to Minister Drednev's Conference Room. This whole scheme was indeed moving faster - much faster - than he had anticipated. Admiral Glutsin had made a career of mastering the art of moving ideas through the gigantic bureaucracies of the Soviet system, where the chief virtues were loyalty, patience and persistence. But this was different. Think whatever he might about his new boss, Vladimir Drednev was a man of action.

The admiral collected his old army parka at the cloakroom and headed for the stairs. Indeed, the pace at which Drednev was pushing this "enterprise" was frightening. And the minister had not yet shared the plan with President Starazhnikoff - this was disturbing. Glutsin had brought the idea to Drednev because the minister of defense was next in his chain-of-command. He rather expected that the appropriate next step would be for the minister to take it on up the chain.

But Glutsin was good at focusing on objectives, and his primary objective was to correct some of the sickening squalor that had overtaken his life, and that of his former comrades. What was, earlier this morning only something of a distant dream seemed now, after his interview with this New Russian Salesman, Vladimir Drednev, to be taking some realistic shape! Frightening, yes, but exciting.

A glimmer of promise, as when turning over an ace in a near-dead game of solitaire.

Chapter Four

<u>Chariots of Fire</u>

December
Cambridge, Massachusetts

"SO, YOU'RE TRYING TO TELL ME that women today are being duped to think that the only way they can be productive in society is to have a career?" TV talk-show host Gregg Bentley scratched his head and smiled knowingly at the studio audience.

Susan Winning had had enough of Gregg Bentley, and of the too-bright studio lights, and of the too-rude studio audience. This audience was a hoax, much tinier than it appeared to the millions who watched Bentley's top-rated afternoon talk show, *Speak Your Mind.* Susan knew she was the token "Conventional Mom" on this panel, and she had soon discovered that she was the only "conventional" mind in the entire TV studio. Bentley was taping this show, part of his series on "Women in America Today" in studios at Harvard University, to be aired the following week.

"I'm not *trying* to tell you that, Mr. Bentley," said Susan Winning, "I *am* telling you that!" Susan's voice was polite, drippingly, sarcastically polite, too polite for the audience.

A few quiet, almost shy "BOO"s came from the audience.

"Now, now, ladies and gentlemen," scolded Gregg Bentley. He had mastered the art of orchestrating the emotions of these audiences and of his guests. "Please remember your manners. And also remember where Mrs. Winning is coming from. She represents the views of centuries of women who have been *duped* to believe that the only way a woman could contribute to society was by having litters of sons."

Laughter, mixed with hearty applause, filled the little studio.

Susan Winning smiled grimly through her humiliation and anger. She surprised herself with the calmness of her response. "Mr. Bentley," she said, "you have summarized my point poorly."

"Well, then, try your point again, Mrs. Winning," said Bentley. He smiled graciously. "Perhaps I shall understand it better this time."

Susan tried again. "I am not saying...never have said...that the only way a woman can be 'productive,' as you put it, is to have children."

"Thank you, thank you," said the talk show host, as he gave an exaggerated, courtly bow. The camera panned back to show the delighted smiles of his audience.

Mrs. Winning continued, "What I am saying is that our society, our schools, our TV programs," Susan motioned toward Gregg Bentley, "make motherhood, and being a housewife out to be an inferior position, one that is tantamount to defeat in life. Everywhere I turn, I hear, 'Oh, you're just a housewife' or, 'Do you work, or are you a housewife?' What a laugh!"

Mrs. Susan Winning, now in her mid-forties, was as attractive as ever, and her eyes sparkled as she engaged in the fight. The TV camera loved it. The show's director called for the crew to pan in on her for a closeup as she spoke.

Susan continued, "My ten-year-old daughter, Lucy, was asked early this year in her fourth grade class to write a paper on what she wanted to be when she grows up. She wrote about being a mother. She said she wanted to have two boys and two girls, and so on. Her teacher wrote a little note on it that said, 'This is fine, but what do you REALLY want to do when you grow up?'"

Susan Winning continued, "Look, I'm not saying that careers outside the family are necessarily wrong for women, and I know that there are many situations where there is no choice in the matter. What I am saying that it is wrong - and dangerous - for our society to give women the idea that staying home and managing a family is an inferior role."

The woman who sat next to Susan had been silent up until this moment in the show. Now she took advantage of the pause and spoke up. "Gregg, I am a teacher, and I'd like to comment on something Mrs. Winning just said."

"Go ahead, Dr. Draper," said Gregg Bentley.

"I want to commend little Lucy's teacher," said Dr. Draper, "for having the courage to challenge the girl to reach for more in life than she is evidently learning at home." The audience erupted again in applause.

"I am the Superintendent of Schools in Byron, Massachusetts," Dr. Draper continued, and I can tell you that in our district, we encourage our teachers to challenge our kids to strive to go beyond the limits with which their parents shackle them. To hear Mrs. Winning talk, you would think that it is a mutually exclusive choice: you must either be a mother or you can have a career. No middle ground."

Susan Winning stared at Dr. Draper as the latter spoke, and slowly, sadly shook her head. She remained silent as the panel and various questioners from the audience joined the chorus. The large electronic timer at the rear of the studio stepped down to less than thirty seconds and counting.

"You have been uncharacteristically silent." Gregg Bentley gestured toward Susan. "Do you have any other thoughts for us, Mrs. Winning?"

Susan Winning was rarely without other thoughts. She said, "Only this: with all due respect to the different and honored professions represented here, I have a feeling that our country needs good moms at least as much as it needs good lawyers or computer programmers, or whatever. And I think that the people who mold public opinion, such as educators and talk show hosts, are doing a poor job of presenting a balanced view of the importance of being a dedicated mom. And I particularly resent the notion of Dr. Draper here, that she, Superintendent of Schools though she may be, and not I, the mother, should prevail in establishing my child's values. And..."

The time on the timer had hit zero. The red light on the camera went off, as did the congenial smile on Gregg Bentley's face. "Okay, okay. That'll do it for today. Thank you ladies." Bentley made a quick exit, stage left.

Susan stepped down from the stool on which she had been seated for the show, and, ignored by the other panelists, she made her way toward the exit. She was met there by Monica Blum, the producer who had contacted her about being on the program. The two women talked for a few moments, and then Susan hurried out the door. She had to get home in time to prepare dinner for her family.

Boston

"You gonna be workin' here all night, Mr. Winning?"

Bill Winning looked up from the stack of papers scattered before him and smiled at the security guard who had interrupted his furious paperwork binge. It was almost nine o'clock, p.m.

"No, Gerald, I'm going to wrap this up in about a half hour, ready or not. The wife and I are leaving tomorrow on vacation. I'm trying to get some of this stuff taken care of before we go."

"You're gettin' out just in time," said Gerald. "One of them Montreal Express storms is headin' into town. Should be here for the weekend. You goin' to Bermuda or the Bahamas or one of them islands?"

"Nope." Bill started making stacks of the papers. He could never get through them all before daybreak. At least he could categorize them so he could hit the ground running when he got back in two weeks. "We're going on a trip to Israel with another couple from our church. Been studyin' about the place. Lookin' forward to seeing it."

"Israel." Gerald shrugged. "At least it sounds warm. They got camels and palm trees over there don't they? Also got a lot of loonies and terrorists and all. You take good care, Mr. Winning."

"OK, Gerald, we'll take care. I'll shut off the lights and lock my office door when I leave. Hey, you be careful, yourself. There's lots of 'loonies' over here, too, you know."

Gerald chuckled, nodding his head as he left Winning's office to continue his rounds.

Bill was glad Susan wasn't around to hear this little exchange about "loonies." His wife was nervous enough about having to fly; always had been a basket case on an airplane. The last thing she needed to hear was another reminder about the unrest that had been building in the vicinity of their destination, particularly between Israel and the new, hard-line government in Syria. It had not yet flared into all-out war, but skirmishes had been fought, troops had been mobilized, and the UN Secretary-General had been commuting to Damascus and Tel Aviv to try to douse the flames. The travel agent had shown Bill the State Department warning about the safety of travel in the area, but the agent agreed with Bill that such a warning would have been appropriate for travel in that region at any time for the last four thousand years.

For its part, the United States was going very far out of its way to remain neutral in the gathering controversy. The American president had made it clear that he intended to break the long-standing policy of strong American support for Israel, even though in this he was facing substantial opposition in congress. The U.S. was continuing to suffer from a sluggish economy, and, as the president put it, "There are social priorities to be dealt with in this nation that do not include another adventure in the deserts of the Middle East."

The American president was encouraged in his position by a growing anti-Israeli sentiment in the media, and by polls that showed a rapid falling-away of America's tradition of sympathy with Israel. This was fueled by a rash of allegations of atrocities committed by Israeli fringe groups against Palestinians, and against neighboring Syrians. Some of the stories had at least some foundation in fact, many did not, but all of them sold newspapers and TV time.

But Bill and Susan Winning had been planning this vacation trip for over two years. This was to be their twenty-fifth wedding anniversary trip. They both needed to get away - together. Things had been pretty tough between him and Susan, ever since their oldest daughter had died in a tragic automobile accident. They both needed the relief, and the refreshment, and the excitement of such a trip. Bill was not about to let worry about Middle Eastern politics get in the way of this vacation.

Not if he could help it.

Bill Winning had left active duty in the Navy over twenty years before. He had gone to work as a nuclear engineer for a small consulting engineering firm, Nuclear Operations Services, Inc. Now he was a vice president of the firm, in charge of the engineering division. Most of his work involved consulting on various issues related to the integrity of concrete reactor containment structures.

Much had changed in his life since those vibrant, sometimes dangerous, always exciting days when he rode the boats in the submarine service. Sometimes he missed it, but he rarely had regrets - either for having done it in the first place, or for leaving it when he did. Now he devoted his passions to other pursuits: his wife, his kids and, as some would say, his "religion."

Some would say that, but not Bill Winning. Those who knew him well would hear him say, not infrequently, "*religion* kills; it's the *relationship* with God that makes you alive."

As he drove his old van out of the garage into the cool, crisp Boston air that December night, Bill could not have known how much he was yet to discover about how, indeed, religion kills.

Weymouth, Massachusetts

Winning pulled into his driveway in Weymouth about an hour later. Many of the lights were on in the house, and Granddad Whitney's old Chevy Cavalier was in the driveway. He had driven up from Washington to spend the two weeks with the kids while Susan and Bill were away.

Susan was in the living room packing a suitcase as Bill walked in. Clothing and travel bags were arrayed over the couch. "Hi!" said Susan. "About time you got home. It's almost eleven o'clock. Here, give me a hand shutting this thing."

Bill threw his coat over a chair and began to work with the suitcase. "How'd it go with the TV show, Suze?"

Susan let go of the suitcase, stood up straight, and began to cry. "Oh, Bill, I really blew it," she sobbed. "I got mad. I clamed up. I got overwhelmed. Nobody listened to me."

Bill stepped over to comfort her, but she backed away.

"And, the worst part is, you're going to say 'I told you so.'" Susan sobbed even louder.

"I told you so," said Bill. He could not resist it. Then he tried to backpedal: "Listen, you knew before you went that you were in enemy country. But if I know you, Suze, you fired a few shots before you went down."

"Yeah, I guess so," said Susan. "But I don't think I hit anything." Susan stopped weeping. "Anyway, that producer Monica Blum says they'd like to get me back."

"I hope you told that producer to fly a kite! Susan, what did you just say to me? You'll just get mad. You'll get overwhelmed. And I'll say 'I told you so' again. You're not serious, are you?" Bill shook his head, grinning, knowing well the determined look in his wife's eye. He changed the subject. "I see your dad made it up ok. Where is he? Maybe I can get him to talk some sense into you."

"He's upstairs tucking in the kids," said Susan. "Don't count on him to help you. He thinks it's great that I'm at least *trying* to speak out on some of these things. He says he's been preaching for nearly sixty years and hasn't spoken to as many people as I did tonight. He thinks I ought to go ahead with it."

Bill extended his arm and gently gripped his wife's shoulder. He said, "Susan, you know I'm proud of you. I just hate to see you get blasted. But, look! You keep it up: *Do not grow weary in well doing...*"

Bill looked up the stairwell, where he heard a growing commotion. "Did you say the kids were still up?" he asked.

"I let 'em stay up late tonight," said Susan. "There's no school tomorrow and, with our going away, it's kind of a special night. Dad got a video movie down at the library to watch with them. It was over about an hour ago and they've been up there talking about it."

"What movie did he get?" Bill was somewhat surprised. His father-in-law, the Reverend Steve Whitney, was not exactly a "movie guy."

Susan answered, grinning, "An oldie-but-goodie that was one the few secular movies I think Dad ever saw: *Chariots of Fire.*"

"Well," said Bill, "I'll go on upstairs and say 'hi' to Granddad - and 'goodnight' to the kids." Bill headed up toward the bedrooms.

Near the top of the stairs, he caught the sound of Lucy's little voice. Lucy, the youngest of the three Winning children, was a ten-year-old question-machine.

"I know, Granddad," Lucy said, "but I still don't understand why they called it 'Chariots of Fire'." Lucy was on to a point, and she wasn't about to let Granddad off the hook.

"Listen, kids, have you ever heard the story of the chariots of fire in the Bible?" asked the Rev. Steve Whitney. He stood in the upstairs hallway near the entrance to Lucy's room, but spoke so the two boys could hear as they lay in their bunk beds in the adjoining room.

"I think so, Granddad." Luke, the oldest, spoke up. Lucy had all the questions, but Luke, at fourteen, had all the answers in the family. "Doesn't it have something to do with one of the prophets, Elijah or maybe Elisha? I forget what happened, but it had something to do with angels winning a war or something."

"That's right Luke," said Granddad Whitney. "Let me fill you in on the details." Just then Steve Whitney caught sight of Bill coming up the stairs. "Hey, kids! Your Dad's home!"

A little pandemonium broke out as the Winning children welcomed their dad. Twelve-year-old Ken climbed down out of his top bunk, but was whisked right back up by the strong right arm of his father.

"At ease, kids," said Bill Winning. "I got here just in time to hear Granddad's story. Let's all pipe down and listen."

Bill pulled the covers back up over Ken, tapped him on the forehead, and returned to the hallway. Steve Whitney extended his right hand. Bill grabbed it and pulled his father-in-law into a firm embrace, warmly patting his back. "Great to have you here, Steve. Thanks for coming up."

Both men sat on the floor, side by side in the hallway, backs propped against the wall.

Granddad Whitney began, "Now remember, kids, this is not a fairy tale or a myth. This really happened. And it happened about two thousand, eight hundred years ago over in the Middle East, where your mom and dad are going for their vacation."

"What country did it happen, in?" Lucy wanted specifics. She also was an expert in expanding bedtime stories to extend awake-time.

"Well the story I'm going to tell happened in a little village called Dothan. It was located in what is now modern day Israel. Back in those days, they called it Israel, too, and the Israelites of those days had pretty much the same enemies they do today. Back at the time of our story, the enemies of Israel were called the

Arameans of Damascus. Today, Damascus is the capital of Syria. Anyone read the paper today?"

"I did." Luke was, as usual, on top of this one. "The Syrians have backed out of their peace treaty with Israel," explained Luke. "Both countries have sent troops to the border. Doesn't look good for the two of them. Dad, are you sure you and Mom really want to go over there when there's so much of a problem between Israel and Syria?"

Bill smiled. "Luke, there's *always* a problem between Israel and *somebody* over there. We'll be OK. You just remember to pray for us."

Granddad Whitney continued his story. "Well, back in about 850 BC, the Syrians were giving fits to the Israelites. They were raiding villages, killing people, stealing sheep, causing huge trouble. They would attack one village, then surprise the Israelites with ambushes and then pull a surprise attack somewhere else.

"But then the Syrians had a big problem. A prophet named Elisha was tipping off the king of Israel about where the Syrian army was going to be. So the Israelite army was prepared for defense every time the Syrians tried to pull a surprise attack.

"Well, when the Syrian king found out about this prophet, he decided the best thing to do was to catch Elisha and kill him. He got word that Elisha was staying in a little town named Dothan. So the Syrians sneaked up during the night and surrounded Dothan with a whole army of soldiers and chariots. They really figured they had him, too, because there were no Israeli soldiers around to rescue him.

"Now, Elisha had a young helper. When the helper woke up the next morning and saw the village surrounded by enemy soldiers, he was terrified. He ran to tell Elisha the horrible news. 'We're surrounded! There's no escape! There's no hope!'" Granddad Whitney paused. "Did you ever feel that way, kids?"

There was no response.

Granddad Whitney continued, "Well, Elisha knew better. He had something that evidently his young helper didn't have: faith. And he told the youngster something that can help us even today, if we remember it. 'Don't be afraid,' Elisha said, 'those that be with us are greater than those that be with them.'

"But the youngster didn't understand. All he could see was the enemy army edging closer and closer. He could see the evil grins on the faces of the Syrian soldiers. He could see the early morning sunlight gleaming off the points of their spears and off the blades of their swords. He was beside himself with terror. So Elisha prayed that God would allow him to see the whole story. At that moment, the young man lifted up his eyes and saw a sight that he would never forget. In fact, it was a sight that none of us should ever forget. The Bible says, 'and the LORD opened the eyes of the young man; and he saw: and behold, the mountain was full of horses and chariots of fire...' God had sent His hosts, his spiritual army, to do battle against the enemy of His people.

"Let me tell you, kids, no matter how bad things seem to get, no matter how strong the enemy seems, God is *always* stronger, and He always wins."

"What happened to Elisha and his helper?" Lucy asked.

"Well, God caused the whole Syrian army to be blinded. Elisha was able to lead them all into the headquarters of the Israelite army, where they were captured. Then the Israelites set them free, so they could go back and tell all the people of Syria how great God is."

After a long pause, Lucy was back on the case: "I still don't see why they called the movie 'Chariots of Fire'."

"I don't either," admitted Bill Winning, ending the conversation. "Good night, Lucy. Good night, boys." Tuck-in Storytime had expired.

———

Less than one month later, Bill Winning would think back on this moment, and on this story, and weep with the memory of it. He would long to hear again the voices of his loved ones, and he would pray fervently, as had Elisha those millennia before, that God would grant them peace and strength, and allow them to see the whole picture.

Chapter Five

<u>Tourists</u>

January
Israel, North of the Sea of Galilee

T HE TOUR BUS DEPARTED THE HOTEL promptly at 7:00 am. It was nearly empty. This was the halfway point of the vacation-tour, and the hectic pace, exotic food, and uncertain water were beginning to claim victims. Most of the tourists had opted to skip the day's event and to sleep in.

The attraction for this day was a bus tour of northern Galilee, including an early morning stop at Zefat and a lengthy afternoon tour of Hazor, now called Tell el-Qedah, the magnificent 200-acre home of the ancient Canaanite King Jabin. The Bible records the fall of Hazor to Joshua and the invading Israelites around 1400 B.C.:

> *And Joshua at that time turned back, and took Hazor,*
> *and smote the king thereof with the sword: for Hazor*
> *beforetime was the head of all those kingdoms.*
>
> Joshua 11:10

Susan Winning had been among those who had chosen to stay behind this day. She had decided to remain with several other ladies to make it a day of shopping and relaxing around their hotel complex at the Sea of Galilee. They would leave exploration of this particular set of ruins to die-hards like Bill Winning and Gary Tarr, the pastor from their church in Weymouth.

Bill and Pastor Gary had taken seats on opposite sides of the bus about halfway to the rear. Two couples from Texas sat near the rear of the bus. Bill and Gary had struck up a good friendship with one of the Texans, a quiet little man named Lem Philpot who had retired after thirty years in the Navy as a Chief Electronics Technician. He and his wife, Aileen, were celebrating their thirtieth wedding anniversary with this tour of the Holy Land. She was in poor health, but determined to make the most of their vacation.

Nearer the front of the bus, there were three men from Pennsylvania whose wives, like Bill's and Gary's, had opted out of the tour. Sitting about halfway down the aisle on the right was an elderly couple from Florida.

Hashim Gehazi, the tour guide, talked quietly to the driver as the bus made its way along the highway leading north. There was considerable traffic on the highway, much of it commercial vehicles: trucks, vans and improbably large trailers pulled behind tiny cars. Most of the tour bus's passengers dozed. Gehazi knew that the magnitude of the tip he would receive at day's end would depend in large part on how quickly he could get off the monotonous highway and out into the meat of the tour. It was the reason the tour's planners had chosen the seven-kilometer wilderness road from Zefat to Tell el-Qedah rather than the easier, but longer and boring, highway that led around to excavation site. There was a quick exit off the main highway to the little road that led to Tell el-Qedah, and Gehazi did not want to miss it.

The bus slowed, and the passengers were jarred out of their slumber by deep ruts as they turned on to the narrow path. Sharp curves wound around the steep, barren hills.

"We only have about five kilometers to go," Hashim Gehazi announced to his little entourage. "You will find that Hazor is well worth the bumps to get there." His voice shook along with the bus.

"Let me give to you some information about the mound we will be visiting. The first excavations of the mound were made in 1928 by Garstang. Professor Yigael Yadin stepped up the work in 1955 with a grant from James A. de Rothchild..."

As the bus rounded yet another curve, the driver let out a loud shriek and pushed hard on the brake pedal. The bus skidded sideways as it shuddered to a stop, just missing a large boulder in the dead center of the path. Bill Winning, staring out his window on the right hand side of the bus caught a brief glimpse of a human figure emerging from a clump of bushes in the ditch that ran along the side of the road. The dark-clad figure tossed a large metal object toward the front of the bus.

"*TAKE COVER! IT'S A BOMB!*" Bill screamed as he dove for the floor of the bus, between the seats.

Just as he hit the deck, the bus was filled with the noise of a shattering explosion. Glass fragments tore through the air, ripping into the back of the seat just above Bill's head. The acrid smell of the bomb's smoke soon filled the bus, and screams of terror and pain followed quickly, only to be choked off by the smoke.

Bill struggled quickly to his feet. He leaped over to the huddled figure in the seat across the aisle to his left. "Gary...Gary...you ok?" Bill coughed the words out.

Big Gary Tarr straightened up, "Yeah, Bill," said the pastor, "I'm ok. Let's get everybody out of here!"

Coughing, sputtering, horror-filled screams could be heard from the rear of the bus.

Bill Winning shouted at Pastor Tarr, "Gary, you take care of the folks up front. I'll go back and get the Texans!" Bill began to crawl along the aisle toward the rear.

Bill found his way to the Philpot's seat. "Lem! Come on! We've got to get out of here!" Lem Philpot sat, cradling his wife. Her forehead was dripping with blood, a gash just below the hairline, evidently cut by the flying glass. She was screaming uncontrollably.

Bill turned to the other side. Jerry and Midge Armstrong seemed in a daze, but unhurt. He pulled Jerry out into the aisle, and Midge followed. "We've got to get out of here before we suffocate, or this thing blows up. Let's go!" Bill urged them forward.

Lem Philpot was moving now, helping his wife ahead of him. Bill followed as the Philpots and Armstrongs crawled forward toward the bus door.

Farther forward, Gary Tarr leaned over a man, one of the Pennsylvanians, in a seat on the left. Bill arrived and looked over the pastor's shoulder.

"It's too late, Gary. He's gone," said Bill as he pulled Pastor Tarr out into the aisle toward the door. To his left, he saw what remained of Hashim Gehazi, leaning against the left-side window of the bus. Bill reached over, grasping the young Palestinian by the shoulders. As he did so, the guide slumped down onto the seat, lifeless. The driver was even more ghastly, barely recognizable.

The sound of automatic weapon fire split the air just outside the bus. As Bill Winning tumbled, coughing, out of the bus door, the sight that greeted him was even more terrifying than the devastation inside the bus. Six men, armed with semi-automatic rifles were pushing apart the huddled survivors of the bombing, methodically shooting some and pushing others toward the ditch from which Bill had first seen the bomb-thrower emerge.

Several bodies lay along the road. Bill recognized the lifeless forms of Lem Philpot and his frail little bride, Aileen. Before he could see more, Bill was struck hard from behind with the butt of one of the terrorists' weapons. The blow landed between his shoulder blades, knocking Bill to the dusty road, face down. He could feel the cold steel of a rifle barrel pressing into the back of his head. Bill heard the voice of his tormentor, wild with rage and speaking rapidly. Bill now heard other voices, shouted commands, all in a tongue Bill did not understand, but he recognized it as the lilting tones of Arabic.

The rifle muzzle now was shifted to Bill's ribs, and the frantic voice was yelling directly in his ear. Bill could not understand a word of it, but he clearly understood the painful jabs between his ribs. He stumbled to his feet, lurching in the direction indicated by the prodding rifle muzzle. He had to jump over another of the bodies in the road, this one recognizable as that of Midge Armstrong.

As he approached the right-hand edge of the road, Winning was shoved again from the rear. Bill tried to steady himself by planting his left foot into the turf, but his ankle gave way painfully, and he tumbled down into the ditch. Rolling over and over, down the three-meter deep embankment, he came to rest at the feet of another of the terrorists. Bill staggered to his knees, and looked up into the face of a youngster, barely a teenager. The young man's wild, black eyes looked almost frightened, in stark contrast to the cruel smile that parted his lips. This one wore no beard, as had the other terrorists he had glimpsed. This one was too young for whiskers. But he was not too young for the AK-47 he wielded with the apparent skill of a veteran.

The youngster shouted at Bill, his high-pitched, adolescent voice screaming the same words that Bill had heard from his first assailant. Bill didn't need a Berlitz book of Arabic to know it meant, *"move - fast!"* He got to his feet and moved off rapidly along the ditch in the direction indicated by the young man's motioning rifle barrel. Bill's left ankle began to throb in pain, but he sensed this was no time to complain. He gritted his teeth and tried hard not to even limp.

Off to his left, and up the embankment from which he had been pushed, Bill saw a flash of light, then felt a shock wave and heard a rumbled explosion. The tour bus was gone.

About one hundred meters down the ditch, the terrain opened out to a broad clearing on the right. Bill and his escort rounded the corner at a trot. There, face down in the dust, were three men, guarded by two of the camouflage-clad attackers. Another of the terrorists was in the process of binding the captives' wrists behind their backs with heavy cord. Behind them was a large van, with the markings of a civilian ambulance painted neatly on its sides.

Bill heard more shouts, felt once again the prodding rifle barrel, and was thrust over to where the three men lay. He dove to join them, face down, literally eating the dust, arms extended back.

Bill's head turned to the man groveling in the dust next to him. It was Pastor Gary Tarr. Tarr's face contorted into a grimace as his antagonist pulled hard on his backward-bent arms, securing the rough knot. "Thank the Lord you're ok..." grunted Tarr. The pastor's words were cut short by a swift kick to the ribs, and a shouted command that was obviously the Arabic equivalent of "*shut up or die*!"

Now it was Winning's turn to surrender to the brutal hog-tying. Bill's arms were wrenched back in painful hammer locks up along his spine, and the wrists were crossed. The cord was pulled so tight that circulation stopped. The rough cord broke skin at the bony portion along the outside edge of Bill's wrists.

The assailant finished his work and stepped off in the direction of the van. Bill shut his eyes, attempting to seal off the pain he felt in his arms and wrists, and the continuing dull throbbing he felt in his left ankle. He fought off a wave of faintness and nausea that began to attack him. He took his breath in huge gulps, stirring up the dust around his head as he exhaled. The dust formed muddy cakes around his tear-filled eyes and at the edges of his mouth. His thoughts ran to Susan, and he mumbled, in his agony, "Lord, protect her. Keep her strong."

Bill Winning opened his eyes again, in time to see polished boots stride slowly and deliberately past the heads of the four terrified souls lying in the dust. The boots then rapidly turned toward the van. The wearer of the boots barked orders that Bill could well guess, even though he knew none of the language.

Immediately, Winning felt again the cold steel of rifle muzzles jabbed in his ribs, and heard the harsh command to move. The four prisoners stumbled awkwardly to their feet, and were herded toward the rear of the ambulance-van. They were pushed up a narrow wooden plank, into the rear of the van, then through an interior door into a small compartment. A metal bench ran along each side. Two armed terrorists sat on the bench to the right. The prisoners were pushed toward the left-side bench.

The first prisoner in line stumbled as he was pushed toward the bench. With his hands tied behind him, he could not regain his balance, or break his fall. He crashed in a clumsy heap at the forward bulkhead of the van, banging his head as he went down. Bill remembered having met the man at the hotel the previous day. He was a dentist from Philadelphia by the name of Gold - Mel Gold. Bill uttered a quick silent prayer for Dr. Mel Gold.

Pastor Gary Tarr, third in the line, pushed past the second man toward Gold, hoping somehow to be of aid. Tarr was met with the butt end of one of the guards' rifles, aimed at his midsection, and the big pastor crumpled over.

By now, Bill had seen enough, and he shoved forward toward the guard, with a stupid, frantic yell, "*STOP!*" Bill received the same rifle butt in his own belly, and he, too, was left writhing, breathless, on the floor of the ambulance-van.

One of the guards shut the small inner door. A single small bulb on the forward bulkhead lit the compartment. Another of the terrorists shut the larger door at the rear of the van, and soon it pulled away. The van sped for a moment over rough terrain, and then on to a road only slightly smoother.

Bill lay on the van's floor, his hands tied behind him, his face pounding against the metal decking. He had nearly regained his breath, but the rapid, violent bumps and turns of the van made it impossible to gain his feet, or to even get to his knees. He tried to lift his head from the floor as long as his failing strength would allow, to keep his face from being battered to a pulp as the van jostled along.

He turned his head to the other side to see Gary Tarr struggling to roll over on his side. He saw that Dr. Gold had actually managed to find his way to the bench, where he sat with his head leaning back against the wall, a large red contusion above his right eyebrow.

The van made a sudden turn to the left, then seemed to slow as it finally seemed to have found a smoother road. Bill realized that they had made their way to the highway. He welcomed the end of the torturous jostling. He struggled to his knees and thence to the bench. The two guards sat on the opposite side, watching their captives, neither smiling nor speaking. The soldiers' weapons lay purposefully, not casually, across their laps, fingers alert at the trigger guards.

The relatively smooth ride did not last long. Less than fifteen minutes later, the ambulance-van again swung sharply to its left, on to another rugged road. The vehicle jostled violently for about five more minutes, when it finally slowed, and then crept forward as though entering a building, and then it came to a stop. The doors of the van were thrust open, and the hostages were prodded back out of the van and down another wooden ramp.

They were inside a large, Quonset-hut-style garage. At the center was a medium-sized helicopter, with ambulance markings on the side. The helicopter was faced toward the doors of the garage/hangar, on a roller pad attached to a small tractor.

The guards hustled the captives into the helicopter. All four hostages were crowded along the bench on one side of the chopper; again the two guards took the opposite bench. The man with the polished boots joined the pilot up front. Clearly this man was the officer in charge of the mission.

The small tractor's engine was running, and it quickly pulled the chopper out to a level spot in front of the garage. In a matter of just a few minutes, the helicopter's engines were up to speed and it lifted off.

The flight was a short one. Less than forty minutes after it had taken off, the chopper landed. Bill could see out the front window that they had arrived at a remote, desert location. Low, gray-brown shrubs stretched as far as the eye could see over the rolling hills.

As the hostages emerged from the chopper, they were herded into a ragged line; their arms still tightly bound behind them. The chopper took off again, in a cloud of sand and dust. The officer with the polished boots walked up to the pathetic little band of prisoners. Bill Winning was the closest of the prisoners to him. The officer reached inside Bill's jacket, removing Bill's wallet and passport.

"What is this all about?" asked Bill Winning. He nearly spit the words out.

The officer reacted with a hard slap to Bill's mouth using the back of his hand. Bill staggered back, but did not fall. He was escorted roughly back to the line by one of the guards. A stream of blood trickled from the corner of Winning's mouth.

"You will not be saying anything. You will please to be shut up! You will do as we tell you and you will then not be harmed!" The officer's English was crude, but he had made his point. Bill was quiet.

The officer went to each of the other hostages, removing wallets, papers, and passports. He then strolled back to a vehicle, the smaller of two that waited beside the dirt helipad, and handed the papers in to someone sitting in the back of the four-wheel-drive vehicle. It looked to Bill like a Jeep CJ-5, which in fact it was... manufactured in Egypt. The officer then stood back from the Jeep, and saluted as it sped away on the dirt road, the only road visible in the entire scene.

The other vehicle waiting at the helipad was a Syrian Army transport truck, an old Russian ZIL-131, with a canvass cover over the rear bed. By now the hostages were familiar with the drill: crowded along a bench to one side, facing the same two armed guards on the other bench. But this time the ride was not short. It stretched on for hour after agonizing hour. As the day grew long, the truck pulled into what Bill assumed was probably a military base. The truck refueled, and two new, tough-looking soldiers, both wearing black berets, replaced the guards.

———

North Shore, Sea of Galilee, Israel

Susan Winning and Lori Tarr returned to the hotel at just after noon from their brief shopping spree. The two ladies had thoroughly enjoyed the leisurely pace of the morning. The shops in the little village that surrounded the sprawling, western-style hotel complex catered especially to American tourists. It was the ladies' plan to leave their bundles of packages in their rooms, to have a bite for lunch at the hotel, and then to return to the village for more treasure hunting in the afternoon. They expected the tour bus to return with their menfolk by about 4:00 PM.

As they entered the lobby, they noticed a noisy commotion near the registration desk. An Israeli policeman and a man wearing a business suit were conferring with the hotel manager and several people that Susan recognized as members of their tour group. Debbie Gold, the wife of the dentist from Philadelphia, was in tears, talking with the man in the suit and gesturing wildly with her hands. She looked up to see Susan and Lori approaching.

"Here they are, now!" Debbie exclaimed to the man. Then, turning and running up to the two ladies, Debbie screamed, "Something terrible has happened!   Something terrible has happened! There has been a terrible accident!" Debbie Gold broke into tears.

"Mrs. Gold, Mrs. Gold, please to be still!" The man in the civilian suit spoke sternly in heavily-accented English. He spoke now to Susan and Lori, who had lowered their packages to the floor. "You are Tarr and Winning, yes?"

"Yes. What is..."

"I am Lieutenant Gal of Israeli Internal Security," said the man. He pulled a plastic-coated packet from his coat, and unfolded it to display his badge and his credentials. "There is accident. We do not know what was...details? We know...little. We do know your bus is in accident. You will please to stay in hotel. We will do what we can do to help you. We will also want to ask questions so perhaps you can help us."

"What about the people on the bus? Were they hurt? Where are they?" asked Susan Winning. A shudder of horror began to overtake her.

Susan Winning knew that paralyzing feeling only too well. It had been only three years previously that she had received that awful call from the state police in New Hampshire:

"Mrs. Winning? Is this the home of Angus William Winning?"
"Yes."
"Do you have a seventeen-year-old daughter named Kathy?"
"Yes."
"I hate to have to inform you of this," the trooper had said, *"but the van she was traveling in lost control on an icy patch of road, and..."*

Kathy Winning, Susan's oldest child, had brought joy to every life she had touched. She had her mother's beauty and fire, and her father's calm strength. She had been a Christian from the time she was four years old, and it was often Kathy, as a little girl, who had rallied the family on to early Sunday School or to Wednesday Night Service when her parents might have found excuses to stay home.

It was Kathy who had organized that Evangel Youth Group Ski Trip to New Hampshire. The trip had led to unspeakable disaster: all six teens in the van and both the adult leaders had been killed in the accident.

The death of her daughter had nearly crushed Susan Winning. She knew that she could not have made it without her faith in God, a loving husband with whom to share the grief, and the steadfast help of her dear friend, Lori Tarr.

It is said, "a friend in need is a friend, indeed." The Bible puts it this way "...let us not love (merely) in word or in tongue, but in *deed* and in *truth*." Lori was like that. It was not just what she said, but what she did - steadfastly, selflessly, and quietly - that made her the most precious of friends.

Lori was once again at the side of her friend. Ignoring the fact that Lori's own husband was also on the Hazor tour bus, she sensed immediately that Susan was on the edge. Still vulnerable from the earlier tragedy, Susan was hardly ready to bear another burden. Lori put her arm around Susan, steadying her, leading her to a chair in the hotel lobby.

The two women sat together and prayed together for a time. When Lori heard her friend praying, not just for their own husbands, but for all the other families as well, Lori knew that Susan had received God's strength for this new trial.

Chapter Six

The Subterfuge

January
Damascus, Syria

WALID EL ZOPHAR WAS WAITING for Admiral Sergei Glutsin where the passengers filed through the gate into the baggage area at Damascus airport. As the admiral approached, Walid ran forward and embraced him. Sergei Glutsin submitted to the embrace, but did not share the Syrian's gregarious enthusiasm.

Walid reached for the large, overstuffed leather case that Glutsin carried. "Here, Admiral," he said, "let me relieve you of this burden!" El Zophar spoke decent Russian, albeit with what sounded to Glutsin's ears like an English accent.

"No, thank you, El Zophar," said the Russian admiral. "I will hold on to the case, myself. Here, you can carry this for me if you will." Glutsin handed El Zophar the heavy parka that he had worn to brace against the weather he had left in Moscow very early that morning. The admiral unbuttoned his wool civilian suit jacket.

"How was your flight, Admiral?" asked Walid. "Pleasant, I trust. We have, at least, no snowstorms here, eh? Here, let me take your suit coat. You have scheduled this trip well, eh? Ha, ha! I hear you took off from Moscow in a blizzard!"

"El Zophar," grunted Admiral Glutsin, without a trace of a smile, "I was born in a blizzard. I am infinitely more comfortable in a snowstorm than I am in this infernal swelter." It was early January, the middle of the rainy season in Damascus. This day it was not raining, but it was unseasonably warm. To the Russian, it was nearly unbearably muggy. "But, we have business to attend, no matter the weather, do we not?"

"Indeed we do, Admiral," said Walid El Zophar. "Please come this way." The two men left the crowd that was milling toward the baggage claim and customs inspection station. They walked briskly toward a door being guarded by a Syrian Army corporal. The soldier, wearing neatly pressed fatigues and a black beret, was armed with an AK-47. As they approached, the soldier snapped to attention, and opened the door to let the Russian and his Syrian host pass through. The door opened into a small room crammed with a desk, file cabinets, and radio transmitting and receiving equipment. At the rear of the office, a door led outside to a parking lot.

Another soldier, older, and without a beret, came to a casual attention as the men entered. He greeted El Zophar warmly, and nodded politely to Admiral Glutsin. Walid and the soldier spoke briefly, evidently exchanging pleasantries.

"Admiral," said El Zophar, "if you will identify your luggage, the sergeant, here, will see to it that it arrives safely at the hotel."

Admiral Glutsin rifled through his papers and found claim checks. "I have only these two bags." He handed the claim checks over to El Zophar, who passed them on to the sergeant. The sergeant waived the two men to the back door, opened it, and showed them out. Another guard snapped to attention as Glutsin and El Zophar passed by. The lot contained a number of military vehicles, four-wheel-drive general purpose vehicles, trucks, and motorcycles. Glutsin saw a black limousine parked at the far end of the lot, near a gate in the chain-link fence that surrounded the lot.

"My driver is waiting over there," said the Syrian. "Let us find you a nice comfortable room in the hotel, eh?"

Glutsin said nothing until they had taken several paces, out of earshot of the guard back at the door, and before they arrived at the limousine. He put out his hand to stop El Zophar. "When do I see Mustafa Mutanabbi?" asked the admiral.

"I have arranged a series of visits for you that I am certain you will find profitable. Mustafa is very eager to continue his discussions with you."

"When do I see him?" persisted the admiral.

"Well," said El Zophar, "let us have a good day of rest today, then tomorrow we will fly north to make contact with our young friend. He is conducting some business in Latakia. We will meet with him there tomorrow."

"Latakia!" exclaimed Glutsin. "El Zophar, that is more than 300 kilometers. Why do we not meet here, in Damascus?" Admiral Glutsin did not appreciate having to cater to the schedules and the whims of these Syrians. After all, these are people who would have ceased to exist as a nation long ago had it not been for the support - yes, the benevolence - of his own (former) country. It had been Soviet tanks, Soviet aircraft, Soviet rifles, Soviet vehicles like the ones in this parking lot, and Soviet training that had kept the Zionists from annihilating these Syrians. And now, as he, Admiral Sergei Glutsin, was coming prepared to make available to them a weapon that would establish Syria as the unquestioned superpower of the Middle East, he had to endure a traveling road show.

"Mustafa has a number of people he wants you to meet," explained the Syrian. "And he must seek your advice about some operational facilities that he would show you. But these things can only be accomplished in Latakia. I will beg your patience in this, Admiral. I will tell you that these operational questions are crucial to the success of our business venture. But first, you will allow me to place you comfortably in your beautiful, air-conditioned hotel room. We have obtained for your pleasure some fine Cuban rum."

"That is good," said Glutsin. At least this El Zophar is a good listener, thought the admiral. He has a good memory from our conversations of my last visit. "But, who are these other people that Mustafa Mutanabbi wants me to meet? I thought we agreed, last time, that it was vital at this stage to keep knowledge of this enterprise under strict security. Let me again be very clear to you. From our side, there is the highest of security precaution being exercised. El Zophar, there is no one in Russia, and I mean *no one*, that knows the details of this plan other than Minister Drednev and me, and my senior security associate, Ivanov. It must be the same here, at least at this stage in the proceedings. You know of it, along with Mustafa, General Zaim, and, presumably, President Zabadi. There must be no one else, or we will have to stop this plan right now."

"Oh, Admiral Glutsin!" gushed El Zophar. "Let me assure you. We are as concerned about the security of this matter as you are. Perhaps more so. You were indeed very clear on this matter when we first met. Mustafa himself has told me that security is the first order of business he wants to discuss. It is one of the reasons that he has requested the meeting be held in Latakia, and not here in Damascus. The men you will meet there are under the impression that you are in Syria to discuss help in establishing a special training program, nothing more. Mustafa will discuss this with you."

"We shall see," groused Admiral Glutsin. He set off for the limousine, striding at a rapid pace. El Zophar scrambled to catch up.

North of Damascus

The helicopter, a Russian-built Mil Mi-34 "Hermit" general purpose light chopper, bounced violently through the morning's low-lying clouds as it made its way north toward Latakia. It stayed in Syrian airspace, to the east of the border with Lebanon. Admiral Glutsin, lulled into a doze by the roar of the helicopter's nine-cylinder Vedeneyev engine, shared the narrow rear passenger seat with a Syrian Army officer, a Lieutenant Colonel Jabri, who carried a large satchel. Glutsin had been around enough to know exactly what the satchel contained: the quick-assembly weapons and communications gear of the security agent. Jabri had not spoken a word since being introduced to the Admiral as they boarded the chopper earlier that morning. Neither did he doze. Jabri occasionally looked out his window on the left side of the aircraft, but for the most part kept his eyes over the pilot's shoulders, scanning the instruments. Walid El Zophar slept soundly in his seat in the front, next to the pilot. El Zophar's snore was loud enough to hear over the din of the engine.

As the chopper approached the northern end of the Anti-Lebanon Mountains, the pilot changed course to the left about ninety degrees from its northeasterly course to a northwest heading that would take his passengers across the Orontes River Valley toward Latakia, the largest city on Syria's Mediterranean Coast. The cloud that had engulfed them ever since their departure from Damascus thinned slightly.

Glutsin straightened up in his seat to look out of his small window. The Orontes was visible below, through a large patch of clear sky. The river, a lazy gray-brown ribbon, ran to the north through barren terrain colored by different hues of the same gray and the same brown. At what Glutsin judged to be about four to five kilometers to the north, the river stopped being lazy. Glutsin could see large irrigation channels that tapped into the Orontes along both the east and west banks. These channels branched out into smaller ditches that fed the many cultivated fields. Near the river's banks on both sides of the river were busy groups of huts. Further north, the city of Homs littered the east bank of the river with its giant Czech-built refineries. Other villages, factories and irrigated fields occupied the attention of the Orontes as far as Glutsin could see to the north.

The cloud closed back in on the little entourage, and the admiral settled back to his doze, leaving the pilot to watch his instruments and Lieutenant Colonel Jabri to watch the pilot. Some time later, Glutsin awoke with a start as the helicopter jarred to a landing at a small helicopter pad. It was raining steadily, and the helicopter's still-rotating propeller whipped a near-blinding wash of muddy water onto Glutsin's window.

A trio of men rushed out of a large, modern building toward the helicopter. Two wore the uniforms of Syrian Army officers. The third wore an open necked civilian shirt. Each carried an umbrella, fighting off the torrential rain that beat down upon them, at the same time skillfully aiming the umbrellas so that the force of the chopper's prop wash would not collapse them.

Walid El Zophar was the first to step out of the helicopter door. One of the Army officers shielded him with his umbrella. "Jabri, you next!" El Zophar pointed at the Lieutenant Colonel who had unbuckled his safety harness and collected his satchel.

Jabri made his way in front of Admiral Glutsin and out of the little door on to the Tarmac chopper pad. One of the three greeters, a security agent of lower rank, shielded him from the rain with his umbrella as they stood back from the doorway to clear the way for the other passengers.

"Admiral Glutsin, if you will step this way please, we will do our best to keep you dry." El Zophar signaled the admiral toward the door.

As Glutsin stepped out, he was met by the man in civilian clothes, a short, powerfully built young man, clean shaven with curly black hair, close-cropped. His dark, exceptional good looks were widely admired, said to be inherited from his mother,

President Hazael's sister. It was Mustafa Mutanabbi. Mustafa offered his umbrella to the Russian admiral.

The admiral carried his leather case in his left hand, placing his right arm around the Syrian. "Mustafa, it is very good of you to meet me out here! No, no! You keep the umbrella. We can share it." Glutsin knew how to be cordial to a recognized person-of-influence. "A little rain never hurt anyone!" The two of them, Mustafa Mutanabbi and Sergei Glutsin hastened into the building. Walid El Zophar and his escort, a Syrian Army colonel, trailed them, followed by Jabri and the other security officer.

The chopper pilot waited until his cargo had been safely delivered into the Ministry of Electricity Production Building, then lifted off the pad, his mission accomplished.

Inside the building, the six men stomped the water and mud off their boots and shed their raincoats and umbrellas, handing them over to the Army corporal that attended the guard's desk just inside the entrance foyer. "Colonel Awad," Mutanabbi spoke to El Zophar's escort, "we will begin the Project Power Pack briefing as we planned at 1300 hours. Have the staff assembled and be sure that the equipment is ready. Admiral Glutsin and I will visit for a while in my office. Assure that we are not disturbed."

"Yes, sir." Awad saluted, and turned to the two security officers, motioning them to follow him. El Zophar joined the soldiers, leaving Mutanabbi and Glutsin alone.

Without speaking, Mustafa Mutanabbi led the way down the long passageway to a large conference room. The building, obviously still in the final stages of construction, smelled of fresh paint and sawdust. Proceeding to a cabinet at the far side of the conference room, Mutanabbi poured two cups of tea from a pot in which the brew was already steeping.

Mutanabbi spoke as he poured. "You take yours with no sweetening, as I recall, Sergei?" Mutanabbi's Russian carried only the slightest traces of accent.

"You remember well, my friend," said Sergei Glutsin.

Mustafa proceeded back into the hall, and unlocked and opened the doorway next to the conference room door. The two men entered a small anteroom containing only an empty desk and chair. Mutanabbi closed and re-locked the door, then turned to

Glutsin and said, with a gracious smile, "Please come in and have a seat, Sergei Leonovich." He led through a second door into a spacious, but sparsely furnished office. "Excuse the lack of facilities. We have only moved in to this building last week, and we are still in the process of delivering equipment and supplies."

"How 'quiet' is this office, Mustafa?" asked Glutsin. His eyes roamed the edges of the walls and ceiling, and inspected the simple light fixture that hung in the center of the room, looking for telltale signs of electronic listening devices.

"There are no 'bugs,' Sergei," said Mutanabbi. "This entire building was designed to my specifications and I have personally supervised every step of its construction." Mustafa chuckled, "And, besides, even if I'd wanted to bug this place, we would, no doubt, be six weeks behind schedule in installing the equipment. I'd have to hire you to come and show us how to install it and how to use it." He took a seat across a small table from Admiral Glutsin.

"But," continued Mutanabbi, "I am very glad that you mention security. Unquestionably you agree that we must take extraordinary precautions to assure secrecy. To assure it absolutely! So much of our strategy depends on keeping knowledge of this enterprise to extreme limits." Mutanabbi leaned forward to press his point on his guest. "Inside our own countries as well as to the outside world."

The two men talked at length about the security precautions that would be taken by both sides. Only the principals would have full knowledge. Others that must be brought into the plan would receive only information germane to the portion of the plan in which they had particular need-to-know.

A subterfuge plan, "Project Power Pack," had been developed. According to the subterfuge, Admiral Glutsin was officially in Latakia to lay plans for providing Syria with the first steps in developing a multiple-unit package of small nuclear reactors for power generation. To be sure, such a development would violate the terms of the Nuclear Non-Proliferation Treaties signed back in the '70's. But that only made the subterfuge plan more credible. It explained the reason for the security provisions that could not fail to draw attention from interested observers.

The only downside risk of discovery of the subterfuge plan would be to incur, perhaps, expressions of concern from the so-called "international community," over such plans to build an outlaw nuclear power plant. At worst, this might ultimately incur some form of international inspection. By that time it would be too late.

The subterfuge plan would also provide a credible, and attractive, basis on which to solicit investment from wealthy friends of President Hazael Zabadi. These were friends with much money and an interest in obtaining access to nuclear technology and by-products. Plus, much of what would be done as part of "Project Power Pack" would be directly useful for the real mission. The crash course in nuclear training, the delivery of spare parts inventories, and even some of the physical plant and facilities constructed for the subterfuge Project Power Pack would certainly benefit the real mission: operation of the *Antyey III* tactical-missile submarine.

Admiral Glutsin was much impressed with the cleverness and almost frightening efficiency with which the young Syrian had approached this mission. Security. Staffing. Training. Supply. Operational policy. Communications. All had been considered, much was already underway. This was totally unlike any dealings he had suffered in the past with his former country's Arab clients. But, despite the exceptional progress that had been made, there were still loose ends. The most glaring, to Glutsin's bureaucratic mind, was that there was no signing-sealing-delivering edict. All these plans had been laid, and were, in fact, well in motion before there was any final, formal agreement.

"Mustafa, you have certainly made progress in preparing for deployment of the system." Glutsin rose and went to the single large window at the rear of Mutanabbi's office. Drawing up a Venetian blind, he scanned the courtyard that was surrounded by the brand-new Ministry of Electricity Production Building. Construction equipment littered the scene, although no workers were evident. The heavy rain, still falling, made ugly brown pools that soon would converge into one large mud-lake. "But, let us not set too quick a pace. I am not aware, for example, that we have a basis for agreement on such a fundamental matter as the price."

"It has been agreed, Sergei." Mustafa wore a strange, smug smile. "President Hazael has been in contact with your Minister

Vladimir Drednev. They have agreed on price and on terms of payment, pending only agreement between you and me that we have a workable plan to carry out the transfer."

Glutsin's mind reeled again. He continued staring out the window, seeing nothing, saying nothing. They have agreed? He thought. Why was I not told of this? This was after all, *my* idea. This is *my* ship! Now Drednev is making the deals without even letting me know. And Mustafa Mutanabbi has nearly raised the Syrian flag up the mast of *Antyey III* before I even know what's going on!

The Syrian continued, "And I am so glad that our two leaders have been able to conclude this matter swiftly. Any delay would only lead to grave difficulty for the whole enterprise."

Reason prevailed in the mind of the admiral as he stood by the window in Mustafa's office. "Of course, that is so." Glutsin spoke softly, then thought, to himself, ...and I am a fool to think it would be otherwise. There is no more Politburo to fight over credit and blame for such things. There is only a desperate need to make a sale. My people are starving. And, besides, setting the price is certainly not my area of knowledge.

It begrudged the admiral to have to admit that, in this end of his own "enterprise," it was he who did not have the need-to-know. It was he that was shut out of the loop of full disclosure. He was no longer one of the *principals*. Reason prevailed, but it was accompanied by an ominous, black cloud of dread.

"Sergei Leonovich," said Mustafa, "you are absolutely right that there are many important things yet to be done!" Mustafa Mutanabbi clapped his hands, his infectious enthusiasm penetrating the gloom. "This afternoon, you will be meeting key members of my team. Tomorrow, I want to take you to inspect the facilities at Damsarkhu. We have nearly completed construction of the wharf and storage buildings there, but we have many questions to ask. Now, in the meeting this afternoon..."

The two men conferred about the goals of the upcoming meeting with Mutanabbi's team, and about the agenda. Mustafa was particularly interested in having the admiral meet each of these men that he had, personally, hand picked. He wanted the advice of this professional submariner about his people. He also would want to know what his people thought of the Russian admiral. Mutanabbi knew full well that his mission depended on the skills of these men, and on the skill with which he used them.

Conference Room, Latakia, Syria

"Gentlemen, we are all together for the first time." Dr. Mustafa Mutanabbi stood before the group of men seated at desks in the fresh, new conference room. "We have, all of us, talked individually about the challenges that face our nation, and what we can do about it. But this is our first chance to come together as a team. And it is *as a team* that we shall succeed!"

Admiral Glutsin, seated behind Mustafa and off to his right, studied the faces of the men in the audience. They were young, all of them. Colonel Awad, whom he had met upon arrival at Latakia, was the oldest man in the room next to himself. Awad and El Zophar were probably the only Syrians present who would have been more than ten years old during the disastrous 1967 War. Lieutenant Colonel Jabri was seated in the back row, as was the other security officer that had met the helicopter at the Tarmac pad. There were two other uniformed Army officers in the room, and two that wore the insignia of Army sergeants. There were three officers of the Syrian Navy, and several enlisted sailors. The rest of the team wore civilian clothing. Several, including Awad, Jabri, the Army sergeants and some of the civilians had the unmistakable look of tough, battle-hardened fighters. Many of the others, including the naval officers, looked more like college students. All were on the edges of their seats; there were no casual smiles, no stray noises. Glutsin could understand none of Mutanabbi's Arabic language, but whatever it was he was saying, these men were drinking in every word.

If there was one common factor that seemed, at Glutsin's first glance, to congeal this team, it was intensity of feeling. What was the feeling? The thought that crossed the admiral's mind: the feeling was *hatred.*

"...and Admiral Glutsin has joined us this afternoon to tell us something about the nuclear reactors that he pioneered for his navy." Mutanabbi was continuing his address to his team, "Now, the infidels of the West will not approve of this idea, but we intend to acquire some of those reactors for Syria, to put them to work generating electricity for our people. Gentlemen, I know I need not remind you of how vital it is to maintain the strictest of security on these matters. You will take no notes. We will have plenty of time later to study the details, as you may require them. This session, today, is for the purpose of an overview." He turned to the admiral, motioning him forward. "A brief description of the reactors, please, Admiral." Mutanabbi spoke to Glutsin in Russian, "Dr. Gurbaal, here, will translate." One of the civilians, seated in the front row, got up to stand next to the admiral. Mustafa Mutanabbi took a seat facing the team.

"Thank you Dr. Mutanabbi." Glutsin turned to the audience. "What we have in mind is a package of six reactors, capable of generating enough electric power to supply the needs of Latakia, Homs and Damascus combined." Admiral Glutsin paused to allow Dr. Gurbaal to translate. "It will allow you to use your oil for more precious applications than to burn it up for your own internal use. These reactors we will provide you are of the 'PWR' - that is 'Pressurized Water Reactor' - type, meaning that the reactor coolant system is a closed loop containing water at high pressure." Glutsin spoke loudly, slowly. He was used to giving such briefings, including briefings that had to be translated. As he spoke, he sketched neat schematics on a chalkboard. It was obvious to the team that he knew what he was doing.

"Since the water is kept at high pressure," continued the admiral, "it can be heated to high temperatures without boiling. Thus, it can be pumped through the reactor core by rather simple centrifugal pumps. As the water is heated in the reactor core, it is pumped to a heat exchanger, called a steam generator, where it circulates through a bundle of tubes, and then back to the reactor. On the outside of those tubes in the steam generator is another system containing water. This second system, however, is at low pressure. So, when this low-pressure secondary water flows over the steam generator tubes containing the very hot, pressurized reactor coolant, the secondary water flashes to steam. The steam is then used to drive the turbines that are geared to the ship's propeller, or in this case," Glutsin lied, "to an electric generator."

The Russian admiral continued his lecture to his potential Syrian clients. "These are reactors that are of standard design. They are identical to those that we install in our large missile submarines. In fact, the first two units have completed their fabrication and are just now completing final testing. These two units were initially intended to be placed in submarines, but we now plan to divert them for use by our friends here in Syria."

At this, there were a few grim smiles, a few heads nodding in appreciation.

Glutsin proceeded, describing and sketching the major subsystems of the Model VM-5 Russian PWR's. He described the pressurizer, reactor coolant pumps, natural convection coolant system, and other engineered safety features and support systems. It was the proverbial drink from a fire hose, but it was a magnificent overview of the machine he was about to sell. His audience paid close attention to every detail.

The Russian then turned to a discussion of the typical operator requirements for the plant. The operators of the reactor system set up to generate electricity would be precisely the same as the operators of a submarine power plant system. There was a single exception: there is no need for a "throttleman" to control propeller speed when there is no propeller. But the duties of the reactor plant control panel operator and the electric plant control panel operator are precisely the same, whether it is a ship-mounted plant or a power plant ashore.

"This allows us," continued the admiral, "to make available to you our standardized training manuals and techniques. In fact, Dr. Mutanabbi and I were discussing it earlier this morning. We will be able to install, on the second floor of this building, a Simulator-Training Unit, 'STU,' for the reactor systems. It will allow you to get valuable hands-on experience before the first operating units arrive for installation. This STU will be identical to the one we operate in Magadan, in our country."

Admiral Glutsin did not mention that the STU to be installed would be identical, not only in the simulated reactor plant and turbine-generator controls of the power plants, but also would include an exact duplicate of the *Antyey III*'s Katapaltes missile systems, her auxiliary systems and her sonar and communications systems. No one else in the room beyond Mutanabbi, El Zophar and Glutsin knew that, yet. That revelation would come soon enough.

———

According to the Mutanabbi/Glutsin plan, the training provided to the Syrians at this stage would be for orientation purposes only. For the first six months of operation, *Antyey III* would be provided with a crew of Russian "buddies" - consultants - that would serve the dual purpose of operating the ship, and of providing what the Americans called "on-the-job training" to their Syrian clients.

During this transition period, the Russians would bring their Syrian counterparts along to the point where they could operate the mammoth vessel on their own. Each of the Russian consultants would be paid handsomely for their half-year's work; each would be able to retire comfortably for life afterward. It was technology transfer in its purest, and most frightening, form.

More frightening yet was the plan that had formed only in the mind of Mustafa Mutanabbi. He had no intention of waiting six months to accomplish his mission. He was a man of great intellect, of great, passionate hatreds, but of little patience.

Chapter Seven

<u>Khokskya</u>

January
Northeastern Russia

A RUTHLESS WIND BLEW DOWN toward the Sea of Okhotsk out of the Kolymskiy Mountains and brutalized the little village. There had been no real cessation of the wind for almost two weeks. The natives call this, in their regional dialect, *Veter Khokskya*, roughly translated, "Our Own Wind." In this remote, desperately forlorn region of northeastern Russia, they refer to this particular time of year, not as January, but as Khokskya. And they know that during the Khokskya time of year, they do not leave their dwellings. This suits the natives, of whom there are very few, because it is also the time of year that the sun is seen for only brief moments, dim and low on the gray horizon at noontime each day.

Sometimes the wind reaches gale force. At other times it backs off to a relatively light bluster, but it is always there. And it is frigid, bone-numbingly cold. Thermometer readings and wind-chill factors are only numbers, and cannot describe what it is like for a human being to stand in the teeth of a thirty-five knot wind pushing air that has been rushed from the Arctic Circle at minus-fifty degrees Fahrenheit.

Such temperatures, in still air, might be bearable for a properly-dressed stalwart. The body generates heat that good wool and fur clothing holds in, near the body. So, the heat transfer rate of BTU's lost by the body out to the surrounding heat sink is within the body's capability to accommodate, for short periods of time. But with such a ripping wind, that layer of warmth is torn away from the body, even through the fibers of wool and strands of fur. The heat-loss rate is far in excess of what the body can generate. So, except for modern, high-tech materials and "heat retention systems," death would ensue in a matter of minutes to anyone exposed to this environment.

The little village also took its name from this annual, deadly phenomenon. The village of Khokskya sits near the shoreline of the Shelikhova Gulf in the northeast quadrant of the Sea of Okhotsk. The village had been established here since ancient times, in spite of January's wind, because the deep waters remain deep all the way up to Khokskya's rocky coastline, and provide for excellent fishing. The Shelikhova Gulf is among the most productive fishing regions of the Russian East Coast, and those Eskimo-like people who are able to survive the grim winters manage to eke out a living by fishing the waters very close to their home shores. The fierce Khokskya-wind is, to them, simply a nuisance that they have to bear for a time each year.

The deep waters and steep granite cliffs held other advantages, for other, newer residents of Khokskya. Submarines could remain submerged right up to the shoreline. They could enter the "pens," caves dug deep in Khokskya's cliff walls, remaining undetected, before surfacing. The advantages were first recognized during World War II, and the pens were constructed, at the cost of countless slave-labor lives, but were never put to use. It was not until some four decades later, when there was a need to develop certain submarine construction programs surreptitiously, that the Khokskya Pens began, finally, to realize their potential.

In the 1980's, when the *Antyey III* program was first conceived, it was evident that secrecy would be a prime factor in the program. A submarine is, speaking generally, the ultimate stealth weapon. A submarine is unseen and undetected until she strikes. But with *Antyey III*, the Soviets intended to go a step further with stealth. Even the existence of the weapon, let alone her location, was expected to be hidden from the enemy. The modified *Plark*-class submarine, grotesque giant that she was, was considered the ideal platform to carry the new death-by-volume Katapaltes weapon system. The deepwater Khokskya Pens, remote and hidden from the prying eyes of American intelligence satellites, were considered the ideal spot to develop the program.

It was with eager enthusiasm that Viktor Rypkin had first reported to his little office in a trailer next to the graving dock in North Pen, thirty-five meters beneath the surface at Khokskya. He had been overwhelmed with pride at having been selected for the assignment: Sonic Navigation Subsystem Project Manager for a hyper-secret new submarine development program, code-named "Project Titus." Before this promotion, he had been a top student of electronics engineering at the universities at Moscow and Kiev, and had spent five years as a project engineer on submarine navigation system development, with assignments in Rostov and back in his hometown, Moscow. This assignment on Project Titus was a real breakthrough for his career.

Rypkin had begun to wonder why he had been held back as other, lesser, engineers got the plum assignments. A friend, who had come from a traditionally Jewish family, had grumbled that it might be because Rypkin's mother had been a Jew. How foolish! His mother had died when Viktor was only seven. Rypkin's father had been a loyal Party man and a capable electrician until the day he died, and Viktor himself had been an exemplary Young Pioneer, not to mention that he was also a Red Star Scholar. He had always been active and loyal in the right things. Rypkin knew that anti-Semitism was still very much apparent in some quarters in his homeland, but certainly not among his well-educated and competent superiors on this program.

Whatever may have been the validity of Viktor's suspicions about the reasons for his late-blooming career, he was, finally, a full fledged project manager. He had proven his loyalty as well as his skill. And, best of all, he was on a project that had been kept going even as the Soviet Union had collapsed. Many of his associates, eminent scientists and engineers, were being cast adrift into the maelstrom of economic distress that gripped his new country. It seemed that every day a new rumor filtered into the Pens that one or another project had been canceled, or that even Project Titus might be in jeopardy. He knew that the project was near completion, and he worried: what would come next?

So, it was with considerable trepidation that Viktor Rypkin answered the call to report to the headquarters of Project Titus, over at Center Pen. He had heard that Admiral Sergei Glutsin himself, the man who had been called the Father of the Giant Submarines in the old Soviet Navy, was paying a personal visit to Khokskya. Admiral Glutsin is the man who, remarkably, had survived the collapse of the old Communist government, and had maintained his status with Yeltsin, Putin and the rest. No one knew where he stood with the new Starazhnikoff-Drednev administration. But, if this rumor were true, and if the Old Man were visiting even now, when the Khokskya-wind was blowing at its worst topside, it must be serious news, indeed. Viktor expected the worst.

Rypkin took the elevator down to the Headquarters Access Passageway that led from the littered, noisy North Pen over to the relatively pristine environment of Center Pen. Here is where the administrative offices were found, as well as living quarters for the eight hundred men and women that comprised Project Titus.

Center Pen was a self-contained, if austere, little community, with a store for necessities, a mess hall, even a barber shop. Rarely in winter did anyone except for Security Department personnel venture out into the topside world. These Titus people, many of them submariners or former submariners, might as well have been at sea, submerged below a thousand feet of ocean.

Rypkin's mood continued to sink as he made the familiar trip home. How absurd! he reminded himself, I'm actually thinking of this cave in the middle of nowhere as 'home.' But, it was true. It was the finest home he had known. As Project Manager of one of the more important subsystems, he rated one of the nicer cubicle-apartments in the complex. Two rooms plus a kitchenette! All to himself! He had done what was probably the best work of his career, hashing out control system problems and design innovations, at the table in that little kitchenette. When Titus was canceled, as he was sure it was about to be, he would miss both the prestige of his quarters and the professional challenges that beckoned nearly every day.

But this was more serious than merely having to give up his cozy cubicle. Viktor had heard all the stories of the utter poverty that had befallen many of his former colleagues. He had been isolated from much of the real world for nearly two years, with only rare sabbaticals, visits to old friends in Moscow and Rostov, to catch up on all the rumors. And, what does one do to try to find a good position - or any position? And what of Tatyana? What would become of her?

Tatyana Patinova was a very bright young woman, a mechanical engineer whom Rypkin had first met when they took an

English language course at the university at Kiev. They had been the only two engineers taking the course, and both had struggled with it. But out of their mutual struggle, they had forged a friendship that had grown over the years, especially when they found themselves working together on Project Titus. It would not be correct to describe their relationship as a romance. Tatyana might have permitted these feelings, but Viktor was simply too involved in his work to indulge in such frivolity. He had heard the warning often: "Do not become involved with workmates -- it clouds judgement, destroys reputations, ruins both careers." He took this proverb to heart. At this stage in his life, Viktor Rypkin wanted nothing to stand in the way of a successful career.

But Tatyana and Viktor did spend a good deal of time together. Many of their associates assumed that they were, in fact, close. Many assumed that they were merely feigning a friends-only relationship. Tatyana and Viktor comprised, indeed, a handsome couple. Tatyana was a little stocky, not a stunning beauty, but neither was she unattractive. She had alert, bright blue eyes and a laughing spirit that was an engaging counterpoint to Viktor's tall, thin, and melancholy darkness. Viktor was actually very handsome, but he had no idea of it. He had been convinced from youth that his only worthwhile asset was his mind.

The time Tatyana and Viktor spent together was mostly in discussion of details of their work on Project Titus, occasionally in pondering the fate of their new-old country, but rarely in discussion of any personal matters. Both seemed to relish the ability of the other to match intellect and insight. They had each become dear to the other, as good friends do.

And now Viktor found himself anxious, not only for the impending doom that he was certain was about to befall him and his beloved career, but also for Tatyana.

A sense of low-grade panic began to dominate his thoughts. Viktor began to think through the list of contacts he had made over the years, people who could possibly help him find a position when he left Project Titus. But he doubted he could ever land another position as rewarding, and demanding, as this one.

As he entered Center Pen and offered his identification pass for inspection by the guard, he headed inboard, toward the

Headquarters Complex. He had to show his ID again and sign in at the guard station leading to the office cubicles. The guard checked Rypkin's name against a list that he had on a clipboard at his desk.

"Yes, Mr. Rypkin," said the guard. "You are to proceed to the director's office. Please go up to the second level and report to Miss Gleneeva, the director's secretary."

This was serious, indeed! Rypkin had never even been to the second level before, let alone visit the director's office! A promotion? No, no. Viktor knew better than to let his hopes outpace reality. Have I made some indiscretion, have I made a mistake somewhere? Rypkin asked himself, refusing to think anything but the worst.

He passed through the large double doors leading to the office of the director, and trotted up the central staircase to the second floor. He saw the secretary's desk behind a glass door across the hall at the top of the stairs.

"Mr. Rypkin?" Miss Gleneeva was waiting for him. She smiled pleasantly, thoroughly confusing the young engineer. "Please go on in," she said. "Director Khalinko and Admiral Glutsin are expecting you." Now Viktor Rypkin was stunned.

"You are certain it is I they wish to see? I am *Viktor* Rypkin of the Ops/Nav Department. There is another Rypkin, in Security."

"Yes, yes, Mr. Rypkin," said Miss Gleneeva. She indicated the door behind her. "You are the correct Rypkin. Please go on in."

Viktor opened the door and timidly went in to the large office. Pictures of submarines covered the walls. A large, framed picture was mounted above the leather swivel-chair that sat behind a grand wooden desk. The picture showed two men, shaking hands, beaming at the camera. Behind the men in the picture was a submarine about to be launched at a shipyard. It looked like a *Plark* or perhaps an early *Granit*-class. The two men in the picture were Director Andrei Khalinko and Admiral Sergei Glutsin. It was to Viktor's continued sense of anxiety to see those same two men seated at the director's conference table, beaming just as in the picture. Director Khalinko stood to greet Viktor.

"Rypkin, yes? It is good to see you, Rypkin," said Khalinko. Turning to Admiral Glutsin, the director continued, "This is the man who has been one of our most productive project managers,

Admiral. He is the prime developer of the new 'Yodel Echo Navigation System.' He has met every schedule milestone we have established, and has stayed within budget. He was even able to stay on schedule with the budget cut we had last year! I am recommending him for a Top Performer Medal."

Admiral Glutsin rose from his chair and offered his hand to Rypkin. "Very glad to meet a Top Performer, Rypkin!" said the admiral.

Viktor's hand was sweating, cold. What is happening here? he asked himself silently. "Thank you, sir," Rypkin croaked as he shook the hand of the admiral.

"Please sit, over here," offered Director Khalinko. He motioned to a seat across the table from where he and the admiral sat. Three other men sat along the table on Viktor's side.

"Rypkin," said Khalinko, "I'd like you to meet Dr. Kaspar Ivanov, of the Ministry of Energy." The director indicated the man seated closest to Viktor. He then continued, gesturing at the other two men, farther down the table, "I believe you are acquainted with Boris Shelepin of our Nuclear Power Engineering Division and with Alexander Karkaraly of the Electrical Engineering Division."

Dr. Ivanov rose part of the way out of his chair, extending his hand for a perfunctory handshake. Viktor did not recognize the name; he had never seen the face. Viktor nodded to Shelepin and Karkaraly. He had known them both for some time, though not well. Both were from the Power Engineering Department offices over at South Pen. He had seen them occasionally when one or the other of them would come over to North Pen where the giant submarine was actually being constructed. He had spoken to them from time to time at the weekly staff meetings. But he had never had any direct dealings with either man.

From all Rypkin could gather, both Shelepin and Karkaraly were good engineers. Both were younger than he, and both had cubicle-apartments nearly comparable to his own. Well, of course Viktor's apartment was by far superior in its location, being nearly at the end of a passageway, quiet, granting some measure of privacy. But, these were clearly top people that had been brought before the admiral. This must be very bad news, indeed! It must be, Viktor thought, the admiral's way of breaking the news to us personally. He has a reputation for caring for his men; this must be the admiral in action, showing his so-called "concern."

When Viktor had taken his seat, it was Admiral Glutsin who began the conversation. "Gentlemen," he said, "I am very pleased to have this chance to meet with you, personally. Tomorrow we get together with the entire project, down in the auditorium."

Here it comes, thought Rypkin. He could not look the admiral in the eyes. Tears began to form in his own eyes as he stared down to his hands, folded in his lap. His heart pounded, his head felt light, dizzy. What will I do? Where will I go? he thought.

"I think you will all be pleased," said the admiral, "with the news I bring you." Viktor barely heard the words. Glutsin continued, "Because of the excellent work you all are doing here in Khokskya, I am very happy to report that, in spite of all the budget axes that have fallen around us, we are able to continue Project Titus, at least for the present time."

Rypkin closed his eyes. "What?" thought Viktor. He dared not believe what he had just heard. He opened his eyes again, lifting them cautiously up and across the table at the admiral, who was still speaking.

"Director Khalinko and you, the Top Performers on Titus," said Glutsin, "have been successful against many odds. And, you have maintained the security of our operation. That is vital. It is, in fact, what allows us to continue the operation."

Glutsin looked straight at Rypkin. "I know the rumors that have been floating around The Pens," said the admiral. "I know the dread we all face in seeing our forces cut back so wantonly. But, fortunately, the axe will not fall on Khokskya, at least not soon." Admiral Glutsin paused for a moment, shuffling a stack of papers that were arranged before him on the table.

"Now, however, gentlemen," Glutsin continued, "I want to get to what is, for you, the truly good news. I know that good, challenging assignments are most difficult to find in our country today. That will change, but today I know the opportunities for professional growth are limited in the extreme. Dr. Ivanov, here," Glutsin pointed across the table to the stranger who sat next to Rypkin, "is with me today to introduce you three Top Performers to a new project for which you have been selected. Personally hand-picked. It is a project that you will find rewarding as well as professionally challenging. Now, I'm going to ask Dr. Ivanov to describe this project to you in detail. But first, I want you to know something."

It was time for the Big Lie.

"When you join Dr. Ivanov's team," said Admiral Glutsin, "you will be leaving mine. I want you to know, I am not happy about that. Viktor Rypkin, Boris Shelepin, Alexander Karkaraly," Admiral Glutsin looked each in the eye as he called their names, "you are truly the best of the best, and I am very unhappy to give you up. But, our country has entered a new era. We must learn to use our skills in pursuits that have more peaceful ends. We must make the transition from machines of war to machines of peace and productivity. Do you understand this?"

Viktor nodded enthusiastically. So did Boris and Alexander. "It is true, everything they say about this Admiral Glutsin!" thought Rypkin. "He knew what I was worried about; he has planned an avenue for my career! I had no idea he even knew my name!"

"Now," Glutsin continued the lie, "the project to which you will be assigned is not at all associated with Project Titus. It is, in fact, not even in this country. You will be going, gentlemen, to help a nation of very good and long-standing friends. You will be helping them to develop a power generating capability. This will help their economy by providing electric power to their farms, and homes, and factories. We, in Russia will earn a handsome fee for providing your expertise. And you, gentlemen, will have taken a major career step in a vital field that will provide you opportunities for a lifetime. Everybody wins."

Later, as he considered this conversation, Sergei Glutsin would feel most remorse for this last lie: "And, gentlemen," said the admiral, "best of all, you will be able finally to leave this infernal cave and the cursed Khokskya-winds. You are going to a vacation spot: the Mediterranean Coast of Syria!"

In fact, Glutsin would have preferred a thousand winters in Khokskya to one miserable week in Syria.

Glutsin turned the proceedings over to Dr. Kaspar Ivanov, whom he presented as Director of "Project Power Pack." The admiral hated having to dissemble so blatantly before his own men, but it was the price of their own survival, as he rationalized it. He was doing them a favor.

Ivanov went to an easel that contained flip-charts. As he removed the cover sheet, a large map of Syria was revealed, with a bright red circle at the upper left, around the port city of Latakia. "What we have in mind, gentlemen," began Ivanov, "is a project that will utilize the Model VM-5 pressurized water reactors, identical to the *Antyey III* power plant, to establish an electric power plant in Syria. We will ultimately build six such reactors, but we will begin with two of the units." Ivanov showed detailed maps of the proposed site, located just seven kilometers north of Latakia at the seaside village of Damsarkhu.

"The Syrian Ministry of Electricity Production," said Ivanov, "has established a modern office complex and training facility at Latakia, which will be your headquarters. Our first order of business will be to establish a first-class training program for the Syrian engineers and operators."

Dr. Ivanov continued, giving a detailed description of the plans for the power plant, and for setting up the administrative and engineering offices in Latakia. Considerable attention was paid to the training facilities that would occupy one whole floor of the huge new Ministry of Electricity Production building. Rypkin was impressed to see that over half the area of the training floor was vacant, labeled "FOR FUTURE USE." Viktor had rarely seen such lavish working facilities, even in the heyday of Soviet military buildup.

After nearly ninety minutes of detailed presentation by Dr. Ivanov, Admiral Glutsin suggested a break for tea. The men headed for the restroom located in the hallway outside the director's office, but little was said until they returned to the conference room where Miss Gleneeva was busy serving the tea.

Admiral Glutsin re-opened the meeting. "Well, men," he said, "Kaspar has talked himself hoarse. Now it's your turn. Any questions?"

No one spoke. No one even budged.

"Look," Glutsin smiled at the young engineers, "this isn't the Soviet Navy any more. We've got to start acting like businessmen." Glutsin had learned quickly from his new mentor, Vladimir

Drednev. "You have a question, you ask. You think you have a better idea, you say it. You, Rypkin, what do you think?" asked Admiral Glutsin.

Viktor almost choked. He was not familiar with being asked a question that called for something other than a specific numerical answer, certainly not from the admiral who was a legend in the Khokskya Pens. "It is a brilliant plan, Admiral. Dr. Ivanov has covered it most thoroughly."

Glutsin still smiled patronizingly at the young electronics genius. "Come on, Viktor," said the admiral, "I want some input."

Ivanov's briefing had stimulated Rypkin's professional enthusiasm, but, in fact, there was one matter that had been puzzling him. If the admiral wanted input, Viktor would obey. "Well, sir," said Viktor, coughing self-consciously, "I am wondering about one thing. Do not take me wrong, sir, I am very much honored to be included in this new project, and I am not suggesting otherwise..." Rypkin paused.

"Go on, Viktor," Admiral Glutsin nodded pleasantly.

"Well," Viktor stammered, "I...I am an electronics engineer. My experience is in sonar and navigation systems. Where do I fit in for this power plant project?"

Admiral Glutsin nodded faintly toward Kaspar Ivanov. Ivanov spoke up, almost as if on cue, "We want you on this project, Rypkin, not just for your electronics experience, but because Director Khalinko has told us that you are an exceptional project manager. It is your experience with budgets and schedules that we are most interested in. There may, indeed, be some need for you to do some work in your electronics discipline in Syria, but your prime responsibility will be to organize a system for planning and scheduling Project Power Pack. I think you will find it..."

Admiral Glutsin interrupted. "Viktor, I appreciate your expressing this concern. I will personally see to it that you will be given opportunities to stay current in your field of expertise." The admiral jabbed his index finger hard into the tabletop to express the firmness of his commitment. "I will promise you that I will call on you for work in sonar navigation systems from time to time, even if I have to pull you away for a few days from my friend Kaspar, here. You will not grow stale in Syria, I will guarantee you that."

"Thank you, sir. It almost seems that you anticipated my question. It is obvious that you and Director Ivanov have thought through every detail of this program. I look forward to getting started on it." Viktor Rypkin's enthusiasm was genuine. Admiral Glutsin's cordiality was not.

An hour later, after the meeting had broken up and the three young engineers had been dismissed to make preparations for leaving Khokskya, Glutsin turned to Dr. Ivanov. "You will do well, Kaspar, to keep a very close eye on this Rypkin. I know that he is considered indispensable in setting up the Yodel Echo navigation system. I realize that the Katapaltes system will not function properly without his expertise, but his questions bother me. He is a bright young man. He will not be easy to convince that he's only in Latakia to plan a power plant."

"He has never been a problem, Admiral." Director Khalinko spoke up. "He has a spotless record for loyalty. As I have mentioned before, his only flaw seems to be a compulsion to advance in his career. And that is certainly a healthy attitude from our perspective."

"That may be so, gentlemen," said Glutsin, "but hear me well." Admiral Glutsin spoke slowly. He spoke now, not as a would-be capitalist businessman, but as an admiral of the Russian Navy. "I also see in the records that Viktor Rypkin's mother was a Jew. You know that in Jewish culture, if the mother is a Jew, the children are considered Jews. Viktor Rypkin is a Jew. If he finds out about the true mission he is being sent to perform in Syria, there may be a problem. We want no problems. I say again, watch him closely."

"Yes, sir," said Ivanov. The head of the so-called "Project Power Pack" realized that now Admiral Glutsin was not inviting comment, but giving an order.

————————

Viktor Rypkin felt nearly like humming a tune as he tripped lightly down the stairs from the second level and out the door toward the security station. What a relief! He had been so sure that he was about to experience the end of everything: his profession, his secure income, his self respect. He had been certain that his life, for practical purposes, was about to end. And now, in the space of the last three hours or so, everything had fallen in place in a most wonderful way.

Viktor had actually met The Admiral. *The Admiral - in person*! And The Admiral seemed to really care about him; really wanted him on this new project. And The Admiral had personally guaranteed him opportunities to advance his career. So what that he, Viktor Rypkin, did not yet fully understand why they wanted him in Syria? So what that Director Ivanov's responses to his questions were a little vague? Viktor's skills were as an electronics engineer, not as a planner and scheduler. Anyway, no matter. He was sure it would become clear soon enough. "Wait until Tatyana hears this!" thought Viktor.

Well, he couldn't tell her everything. Admiral Glutsin and Director Ivanov were very clear that no one was to know the location or nature of the work. But he could pass along that he had received a handsome promotion and the personal assurances of Sergei Glutsin for special treatment in his career.

Rypkin signed out at the Headquarters Complex security station and headed for the Living Quarters at the far end of Center Pen. Tatyana would be getting off her shift in less than a half hour, so he would go have a cup of tea and share the good news with her.

There was a small shop near the entrance to the Living Quarters where Viktor often stopped to get hot tea to go, in large paper cups. He entered the shop, crowded with workers on the way to begin their shift.

"The tea will be cold by the time Tatyana gets here," Viktor murmured to himself, as he absently looked at the shelves of the shop. "Besides, this is a special day. I wonder what they have that's special." Russian stores are not known for variety or elegance, especially little concession shops in Siberian shipyard-caves. But Viktor's eyes fell on something distinctive: a small box of chocolates, imported from Denmark. Viktor knew that Tatyana loved sweets. Loved them too much, perhaps. It was likely that she had never tasted anything quite so exquisite as these chocolates. What a perfect way to celebrate the good news!

Tatyana was right on time. Tired from a long shift at North Pen, she brightened at the sight of Viktor waiting in the small lobby of her dormitory building. "Viktor!" exclaimed Tatyana. "It is wonderful to see you." Her voice rang with delight at seeing her friend. "Come on up to my room while I put this stuff away and tell me what happened today!" She carried a box full of papers, evidently intending to do some homework.

"Here," said Viktor, "let me carry this box for you." Viktor took the heavy box from Tatyana, and handed her the bag containing the surprise. "You take this," he said. "It is for you." The wide grin on Viktor's face was a rare sight, indeed.

The two of them proceeded up a flight of stairs to the hallway. Tatyana's room was the first door on the right.

"For me?" asked Tatyana. "Viktor, what...?" It was not the habit of this brooding young man to give presents. An occasional paper cup of tea, perhaps. And, at that, he usually expected her to take her turn at buying. "Oh! These are *wonderful*! Chocolates! For me? What did you find out at the meeting at Headquarters Complex? It must have been magnificent news. Please tell me about it, Viktor!"   All signs of fatigue from her job had disappeared. Tatyana was aglow with excitement at this uncommon expression of affection, or generosity, or whatever it was, from Viktor Rypkin. Tatyana's own beaming face matched Viktor's smile.

Viktor noticed the beauty of her countenance, the charm of her delightful laugh. He placed the box of papers on the table inside Tatyana's room and then reached over to embrace her. He kissed her, for the first time, and marveled at her warmth and softness, and at how delicate she seemed in his arms.

He held her at arm's length for a moment, continuing in an excited voice, "Tatyana," said Viktor, "you can never guess what has just happened to me!"

"I am waiting for you to tell me!" said Tatyana. "So tell me!" Tatyana's heart raced with delight to see such happiness and apparent affection from her friend.

"Tatyana," explained Viktor Rypkin, "I have just come from a meeting with Director Khalinko, and with Admiral Sergei Glutsin, *himself!"*

"I had heard that The Admiral was in Khokskya," said Tatyana. "You met him, personally? Oh, Viktor, that *is* wonderful!"

"That is only the beginning, Tatyana!" said Viktor. "Wait until you hear what was said." Viktor continued, excited, nearly breathless. He told of his apprehension about going to the second floor. He told of the others who were in the room. He told of Khalinko's calling him out as a Top Performer. And he began to tell of the new project to which he was to be assigned. "Now," Viktor cautioned, "I am not at liberty to say anything specific about where this will be; not even what kind of job it is."

In his fervor, he did not notice the change in Tatyana's mien. She still smiled, she still nodded with apparent enthusiasm at the unfolding news. But the sparkle had left her bright blue eyes. The exhilaration had suddenly fled, and she felt as though her heart had tumbled into an abyss.

"And...Tatyana...and listen to this!" Viktor went on, speaking with uncharacteristic excitement, "Admiral Glutsin gave me his personal assurance - 'guarantee,' he said - that he will see to it that I am able to get good assignments in the future in my field of sonar navigation. Isn't that fantastic?"

"Yes, Viktor," responded Tatyana. "It is truly fantastic." Tatyana backed gently away from Viktor; he released his loose embrace.

"And, Tatyana," continued the excited Rypkin, "perhaps one day I will be able to work with you again. Listen, if anything happens to Project Titus, you know you can call me, right? Perhaps with the new contacts I make I could help you find a more secure position, too." Viktor headed for the door to Tatyana's room. "I must go now. We are to be ready to leave Khokskya by 0600 in the morning. I have much to do. I will hope to see you before I go. See you later!"

Viktor departed with a wave.

Tatyana closed the door behind him. She leaned against it, still clutching the rumpled bag and its precious Danish chocolates. Tears filled her eyes.

Chapter Eight

Amazing Grace

February
Jabal ad Farabi, Northwestern Syria

BILL WINNING AWOKE with a shudder. Pain stabbed along the entire left side of his body. The throbbing ache in his ankle and lower leg would not go away. The pain seemed to intensify at night. He had been asleep for what he estimated to be a couple of hours, lying on his left side on the cold concrete floor. His left wrist was manacled to a chain attached by a padlock to a bracket in the concrete wall. His wrist, galled badly by the manacle, sometimes ached so badly that it helped Bill to forget the throbbing in his ankle.

A noise had aroused him from sleep. It was the noise of footsteps, of keys clanking and of a door opening. In the darkness, Bill could see little. The door to his cell remained closed. Suddenly, a bare light bulb in the center of the cell's ceiling clicked on. Bill quickly closed his eyes, covering them with his unmanacled right hand, shielding them from the abrupt onslaught of light. The small inspection port in the door opened; two dark eyes peered in. The cell door opened and a black-bereted Syrian soldier appeared, carrying an AK-47 assault rifle in one arm, and a bucket in the other. The soldier glanced around the cell as he placed the bucket down by the door. He saw four miserable souls shackled to the wall. Bill Winning was along the wall to the right of the door, Pastor Gary Tarr next to him, along the same wall. On the other side of the cell lay Dr. Mel Gold, opposite Winning, and Bucky Albostini, opposite Tarr.

The cell was designed for six prisoners. Two unused sets of manacle-chains and brackets occupied the space at the rear of the cell, one on either side of the cell. The only other furnishing in the room was a large metal canister, which the men had appropriated as their toilet and placed near the back wall.

The soldier, evidently satisfied that all was in proper order, shut the door, locked it, bolted it and flipped the light back off. His footsteps could be heard leaving the cell area and closing another door behind him.

Bill crawled over to the bucket that the soldier had placed by the door. "Water!" he exclaimed as he cupped his hands and guzzled large, refreshing gulps. "Who's next?"

"Here!" Bucky Albostini cried out in a weak, pitiful voice. Bill slid the bucket to Gary Tarr, who shoved it across the cell to Albostini, slumped with his back against the wall. Albostini eagerly leaned forward to grab the bucket. He began to gulp from cupped hands.

Their last drink had been the previous afternoon, as they had filed, blindfolded, out of the back of the Syrian Army truck that had brought them to this forlorn camp. At that time, they had been allowed to visit a latrine and then to slake their thirst from a bucket of water. They then had been brought in to this concrete cell building, where their handcuffs were removed, only to be replaced by the manacles and two-meter-long chains that bound them to brackets in the walls.

Bill estimated the time of the guard's arrival to be about five o'clock in the morning. The barest hint of sunlight appeared at the eaves of the building. A thin gap between the roof structure and the walls was the only opening to the outside world; there was no window in the cell. Confused and disoriented since their capture at Hazor, his watch having been confiscated along with his wallet and passport, all Bill could do was to guess, even as to what day it was. By his reckoning it was Saturday. The men passed the bucket around until all four had quenched their thirst. Albostini spoke in a near-whimper, "I wonder if they are planning to feed us here."

"Well," Bill responded, "they wouldn't waste water on us if they didn't have some reason to keep us alive. And they can't keep us alive if they don't feed us. So, I think the chances are pretty good they'll give us something to eat. I wouldn't expect *hors d'oeuvres* though." Bill grinned through his pain.

"Why has this happened to us? What are they going to do to us?" Albostini whined. He had been near to tears most of the time since their capture three days before. This was the first time in those three days that the men had been left alone, able to talk.

"Look, Bucky," said Mel Gold, "you've got to get a grip." Gold was Bucky Albostini's brother-in-law, and he had heard enough of the mewling. "None of us knows what's going on here."

"Mel's right, Bucky." Gary Tarr spoke up. "All we know is the Syrians and the Israelis are nearly at war. Maybe they are in a full-scale war by now, I don't know. Somehow we are going to be used as pawns in this thing. Remember those hostages that were taken in Lebanon several years ago? Terry Anderson and Terry Waite and those guys? They became the keys to negotiations between the U.S. and Iran and who knows who else? Hey, the whole Iran-Contra thing involved trying to swing a deal to get those hostages released. You can bet there are a lot of folks back home who will be pulling every string in the book to get us out of here. We'll get out of here, all right, Lord willing."

The men settled back down to the hard floor. A long silence followed. The only noise was the muted, low growl of a diesel engine, an electric power generator, off in the distance. The faint light struggling through the eaves slowly became strong enough so that the men could see each other dimly in their pitiful, stinking, cell-room.

Bucky Albostini, curled in the corner, began to weep, softly.

No one spoke for a long time. Albostini was beyond comforting with words. Then, a rich, baritone voice began to fill the room. "A-ma-zing grace, how sweet the sound, tha-at saved a wretch li-ike me! I once wa-as lost, but now am found; wa-as blind but now I see!" Gary Tarr sang the familiar tune, joined by Bill Winning on the second verse: "T'was grace that taught my heart to fear, and grace that fear relieved. How precious did that grace appear, the hour I first believed." No violins, no guitar. Not even professional voices. But never had music sounded sweeter.

The two men sang a third verse, then began to hum the melody. Mel Gold hummed along with them. He had remembered the tune from an old Judy Collins record he'd heard as a youth. He had never thought much about the words.

"It's a beautiful song. What does it mean, 'Amazing Grace?'" Mel asked as they finished a last chorus.

"Grace," Gary Tarr spoke quietly, "is the love that God gives us, even though we don't deserve it. It *is* amazing, when you think about how rotten we are as mankind that he would ever give us a chance to come into his presence, let alone offer us eternal life with him."

The men fell silent again for a time. The only sounds were the faint hum of the diesel generator and the barking of a dog in the distance.

Bill Winning spoke up. "As the song says, it was grace 'that saved a wretch like me.' I'll tell you, I was a real wretch when God's grace saved me. I wasn't an alcoholic or on drugs or any of that, but I was worse: I didn't even think there was such a thing as God. But one day he really got my attention and I began to think seriously about God."

"How did God 'get your attention,' Bill?" asked Mel Gold. Gold shifted his position, rattling his chains. Bucky Albostini had stopped his sobbing and sat up along the wall.

"Oh...I was in the Navy, and...well...I nearly sank my submarine. It was a long time ago, I was in my early twenties, just a junior officer running deep in a submarine for the first time. It's a long story, but I nearly caused us to sink the ship. I honestly thought for a moment that I was going to die, and the whole ship was going with me. We did have one man get killed that day. Well, it really caused me to think, 'what if we had gone down? Where would I be now?' Seriously, Mel, if you were to die today, where would you be tomorrow?"

Gold shook his head, thoughtfully.

"Well," Bill continued, "I had heard a preacher talk about how the answer to this question is found in the Bible. So, I figured I had spent plenty of time reading other books, why not try the Bible? So I did. Cover to cover. By the way, that preacher later became my father-in-law."

"Did you find the answer to your question?" Gold asked.

"Yep," said Bill Winning. "It's very simple. First, the Bible makes it clear that everyone...I mean *everyone*...falls short of God. The Bible calls that 'sin.' The Bible says, '...all have sinned and come short of the glory of God.' Second, the penalty for sin is death. It says, 'the wages of sin is death,' and 'it is appointed unto man once to die, but after this, the judgement.' And there's nothing that anyone, on his own, can do about it. I don't care if someone is a priest or a pope, or a rabbi, or a mullah. I don't care if he gives all his money to the synagogue, or goes to church every day of his life, or bows to Mecca three times a day, or lives in a monastery, or whatever. There is absolutely nothing we can do to obligate God to give us eternal life, to let us in to his heaven. The Bible says, 'all our righteousness is like filthy rags' in God's sight. It's as though we've all been convicted by a judge for breaking the law, and the sentence is death. That's the bad news.

Bill longed for his Bible. That, he knew, was where he could count on words of truth to share with his new friend. But he was glad that he had been part of a *Navigators* training group that his father-in-law had led years ago, when Bill was a brand new Christian. He was glad that he had learned to memorize important verses.

"What's the good news?" asked Mel Gold. "We could use a little good news right about now." Gold smiled a grim smile and rattled his chain again. "And, remember, Bill, I'm Jewish. I hope your 'good news' doesn't leave me out."

"Hey...quiet a minute!" said Bucky Albostini, bolting to his feet. He pulled his manacle chain tight to keep it from rattling. "Listen, something's coming into the camp!" The four men listened for a moment in silence. The dog's bark could be heard again, this time sounding closer. And there was the sound of a vehicle, growing louder, more distinct.

"Here, Bill, get up on my shoulders and see if you can see out through that gap up there." Gary Tarr pointed toward the eaves, where the rafters lay on top of the wall, the light now filtering in boldly. Big Gary Tarr crouched down so Winning could climb up on his broad shoulders. Tarr stretched his chain tight, moving as far as he could toward the right so that Bill could have enough slack in his own chain to straighten up to full height above them. Winning's eyes barely reached the eaves.

Bill could see out! Victory! A tiny victory, but how exhilarating!

What he saw, however, was not in the least encouraging. "It's a Jeep," reported Bill Winning. "Looks to be the CJ-5 we saw when we got off that helicopter, or else one just like it. The Jeep's heading down a road that's across a little gully below us. Looks as if he's coming this way."

Albostini was excited. "Who's in the Jeep? Is there a flag on it or something? Maybe it's somebody coming to get us out of here."

"Don't count on it, Bucky." Winning scanned as far as he could see to his right and to his left. A tall chain-link fence surrounded the compound, topped by razor wire and what appeared to be electrically charged wires. Directly across from the cell building, and about thirty meters away, was a two-story concrete-block structure that probably served as headquarters for the compound and possibly as barracks for the guard troops. To the right of the headquarters building was a gatehouse, manned by two armed guards. The gate structure actually consisted of two gates, one outside the other. A utility shed was off to the far right, a backhoe vehicle parked off to the side of the building. The utility shed also appeared to house the electric generator that continued to hum.

The entire compound was small, no more than about four barren, rocky acres. A few dismal shrubs grew beside the utility shed and along the fence to Bill's left. Outside the fence, on the left side, were parked a couple of general-purpose trucks, old Russian-manufacture ZIL-131's. Another of the Egyptian Jeeps was parked on the far side of the trucks.

"What's he doing now?" Albostini asked.

"He's coming to a little guard shack that's down along the main road," said Winning. "I'd say it's less than a quarter mile away, on the other side of the gully. The guards are coming out of the shack. There are two of them. They're saluting. This must be a top dude. The Jeep has turned off the main road and he's heading across a culvert over the gully and up this way. Looks as if he's heading toward our little playground, here."

The main road headed past the guardhouse and on down the narrow valley. It then crossed up and over the mountain called Jabal ad Farabi toward the Jari district of extreme northern Syria. The terrain here consisted of rugged, rocky hills. Vegetation was sparse in spite of the rainfall the area received during this, the rainy winter season. The soil, what little there was of it, was too poor, and the terrain too angular to support farming. This spot on the Jabal ad

Farabi was too far from the Orontes River, nearly thirty-five kilometers to the east, and from the Mediterranean Sea, over fifteen kilometers to the west, to support any kind of trade or commerce. The nearest permanent settlement of any sort was the wretched little village of Q'adi, some twenty kilometers to the south. Except for some nomadic shepherds that occasionally strayed into the area, and a British archaeological dig about fifteen kilometers to the north, the location was totally isolated. The Syrian High Command regarded Jabal ad Farabi as the ideal spot for their newest detention/execution compound.

"OK," Bill continued as he peeked out the crack at the top of the cell wall, "now he's pulled into a parking lot next to another Jeep. There's a couple of old trucks there, too. There are two officers in the Jeep. Hey, what's this? We know this guy! Remember the officer with the slick-polished boots? Hey, he's the one that gave me a boxing lesson. I might've done a little better if my hands hadn't been tied behind my back. Boy, what a thrill to see him again!" No one laughed at Bill's attempts at bravery-by-joking.

Winning watched the two men go around the outside of the fence and enter the two gates, opened one at a time. The guards at the gate saluted smartly as the officer, a colonel, strolled through. He was met there by a lieutenant, who saluted and accompanied the colonel and his aide into the headquarters building.

"What do you think it means, Bill?" Albostini asked as Winning climbed down off Gary Tarr's shoulders. "Do you think they'll move us again?"

"There is no way to know." Bill sat again on the concrete floor. Pain surged through his body. He was conscious again of the dull, aching throb in his ankle. And the sharp, burning chafing of the manacle on his wrist had been made worse as he had stretched the chain tight to get his glimpse over the top of the wall through the eaves. "Colonel Boots is obviously the man in charge of this little operation. He's a pretty brutal guy. He didn't have much mercy on Lem and Aileen Philpot, or the Armstrongs or the others on our bus tour. I wouldn't be too encouraged about what he's here to discuss."

"Oh, my God!" Albostini broke into a near whimper again. He had been standing, but he collapsed to the floor, then stretched out on the floor along the side of the wall, head buried in his unmanacled right arm.

"What about *your* God, Bill?" Mel Gold ignored his brother-in-law for a moment and directed the question at Winning. His tone was not cynical or bitter. He honestly wanted to know. "You told me the bad news. You said the Bible tells us that everyone is doomed to die because they don't live up to God's standards. I can buy that. And you said that nothing we can do, no matter what, can change the death sentence. OK. But what's the good news? Is there any?"

Bill was silent for a moment. He stared down at his chains, then looked up at Dr. Gold. "Mel," Bill spoke quietly, slowly. "I'm going to mention a name that is the probably the most abused, misunderstood name in the world. I know you've heard it, but probably only when somebody was cursing. It's the name of the man who is also God. It's the name of the One who does the judging when we die. You said you are Jewish; so is this man. In Hebrew, His name is *Yeshua*. In English, we pronounce it 'Jesus.' He is the Messiah. Or, to use the Greek title, He is the Christ." Bill paused for a moment, shifting his weight and adjusting his chain.

He continued, "The great Jewish prophet, Isaiah, said, '...unto us a Child is born, unto us a Son is given: and the government shall be upon His shoulder: and His name shall be called Wonderful, Counsellor, The mighty God, The everlasting Father, The Prince of Peace.' Mel, this is the most important thing in the world to know: Jesus was that Child, that Son. Jesus is the mighty God!"

Mel Gold looked at Bill. There was no change in his expression, but a slight shake of the head indicated he was, at best, confused.

Bill Winning knew the feeling. "Now, God knows that there is nothing *we* can do to pay the penalty we deserve to pay for our sin. But He loves us so much that *He* paid the penalty for us. Again, in the words of the Jewish prophet Isaiah, '...the Lord laid on Him the iniquity of us all.' In other words, the Judge, Himself, bore the penalty of death on our behalf. He was tortured to death in what was regarded as the most agonizing torture device ever. The Romans invented it. It was a wooden cross. *Yeshua* died on the cross. He paid the price for us."

Mel interrupted, "A little like the 'Day of Atonement' that we

Jews celebrate?" Mel did not grasp what Winning was saying, but he did hear some things that had a ring of familiarity. He had learned of the concept of the 'Sacrifice of Atonement' from a rabbi somewhere in the distant past.

"Exactly," answered Bill. "The sacrifices conducted by the ancient Jewish priests were set up to be a sort of preview of what the real thing would be like when the Messiah came. Just after Jesus had died on that cross, a Roman soldier stuck a spear in His side to make sure He was dead. It was the Messiah's blood that ran down from Him that day that was the ultimate 'sacrifice of atonement.' Then they took Him down off the cross and buried Him in a tomb."

Mel Gold shook his head, sadly. "The Messiah we were taught about is a king. He'll rule the whole world. You said yourself, '...the government will be on His shoulders...' or something like that." Gold again sat back against the wall. He closed his eyes in disgust, his face ashen, sunken-in, touched with the ghastly appearance of death. "Our Jewish Messiah is a king, not a dead man." Gold was not bitter at Bill's statements, but he was sadly disappointed; a wave of hopelessness spread over him.

Bill smiled, and flipped his chain. "Mel, I haven't finished telling you the 'good news' yet. And, listen, when God plans for good news, He really means *good news!* Jesus was dead. They put Him in a grave. But..." Bill paused. Dr. Gold opened his eyes slightly. *"...HE CAME BACK TO LIFE!"* Gold bolted upright. In an instant, the color returned to his face. His eyes flashing, charged with excitement, he exclaimed, "Oh, yes! *I GET IT!*" Gold struggled to his knees, and he leaned forward to hear more. "I had heard something like that before, but I never thought it was...but now I see! I get it!"

Bill continued, "He came back to life, and He still lives, today, in Heaven. And, Mel, the Bible says that whoever believes in Jesus will have their sins forgiven. This Jesus, the same One that judges us, also paid our penalty on the cross. *We will also be raised from the dead!* He proved it could be done, and we can receive the same power that did it. God's power. It's what the Bible calls being 'saved.' Even His name, *Yeshua* – Jesus – means "One who saves." Saves from death and from God's judgement. It's available to anyone who puts trust in Him. Those that don't believe Him, they still are left to pay their own penalty.

"The decision is ours. The power is His."

Bill paused, looking directly into the eyes of Dr. Mel Gold.

"And Jesus will return one day, perhaps soon," continued Bill. "When He does, it will be at that time that He takes over as the King you were taught about."

"What do you have to do...to be 'saved?' " Gold gestured enthusiastically, his pathetic chains rattling.

Bill answered, "Mel, the Bible tells the story of a man that asked the very same question. And the answer is the same for you and me as it was for that man. 'Believe on the Lord Jesus Christ and thou shalt be saved....' That's it. No fancy stuff. Just believe in your heart what the Word of God says about Jesus. He's the Messiah, the mighty God. He paid the penalty for your sins. He gives you eternal life. You put your faith in Him, turn from your own self-centeredness and sin, and go in God's direction instead of your own. He assures you of your ultimate victory."

There was a pause. A noise could be heard outside the cell: The sound of voices, the sound of a vehicle engine – the backhoe - starting up, in the direction of the compound's utility building.

Dr. Mel Gold looked over at Gary Tarr, who nodded his head encouragingly. He then looked straight into the eyes of Bill Winning. "I believe it." He smiled at the two men across from him. "*I believe it!*" He turned to his brother-in-law, who still lay along the wall, his head buried in his arms. "Bucky, did you hear this? This is amazing!"

Bucky Albostini looked up, his eyes red, his voice trembling, "The only thing I hear is noise outside. Something's happening out there. Bill, don't you think you should go back up there and check what's going on?"

Before Winning and Tarr could get in position to mount the wall again, the voices suddenly came closer. The noise of the keys and the opening of the cell's outer door could be heard. The light bulb in the overhead flashed back on, and the inspection port in the door opened. The cell door was then unlocked and slammed open.

The prison guard entered first, placing his key ring back into the pocket of his fatigue trousers. He was followed by an armed soldier and by "Colonel Boots." The colonel's neatly pressed trouser-legs were tucked into the highly polished black boots; his black beret was pulled down rakishly over his right eyebrow. The colonel held a folder containing documents and several pages of computer-printout information.

"You are Winning," proclaimed Colonel Boots, "from city of Way-Moot." He compared the man on his right with the passport photo he had in his folder. Going to the next man, he studied the photographs and papers in his folder. "You are Tarr, also from Way-Moot." The Colonel spoke with a heavy accent, barely recognizable as English. Going on, "You are Albostini," he mangled the pronunciation, "from Peel-a-del-pee-a."

The colonel then came to Mel Gold. He motioned to the prison guard, who came over to Gold, producing a set of handcuffs from his belt. "You are Gold. You are Jew!" The colonel spit out these last words. The guard fastened the handcuffs to Gold's wrists. He then retrieved his key ring from his pocket, searched for the correct key, and unlocked the manacle that connected Gold to the chain and the wall bracket.

The soldier pushed Mel Gold through the cell door, and followed him out, steering him to the left, toward the building's entrance door. The colonel followed, trailed by the prison guard who closed and bolted the cell door behind him.

The three remaining hostages sat on the floor of their cell, backs against the concrete wall, with eyes staring blankly across the room. Gary Tarr uttered a brief prayer. Bill Winning closed the prayer with a softly spoken "Amen." Four loud rifle shots rang out, followed by the sound of the backhoe shoveling dirt.

"No! Oh, no!" wailed Bucky Albostini. Then in a hushed, frantic whisper, "My God! I am married to his sister. Do you think they'll find that out? I'm Italian...surely they can tell that from my name? If they try to take me, be sure to tell them I'm not Jewish..."

"*Shut up*, Albostini!" Bill's tone was harsh. He stood suddenly and, in his frustration, jerked at his chain with a ferocious tug. A thin sliver of concrete shattered away from the wall near the bracket and clattered to the floor. The bracket did not budge. Bill pounded a fist on the wall, shook his head, shut his eyes.

"Easy, Bill" Gary Tarr's quiet voice spoke up. "Listen, remember what Mel said just a few minutes ago? He said, 'I believe it!' What does the Bible say? '...whosoever believeth in Him shall not perish, but hath everlasting life.' Mel Gold is in the presence of the Lord right this moment, and his debt is all paid. And, Bucky, remember what he said to you? 'It's amazing!' It sure is: amazing grace."

Bill sat back down along the wall. "You're right Gary," he said. "Thanks." Bill Winning and Gary Tarr began to pray again, this time in an extended conversation with the One they called "Father."

Chapter Nine

<u>Cobalt Sixty</u>

January
Latakia, Syria

WALID EL ZOPHAR had rarely seen Mustafa Mutanabbi so visibly angry, and this was closer to rage. Never before had Mutanabbi's wrath been directed at Walid, and it was frightening to the old Syrian.

"El Zophar," said Mutanabbi, "I do not want to hear your excuses! I have asked you to accomplish this task, and you will be handsomely rewarded to accomplish it. If you can not do so, I will find someone who can. Your usefulness to me will have ended." Mutanabbi's rage did not lead to a raised voice or a pounded fist. Instead it was a chillingly quiet, slowly spoken voice that sent shudders down the spine of Walid El Zophar.

Mutanabbi continued his tirade. "Let me put it in perspective. If you fail the mission to bring back the material that we seek, I will call off the entire program. We do not need a delivery system if we have inadequate materials to deliver. Do you understand, Walid, that there will be grave consequences if this venture fails?"

El Zophar nodded his head, his mouth set with grim determination, his eyes focused on a piece of paper before him on the table.

Mutanabbi's tone softened briefly. "Now, Walid, I do appreciate what you have accomplished so far. It has cost my uncle's treasury much, but we have come close to meeting our objectives. I am very pleased, so far, with progress toward acquiring the Russian submarine. We were also successful in purchasing that plutonium waste from China. It forms the heart of our stockpile. You have acquired nearly enough cobalt sixty waste to complete our plans. Nearly enough - but not enough!"

Mutanabbi suddenly sat forward again, and looked directly into El Zophar's eyes. "Now you tell me, El Zophar, that your initiative with the Pakistani nuclear plant has failed." Mutanabbi's voice, dripping with threat, returned to that terrible, forced calm. "Failure! I do not want to hear such talk!"

Walid El Zophar, in his line of work, enjoyed lucrative reward for jobs well done. He also understood that the great reward was often accompanied by just as great a risk. He knew that, on this particular project, the downside risk could well include his life.

El Zophar shifted uneasily in his chair. "I did not use the word, 'failure,' Dr. Mutanabbi," he said. "I have never failed you and I have never failed your uncle. I am not about to start discussing failure now! What I have told you is that my contacts in Pakistan have not been able to find an opportunity to directly purchase the material. But, if you will hear me, I believe there may be a way to obtain it by alternative means. It could be risky, but it could produce what we need without further delay."

While El Zophar had not succeeded in obtaining the desired materials by his so-called "ordinary" procurement methods, he had a plan. One of his agents working in Pakistan had been able to establish a relationship with a shift supervisor at the nuclear waste storage site at Turbat, Pakistan. Turbat was the repository for the low-level radioactive waste generated by Pakistan's nuclear power station. Mutanabbi listened intently to El Zophar's plan, formed from what Walid had learned from the Pakistani contact.

Mutanabbi liked what he heard. The plan was direct and the plan was quick.

Later, as he left Mutanabbi's office and walked down the long passageway toward the lobby of the Ministry of Electricity Production Building, Walid El Zophar exhaled deeply and shook his head. El Zophar had confronted many remarkable individuals in his life, but none to compare with Mustafa Mutanabbi. Mutanabbi's brilliance of mind was stunning; his singleness of purpose, terrifying.

Walid El Zophar was not a technically trained man. He had only a vague notion of what Mutanabbi had in mind to do with the contraband material he was obtaining from these various sources. Of course, Walid knew that nuclear waste was generally regarded as dangerous, though it was incapable of being used to manufacture nuclear bombs. Certainly, Walid had a clear understanding of the fear that could be generated if the Syrians had access to such material, along with a weapon like the submarine *Antyey III*. To Walid, this was a delicious irony: the superpowers had, for years, wielded nuclear blackmail over the heads of a cowering world. Now, let those so-called superpowers sweat the implicit threats! And, reasoned Walid to himself, think what this will do for us at the negotiating table with the Israelis! With this, we should be able to get back the Golan Heights without firing a shot!

But Mustafa Mutanabbi's plan was more diabolical than perceived even by the cynical Walid El Zophar. Mutanabbi had an obsession that went far beyond using his weapon for political extortion.

Mutanabbi recognized that it was totally impractical for him to develop the capability to produce nuclear fission devices. Even if he could get access, somehow, to adequate quantities of fissionable material, he would require a team of experts and fabrication facilities that were simply beyond his grasp. Mutanabbi was a practical man. He was also an impatient man. The time that would be required for such an undertaking simply was not acceptable to him. Besides, he had a better idea.

Mustafa knew that the initial blast of a nuclear bomb was truly devastating. The unimaginable force of the explosion, and the dreaded mushroom-shaped cloud were specters that had haunted the nightmares of all generations since the second World War. But he also knew that, in the longer term, perhaps even more to be feared was the devastating radioactive contamination that would be spread for miles by the explosion of a nuclear bomb. It was this aspect of the nuclear nightmare that Mutanabbi had it within his grasp to duplicate.

It was true that the conventional explosive charges he was buying from the Russians might not be able to achieve the same kind of total devastation of structures within Israel that would be accomplished with a nuclear fission device. But, by using those explosive charges to spread radioactive contaminants throughout populated areas of Israel, Mutanabbi could slake a blood-thirst he had suffered since he was a child. He could accomplish his life's mission: spreading devastation in that land. And much of the hated land would be unfit for human habitation for generations to come.

Yes, many of the Faithful would have to die in the process.

The lives of Muslim Palestinians living in Israel would have to be sacrificed. But was not their plight hopelessly miserable as it was? Was not this *mujaheidin*, a holy war? Would not all those Faithful who died be received immediately into heaven? Did not Koran promise this reward?

Besides, as he saw it, his plan held another, subtle advantage. He reasoned that, even if he could, somehow, deliver a nuclear fission warhead - or chemical or biological agent, for that matter – he would not do it, at least not at this juncture. The response would be immediate and massive retaliation against his own land. He knew that other world powers, particularly the U.S.A., would be stirred into action by an overt use of such "weapons of mass destruction."

But Mustafa Mutanabbi had been very successful, so far, at keeping the Americans out of this conflict by cleverly applying political pressure and misinformation. The Hazor Hostages tactic had been a brilliant stroke. Just enough implication of Israeli involvement had been introduced in the media to keep the Americans at bay: their president needed only the barest excuse to stay out of this fight in the desert.

So, reasoned Mutanabbi, if I can deliver conventional weapons that release nuclear waste materials, and prepare a media blitz that contends that the waste comes from Israeli nuclear weapons sites, then enough doubt will be spread to preclude a retaliatory strike. There might even be sympathy for our cause: "ridding the Israelis of their illegal nuclear weapons."

El Zophar had learned from his contact that the Pakistan Atomic Energy Agency was under pressure to make modifications at what the Pakistanis called the "Turbat Nuclear Waste Storage and Monitoring Facility." Located several hundred kilometers away from the nuclear power plant itself, Turbat was in the southwestern corner of Pakistan, in the Baluchistan Province.

At Turbat, the nuclear waste was stored in simple, steel clad, lead-shielded cylindrical containers. These were laid out on concrete pads, in large concrete-block sheds. It was not very sophisticated, but it was effective.

In its most recent review of the Pakistani nuclear power program, the International Atomic Energy Agency ("I.A.E.A.") had urged, in a strongly worded memorandum, that improvements be made at Turbat. I.A.E.A. insisted that the wastes stored at Turbat be re-encased in stainless steel-lined fiberglass cylinders. The cylinders then were to be buried in the earth, with installed leak-detection monitors, instead of simply filed away in sheds. The I.A.E.A. had expressed concern about the growing hazards, worldwide, of the relative lack of control of "low level radwaste." They reasoned that below-ground storage not only would provide for more, natural, shielding, but also would add to security against theft and the horror of possible widespread release of the material.

Ironically, it was this concern for the security of the nuclear waste material that gave El Zophar the opportunity he needed to get his hands on it.

The Pakistan Atomic Energy Authority planned to issue a Request for Proposals to various engineering and construction firms to compete for the job of re-encasing and burying the waste materials. Phase One of the project would be to re-encase the waste in "Building Alpha" and to bury it. Building Alpha housed the wastes containing the most dangerous of the materials at Turbat, "cobalt sixty." This isotope of the element cobalt, having been irradiated in the power plant's nuclear reactor, is highly radioactive, giving off high-energy gamma radiation as it decays with a half-life of 5.2 years. Thus, in about five years, the material stored in Building Alpha would still be half as deadly as it is today. A generation would pass before the material would be reasonably stable.

El Zophar had been tipped off by his Pakistani contact as to the requirements that would be specified in the Request for Proposal. With other contacts that he had in the engineering-construction business in Europe, El Zophar was ready to grab the opportunity.

The Italian consulting engineering firm, RPIT SpA, was well-known for designing and managing power and industrial construction projects around the world, especially in Europe and the Middle East. They often worked through sub-contractors who could provide special areas of expertise, especially if the subcontractor could accomplish portions of the work at lower costs, and thus increase RPIT's overall profitability. The manager of marketing for RPIT, Guido Scaroli, was an old acquaintance of Walid El Zophar.

For his part, El Zophar had the perfect man for the task on his own team. One of his brightest young Syrian associates was an engineer known as Shafiq Talas. Among Talas's many credentials was that he spoke passable Urdu, the official language of Pakistan.

Walid introduced Talas to Scaroli with a simple tip. "Listen to him Guido. He may have an attractive deal for you." Talas, now posing as an executive of "Leb-Tek," a Lebanese firm that had been set up as a front for Syrian operations, told the RPIT man about the upcoming competition for the Pakistani job. He offered this: his firm, Leb-Tek, eager to establish its reputation in the business, would offer the service of re-encasing the first phase of waste canisters at Turbat at well below cost. This would allow the total RPIT bid to be considerably under the competition, and RPIT would make its normal profit on the balance of the project, designing and constructing the burial site and then actually performing the canister burial operation.

The Pakistan Atomic Energy Authority had budgeted the equivalent of $105 million for Phase I, with funding to come from international bank loans. The "RPIT/Leb-Tek Plan" would allow RPIT to submit a total bid of nearly $1.8 million under that budget, virtually assuring them of winning the competition for the work.

The job plan was developed by Talas, and sold to RPIT and to the Pakistanis. The plan was then secretly revised by El Zophar and Talas to accomplish the Syrians' special, ominous mission. In this they worked closely with Mustafa Mutanabbi's head of special operations, Colonel Adib Bildad.

In Talas's original, legitimate, plan, encasement cylinders would be fabricated of a fiberglass sheath enclosing a stainless steel liner. There were twenty drums of highly concentrated radioactive material in Building Alpha at Turbat. Each drum was a cylinder 1.50 meters in diameter and 1.25 meters in height. The new encasement canisters were to be sized so that the existing drums, complete with their steel-and-lead shielding, could be slipped inside them. The canister then would be secured with a fiberglass cap, and epoxied into place. Finally, to meet the I.A.E.A.'s new requirement, a radiation monitoring device would be installed in the lid of each canister to warn of any breach of the containment device. The containers would then be ready for burial at a later time, after RPIT had completed the burial site project.

Leb-Tek, under the supervision of Talas, was to conduct the fabrication of the twenty replacement fiberglass canisters to the exacting tolerances specified by the Pakistanis. They were then to ship the canisters by shallow-draft freighter to the small Pakistani waterfront village of Pasni. A special convoy of six trucks would then transport the canisters to Turbat, in the Makran Coast Range of hills, some 100 kilometers to the northwest of Pasni. Five of the trucks would be flatbeds, each carrying four canisters. The sixth truck, the utility vehicle, was fitted with a crane at the rear and an aluminum box-van section just forward of the crane. The van section was billed as the project's Radiation Control ("Radcon") Center for the project. It contained the Geiger-Mueller tubes, scintillation counters, thermo-luminescent devices for monitoring personal radiation dosage, contamination protection ("Anti-C") clothing and other material and devices required for the project.

Talas estimated that the process, if conducted strictly as proposed, would take about one twelve-hour shift. Throughout the process there would be close monitoring by a Leb-Tek radiation protection specialist for any sign of excessive radiation dosage to which the workers might be exposed. Talas had proposed that the job be performed at night, "to avoid possible problems with other work crews that would be at the plant during normal working hours." Performing the job during the night shift also assured a minimum of oversight from plant management, and greatly simplified Talas's real mission.

The job would be conducted under the eye of the Pakistani night shift supervisor. It was scheduled for a night when the night shift supervisor was El Zophar's "contact."

Chapter Ten

Suspicions

VIKTOR RYPKIN HAD COMPLETED the first week of his assignment in Syria. He still was in a considerable state of confusion: a new apartment, new colleagues, a new supervisor and a new mission. But what was his mission? It was not yet clear to Viktor what, exactly, he was supposed to be doing. Compared to the discipline, unity of purpose and sense of fulfilling a grand purpose that he had felt on Project Titus, he saw none of this among his new colleagues on Project Power Pack.

He had understood from his conference with Admiral Glutsin in Khokskya that he had been selected to come to Latakia because of his strong performance as a project manager on Titus. This recognition had surprised him. True, he had come up with a rather clever project budget- and schedule-tracking program, but these programs were, to him, simply ways to work more efficiently. It enabled him to spend more time with his beloved one-line diagrams and electronics system operator manuals. He always thought his professional reputation would develop from his expertise in sonar navigation systems. He was puzzled to have been selected for a job that was to be exclusively scheduling and budgeting. He was not yet sure he liked the idea. But, Admiral Glutsin had made him a personal promise, and who could refuse The Admiral?

He had been rushed from Khokskya to Latakia. There had been insufficient time for him to contact friends in Moscow before he departed. He had not even been able to see Tatyana one last time. He had been hustled out of the caves and into a waiting airplane that whisked him and his associates away from *Veter Khokskya*, to the naval base at Magadan. A military transport jet was waiting for them at Magadan, and the men were barely settled in their seats when the huge jet was rumbling down the runway, bound for Damascus. Viktor caught up on his sleep on the long plane ride. He slept even more on the bus as he made his way from Damascus to Latakia.

Viktor spent the first two days at Latakia in briefings with Director Ivanov and his staff. Little was said at the time about Rypkin's role in the project. Ivanov introduced Rypkin to the other members of the project team as a "project management specialist." Rypkin himself could only guess what that was intended to mean. He assumed from what had been said that he was expected to implement a scheduling and budgeting system for Project Power Pack similar to that which he had developed earlier for Project Titus.

Viktor was pleased with his new office. To Rypkin, this was truly a castle compared to the tiny space allotted to him in the trailer at Khokskya's North Pen. The office was on the second floor of the new Ministry of Electricity Production Building. It had two windows that overlooked the central courtyard. The furnishings were sparse, but brand new. There was a metal desk, a swivel chair, a chart table, and file cabinets. Two other, simple metal chairs were provided with the chart table.

Ivanov assigned to Viktor a staff of two. One was a young, inexperienced, Syrian engineer named Omar Fassad, who was to be Rypkin's "client-associate." Omar Fassad could seem to manage none of the Russian language, and seemed to have nearly as little proficiency as an engineer. The other member of Rypkin's staff was a much different story, the brightest spot so far in his Latakia experience: a lovely young Syrian woman named Jadeel Dovni.

Jadeel was actually half-Syrian. Her father, a Soviet diplomat, had been stationed in Damascus for a number of years. Jadeel was fourteen years old when her father was transferred back to Moscow. Neither she nor her mother had ever heard from him again. But Jadeel had learned enough Russian to land a position as an interpreter while she was a student at the university in Damascus.

Rypkin's major problem in working with Jadeel was to keep his mind on his work. She was an extraordinarily beautiful young woman, although she would have been considered a classic beauty neither in Russia nor in Syria. She was too tall to fit the traditional Syrian mold. She had too broad a forehead; she had too-high cheekbones. And, to most Russians, she would have been considered too skinny. Her Arab-tan skin, penetrating dark eyes and thick black hair would have spoken of "impure" heritage. But the combination of Semitic and Japhetic features produced in Jadeel the cosmopolitan beauty so often sought on the covers of magazines in western countries.

Viktor Rypkin soon realized, to his delight, that Jadeel also seemed to understand his concept for establishing a planning and scheduling system for the design and construction of the nuclear power plant. Her grasp of the concept, in fact, seemed considerably superior to that of the young engineer that had been assigned as his client-associate.

Rypkin sat at the chart table in his office thumbing through a roll of Mylar prints that showed the plan and instrumentation drawings for a portion of the power plant site.

"Two days!" groused Rypkin. "It has been two days since I asked for this very simple information." Viktor Rypkin was not accustomed to such ineptitude. "Miss Dovni, please ask Mr. Fassad what could possibly have prevented him from accomplishing this simple task. It has been two days!" Rypkin was not one to raise his voice in anger, but the level of his consternation was evident to his interpreter. "Please ask Mr. Fassad if it is that he does not understand the question. Or perhaps he does not know the answer. Or perhaps it is that he simply does not care!"

Jadeel nodded at Viktor, shrugged her shoulders and smiled sheepishly. She turned to Omar Fassad and spoke in Arabic, attempting to subdue the Russian's irritable tone as much as possible, "Mr. Fassad! Excuse me, Mr. Fassad," she said.

The young Syrian engineer had been standing by the window, casually staring out into the courtyard below them. He had seemed to take little notice of the conversation. He now turned to the interpreter, a polite grin on his face. "Yes, Miss Dovni. You wish to speak to me?"

"Sir, Mr. Rypkin is interested to know what can be done to get the information he asked about two days ago," said Jadeel. "He wants to know if there is any way he can help you obtain this information."

"Information? What information is it that is required?" asked Fassad. He continued his polite smile, and adjusted his glasses to look down at the table to the papers that lay before them.

"This information." It was Jadeel whose voice now rose in impatience. "The milestone networks for the project," she said. "It was two days ago that you were asked to obtain these milestone dates." Jadeel rotated the papers around so that they were right-side-up to Fassad's sight. "Without the milestone dates, it is not possible to construct a schedule."

"Of course, of course," said Fassad. "Please tell Mr. Rypkin that to get these dates, he must contact, directly, the office of President Zabadi, himself. I do not know these dates. No one that I know has any idea what these dates are." Fassad spoke the words casually, and glanced again back outside the window.

"Mr. Rypkin," Jadeel turned back to Viktor, and spoke again in Russian, "Mr. Fassad explains that he does not have access to that information. He says that it is available only through the office of President Zabadi. Sir, perhaps you would allow me to comment on this matter?"

"Of course," said Viktor Rypkin.

"Sir," ventured Jadeel, "last week when Director Ivanov briefed me about this assignment, he mentioned that Project Power Pack was expected to be completed in forty months from the day you and the other members of the Russian team arrived. Is that the kind of information that you mean by 'milestone dates?'"

"Exactly!" said Rypkin. "It is only when we have such dates in mind that we can establish a more detailed schedule. Our objective is to develop a detailed work breakdown structure. It will include many elements, and each element will have its own little schedule. Eventually all of the schedules for all of the elements will come together to produce a finished project. But, of course, before we can put this together, we have to know what the milestones are. We also have to know the limits on our resources for accomplishing them." Viktor looked admiringly at his young interpreter. Was it possible that she might be as intelligent as she was attractive?

Jadeel reached for the papers she had placed in front of Fassad, and brought them back over to Rypkin's side of the table. "Well," she said, "another date that was mentioned to me last week was that I could expect to be assigned in this position until construction begins one year from now. Does that help any?"

"Jadeel," said Viktor, "it's more than anything else I've had to go on." Rypkin frowned as he looked at the schedule-chart sketched before him. "Does our engineer-friend have any idea whom we can call in Zabadi's office?" Rypkin gestured at Omar Fassad, who continued to stand by the window, oblivious to the conversation.

Jadeel turned again to the Syrian engineer. "Mr. Fassad, do you know anyone in the office of the President who can give us the milestone dates?"

Fassad turned from the window. "You know," he said, "this building was constructed in less than twelve months! It is the most advanced-technology building in all of Syria! Look down there!" Fassad pointed back to the window, "They are bringing in the new computers to be installed here in the training facility. Now...what is it you ask, Miss Dovni?"

Jadeel spoke sternly, in Arabic. "Mr. Rypkin points out that it is our task to develop a project schedule. To do this, we must have the dates that you were asked for two days ago. Do you have any idea whom we can call to get that information?"

Fassad shrugged his shoulders, shook his head and wandered back to the window where he continued to observe the work proceeding below.

Jadeel looked back at Rypkin, and shook her head. She seemed to share Rypkin's annoyance at the lack of interest shown by their colleague. Rypkin and Dovni continued talking in Russian for some time. Viktor laid out several sheets of paper on which he sketched a series of dots connected by arrows. He explained that the arrow lengths were proportional to the elapsed times expected for each of the tasks that would be required to complete the power plant project. Before Project Power Pack would be able to provide electricity to Syria's power supply grid, he explained, more than ten thousand tasks would have to be performed. And each of these tasks would be scheduled in his system.

Jadeel continued to ask questions. She had no engineering degree, but her innate common sense enabled her to perceive much of the plan that Rypkin had in mind. Viktor found himself fascinated...more than fascinated...with this half-breed Russian-Syrian girl.

But Viktor Rypkin was no fool. A little alarm went off in his mind as he contemplated these feelings. There was the old admonition about avoiding romantic relationships with workmates. And, perhaps of greater concern, this was a very sensitive, top security project. He knew that. For the Syrians to be building a nuclear power plant very likely was in violation of international nuclear non-proliferation agreements. Much was at stake here. Viktor knew that he must be very cautious about any relationship he might develop with this girl. He knew nothing more about her than what she had told him. As strongly as he felt drawn to her, and as much as he sensed she felt the same about him, he knew that he must let caution rule his actions.

The afternoon was drawing to a close. Viktor dismissed his little staff. In view of the disappointing start to this project, Rypkin had in mind to pay a call on his boss, Project Director Ivanov.

Viktor Rypkin left his office, exiting into the hall. He had to crowd against the wall of the passageway to maneuver past a large instrument panel that construction workers were laboring to move down the hallway. An opaque plastic sheet covered the panel, but Rypkin could see through gaps in the plastic that the panel held an impressive array of gages, meters, and switches. It reminded him very much of the instrument panels he had seen in the operations spaces of the *Antyey III* submarine back in Khokskya.

Shaking off his curiosity, Rypkin proceeded down the hallway. He stepped into the stairwell and skipped down the stairs, not bothering to wait for the elevator. As he exited the stairwell at the large rotunda area on the first floor, a bustle of activity at the building's main entrance caught his attention. A limousine had arrived just outside the door, and armed guards escorted the occupant of the limousine into the building.

As Rypkin watched, the sentry at the building entrance snapped to smart attention and saluted. Two armed guards entered the building first, followed by a dapper young man in a western-style business suit, accompanied by a Syrian army colonel wearing highly polished black boots. A single armed guard brought up the rear of the group. The five men headed rapidly down the hallway, past Director Ivanov's office.

Rypkin followed the little parade at a distance. He could not understand what they were saying, but it was evident that the young man was the one in charge. Rypkin stopped briefly at the entrance to the project director's office. He watched only long enough to observe the party enter another office, two doors down from where Rypkin stood, perhaps twenty meters away. The two lead guards stayed outside the door, with the neatly dressed young man entering first, followed by the colonel and his aide.

Viktor proceeded in to the anteroom of the director's office. He reported his name to the secretary at the reception desk. She, in turn, relayed his name through the intercom to the director. As he waited, Viktor mused: he was here to express his concern about the inefficiency of Syrian support for this project, but there was certainly nothing inefficient about the Syrian security system. The Syrians were good at security.

About five minutes later, Ivanov appeared at the door of his office. "Come in, come in!" The director seemed genuinely pleased to see his young project management expert. Rypkin followed Ivanov to a large chart table that sat across from the director's desk. They both took seats at the table.

"It is very good to see you Viktor," said Ivanov. "How is the program proceeding for you?"

"I must say, Director, it has been somewhat disappointing." Viktor was not in a mood to play bureaucratic word games. "I am having difficulty getting even the most fundamental information for developing a milestone network schedule."

"What information do you require?" Ivanov looked directly into the eyes of Viktor Rypkin. The director's smile had disappeared.

"All I have been able to find out," said Rypkin, "is that the project is expected to be completed in forty months, and that construction is expected to start in twelve months. And this I discovered only because my interpreter happened to have heard it, when she was briefed on this assignment. I have heard nothing about when you expect to complete conceptual design, or about when you will have design basis information available, or when you expect to accomplish any of the other project milestones. I need to know this before I can even begin to develop a work breakdown structure." Rypkin paused, shaking his head.

Ivanov continued to look directly at Rypkin. The director stroked his white goatee beard. "These are decisions, Viktor, that will be made by the Syrians," said Ivanov. "You have been assigned a client-associate to help you get that information." Ivanov removed his glasses and looked at Rypkin in a way that emphasized that his advice was, in fact, a command.

"Well, sir," said Rypkin, "that is what I had hoped. But, so far, Mr. Fassad has shown no inclination to provide any such help."

"You must understand, Viktor, there has never been any project of this complexity in the history of Syria," said Director Ivanov. "None of the Syrians has any experience in such things. Our job is to hold their hands. They are paying us quite generously for it. If they show no interest, it is their own money that is wasted. Right now, our priority should be to establish training programs for their personnel. The focus on the actual design and construction effort will have to come later. Now, I can give you some of the information you seek, but you will simply have to be patient about the rest of it. Do you understand?"

"Yes, sir." Rypkin got the message. He would do the best he could.

The two men discussed what little information they had at hand. They made assumptions about certain dates and projected elapsed times for project functions. The director's bearing softened. He seemed to listen closely to Viktor's conscientious questions. Viktor sketched the information on a pad of graph paper.

"What about the site, itself?" Viktor asked. He was a thorough engineer, and he wanted his supervisor to know it. "What about the geotechnical attributes at the site? What about the underground utilities?"

"Viktor, Viktor," Ivanov said, waving his hands in a "slow down" signal, "you're getting way ahead of yourself. Let's get the basic information down first, and then we can consider more of these details." Ivanov smiled patronizingly at his young colleague.

"Yes, sir," replied the stubborn Viktor Rypkin. "But we must do whatever we can to encourage our Syrian client to consider these 'details' as rapidly as possible. Director, you know, certainly better than I, how such details can kill a project. From what I have seen, the only thing that the Syrians seem to be taking seriously is security."

"What makes you say that?" Ivanov smiled at Rypkin, encouraging the young engineer to voice his insight.

"Well," said Viktor," for example, just before I entered your office, I saw one of the Syrian managers arrive. He was met at the door by two armed guards who marched him down to his office. The guards are standing at parade rest right now. I don't know who he is; he appeared to be fairly young. They sure do know how to provide security around here." Rypkin managed a smile.

Director Ivanov sat forward again. "That young man, Viktor, is Mustafa Mutanabbi," said Ivanov. "He is the top dog around here. He is the minister of electricity production for the entire nation of Syria. This project is his baby. It is his dream to bring adequate electric power to his people, and it is my job to keep him happy. I hope, Viktor that you will continue to do your part to help me keep him happy."

Viktor could tell from the director's tone that the interview was over. He got up to make his exit. "Yes, sir," said Viktor. "I will do everything I can to keep our client happy." Viktor stepped toward the door. "Do you wish me to close the door as I leave?"

"Yes, please, Viktor." Director Ivanov stared at the closed door after Rypkin had departed. He waited for a few moments, thinking, nervously tapping his pencil on the table. Abruptly he got up from his chair, and strode to his desk, where he picked up the telephone. He punched in a number, and waited for a response. After a few moments of preliminary conversation, Ivanov got down to business: "Listen, our young friend Mr. Rypkin is asking many questions. Perhaps too many questions. I believe we must move quickly to the Yodel Echo placement phase." Ivanov waited for a few moments listening to conversation from the other end. "I understand that, but it is necessary to move it more quickly. I believe you were right: we must keep a close eye on Mr. Rypkin..." another pause. "Yes, you are correct: it is most important that we keep up that level of surveillance. And I want to assure you, we do have surveillance in place."

Chapter Eleven

Shell Game

January
Turbat, Baluchistan Province
Pakistan

THE CARAVAN ROLLED TO A STOP near the security station at Turbat. Shafiq Talas collected his folder of papers and entered the guard shack. "I am Doctor Talas." he announced, speaking in the Pakistani's Urdu language. "Here are my papers. I am project director for the canister replacement at the Turbat Nuclear Waste Storage and Monitoring Facility."

"Yes. We have been expecting you." The senior security guard took Talas's packet of documents and looked carefully at each page. The guard then removed a three-ring binder notebook from a bookshelf on his desk. The notebook contained a copy of the contractor's proposal, including the project procedures, and a contract document. The guard turned to the pages that listed the project personnel. He compared the list with the records in Talas's packet. The guard then went to his window, and looked out at the caravan that had pulled to the side of the dusty road leading into the Turbat site.

"Doctor Talas," said the guard, "perhaps you can explain this to me: the procedure that I have been given specifies that you will have five trucks for this program. I believe I see six trucks outside my window."

"What? Let me see your procedure." Talas grabbed for the notebook containing the project procedure. It occurred to the Syrian as he fingered through the pages that this mission might not be so simple as he had expected. Nothing is so troublesome to a delicate mission as a security guard who takes his job seriously. "No, no," comforted Talas, "look at this." The equipment list did indeed show, after the heading "Canister Truck Rigs" the number "5." And, sure enough, there were *six* tractor-trailer rigs outside the window. "*This* is the sixth vehicle." Talas pointed at the equipment list item labeled "Equipment\Manipulator Crane Rig" with the number listed "1."

"You see, Sir," explained Talas, patiently, "they do appear very similar, but look more closely! My lead vehicle is not the same as the other five rigs. That one is the equipment and manipulator crane rig. The others contain the replacement canisters. I am sure you will want to inspect them." Talas set the procedure notebook back on the desk.

"Yes, of course," grunted the guard. He turned to one of his assistants, who sat at a desk near the door. "Come, Jinnah, help me to examine these rigs." Turning to a third guard, he said, "You, Safed, stay here and keep an eye on things."

Talas accompanied the two guards out to the lead vehicle. Colonel Bildad and his aide, Sergeant Baydoun, both dressed in the white smocks of radiation protection workers, waited near the front of the lead vehicle.

Talas introduced Bildad and Baydoun to the security guards. "These are two of my assistants," said Talas. "They will be glad to show you into the rigs."

Turning to Bildad, Talas said, with an arrogant flourish, "Bildad, see to it that you fasten the canvas covers properly when you are finished showing the guards through the rigs. I want no more flapping canvas, do you understand?" Young Talas rarely had the opportunity to speak in such superior tone to the feared Colonel Bildad, the highest-ranking officer in Mutanabbi's Special Operations Force. Talas would enjoy this while he had the chance.

"Yes sir," responded Bildad. "I will remember, sir." The colonel was properly subservient.

"I'll bet you will," mumbled Talas, under his breath, smiling as he walked away. He strolled over to the cab of the lead vehicle and removed another packet of documents. Bildad and Baydoun had started toward the rear of the lead rig, accompanying the two Pakistani guards. Talas caught up with them again.

"Excuse me, officer," said Talas, addressing the senior guard. "Do you have a restroom in your guard station that I may use? It has been a long trip from Pasni."

"Yes, yes," responded the guard. "It is to your right after you enter the main door." The guard turned back toward his assistant, and continued with the business at hand. "We will begin by inspecting this vehicle. I will check items off the equipment list as you call them out to me."

Talas strode briskly back toward the security station. The third guard, Safed, was in the station, staring absently out the window at the line of trucks. This guard seemed to take little interest in the situation. He appeared to be a junior member of the group, and he looked to be thoroughly bored.

Talas briefly looked around the interior of the security station and quickly spotted what he was seeking: the notebook containing the contractor's Canister Replacement Procedure. It was lying where he had placed it earlier, on the desk, near the young guard.

"Your boss says he needs the procedure." Talas mumbled, as he casually moved toward the desk. "Oh, here it is." Talas took the folder from the desk and started to head toward the door to exit the building.

Before he stepped out the exit, Talas turned and asked Safed, who was still staring out the window, "Mind if I use your restroom facilities?"

"Certainly not. Go ahead. It is unlocked." Safed indicated the door to Talas's right.

Inside the cramped bathroom, Talas reached into the packet of papers he carried and withdrew a document that looked, at first glance, exactly like the copy of the contractor's procedure that was contained in the Pakistani security guard's folder. Talas removed the old procedure and quickly clipped the new, "revised" procedure into its place. He tucked the old procedure into the manila envelope he had carried with him. Before leaving the room, Talas flushed the toilet, and ran water in the tiny sink to make his bathroom visit sound more authentic. He slipped on out the exit door without further words to the guard.

Talas proceeded to the front of the lead vehicle, and around to the opposite side, out of the sight of the guard house. The senior guard and his assistant were busy at the back of the vehicle. Talas opened the door of the cab, and placed the manila envelope containing the old procedure on the seat in front of him. He scanned quickly through the procedure, noting that at several steps in the document, pencil marks, circles around procedure step numbers, had been made. He took a pencil from his pocket, and found the comparable spots in the new, revised procedure and made identical-looking pencil marks. He then collected the notebook, with its revised procedure, and walked with it back to the guard station. The old procedure, in its manila envelope, was stuffed with a collection of trash under the front left seat of the truck.

Entering the station, Talas addressed the young guard, casually. "Guess your boss has all he needs, for now." Talas placed the notebook back on the desk. "I believe it goes here?"

Safed nodded.

Talas produced a pack of cigarettes from his shirt pocket. "Care for a smoke?" he asked the youngster.

"Sure, thank you."

The two men stood near the window, talking casually. Talas discovered that Safed was an erstwhile student at the university in Karachi. He had been forced to drop out of school for a time so that he could earn enough money to continue his education. He was hoping to earn a degree as a mechanical engineer. The two chatted at some length about the kinds of opportunities that were open for Mech-E's in the nuclear waste treatment business.

"Do you not have opportunities to get involved with some of the operations on the site?" Talas pushed the youngster for some tidbits of useful information. "Surely you guards have to be well-informed as to the details of procedures being conducted during your shift, do you not?"

"Not at all! We are kept completely in the dark!" Safed shook his head in disgust. "When we try to get more detail, we are pushed aside with, 'you have no need to know, and you would not understand it, anyway.'" He shrugged his shoulders. "About the only thing we are able to do is to see what comes in and what goes out. That is hardly any way for me to learn how to be an engineer!"

Safed continued to talk about his schoolwork, the courses he had taken and those he hoped to take. It was obvious that the youngster was lobbying for a possible job with Talas's "firm."

"Anything would be better than being a security guard," the young man said, wistfully.

"I understand that. Here is my card," Talas handed him a neatly printed business card. "Call me when you get your degree. We are always on the lookout for bright mechanical engineers with an interest in nuclear waste management."

As the conversation continued, Talas learned much more about the Turbat security guards' schedules. He also encouraged the young would-be engineer to venture his opinions as to the foibles that he perceived in his various supervisors.

"This fellow Khan," said the youngster, "the one who is on duty now, he is not too bad. He does not mind if I study my books when there is nothing happening. But, you should meet Kasur! He comes on during the morning shift. He is just hopeless. He will do nothing unless it is by procedure. I can never accomplish anything when I serve on a shift with Kasur."

"Really?" said Talas, with sympathy. "When does Kasur come on duty? No doubt you are glad you are not on his shift now."

"He takes over the shift at eight o'clock tomorrow morning," said Safed. "I will be home in my bed by that time. But I will not be so fortunate for long. Next month I rotate into Kasur's shift."

Talas took one last drag from his cigarette, and stubbed it out in the ashtray that sat on the desk. "Well, I should get back to see how the inspection is going." Talas got up to leave. "Do not forget to send me a note when you get your degree."

"I will not forget," said the young man.

As he strolled back over toward the convoy, where the inspection team was now looking through the rear opening of the second truck, he reflected on what he had learned. It was not good news. The plan was to complete the procedure by 9:15 the following morning. Kasur, evidently the most thorough of the security chiefs, would be on duty. Talas filed this intelligence in his mind. This could prove to be a major difficulty. Talas hoped that the revised procedure he had managed to place in the guard shack would enable them to make a clean exit from the plant. If not, Bildad's alternative plan would have to be executed, and that could get ugly.

———————

The first part of the plan had gone smoothly, even though the stop at the security station had lasted twenty minutes beyond what had been expected. Talas and his convoy and crew had been met by the station manager, Doctor Shahdapur, and by the duty shift supervisor, Mr. Mirza, as they arrived at Building Alpha.

Talas knew that it was normal procedure for Doctor Shahdapur to personally observe the first step of such projects, sometimes staying around for a second step. Talas and his team were prepared to encase as many as three canisters, legitimately, if Shahdapur had decided to linger. Three of the canisters were authentic; the other seventeen were "trick" canisters.

The manipulator crane was maneuvered into place by one of Talas's technicians. It grabbed the new, stainless steel-lined fiberglass container in position Number One on the first canister rig, and lifted it slowly over to a four-wheeled dolly.

A small tractor that had been carried aboard the equipment rig was used to maneuver the dolly and its empty, new canister over to the drum storage area. The idea, of course, was to simply place the old steel-and-lead storage drums into the new canisters.

It was a simple procedure. The manipulator crane picked the first of the old waste drums off its position on the concrete pad, and set it gently on a second dolly. The crane then took the new canister and placed it at the vacated spot on the concrete pad. The old waste drum was then hoisted into place just above the new canister, and two of Talas's technicians guided it, gently lowering it into the new canister.

A fiberglass lid was epoxied in place with a specially-adapted machine. A radiation detection device, previously fabricated into the lid of the canister, was connected to the local power supply circuit, and energized. The entire procedure took less than forty minutes, including the inspection of the Pakistanis, Plant Manager Shahdapur and Shift Supervisor Mirza.

Fortunately for the Syrians, Shahdapur was content to observe only one of these canister-sealing evolutions. He then turned the observer's role over to Mr. Mirza.

Mirza was El Zophar's "contact." He had been paid a fat advance on his fee. His only obligation was to disappear, for the duration of the shift, from the operating floor of Building Alpha. He would receive the balance of his fee upon completion of the project. Mirza retreated into his small office near the building's entrance door. To provide an added measure of confidence for the project, Mirza had arranged to stay on an extra two hours the following morning.

Once again, Talas's crane swung into action. This time, however, in the absence of Shahdapur, it passed by "legitimate" canisters Number Two and Number Three, and selected canister Number Four. This one was not hollow. It was filled with sand and lead ballast to approximate the weight of one of the real waste drums plus its lead shielding. The heavy, fake canister was maneuvered slowly over to the storage pad. The manipulator crane removed the old carbon steel waste drum, as before, and placed it on a dolly. The new canister, sand, lead ballast, and all, was placed in its position on the pad. Again, the radiation monitoring device was energized. Thanks to a very small gamma source placed near the monitor's detecting head, it indicated just the right amount of radiation above background to make it look "real."

The old carbon steel drum, full of cobalt-sixty-laden waste material, was placed back on the flatbed of the truck, in space Number Four. The hoop-and-canvas cover was placed back over the flatbed, and the truck was pulled out of Building Alpha. The next truck rolled in.

Work progressed smoothly through the night and early morning hours. From time to time, shift supervisor Mirza left his cubical to visit the bathroom, or to get a cup of tea. He chose not to watch any of the procedure that was going on at the far end of the building. After all, this would be his last day on the job at Turbat.

Mirza would receive enough for this night's "work" to retire comfortably. Of course, he would have to leave his native Pakistan. But, ever since he had heard from his relatives who had settled in the U.S., it had been his dream: to move to California. By the time the dummy canisters were discovered – if they ever were – he would be enjoying his new home in Los Angeles. He had seen pictures of Disneyland. Now he would be able to see it for himself!

It was 9:10 a.m. when the last canister was put in place. Canisters Number Two and Three, which had been held in reserve in case of a surprise visit from any of the plant officials, were placed last. The waste drums were dutifully placed inside, the lids carefully epoxied in place, and the radiation detection devices energized. Everything had gone well. Now, it was gut-sucking time. Time to move the convoy out past the security station.

It had been Bildad's and Talas's hope in developing this plan that the exit stop at the security gate would involve no more than routine personnel identification checks. From the intelligence gathered by Talas the previous morning in conversation with young Safed, it was clear that a simple exit was not likely. So, Bildad and Talas had rehearsed the contingency plans in detail with their crew during the long night of canister replacement. They were ready for anything, but they knew their chances for completing their mission successfully diminished with every step they took away from their base plan.

The caravan pulled up the hill from Building Alpha to the main access road and toward the security gate. Arriving at the checkpoint just inside the gate, Talas got out from his position in the cab of the lead vehicle and walked over to the security station. A short, stout Pakistani dressed in a neatly pressed uniform met him. It was Iskander Kasur.

"Your papers, please." Kasur took the folder of papers and looked carefully at each one. "I was told to expect you at about ten thirty to eleven o'clock this morning," he said. "You have evidently managed to exceed your schedule expectations." Kasur looked up at Talas, one eyebrow raised.

"Yes!" exclaimed Talas, cheerfully. "We did very well! My supervisors will be pleased. We pay our crew on an hourly basis, you see, and time is money!"

Kasur did not share Talas's smile. "I must request," said the guard, "that you have all your crew come in to the security area for inspection."

"Is this necessary?" Talas objected. "It has been a very long night for all of us. I am sure you have found that our papers are in order. We would like very much to proceed home as quickly as possible. We have worked very hard to stay within our time limits..."

"I understand fully," Kasur said sternly, impatiently. "But you must also understand that I have my instructions. Now, the sooner you bring your people in here for inspection, the sooner we can begin our search. Please be sure each of your men brings his personal notes, bags, and briefcases. We want to inspect them all. It will go more quickly if you bring them to us."

Talas went back to the command vehicle and spoke in hushed tones to Colonel Bildad and Sergeant Baydoun who were waiting in the cab. Bildad went to each of the other truck cabs to give instructions to each of the other personnel in the team. Meanwhile, Talas and Baydoun returned to the guard station.

Kasur directed his two assistants to check each individual against his name as listed on the personnel roster. The guards carefully perused each notebook, and emptied and inspected each briefcase and personal bag. When this process was complete, Kasur directed the men to wait at the security station while they inspected the trucks. "At least," pondered Talas to himself, "they have stopped short of a frisk-search."

Bildad's men watched, trying to suppress their anxieties, as the three guards approached the trucks. Kasur approached the last truck in the convoy, and pulled at the canvas flap near the rear. He pointed the beam of his flashlight around the truck's interior, observing its contents of old, slightly rusted waste drums. He continued staring for a long moment.

Kasur looked confused, but said nothing as he re-fastened the canvas flap. He went around to the forward corner of the flatbed trailer, where he repeated the process, looking at length with his flashlight into the flatbed, its four waste drums in plain sight.

Kasur turned to his second in command, and spoke in low tones. Colonel Bildad, standing about six meters away, reached inside his technician's cloak and gently gripped the handle of the automatic pistol he kept in his shoulder holster. Bildad did not speak Urdu, but he knew that there was something potentially amiss. The guard began to search in the cab of the truck. Nothing was said about the contents of the flatbed. Kasur went to the next truck, where the third guard was looking into the canvas-covered flatbed.

The younger guard spoke to Kasur. "I was expecting to see empty trucks departing, sir. I did not realize that they were to be taking away the old drums."

Bildad's grip grew tighter on his weapon. It was a SIG-Sauer P-

220. Bildad regarded it as the best .45 caliber double-action combat pistol ever made. The colonel had to fight an urge to move immediately to the Alternative Plan. His SIG-Sauer needed the exercise. But plans were plans and they must be followed exactly.

Kasur shook his head, confused. "Get the procedure from the desk, Yahya," Kasur ordered his young assistant. Yahya hurried off to fetch the document.

"Is there a problem?" Talas asked the question casually.

"If I understood your procedure correctly, you were to leave the drums in place. You were to be leaving with empty trucks." Kasur's voice betrayed a trace of confusion.

"No, no, no." Talas protested, just a note of irritation in his voice, "you have not read the procedure correctly. Let us take a look. I will show you."

Yahya returned, rushing forward with the notebook containing the clipped-in packet of procedures. Kasur flipped quickly through the pages, coming to the last page. "Here, it says that...wait! I thought for certain it said you would be leaving the drums in Building Alpha!"

"Where did you get that idea?" Talas began to push. "Look! Look right here." He jabbed his finger into the procedure. It clearly stated "remove old waste drum, place in proper position on truck flatbed. Do not exceed four drums per flatbed."

Talas turned to the convoy, and said, impatiently, "Check our trucks! See if you can find where we have exceeded four drums per flatbed! Follow your procedures, Sir!"

"I...I...I think I should call the head of operations. I was sure..." Kasur was not at all sure. He stuttered as he spoke.

"Now, listen here!" Talas spoke with indignation. "You have already delayed us nearly fifteen minutes. I am hereby notifying you, Sir, that for every minute you delay us from this point on, we will charge a contract extra to your plant. Now, I must have your name and identification number. If you do not give me this information immediately, I will call your manager of operations, myself, personally!"

"But...I..."

"I tell you, you should leave the technical operations of this plant to the technical experts. I will not tolerate any more delay. If you have a security matter to discuss, fine! But, if you begin to question my following of explicit procedures ... you have them in your hand ... I will call myself." Talas began to walk into the guard shack as though he meant to place a call.

"No, no." Kasur backed down. "There will be no need for you to call. You may proceed. You are correct. It is as written in the procedure. You may proceed."

Months later, after the entire, terrifying story had unfolded, it was discovered that most of the canisters in Building Alpha at Turbat were phony: filled with sand and lead. Kasur, the most experienced security guard at the site, was found to have been grossly negligent in allowing the Syrian impostors to escape with their load of nuclear waste.

His moment of indecision would cost Kasur his job. It would almost send him to prison. But it saved his life.

Chapter Twelve

Caution

January
Latakia, Syria

VIKTOR RYPKIN ARRIVED AT HIS OFFICE at 7:30 a.m. He was surprised to see that Omar Fassad was already there, along with Jadeel Dovni. Office hours were supposed to begin at eight o'clock a.m., and up to this day, Fassad had never yet arrived on time. It occurred to Rypkin that, possibly, his little chat with Director Ivanov had served some useful purpose, after all. The Syrians were, indeed, the client, but was it not reasonable to expect some level of effort from them?

Jadeel had also arrived early, but that was to be expected. This remarkable woman served not only as interpreter for the two engineers, she also performed many of the functions of a secretary. She had arranged the schedule-charts in neat order along the chart table, and had also managed to obtain a set of prints, plot plans showing the project site at Damsarkhu.

Viktor looked forward eagerly to getting to work each morning. He was strongly motivated by ambition to make a mark professionally with this project. More and more, however, his aspirations also began to include spending time with Jadeel Dovni. Her wit, her intelligence, and, yes, her extraordinary beauty captivated him.

Viktor beamed broadly as he entered the office. He exchanged greetings with his two associates, and then announced, cheerfully, "We have had enough of desk work for a time, what do you say? Let us take an excursion up to Damsarkhu and collect some site information."

Jadeel relayed the message to the Syrian engineer, who nodded with a bland smile.

The trio made their way out of the office, and down to the first floor security station. They signed out in the security log, and headed for the project auto pool. Fassad checked out a car, and took the driver's seat. Viktor and Jadeel sat in the rear.

Viktor's heart raced as never before to be so near this exotic Syrian woman. Was that a new perfume she was wearing? Viktor had a difficult time keeping his mind from racing as fast as his heart.

As they drove through the city streets of Latakia toward their destination some six kilometers to the north, Jadeel pointed out a place where her father had brought her, years before, to visit the Mediterranean shore. It had been the first time she had ever seen any body of water larger than the Orontes.

She made Fassad stop the car so she could get out to show Viktor the very spot where she had first glimpsed the sea. She ran up a hill where a footpath led from the street below. At the top, she stopped, once again a delighted child, and pointed excitedly to the west. She motioned for Viktor to join her. From the crest of the hill they could see it: the Mediterranean.

Known to the ancients as "The Great Sea," on this day the Mediterranean deserved the title. Its color was a study in blues: light, nearly turquoise near the beach; darkening, turning a deep sapphire blue at the western horizon where it met the azure sky. To the north, a breeze stirred the sea into a frothy blue-violet. The Port of Latakia lay below them, to the south, in a stagnant, bluish gray inlet.

Jadeel, breathless from her dash up the hill and from exhilaration at reliving this treasured moment from her past, grabbed Viktor's hand and squeezed tightly. "Oh, Viktor!" she exclaimed. "It is still as grand as it was when I was fourteen years old and my father showed it to me! Have you ever seen anything so beautiful?"

"No," Viktor responded. He was not looking at the sea, but into the brilliant black eyes of his interpreter.

Jadeel continued, "My father used to tell me of the things that lay beyond here." She gazed out at the horizon as she spoke. "He told me about times he had been to Africa, to Southeast Asia, even to Cuba! Almost to America itself! It is easy to imagine oneself traveling to those places." She turned to Viktor and took up his other hand.

Viktor's mind was barraged with messages. He, too, had dreamed of far-off places. He had dreamed of places just like the Latakia shore on which he now stood. He was nearly overcome with the sheer pleasure of sharing the moment with such a delightful, beautiful girl. But, in addition to the messages of enchantment and excitement there was another message. A flashing red sign accompanied this message: "caution!"

Viktor led the way back down the hill to the waiting car. No further words were spoken until they had reached Damsarkhu.

Damsarkhu, Syria

Omar Fassad pulled the vehicle up to the guard shack that stood at the entrance to the Damsarkhu site. Fassad rolled down his window and spoke a few words to the guard, showing the armed soldier his identification pass. The guard signaled to the two occupants of the rear seat that they should produce their passes. Viktor Rypkin and Jadeel Dovni hastened to comply. The guard carefully checked names, numbers, and identification photos. He sternly instructed them that they were not authorized beyond the Pier Area Interior Guard Station, and then signaled them through the gate.

A tall berm obstructed any view of the site from the outer perimeter fence and the guard shack. Omar drove away from the fence toward the berm, along a dirt road. As they proceeded through a gap in the berm, the site came into full view. The land sloped gently down to the shoreline. At the extreme northern end of the site, the Syrians had recently constructed a long pier structure. The pier extended nearly seven hundred meters out into the sea, and was nearly thirty meters wide. The topographical plans that Jadeel had obtained showed that the depths of the water along this pier had been dredged to accommodate deep draft vessels.

A large corrugated metal shelter was under construction at the far extremity of the pier. Several other small metal sheds and office buildings were grouped along the pier near the large shelter.

At the base of the pier, just inland from the shoreline, was an enormous concrete structure. It looked like a giant warehouse, but it was very sturdy, constructed of reinforced concrete. It was shown on the plans simply as "storage shed." But the building was considerably larger than the dimensions indicated on the plans, and "shed" was hardly the term to describe this immense building. A heavy chain-link fence surrounded the concrete warehouse, and also protected the entrance to the pier. A second guard station, similar to that which they had passed to gain entrance to the site, provided additional protection for the pier and warehouse area.

"Syrian security," muttered Rypkin. "If there's one thing they're good at it's security." Rypkin thought briefly of his own country, of the exceptional security measures at Khokskya, and conceded that, during the Cold War years, the Syrians had hired good teachers in this matter of security.

Rypkin also admitted to himself that the construction of these structures along the pier appeared to be of excellent quality, from what he could see. This, at least, was a good sign. Perhaps there was hope for this project, after all.

Back in Latakia, the morning sun had burned off the haze, and the sea had sparkled like a jewel. But, here at Damsarkhu, a gray mist still lay over the crescent-shaped shoreline. Here, the Mediterranean struck a more menacing pose, her gray waves lapping hungrily at the bulkhead that had been constructed along the front of the site.

Rypkin stretched out a print of the site, identifying the planned location of major components of the power plant. He spoke directly to Jadeel, who passed his comments along to Omar Fassad.

"There, to the south," Rypkin pointed, "is where the cooling water intake structure will be located. We will have to level this hillside just in front of us for the power plant foundations. That pier will be an excellent asset to bring in equipment and supplies." Rypkin studied the chart again. "Can we get down closer to the shoreline? I want to get a feel for the bulkhead construction."

Fassad eased the automobile down the sloping road toward the shoreline. The road took them toward the north, closer to the pier facility. Rypkin noticed a considerable commotion that was attending to a small, shallow-draft freighter, tied to the pier, only about fifty meters out from the shoreline. It appeared that the freighter was off-loading trucks from its cargo deck onto the pier. One of the trucks was already moving landward, escorted by two military vehicles. Fassad pulled the car to a stop at the shoreline, not far from the security fence that protected the pier area.

Rypkin got out of the vehicle, and wandered down to the bulkhead. He signaled for Omar and Jadeel to join him. Although the bulkhead had been constructed only recently, several large cracks appeared in the earth just landward of it. At one point, near where Viktor stood, several of the beams that formed the bulkhead structure had collapsed. "You see, here," Viktor pointed to the damaged area "we will have to plan for considerable rework of the bulkhead structure before we can even begin to set foundations. This will be an important factor as we establish the conceptual design schedule. The civil engineers will have to get involved in this, but I suspect we may have to move the entire plant further inland, if we cannot stabilize this shoreline."

Jadeel nodded and translated Rypkin's comments into Arabic for the client-associate, Omar Fassad. Rypkin's eyes were drawn again to the activity along the pier, now only a few meters away from him. One of the trucks that had been taken from off the freighter had been driven slowly down the pier, and off onto a paved lay-down space near the huge concrete storage building. A crane was in the process of removing a large cylindrical canister from the flatbed trailer of the truck onto a set of dolly wheels. A technician emerged from the cab of the truck, and began to sweep around the canister with an electronic instrument shaped like a pistol, with an exaggerated, wide barrel. Viktor recognized the instrument immediately: it was a scintillation counter, a radiation detection device. He had seen identical instruments countless times at the radioactive control checkpoints set up all over the *Antyey III* project. What was a radiation detection device doing here?

Before Rypkin had a chance to mention his observation to his colleagues, a loud voice approached from the rear.

"What are you doing here?" An armed guard ran at full speed from the direction of the security station. "You are not authorized here!" screamed the guard.

Omar Fassad took out his identification pass. "We are from the ministry in Latakia..."

"I do not care if you are sent from Allah, himself!" the guard continued to scream. "You will depart immediately!" The guard lowered his rifle, pointing it in the direction of the three visitors.

Omar leaped immediately into the driver's seat of the automobile; Jadeel and Viktor scrambled into the rear seat. The car lurched forward up the hillside and rapidly moved away from the menacing guard. Fassad's hands shook nervously as they gripped the steering wheel. Fassad turned his head quickly to the right, and to the left, looking carefully along the road, seemingly in a panic. Seated in the back seat, Viktor could see Fassad's eyes in the rear view mirror. They were eyes filled with terror. Fassad mumbled something in Arabic, nervously repeating the same phrase.

Viktor leaned over to Jadeel, "What is he saying?" Viktor whispered.

Jadeel shook her head gently. "Only that he is afraid they will get our names and we will be in trouble." Jadeel whispered back to Rypkin. "It is nothing. This is just a typical security precaution." From the tone of her voice, Viktor was unable to tell if this was a statement of knowing reassurance, or if perhaps Jadeel, too, was concerned about the abrupt end to their site visit.

Fassad slowed at the outer security gate, and then accelerated rapidly onto the main access road, relieved that he had not been further detained or questioned at the guard station.

Few words were spoken on the short trip back to the Ministry Building in Latakia. Viktor Rypkin was deep in troubled thought. What was it he had seen? He knew only two things for certain: those canisters were definitely being monitored with radiation detection instruments, and the Syrian guards were not at all happy that this had been observed. Why would there be radioactive material at the site now? This plant would not be receiving any kind of nuclear fuel for years. Furthermore, that was not nuclear fuel in those canisters. The canisters looked more like the shielded radioactive waste containers he had seen many times at the nuclear submarine pens at Khokskya. But why would the Syrians be bringing radioactive waste into this power plant site? Why the hyper-sensitivity of Security? Rypkin tucked these thoughts into his mind's files as Omar Fassad pulled the automobile into the parking lot at the Ministry of Electricity Production Building.

It was a simple invitation, given casually, but it inflamed the soul of Viktor Rypkin. It was a feeling that he never before in his life had known.

Viktor, Jadeel Dovni, and Omar Fassad had nearly completed their work for the day. Omar was busy filing scheduling charts in a cabinet at the far side of the room while Viktor and Jadeel, at the chart table, arranged documents that would be used for the next day's efforts. Jadeel caught Viktor's attention, lightly touching his hand, and speaking softly, "Viktor, I have been invited to dinner this evening with friends from my college. Their apartment is not far from here. Can you join me?" Jadeel's manner was halting, almost shy.

"I would love to, Jadeel!" Viktor gushed, "Where shall we meet? What time?"

"My dormitory is only about three blocks from yours," said Jadeel. "I will stop by and meet you in the lobby of your dormitory. We can walk to my friends' apartment from there. It is only a few blocks, toward the center of Latakia. Will seven o'clock be convenient for you?"

Omar Fassad turned from his file cabinet and complained sharply to Jadeel. Viktor could not understand his Arabic language, but he could tell that Omar was, once again, frustrated by the details of his work. No matter. To Viktor, Jadeel's invitation had made this day an unqualified success.

"Miss Dovni," said Fassad in Arabic, "please ask Mr. Rypkin to tell me the file in which I should place this document." Fassad handed a report consisting of several pages to Jadeel. "There is no category in our files which seems to fit."

Jadeel took the document from Fassad and handed it to Viktor, explaining Fassad's problem. Viktor looked briefly at the papers, then withdrew a blank manila file folder from a box on his desk, and wrote a number on it.

"There," said Rypkin, "I hope that this may be the most difficult problem we have to face on this project, Jadeel." Viktor chuckled as he handed the new file to Jadeel, who passed it on to

Fassad.

Fassad grumbled as he put the file in its place in the cabinet. Viktor could not understand Fassad's words, and he thought it was just as well.

"Well," said Viktor Rypkin, "we have had enough for this day. Jadeel, tell Mr. Fassad he may go as soon as he has filed that document. Then, may I walk you to your dormitory?"

Jadeel gave the instructions to Fassad, then turned back to Viktor. "No, that will not be necessary," she said. "I must finish organizing things here for tomorrow's work. But I will very much look forward to seeing you this evening. At seven o'clock then?"

"Yes, Jadeel," said Viktor, "that will be fine."

Rypkin left the office, and headed rapidly down the stairs and off to his dormitory. He wanted to shower, to shine his shoes, and to prepare his best suit of clothes for this evening with Jadeel. Viktor was no musician, but his heart felt like singing as he left the Ministry of Electric Power Production.

Viktor Rypkin had been identified early in the Soviet educational system as a potential "Red Star Scholar," children who were singled out for very special, intensive academic programs. Rypkin was pushed, twelve months a year, for eighteen years, in the best schools that his government could provide. For these young Red Star Scholars, the schools were fine, indeed. The competition was fierce. An unsatisfactory mark for but one semester in one course could result in dismissal from the program. This would bring unthinkable shame and failure to the young students. Viktor Rypkin, totally absorbed in his studies until he was twenty-four years old, had never had time for girls. He was interested, to be sure, but he simply could not afford the time.

Except for professional friendships such as he had with Tatyana Patinova, he had rarely spoken privately with any female. And he never had felt this way before about any girl. Such a thing as this night, to be with Jadeel, was something that had lived, up to now, only in Viktor's dreams.

Viktor was waiting for Jadeel when she arrived in the lobby, promptly at seven o'clock p.m. He had, from the very beginning, thought Jadeel to be a strikingly beautiful woman. She always dressed properly for work, in modest business attire, hair bound tightly up on her head. For this evening, Jadeel had dressed more casually than Viktor had seen her before. She wore a simple, brightly colored cotton dress, and her dark hair fell loosely about her shoulders. Viktor caught his breath at the sight of her. He had never seen anything so lovely.

Outside, it was unseasonably warm. A slight breeze blew in from the Mediterranean; stars filled the dark, cloudless sky. There were no street lights, but the little shops along the narrow streets were brightly lit. The wild strains of Middle Eastern music blared out of some of the cafes along the way, lending a carnival feeling to the evening. The Syrian Army heavily patrolled this particular section of the city, as did the city police, so there was little to fear, in this quarter at least, from street criminals.

As they strolled along, Jadeel spoke excitedly about the friends they were about to visit. "Risa was my roommate for the first two years I was at the university," said Jadeel. "She was my very best friend when I really needed one. We dated lots of boys together then. I never found anyone, but Risa did. She married Husni during our third year. I have only seen them occasionally since then. Husni seems like a nice fellow. He's not exactly my type, but I think he has been good for Risa."

"What is your type, Jadeel?" asked Viktor Rypkin. He stared straight ahead, not noticing as she shot a quick glance at him.

"I do not know," she said. "I have yet to get to know such a man...not yet."

They proceeded along this street, Jadeel pointing out favorite shops, suggesting cafes to avoid and others to enjoy.

"Before the war began," she said, "this street was much more festive. Most of the young men have now gone off in Zabadi's army. Now the girls have nothing to draw them here. Look! There is Risa's apartment building." Jadeel led Viktor into an ancient, two-story stucco building. They went up a narrow flight of stairs, knocked on a flimsy wooden door, and were greeted by a short, stout Syrian girl. Risa squealed with delight and hugged her college chum, Jadeel Dovni.

Risa smiled knowingly at Viktor as Jadeel introduced him. She spoke to Jadeel, asking her to translate her Arabic words of welcome for Jadeel's Russian friend.

"Risa wants me to tell you that you are very welcome in her home," said Jadeel. "She also insists that I tell you that she has heard many good things about you." Jadeel smiled, "But I cannot really tell you that without embarrassing myself, can I?"

Viktor laughed warmly. It was obvious to Risa that Jadeel had properly relayed her greeting.

Risa's husband, Husni, was not home from work. He evidently had some sort of position at the local government radio station. His work there was important enough to keep him out of having to serve in Zabadi's army, but it often required late hours of toil.

Risa had prepared a simple, but copious meal for her guests. Wartime restrictions prevented more elaborate fare, but she had prepared a delicious dish of rice and fish, which Viktor thoroughly enjoyed.

Jadeel and Risa barely stopped talking throughout the dinner. Only occasionally did they pause to acknowledge Viktor's presence, or to recognize that their giggling and gossip in Arabic was totally unintelligible to him. But Viktor enjoyed it all. He would have been delighted to spend all evening, simply watching Jadeel: fresh, animated, beautiful.

It was shortly after eleven o'clock p.m. that Husni finally returned to his home. Tall, by Syrian standards, and very thin, he looked haggard and worn. He made apologies for being so late, and slumped into a chair at the table waiting to be fed. Viktor surmised from his appearance that he probably had not eaten anything else that day. It was obvious to Viktor that the time had come for him and Jadeel to depart.

As they reached the bottom of the stairway, Jadeel stopped, took both of Viktor's hands in her own, and said, "Thank you, Viktor, for being so nice. You did not understand a word we said, did you?"

"Well, no," admitted Viktor. "But, Jadeel, I enjoyed every moment of it. And your friend is really a very good cook."

Jadeel gave Viktor a brief hug and continued to hold his right hand tightly, tugging him down the street. "Come, Viktor," she said. "I will show you another a beautiful view of the sea!"

The two made their way through the narrow streets. Viktor had never experienced such a feeling: bathed in the warm breeze from the sea, and in the exotic sounds of the Latakia streets, and in the presence of the beautiful, spirited Jadeel Dovni. Her hand gripped his tightly as they made their way across one last street to the dunes that led down to the Mediterranean shore.

The moon was not bright, as it should have been for such a romantic evening, but a quarter of it sat high overhead, casting a faint shimmer on the waves. The tangle of sounds that passed for music back on the streets faded, giving way to the rush of the waves against the shore. The euphony of the seashore was much more pleasant than the noise of the streets to the ears of the Russian boy and the Russian-Syrian girl who strolled, hand in hand, barefoot, along the beach.

Suddenly, Jadeel broke free from Viktor's hand, and ran headlong into the surf. She turned and called to Viktor, tauntingly, to join her.

Viktor was not given to such impulsiveness. He generally disliked being in the water. Besides, he was wearing his best suit! But then he looked again at Jadeel, illuminated only by the faint moonlight, and heard her laughing voice. He dropped the shoes he was carrying and raced at top speed down to the breaking surf and dived in, head first, suit and all. Jadeel gave a delighted shriek, and dived in the surf after him.

They both surfaced a few meters beyond the surf, standing in waist-deep water. Jadeel took Rypkin's hands to steady herself, and then embraced him around the neck. She stood on her toes and kissed him, with all her might. Viktor held her close, lifting her up as a wave broke about their shoulders.

Suddenly, the idyllic scene was shattered by a screeching siren sound. A searchlight focused on the couple, pointed at them by police officials in a beach-patrol vehicle. A voice growled at them through a bullhorn. Viktor could not understand the words, but he got the message. He and Jadeel ran in toward the beach.

"I am so sorry, Viktor," lamented Jadeel Dovni. "This beach is closed at night. I should have known. I am so sorry."

"Sorry?" Viktor laughed. The shore police had moved slowly on down the beach. "Jadeel, do not apologize for this. Let us wait until the beach patrol goes on further and then we can..."

"No, Viktor," said Jadeel, "The last thing we need to do is to get in trouble with the authorities. Oh! I am so sorry I have acted like a stupid child!" Jadeel raced up the beach toward the street from which they had come.

Viktor, ever practical, picked up their shoes and followed.

Chapter Thirteen

The Trawler

January
Latakia, Syria

VIKTOR RYPKIN AWOKE EARLY. He had not slept well. Troubling thoughts of radioactive waste containers competed with the much more pleasant imaginations of Jadeel Dovni.

Viktor's dreams of Jadeel were not the same as those he had dreamed of Tatyana. Indeed, Tatyana was a wonderful friend. She was a person with whom he could share his innermost thoughts. She was truly a "comrade," to use the now-archaic term. She was a buddy.

But, Jadeel! Her dark, mysterious beauty captivated Viktor. The agility and depth of her mind awed him. And her tendency to shift in an instant from the cold, businesslike interpreter to the coquettish, giggling schoolgirl confused him. Unlike with Tatyana, he felt he could share nothing of his personal feelings with his enigmatic interpreter. He felt he had to remain on guard in her presence. Captivated, awed, confused, Rypkin gave up on the idea of sleeping. He checked his watch: five forty-five a.m. Viktor had slept all he was going to sleep this night. He staggered out of bed and prepared to go into the office.

It was shortly after seven o'clock that Viktor arrived on the second floor of the Ministry Building. He was delighted to see that Jadeel was, as usual, early.

Jadeel looked up, smiling at the Russian. "Oh, hello!" she said. "I thought perhaps it was Omar coming in early. He has been more punctual lately. Did you sleep well last night?"

"No, Jadeel," said Viktor, "I did not sleep well at all. I...I..." Viktor stammered, blushing like an adolescent. "Listen, Jadeel. Would you join me for breakfast? Have you eaten breakfast this morning?"

"I have eaten breakfast, Viktor," said Jadeel, "but I would be pleased to have tea with you while you eat. Perhaps you may need an interpreter." Jadeel continued to smile cheerfully at Rypkin. The two left the office, heading for the small cafe located in the building's basement.

Viktor bought Jadeel a cup of tea, and one for himself. He also picked up a small basket of hard, flat biscuits that would serve as his breakfast. The two of them took a table at one corner of the crowded cafe. Their conversation began with a review of the upcoming day's tasks, but soon led to more personal issues.

Viktor was fascinated by Jadeel's family history. Jadeel shared with him her childhood dream of one day going to find her father in Russia. She had imagined visiting the storybook spires of St. Basil's in Moscow. "Now that your country is no longer run by the communists," reasoned Jadeel, "there may be more opportunity for me to visit, one day."

The naive sincerity of his beautiful young interpreter charmed Viktor Rypkin. "I am not too certain of that, Jadeel." Viktor shook his head sadly. "In fact, nothing is certain now about my country. There is so much talk about freedom, about democracy, about this so-called *free enterprise*. But, meanwhile, the people starve. My country is beautiful, yes. But I would not advise that this is a good time for you to see it. Besides," Viktor looked for an instant into the sparkling dark eyes of the Syrian girl, and then turned his own glance away, sheepishly, "I have found much more beauty here in Latakia than I have ever seen, anywhere."

Possibly Jadeel did not fully understand Viktor's meaning, or possibly she was just being coy. "Oh, Viktor," she said, "I know that we do have some lovely places here, but mostly it is squalor. That, or desert. I remember pictures my father showed me of Moscow. And also of your Ural Mountains. They are *real* mountains! Perhaps one day..."

Just then, Omar Fassad entered the door of the little cafe. He spotted Jadeel and Viktor and hurriedly made his way through the crowd to greet them.

"Jadeel, Jadeel!" called Fassad. "You must tell Mr. Rypkin that he is wanted immediately at the director's office. They sent a messenger to our office just a moment ago to get him."

Jadeel turned to Rypkin and translated, "A messenger has come from the director's office, Viktor. It is requested that you go at once to see the director."

Rypkin grimaced and shook his head. He wiped the corners of his mouth with his napkin, and tossed it down on the table before him. "I will go up to see Ivanov. I will meet you two back in the office later." Viktor stalked out of the cafe and headed up the stairs toward the director's office.

———————

"Viktor, come in, come in." Director Ivanov stood graciously and ushered Rypkin to a chair that sat beside his massive wooden desk. Another man, stern-looking, obviously not a Syrian, sat nearby. The man wore a civilian suit.

"Viktor," said Ivanov, "I would like you to meet *Kapitan Pervogo Ranga* Yevshenko." He indicated the still-unsmiling stranger who nodded very slightly at the introduction. "Captain Yevshenko is on the staff of our good friend Admiral Glutsin." Ivanov walked over to his office door, and shut it. He then sat at his desk and spoke in hushed tones. "Do you remember Viktor, that Admiral Glutsin told you in Khokskya that he would see to it that you had opportunities to stay involved in his submarine programs?"

Rypkin nodded, eagerly.

Ivanov continued, "I had to promise the admiral that I would permit you to be spared from time to time from my Project Power Pack to allow you to work directly for him. Evidently, this is to be one of those times. I am instructed to let you go with Captain First Rank Yevshenko, here, to work on some project that Sergei Glutsin has going on. I am not cleared to know any more about this, but I am sure that Captain Yevshenko will fill you in on the details." Ivanov motioned to the captain.

The captain did not smile, and he did not waste words. "Not here," said Yevshenko. "We will talk later. I will go with you to your apartment to get your things. Then we will depart."

"How long will I be gone, Sir?" asked Rypkin. "How much of my clothing should I pack?" Viktor directed his question at the captain.

It was Ivanov who answered. "Admiral Glutsin told me to expect you to be gone for no more than five days. You should expect to be gone for about five days."

"Let's go," said Captain Yevshenko. He stood and went to Ivanov's office door. He opened it and signaled for Rypkin to follow him. Rypkin stood, nodded politely to Director Ivanov, and followed the captain out the door.

As they stepped out into the main passageway, Rypkin noticed the two armed guards at the office door just down the hall. Mustafa Mutanabbi must be in, Rypkin thought to himself. He was glad, in a way, to be leaving Mutanabbi's madhouse project for a time. He was undeniably excited to hear that Glutsin had not forgotten his promise. At the same time, however, Viktor felt a tinge of frustration. He had so much more that he wanted to say to Jadeel Dovni! Now, he would have to put that off for another week.

Captain First Rank Yevshenko relaxed somewhat after he and Viktor left the building, and were safely in a Russian vehicle, driven by a Russian Navy seaman.

"You cannot be too careful, Rypkin," said Yevshenko. "It is never good to discuss sensitive matters inside a building in a foreign land. Especially a new government building." Yevshenko took a pack of cigarettes from his breast pocket, and offered one to Rypkin. Viktor shook his head, refusing politely. Yevshenko took a cigarette for himself, lit it, and began to explain the purpose of the five-day mission.

The two of them were to board a Russian trawler, called *Zaytsev*, that was now docked at the main wharf in the port of Latakia. Of course, as with many such Russian "trawlers," this vessel was equipped for much more than fishing. In fact, she was loaded with the very latest in sonar and electronic navigation equipment. It was the kind of equipment that Viktor Rypkin had spent his career developing. And there was more: the ship carried 144 Yodel Echo transceivers.

These transceivers were the very devices that had been Viktor Rypkin's brainchild at Khokskya. This was truly exciting for Rypkin! He had placed grids of these sonar transmitter-receivers in Russian waters for experiment, but this would be the first time they were placed in something other than "hometown" environments.

The idea of the system was simple. It was a clever solution to what had become a prohibitive problem in the development of the Katapaltes weapon system. The success of Katapaltes depended on being able to launch a massive volume of firepower while submerged, undetected. To do this, it was vital to know, with a high degree of accuracy, the precise location of the launching submarine. Otherwise, the firepower might be totally misdirected, and miss its mark entirely.

Satellite navigation, using the information broadcast down by orbiting navigational satellites, was a highly accurate means of navigating. However, satellite navigation required exposing the receiver antenna at the ocean's surface. The Americans had become expert in quickly detecting such antenna broachings. Furthermore, the giant *Antyey* submarines were extremely difficult to control near the surface. It was practically impossible to maintain periscope depth without broaching, exposing much of the giant submarine's profile in the process. Nothing short of a sitting duck is more vulnerable than a submarine at the surface. Viktor Rypkin, leading his team of sonar navigation technicians, had developed another, better way to acquire positioning data for the launch submarine.

Viktor's idea was to place specially designed sonar receiver-transmitters at precisely specified points on the ocean floor. The accurate position of each transducer would be fixed in advance by using satellite navigation data. Rypkin's system placed 144 such transducers, in a twelve-by-twelve grid at potential "launch points" to be located secretly at sensitive areas around the world.

When a launch became necessary, the giant submarine would be able to creep into the area, running at its preferred launch depth of about sixty meters. When in the vicinity of the Yodel Echo transducers, it would send out a very low power "trigger pulse." The trigger pulse would be directed straight down, toward the approximate location of the grid. The pulse was so focused in its direction, and of such low intensity, that it would be practically undetectable by enemy ears that might be listening. When the waiting Yodel Echo hydrophone collected a trigger pulse of the correct pre-coded frequency, it would then click in to its active mode. A highly directional, low intensity sound pulse would be sent back to the Russian submarine from the long, narrow, conical "horn." Again, the signal was carefully designed so that only a sonar receiver on a launch submarine directly above the transducer could hear it. The submarine's receiver had to be precisely tuned to the proper pre-coded frequency. By receiving the return signal, and those of other transducers in the grid, the Russian submarine's computers would be able to triangulate an accurate navigational position.

In trials conducted in the Sea of Okhotsk and in the Black Sea, the system had proved incredibly accurate. Thus armed with accurate data, the appropriate correction could be made to the submarine's inertial navigation system, the fire control system could be engaged, and Katapaltes launch could commence.

Viktor Rypkin and Captain First Rank Yevshenko arrived at Port Latakia at about 10:30 a.m. It was a gray, chilly day along the piers. Dark clouds hovered in the east. A stiff breeze blew in from that direction. A misty rain was falling and it was obvious that more difficult weather was on its way. Leaving the car, Rypkin and Yevshenko made their way, quickly but carefully, along the waterfront. The wharf was greasy and cluttered, now made treacherous by the slippery, wet weather. Arriving at the *Zaytsev*, the two men hurried up the gangplank to go aboard.

Before they could set foot on the metal deck of the trawler, they were stopped abruptly by a well-armed Russian sailor. "My orders," said the sailor, "are to let no one aboard without positive identification."

The rain was beginning to fall in earnest, driven by a sudden gust of wind. The captain yelled above the noise of the wind and rain, "I am Captain First Rank Yevshenko, sailor! This is Engineer Rypkin. Now let us get in out of this rain!"

"I must see your identification, sir! I have my orders!" repeated the sailor.

Captain Yevshenko nodded, grunting as he pulled his identification pass out of his pocket. Viktor Rypkin also produced his identification card. The sailor checked both names against a plastic-covered list. Satisfied that they were on the list, he saluted smartly and ushered them aboard. All three men were, by now, soaked from the heavy rain.

Captain Yevshenko smiled at the young man, "Good work, sailor! Stay alert! And you'd better get some raingear!" He patted the sailor on his rain-saturated shoulder.

The two men walked forward to a door that opened into an inboard passageway. They made their way along the passageway, finally entering a small wardroom. Dripping from the rain, they removed their caps, and their outer jackets, and placed them on a stainless steel bench that lay along the bulkhead of the wardroom. Across the small room, a door opened. Admiral Sergei Glutsin stepped forward.

The sight of his mentor fueled Victor Rypkin's enthusiasm. The knowledge that The Admiral, himself, was taking such a personal interest in this project was enough to stall Rypkin's anxieties. The admiral stepped over to greet the two dripping-wet men.

"Rypkin, Rypkin," said Admiral Glutsin. "It is good to see you. We must get you some dry clothing!" Turning to Yevshenko, he laughed, "You too, Yuri! You go now and show Viktor to his stateroom. I will have some dry clothing sent down for both of you. We are scheduled to get underway in about thirty minutes. Let us meet back here in an hour."

Captain Yevshenko led the way down a ladder that dropped below the main deck to a narrow passageway, on either side of which were two tiny staterooms. Rypkin's was the after stateroom on the port side. As they came to the base of the ladder, Rypkin noticed a much larger stateroom that lay forward of the passageway. Rypkin assumed it must be the admiral's.

In Rypkin's stateroom were two bunks, each consisting of a thin mattress placed on a stainless steel shelf cantilevered off the bulkhead. There was no one else in the room, but a satchel had been placed on the bottom bunk. Neatly stenciled across the satchel, in Cyrillic, were the words, *Kovalchuk, Kapitan Vtorogo Ranga*. It was evident that Viktor would be sharing the room, and his roommate had made the first choice. Rypkin placed his wet duffel bag on the deck, beside the chair that was the only other piece of furniture in the room.

Rypkin began to remove his rain-soaked shirt, when a steward knocked at his door, and handed him a bundle of dry clothing. It pleased Viktor to see that the clothing consisted of dark blue coveralls, identical to those that he had worn to work at the Khokskya Pens. He was beginning to feel at home.

Rypkin changed into his dry coveralls, and finished unpacking his bag, neatly stowing its contents in a small cabinet above his bunk. Rypkin could feel the lurch of the ship as it began to move away from the wharf, fighting the strong wind. Rypkin found a foul weather jacket in the stateroom closet. He was not expected back in the wardroom for another thirty minutes, so he decided he would go topside to observe the process of getting under way.

As he stepped out into the dimly lit passageway, he caught sight of a man coming down the access ladder. The man entered the large stateroom at the forward end of the passageway, the one Viktor assumed would be occupied by Glutsin. Perhaps he was a consultant, come to brief the admiral on some matter. The man was short and stockily built, and he had dark, curly hair. In the brief moment that Rypkin glimpsed him in the faint light, he had the feeling that he had seen the man somewhere before. In an instant the man had shut the door behind him. Rypkin thought little more of it, and he headed topside to watch as the trawler pulled out to sea.

Admiral Glutsin's meeting took place as scheduled in the wardroom. Glutsin introduced Viktor Rypkin to other members of the crew. All were Russians, but Viktor knew none of them. They discussed technical details of the mission. Rypkin's input was sought on such matters as depth and spacing of transducer placement and the frequency settings for the instruments.

Rypkin met his cabin-mate, the project navigator, Captain Second Rank Valeri Kovalchuk. The two men engaged in a lengthy conversation about grid placement. They poured over sheet after sheet of bottom contour navigation charts. It sparked Rypkin's curiosity to note that the location of the Yodel Echo grid placement was in the relatively shallow waters off the coast of Israel, less than sixty kilometers west of Tel Aviv. Caught up in the spirit of the technical exercise, however, Rypkin's inquisitiveness was contained. His curiosity was placed in the background as he discussed adjustments to the electronic components that formed the heart of his precious system. Viktor relished this opportunity to work once again with technically competent colleagues, a feeling he had not enjoyed since leaving Khokskya.

After the meeting, Viktor went below to inspect the equipment in the project control room, accompanied by Captain Second Rank Kovalchuk and two of the technicians. The men worked into the night, as the trawler made its way south along the eastern edge of the Mediterranean. They checked and re-checked instrumentation, nearly oblivious to the pitching and rolling induced by the storm passing by outside. It was almost dawn the next morning when Rypkin tumbled into his bunk, exhausted, elated to be doing productive work once again.

The following day was spent much like the first: more checking of the instruments and transducers, more discussion of navigation charts, and more insertion of data into the Yodel-Echo control system computers. Several dry-runs were conducted to practice the intricacies of the drop procedure. By early in the morning of their third day at sea, they were in position, ready to install the transducer grid.

There was, however, a problem. A pair of Israeli patrol craft had been shadowing the trawler since early the previous evening. Admiral Glutsin ordered the trawler's skipper to turn to the southwest and to make standard speed. After about four hours on this course, the Israeli vessels turned back to the east and soon disappeared over the horizon. *Zaytsev* continued on her southwesterly course for another three hours, but then Glutsin directed that the trawler turn back to retrace the course toward the placement point.

Rypkin and most of the other Russian technicians took advantage of the extra time to catch up on lost sleep. Early in the evening, Viktor was awakened by a ship's steward, brandishing a pot of tea. Viktor took the tea, slipped into his coveralls, and made his way out into the passageway to head down to the project control room. As he passed by the open door of the small stateroom next to his own, he was surprised to see it occupied by Admiral Sergei Glutsin. He had assumed that Glutsin resided in the large forward cabin.

"Good morning, Rypkin." The admiral looked up from the

papers he had been studying. "We are nearly at the placement point. How is it going with the transducer settings?"

"Very well. Very well, indeed, Admiral." Viktor paused at the open doorway, "We have one more set of satellite verifications to get inserted into the computer, but then we will be ready to make the drop. I am going down now to be sure that Captain Second Rank Kovalchuk is ready."

"He is ready, Rypkin," said the admiral. "I just spoke to him a moment ago. I will be up on the bridge when we make placement. Good luck, Viktor. This will be an important test of our system. You are doing fine work."

"Thank you sir." Viktor made his way down to the project control center, his heart pounding with pride.

As he entered, Viktor could see that all preparations had been made for the drop. The entire center was "rigged for red": no white lights were lit that would have hindered the men's night vision. The technicians were all in place, wearing sound-powered phones. Many were involved in making last minute adjustments to the equipment. Captain Second Rank Kovalchuk, the officer in charge of the project control center, was in direct communication with the bridge. The drops would commence at his command.

The timing had to be perfect: they had to arrive at the desired drop point at precisely the same time as information became available from the hyper-accurate Soyussat Navigational Satellite scheduled to make a pass overhead within the next twenty minutes. This would enable a final, highly accurate adjustment to the grid positioning system.

Rypkin went to his control station. He was second in command in the room, responsible for final adjustments to the transducers, and for executing the actual drops by pressing a release button on his control panel. The idea was to lay twelve rows, each consisting of twelve transducers, as equally spaced as possible. The operation required keen skill, both in the project control room where Rypkin sat, and in the ship's control station on the bridge. Rypkin had no doubt that Admiral Glutsin would see to the competence of performance on the bridge.

Tension mounted as the red-lit faces scanned instrument panels and listened for orders on their headsets.

"Ten seconds to first drop," Kovalchuk spoke into his headset. "Five, four, three, two, one, MARK! MARK! MARK!"

Rypkin pressed his button at the sound of the first "mark." At the same time, he pressed the timer-button on his console. He carefully watched the ship's speed indicator on the instrument panel before him. Rypkin rapidly made an adjustment with the selector switch, watching the readout change from "A-1" to "A-2." He continued to scan his control panel as he placed his finger back on the "release" button.

"Stand by for release of alpha-two." Rypkin spoke calmly into his mouthpiece. "Stand by. Five, four, three..." Rypkin was now in tactical control of the operation.

It would be Rypkin's responsibility to release the remaining 143 transducers. He would also be giving the orders to make the turns at the end of each row. Kovalchuk, meanwhile, would supervise the inserting of navigational information into the control system computers. The only voices on the communications circuit were those of Rypkin and Kovalchuk as they relayed data back and forth, with an occasional word to the ship's bridge. It was a tedious operation, but the men were well rehearsed, and *Zaytsev* completed her mission, as planned, in just over three hours.

There was a jubilant mood in the control room as the crew stowed their sound powered phones, and secured their instruments and control panels.

"Nice work, Rypkin." Kovalchuk extended his hand to Viktor. "The admiral asked me to pass along his congratulations to you for a job well done. Now we take station to the west. We will return tomorrow to get final verification data, then we can go home. What do you say we go topside for some tea and some fresh air?"

Kovalchuk and Rypkin made their way out of the project control room and up the two sets of ladders to the main deck. As they approached the wardroom door, looking to acquire some freshly brewed tea, they were surprised to find the door closed. They unlatched the door and entered, finding three men seated at the wardroom table, mulling over papers and charts. Admiral Glutsin sat on one side, and Captain First Rank Yevshenko on the other. In the middle was the mysterious young man whom Rypkin had seen on the first day out, entering the large stateroom. He knew he had seen the man before, but he could not remember where.

"Excuse me, Admiral, we did not know the wardroom was occupied." Kovalchuk made a fumbling apology. "We merely wanted to get some wardroom tea."

Captain Yevshenko quickly got up from his seat, and escorted Kovalchuk and Rypkin forward, into the wardroom galley.

"Come on gentlemen," said Yevshenko, "I'll get you a pot of tea." He shut the galley door behind them. "You have done good work, gentlemen. We are merely discussing our plans for tomorrow."

Yevshenko brought out two mugs. Rypkin grabbed the teapot and poured the two mugs full. Yevshenko then opened the galley's other door, and ushered Rypkin and Kovalchuk back out to the main deck by way of a storage room. Yevshenko returned to the wardroom through the galley's main door.

The weather had changed completely since the storm of two days before. The evening was still and clear. Kovalchuk and Rypkin sipped the hot tea and enjoyed the fresh air. They began to unwind from the exacting tasks they had been performing for the last several days.

"Who was that with the Admiral and Yevshenko?" asked Rypkin, "I think I may have seen him somewhere before."

"I have never seen him." Kovalchuk took a long sip from his mug. "He must be some consultant. I do not get the feeling we should ask too many questions about him, though. Yevshenko was unusually eager to get us out of the wardroom."

Rypkin nodded. He contemplated the short, curly hair, the dark features. Where have I seen him before? Rypkin's mind pondered the question as he gazed out over the placid waters. He watched the trawler churn up a luminescent phosphorus wake. A consultant? No, thought Rypkin. A consultant would not occupy the ship's largest stateroom, relegating the admiral to a smaller one.

A bright crescent moon cast its shimmering beam across the water. Rypkin toyed with his memory, enjoying the mind game of trying to remember. This mystery man's features were dark, much like the Syrians with whom he had been working lately...Wait!

Rypkin's mind had clicked in recognition. He remembered having seen the short, dark, muscular man before. It was several days before, as he had been visiting Director Ivanov's office back in Latakia. On that occasion the young man was wearing a dapper western suit. This was the man that headed up the Syrian end of Project Power Pack. This was Mustafa Mutanabbi! What in the world was the Syrian doing on this Russian trawler?

Rypkin turned to Kovalchuk, "I believe you are right, Captain," said Rypkin. "We should speak no more of this." Viktor Rypkin started down toward his stateroom, "We have much to do tomorrow. I think I will turn in. Good night, Captain."

Chapter Fourteen

<u>Six O'Clock News</u>

January
Weymouth, Massachusetts

"**M**OM! QUICK! *IT'S DAD!*"
Luke yelled from the family room in to where Susan, Lucy and Ken Winning were putting away dishes from the evening's meal. A pot clattered to the floor as Susan rushed around the corner to the room where the oldest of the Winning children was performing the evening ritual of scanning the TV news shows for word of the Hazor Hostages.

The picture being shown by CNN was not a pretty one. The man had a defiant scowl on his face. The face was swollen, covered with abrasions. The man's hands gripped a newspaper, held before the camera. Then he thrust the paper down to the floor. The poor quality home-video footage suddenly terminated at that point. The man was Bill Winning.

The CNN news anchorman was saying, as Susan raced into the room, "This footage was just received moments ago at our news desk in Jerusalem, and was beamed to Atlanta by satellite. It clearly shows yesterday's date on yesterday morning's Jerusalem Hebrew-language newspaper. This tape was unquestionably filmed sometime within the last thirty hours. There is no talking on the tape, and we are not yet certain which of the hostages is pictured..."

As the announcer spoke, the pictures of two other hostages briefly appeared, each in turn holding up what looked to be the same newspaper. The three wretched men spoke no words. Susan stood, stunned, as she watched these pictures of her husband and of Gary Tarr and of Bucky Albostini flash by on national television. It had been nine days of nearly unbearable agony since her world had collapsed.

The news program was not yet complete...an interview with a U.S. State Department official...when the phone began to ring. The first call was from Lori Tarr. Yes, those pictures were certainly those of Bill and Gary. Yes, they looked horrible, but, praise the Lord, they are still alive. Yes, the other picture looked like that fellow from Philadelphia, Bucky Albostini. The two women cried together and prayed together over the phone.

More phone calls: several from friends at church, from Bill's office, from family. Bucky Albostini's wife, Ruth, called from Philadelphia. Had Susan heard anything more from the State Department? No, she hadn't. Had Susan heard anything about Ruth's brother, Mel Gold? No, she hadn't. But Susan sensed in Ruth Albostini a desperate need to talk to someone, so she stayed on the phone for over an hour, talking about the possibilities, attempting to comfort her. Susan had only one loved one to worry about. Ruth was missing her husband *and* her brother, and the latter had not even appeared on the TV broadcast. Mel Gold was the only passenger on that ill-fated tour bus who had not been accounted for. Susan sensed Ruth's growing panic. Ruth Albostini had no children, and she seemed estranged from what family she did have in the Philadelphia area.

Susan Winning had an idea. "Listen, Ruth. Why don't you come up here to Weymouth and stay with us for a while? We have a spare room you'd be welcome to use. Lori Tarr lives just a few blocks from here, and we three sure do have something in common! At least we can cry on each others' shoulders."

Ruth Albostini nearly broke out again in tears of gratitude. "Someone finally cares!" she seemed to sob. "I...I'll have to take some time off at the bank. Oh, they'll get by somehow. Oh, yes, Susan, I'd love to come. I can catch the Amtrak train tomorrow morning. I'll call you when I get my ticket. Oh, thank you!"

No sooner had Susan put the phone back on the hook than the phone rang again. "Is this Mrs. Susan Winning?"

"Yes, it is," Susan responded.

"Would you please hold for a call from Admiral Robert Copper in the Pentagon?" asked the voice.

"Yes, of course."

"Susan, is that you?" asked a new voice, the voice of Bob Copper.

"Bob! Yes!" Susan exclaimed. "Thanks for calling!" Susan had heard much about Bill's old shipmate. She had thoroughly enjoyed visiting with Bob Copper and his wife Maria during homecoming visits to Annapolis.

"Susan," said Admiral Copper, "I just heard a few minutes ago that Bill was among those hostages taken in Israel last week. I was at sea over in the Med all last month and only got brief news reports. But then I got back to the office this morning and had a call waiting from our old buddy Dave O'Leary. Dave said he saw Bill's picture on the news earlier this evening. I made a few calls to some friends over at the CIA. They confirmed it: it's Bill.

"Listen, Susan, I know your phone has probably been ringing off the hook, and the last thing you need is to hear from old geezers like me. But one thing I also know is that sometimes when you're trying to get 'help' from a bureaucracy like the State Department, it can be good to have friends. Susan," said Admiral Copper, "I'm a friend, and I want you to call me whenever you need some help. OK?"

"OK, Bob." responded Susan Winning. "I really appreciate your calling. The State Department guy called earlier. His name is Mr. Miller. He's located here in Boston. He has been as nice as can be. But I'll remember your offer. Thank you so much."

"Susan," persisted the admiral, "nice is one thing; help is another. I don't pretend to have any pull in the State Department, but I just hate to see you get any run-around. So, stay in touch, hear? Maria is available to help you watch the kids, and you're sure welcome to stay at our place if you need to come to the D.C. area for anything. Listen, what can you tell me about what happened?"

Bob Copper and Susan Winning talked on for a few moments. Susan explained all she knew about the capture. Most of the people on the bus had been killed, including the driver and the guide, who were both Palestinians. It appeared that several of the passengers had been shot, but they were all burnt so badly that it was hard to tell, or even to get positive identification. Only four of the tourists had been missing from the initial body count when the burning bus was discovered. Now that three had shown up on this morning's TV news report, only one, Mel Gold, was still missing. There was still no real solid clue about who was behind this, except that the videotapes that were shown on the news were said to have been received from an Israeli extremist group. That was hard to figure, but that's all Susan had heard.

After Susan had thanked Bob Copper for his concern, she placed the phone back on its hook, and hastened to set the answering machine on "AUTO ANSWER." She had to get away from the phone for a minute to get the kids to bed. It was getting late.

As hectic as it had been to get such a barrage of phone calls, it was truly comforting to know that so many people cared so much. All the calls helped keep her mind off a mounting sense of hopelessness and panic.

The sight of her husband on national television, obviously mistreated, covered with abrasions, defiantly staring into his captors' camera, was enough to shake the normally valiant Susan Whitney Winning to her foundation. But that foundation was a Rock. And, she had finally seen at least one answer to her prayers: Bill was still alive!

Dr. Steve Whitney had stayed in Weymouth to be with his daughter and his grandchildren to help them in this trial. He had asked for, and received, an extension of his leave of absence from his position as Professor of Old Testament Studies at Washington Bible College in Lanham, Maryland. He would have to return to his work soon, but his first priority was to see that life had stabilized for Susan and the kids.

Granddad Whitney, his daughter, and his grandchildren spent many hours together in prayer during these days. It was not something that was planned, or even well-organized, it just sort of happened, usually in the evenings, as the family came together after the day's events.

Their ordinary pattern was to turn off the television after the news program-scan was completed and the dishes were put away. The little family would collect in the family room. Steve would usually start with a brief opening prayer, and then read a passage from the Bible. Then Susan would pray, in gentle, softly spoken conversation with God. Then each of the kids would pray. Lori Tarr often joined them, for dinner and for prayer. Ruth Albostini, during her visit, often sat in the room and listened. She said she was comforted by it, but she did not feel inclined to join the prayers.

When everyone had finished, Steve Whitney would close, often with a reminder to the kids, "Remember, even when we say, 'Amen,' it doesn't mean we stop praying. The Bible says, 'Pray without ceasing,' so that's what let's do."

The prayers were mostly simple, sometimes lengthy, always fervent, and often profound. Little Lucy had brought her mother and her grandfather to tears when she prayed: "God, I don't understand why you let this happen to Daddy, but Granddad says, 'whatever happens that brings you closer to God is, in the end, a good thing.' So, I know that you are going to do something good. Thank you, God."

Sometimes Dr. Whitney marveled at how wise, but how hard to put into real-life practice, are the precepts of God's word.

Meanwhile, during those first two weeks after the taking of the Hazor Hostages, Steve Whitney had spent considerable time in Boston, at the J.F. Kennedy Federal Center, meeting with representatives of the U.S. State Department, and talking on the phone with State Department officials in Washington. Until just prior to the newscast, when CNN had called State to let them know about the videotapes, there had been no clue about the four missing tourists.

Dr. Whitney had provided detailed descriptions, family histories, background references, possible contacts, and as much information about Bill as he could give. Even though the first contacts with the State Department representatives were cordial enough, it had begun to seem to Steve that his son-in-law was being treated more as a suspect than as a victim of this heinous crime. But he kept his feelings to himself and sought to cooperate as much as he knew how. At least now that the tape had been shown, so he thought, they would get on with the business of freeing hostages.

Boston
February

It was unusually warm for a mid-winter day in New England. Much of the snow and ice that had collected from the previous week's blizzard had melted. Great heaps of snow that had been plowed aside from roads and parking lots blocked passage along the narrow sidewalks near the J.F. Kennedy Federal Center. The color of the snow piles was a dirty, city-gray. It would be three more months until the larger of these mounds would completely melt. They would then become slush ponds that would flood the streets until Boston's antique storm drainage systems could slowly carry the mess away to the harbor.

Susan Winning had left her car at the parking lot at a shopping mall near the subway entrance. She knew it would be easier to take the Red Line subway into the city than to try to cope with traffic and downtown parking. Her appointment with Mr. Herb Miller of the State Department was at ten o'clock a.m. on the third floor of the Federal Center.

Ruth Albostini had returned to her work in Philadelphia. Susan's father had returned to Maryland, but he had given Susan detailed instructions for getting to Miller's office. Lori Tarr was at Susan's house to help get the kids off to school, and to be there for them if Susan ran late getting back in the afternoon. Susan welcomed the opportunity to get involved personally with these government officials, and with the program to get the hostages back. The shock was over, and it was replaced by determination.

Susan crossed the street and entered the plaza that led up a broad set of stairs to the entrance to the JFK Center. Several people, over a dozen of them, stood by the entrance, casually talking among themselves, smoking cigarettes, enjoying the mild-weather break in what had been a grim winter. They all wore federal identification badges either clipped to their clothing or fastened to their necks with a light chain.

Susan stepped inside the spacious lobby of the JFK Center. The entire area was nearly empty, except for receptionists, security guards, and a few well-dressed young men and women scurrying to and from the elevator bank, armed with expensive briefcases and bright ideas. In the center of the lobby were four large desks, arranged in a circular pattern. A receptionist sat behind each desk. Susan approached the nearest of the reception desks and stood waiting while the attendant spoke on the phone.

The receptionist mildly, but irritably, scolded Susan for

interrupting her conversation. This call was personal, it was private, and she did not appreciate Susan's insistent interference. She brusquely waved Susan over to the next desk around the circle. The second receptionist put down her copy of the Boston *Globe* as Susan approached.

"I have a ten o'clock meeting with Mr. Miller in the State Department," said Susan Winning. "I know I'm early, but I hoped he might be able to see me now, anyway." It was 9:25 a.m.

"The number?" The receptionist held her place in the *Globe* with her left hand while she reached for her telephone.

"The number?" Susan repeated, "...Oh, you mean Mr. Miller's telephone number?"

"That's the person you said you wanted to see, isn't it?" The receptionist was annoyed: she had not had the chance to finish reading her horoscope in the morning paper.

Susan fumbled through her purse and found her address book. She flipped through its pages until she found the number. "Here it is," said Susan, "let's see, it's 617-422-3866."

"Only the last four digits, please!" muttered the receptionist. She was constantly amazed at how ignorant these people were who came in to talk to government officials. These people seldom had the numbers ready. Sometimes they demanded that she break out her Building Directory to look up the numbers for them!

The receptionist punched the numbers into her telephone, spoke for a moment to the party on the other end of the line, and turned to Susan. "Mr. Miller is out just now. He should be here shortly. Please have a seat over there." The receptionist gestured to a group of seats that were not far away from where Susan stood. The receptionist returned, at last, to her horoscope.

Susan watched people come and go as she waited. Most of the traffic was in and out of the office along the wall to her right. At the door was a large plastic sign: "Employment Office."

The receptionist nearest Susan continued to talk on the phone. Whatever the conversation was about, it must have been a pleasant one. The receptionist frequently broke into peals of giggling laughter. The other receptionist with whom Susan had spoken was still absorbed in her newspaper. The two receptionists on the far side of the circle were engaged in a conversation that seemed to mostly include complaints about the job, their supervisors, the low pay, and how boring it was to work in this place.

Susan spent the time going over what she hoped to say to Mr. Miller, and what she hoped to hear from him. She checked her watch. It was 9:50 a.m. Susan collected her papers and went back over to the reception desk. "Could you check to see if Mr. Miller has returned yet?" asked Susan.

"What time is your appointment?" asked the receptionist, the one with the newspaper. "I thought you said it was at ten o'clock. Why don't you wait until ten o'clock? They will call you when Mr. Miller is ready to see you."

"Thank you." Susan went back to her chair. She made the countdown as the second hand on her watch ticked toward ten o'clock. At the stroke of ten, she got up once again to approach the reception desk.

This time the receptionist was ready for her. The receptionist shook her head vigorously and said, "They will *call* you when he is *ready* to see you!"

By now, Susan was seething with frustration. She sat again, pulling a small pad of paper from her purse. She began to make a list. Susan Winning was a list-maker. It helped her sort through problems, ease her frustrations, and get things done. She made to-do lists, prayer lists, prayers-answered lists, people-to-call lists, and things-to-fix lists. As she began to jot down items she had observed this morning, she had the feeling that her experiences so far with the government bureaucracies should be placed under the "things-to-fix" list.

At 10:18 a.m., the receptionist called over to Susan, "Mrs. Winning, you may go on up now to see Mr. Miller. He is in suite 3240, on the third floor."

Susan again collected her papers, and headed for the elevator bank. As she passed by the entrance door through which she had come, nearly an hour before, she looked outside, noticing that another group of smokers had gathered. Susan also recognized among the group some who had been there since before she had arrived. "Our budget deficit in action!" Susan thought to herself.

As Susan entered the glass doors to suite 3240, she checked in with the nearer of the two receptionists in the waiting area.

"Oh, you are the wife of one of those Hazor Hostages!" said the receptionist. "Oh, dear! Bless your heart! I do hope they are able to find them and bring them home safely." She got up to lead Susan to a chair near a table in the corner of the waiting area. "Here, can I get you something to read? Mr. Miller will be with you shortly."

Before Susan could take her seat, a tall young man appeared through the doorway to Susan's left. He wore a finely tailored wool suit and a fashionable silk tie. He held a large mug, emblazoned with an emblem and the words "Harvard Law," full of coffee. On his head was an elegant, white, western-style hat.

"Good morning Mrs. Winning," said Herb Miller, removing his hat. He shook Susan's hand warmly. "It is good to see you in person after all I have heard about you from your father. Let's go into my office."

Miller led Susan down a long corridor cluttered with cabinets full of books and papers of all sorts. Giant reams of computer printouts were stacked on the floor against the walls. Miller's office was at the end of the corridor, on the left. The office was more cluttered than the hallway. Miller removed a stack of papers from the chair that sat across from his desk, and invited Susan to have a seat.

"I am sorry I was late, Mrs. Winning," said Miller. "It is next to impossible to find a parking place around here! I have a spot in the basement, here, of course, but someone else was in it this morning! I had to go out in the streets and find a public parking spot! Takes forever! Say, can I get you a cup of coffee?"

Susan took her seat in the now-vacant chair. She glanced at her watch. It was 10:28 a.m. "No, thank you." Susan responded. "What have you learned about the location of the hostages?"

"Mrs., Winning, Mrs. Winning," said Miller. "There is one thing we must learn in dealing with this matter: patience. Of course, we are doing everything in our power to find out what we can, but we must also recognize that the people we are dealing with here are masters of their trade."

"Well, Mr. Miller," said Susan Winning, "I certainly hope that you are a master of your trade, also. I realize that this is a terribly difficult situation for everyone, but at this point all I really am asking for is information. I just want to know about where my husband is, and how he is being treated. So far, the only thing I have been able to find out has been from CNN. And I learn it along with forty million other people!"

Herb Miller shifted nervously in his chair. He picked up a file that was buried in one of the stacks in front of him, tapped it lightly to straighten its pages, and set it down in front of him.

"Mrs. Winning," said Miller, "you can be assured that this agency is doing everything it can to find your husband and to secure his release. We simply are not free to discuss with you all that we know. We just cannot share with you all that we are doing to accomplish our objectives. Surely you can understand that."

Miller sat forward, as if to share a confidence. "Now, here is what I can tell you," he said. "We know that your husband was taken alive, along with at least two other passengers that were with him on the tour bus at Hazor. Your husband, plus the Reverend Gary S. Tarr, and a Mr. Richard B. Albostini, Jr. were evidently the only survivors of the bombing of the bus. A fourth bus passenger, Dr. Melvin A. Gold, is unaccounted for. The three, possibly all four, are thought to be held as hostages." Miller shuffled the papers again, and opened the file to extract a memorandum.

"We are not certain," continued the State Department official, "but we believe that this may be the work of an extremist Israeli group." Miller showed Susan the memorandum. It contained excerpts from the text of the note delivered to CNN's Jerusalem Desk. The words, full of invective against Syria, demanded immediate US statement of support for Israel in the unfolding Israel-Syria war.

"We have reason to suspect that the hostages are being held somewhere in the area of Jerusalem," said Miller. "We have been engaged in very tough and difficult talks with the Israeli government. They do not hold to our view of involvement by Israeli extremists, but we are pushing hard on that."

"Is there any other possibility?" asked Susan. "Are you considering that any other groups might have been involved in this? Have you weighed any other possibilities?"

"Mrs. Winning," cautioned Miller, "We can tell you no more. Of course, we are considering all possibilities until all are ruled out.

But, you must remember also that there is a very dangerous situation developing in that region of the world even as we speak. The war that is now going on between Israel and Syria threatens to envelop the entire region. Our country is simply not prepared...*we cannot afford*...to get involved in that war."

Susan Winning and Herb Miller continued their conversation for some minutes. Susan went down her list of questions, but found that the answers were nothing more than she had already learned on the evening news. As many questions as Susan had, Miller had more. He was particularly interested in what Susan might be able to tell him about Melvin Gold, the dentist from Philadelphia.

"Did Gold ever talk politics with you?" Miller wanted to know. "Did he ever mention his involvement with Zionist organizations?" Susan saw exactly where Miller was headed with this line of questioning, and she resented the implications.

"Mr. Miller," said Susan, "the thing Mel Gold talked most about was how he thought the Flyers were going to do in the hockey playoffs and what the Eagles needed in the upcoming NFL draft. He never once mentioned politics that I can remember. He enjoyed visiting the excavation sites. He seemed to have an interest in archaeology. He seemed to be a very nice man. What are you suggesting?"

"We are suggesting nothing," said Miller. "We are simply investigating every possibility, as you have indicated we should. Mr. Gold is now the only person on that bus who is unaccounted for. That is all."

Herb Miller stood and walked to the door of his office.

"Mrs. Winning," said the State Department official, "I assure you that we are doing everything we can. Please understand that sometimes, in a situation like this, the harder we push, the more difficult it becomes to accomplish what we want. And, if we are not extremely careful, we may get drawn into a war that we cannot afford to fight! No one wants to see your husband released more than we do, but we have our limitations. We are doing everything we can to see to it that your husband is returned safely."

Susan Winning took the hint. The interview was over. She stood to leave. "Mr. Miller," she said, "I hear your words, but I do not believe you. Please do not insult me with words like, 'no one cares more than we do,' when you can't even seem to get to work before ten o'clock in the morning. If you cared as much as I do, you, too, would be up all night looking at maps, trying to figure possible scenarios of how he was captured, and how he might be released. If you are doing that, please tell me! If you are not, please introduce me to someone who is!"

Chapter Fifteen

The Agent

January
Latakia, Syria

T HE TRAWLER *ZAYTSEV* pulled into Latakia at approximately noon. The verification tests had gone well. The placement of Yodel Echo hydrophones had been a successful operation by any account.

During the long transit, Viktor Rypkin had nothing to do but to sleep and to think. In fact, he did little of the former, much of the latter.

Viktor's thoughts were complex and troubling: thoughts of his own sudden transfer from the *Antyey III* Project; thoughts of a weapons system console being moved into the training area of the so-called Ministry of Electricity Production Building in Latakia; thoughts of nuclear waste drums being brought into the new pier at Damsarkhu; and thoughts of the dark figure of Mustafa Mutanabbi, accompanying a top-secret Russian navy mission. Rypkin's mind had always been good at mathematics. He loved to find the unique solutions that fit complex equations. But, as he calculated the possible solutions to the complex formula that was unfolding in his life, he did not like the answer. There was only one answer that seemed to be the unique solution to this equation, and it was staggering. Worst of all, he was playing the fool in it all.

Over all these thoughts was one other great unknown quantity: Jadeel Dovni. Was this beautiful, intriguing woman all that she seemed to be? Or was she more? Was his entire power of reasoning being thrown off by his emotions? Was he a fool being used in a hideous international plot, or was he merely a love-struck dunce to whom adolescent feelings and fears were merely coming late in his life? Viktor had no answers to these questions. He did know, as the trawler eased closer and closer to Port Latakia, that his thoughts were dominated more and more by Jadeel.

Admiral Glutsin had called the Russian technicians together

for a debriefing before they were dismissed. The admiral complimented his crew on a job well done, and he cautioned them again regarding the extreme high level of secrecy that surrounded this mission. Viktor saw no sign of Mutanabbi, and his presence aboard the trawler was never discussed or explained.

Captain Second Rank Kovalchuk drove Viktor back to his dormitory. Viktor nearly leaped out of the car in his haste to change his clothing and to make his way into his office. He briefly wondered if it was possible that Jadeel longed to see him as much as he did to see her.

In very little time, Viktor had showered, shaved, and changed into his normal work clothing. He walked and, mostly, ran from his apartment to the Ministry Building and up to his office.

"Viktor, Viktor!" exclaimed Jadeel as she saw Rypkin enter the office. She got up from her chair and quickly moved to meet him. She clasped both his hands in hers and held tightly. "I was hoping you would be back today!" The smile on her lips, the sparkle of her eyes, and the melody in her voice drove away all of the dark, suspicious thoughts that Viktor had held regarding his interpreter.

"I have missed you, Jadeel," said Viktor. He wanted desperately to embrace this lovely girl, but the engineer Omar Fassad hovered nearby, over a set of charts. Propriety, or perhaps it was simple shyness, dictated patience, caution. But Viktor held Jadeel's little hands tightly.

Jadeel, too, looked over at Omar, "We have been able to make some progress," she said. "Come and see!" Jadeel led Viktor over to the chart table. Viktor, Jadeel and Omar spent nearly an hour going over a schedule chart they had been preparing according to Viktor's instructions. Omar continued to have difficulty understanding the concept of the network charts. But Jadeel, in her stern Arabic voice, was able to coach him, as prompted by Viktor. Omar and Jadeel continued to work on the charts as Viktor went back over to his desk to check his correspondence.

Viktor read through some of the letters and messages that had come for him while he was absent. He picked up a copy of a Syrian newspaper that had been left on his desk.

"Jadeel," Viktor called, "could you come here and help me

read this?" Jadeel came over to his desk and took the paper in hand. She translated the article for Viktor, her voice expressing concern about the deepening conflict between her country and Israel. One article described troop movements, as the border clashes were escalating rapidly into all-out war.

Jadeel looked up to Viktor, "It appears that there is no stepping back from disaster, Viktor." She shook her head sadly.

"What of the Americans, Jadeel?" asked Viktor. "Is there any idea about what they are likely to do? It is not like the Americans to let their friends, the Israelis, get in too much trouble."

"From what I have seen," responded Jadeel, "the Americans are staying far away from this fight. In fact," she turned the page of the newspaper, "here is a story about hostages, American hostages, who have been taken by *Israeli extremists*!" Jadeel shrugged her shoulders.

"*Israelis*!" Viktor exclaimed. "They could not be so stupid!" Rypkin glanced over at Omar Fassad, who continued to bungle along with his charts. Rypkin lowered his voice. "Jadeel, it is a most confusing world in which we live." Viktor continued, "Let me change the subject for a moment. Let me ask you something else. Do you know this man they call Mustafa Mutanabbi?"

"Mustafa Mutanabbi?" Jadeel repeated the name, a touch of nervousness in her voice. "I have never met him, of course, but I know he is the head of our project. He is the head of all of Syria's electric energy projects. He is a very powerful man." Jadeel looked genuinely confused, "Why is it you ask about Mustafa Mutanabbi?"

"I am merely wondering why...what other responsibility he has in the Syrian government," stammered Rypkin.

"I do not know, for sure," Jadeel answered. "I do know that he is a relative of President Zabadi, I believe he is a nephew. But I do not know what other function he might have, except that he is in charge of electricity production."

"Jadeel," said Viktor, "do you remember the other day, when we went to look at the site at Damsarkhu, do you remember what was going on at that pier?"

"No," answered Jadeel, "only a ship unloading supplies." Now she seemed completely confused by Viktor's questions.

"Jadeel," stated Viktor Rypkin, "they were bringing in

radioactive waste barrels!" Viktor lowered his voice again, "Why would they be doing this?"

"I do not know, Viktor," Jadeel whispered. "Are you sure that is what they were doing? What has this to do with Mustafa Mutanabbi? Why is it that you ask these questions? Maybe you should go to Director Ivanov. It is possible he may be able to answer your questions."

"No, no, Jadeel." Viktor said, speaking now in hushed tones. "Before I would talk to the director, I would want to know more. I will try to collect more information, then I will be able to ask more intelligent questions."

Viktor went back around his desk, and walked over to the chart table where Omar continued to struggle with the charts. Rypkin picked up one of the large sheets of paper.

"Let me see how this looks," Viktor spoke to himself. His voice was calm, but his mind was in turmoil. Had he asked too many questions? Was he certain he could trust her? Did it really matter, anyway?

Maybe the best thing to do, thought Viktor, was to simply focus on his job: work breakdown structures, milestone networks, and project plans. He had not slept well for the last couple of days. Perhaps a good night's sleep would help clear his mind. The next day might bring a new perspective to his situation.

Later that evening, as he stumbled, exhausted, into his bed in his apartment, Viktor could not have imagined how much, indeed, his perspective of the situation was about to change.

Rypkin had not bothered to eat dinner; he merely tumbled into bed, fully clothed. He fell asleep almost immediately. He slept so soundly, and it all happened so suddenly, that for a brief period, he actually thought he was in a dream. A nightmare.

The door burst open. Figures armed with flashlights and weapons moved rapidly into the room. Viktor thought there were three of them, but he could not see well in the darkness through his still-sleepy eyes.

Before Viktor was fully awake, someone had grabbed him by

the arms; someone else had clamped painful, sharp cuffs about his wrists, binding his arms behind his back. As the pain of the tight handcuffs stabbed at him, Viktor realized he was not dreaming. One of the intruders pushed him through the apartment door into the grip of another. Now, in the brightly-lit hallway, he could see his attackers: Syrian Army soldiers dressed in fatigues, black berets, and black boots. The soldiers muscled Rypkin down the back stairs of his apartment building, out into the clear, star-filled night. Viktor saw again the crescent moon and the stars that, only a few evenings before, had been so beautiful, so peaceful.

The attackers pushed Rypkin roughly into the back seat of an army vehicle. One of the soldiers got in on the other side of the back seat with him. The soldier pulled a black cloth from the pocket of his fatigue trousers. He bound it tightly about Rypkin's head, binding his eyes so that, for Viktor, all was now darkness.

Soon the blindfold was damp from Viktor Rypkin's tears; his shoulders lurched in heavy sobs. Rypkin wept, not from the pain, nor from the terror. But he wept the most bitter tears of his entire life – more bitter than the child's tears he had wept when his mother died. He wept because in his heart he knew that a woman with whom he had fallen deeply in love had betrayed him.

It was barely past dawn; much earlier than Director Ivanov was accustomed to coming into the office. But this was an emergency, a security matter. And Ivanov had been summoned by Mustafa Mutanabbi, himself. Ivanov sat in Mutanabbi's office, speaking on the phone. The two men were accompanied by Mutanabbi's top security chief, Colonel Adib Bildad.

"No, no," said Ivanov, speaking in Russian. "You did exactly the right thing. It would be better if you came on down to Dr. Mutanabbi's office. It is better not to discuss such things on the phone." Ivanov placed the phone back on its hook. Bildad and Ivanov sat in front of Mutanabbi's desk. Mustafa Mutanabbi drummed his fingertips impatiently as he sat in his chair behind the desk. Ivanov got up, taking a chair from the chart table across the room, and brought it over to the desk.

"It will be just a moment, Dr. Mutanabbi. The agent is on the way down now." The three men continued to talk about the emergency that had developed.

"Admiral Glutsin is in full agreement, Sir." Ivanov continued speaking to Mutanabbi. "He certainly regrets losing such a good man as Viktor Rypkin, but, as you have pointed out, he has already performed the most important service we were hoping to get from him."

"And, he is a *Jew*!" exclaimed Mutanabbi. "You should have told me about that, before, Ivanov! I know you told me he was excessively curious, but you did not tell me everything." Mustafa Mutanabbi was not happy.

"Yes sir," said Ivanov, "his mother was Jewish, but we had no reason at all to think..." Ivanov was interrupted by a knock on the door.

"Here is our agent," Mutanabbi said, getting up from his chair. As he moved toward the door to open it for the agent, he said, "Ivanov, it is certainly a fortunate thing you had the wisdom to request that we place one of our agents with this Jew, Rypkin. That may have saved our project. But we should not have been in this situation to begin with. You should have told me he was a Jew."

Mutanabbi reached for the knob and opened the door. He spoke through the doorway to where the agent waited, "Good work!" said Mustafa Mutanabbi. "Good work. Please come in. I understand you have another idea." Mutanabbi beamed as he motioned the agent into his office.

The agent marched confidently into the office, taking the chair that had been placed by Director Ivanov. The agent took the black-rimmed glasses from his eyes and tucked them into his pocket. It was Omar Fassad.

Fassad turned to Director Ivanov. "Ivanov," said Fassad in fluent, unaccented Russian, "your man Rypkin almost torpedoed this project! I hope next time you will listen to me earlier when I tell you someone is getting too curious!" Turning to Mutanabbi, he continued, now speaking in Arabic, "Dr. Mutanabbi, what I was trying to tell Ivanov a few moments ago on the phone is that we may have gotten rid of one fox in the chicken coop, but I believe now there is another."

"Continue, Omar," Mutanabbi said to his agent.

"The interpreter, Jadeel Dovni," said Omar Fassad. "She is a lovely, intelligent girl. But, I think she is involved romantically with the Jew. I think she knows far too much."

Colonel Bildad, who had been silent up to now, spoke up. "And, of course, Dr. Mutanabbi, she, too, is a half-breed." Looking directly at Director Ivanov he sneered, "She is half Russian."

"What do you recommend?" Mutanabbi directed his question at Colonel Bildad. "The extermination camp? Do we send her along with Rypkin?"

"Probably, ultimately," Bildad nodded, "but I think first we should see what she knows. We must find out if anyone else is aware of the suspicions of the Jew, Rypkin. We should send Jadeel Dovni first to interrogation, then to extermination."

"As you say, Bildad," said Mustafa Mutanabbi. "So let it be."

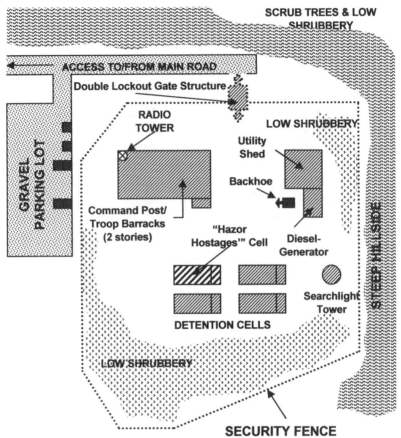

SCRUB TREES & LOW SHRUBBERY

ACCESS TO/FROM MAIN ROAD

Double Lockout Gate Structure

RADIO TOWER

LOW SHRUBBERY

Utility Shed

Backhoe

GRAVEL PARKING LOT

Command Post/ Troop Barracks (2 stories)

"Hazor Hostages'" Cell

Diesel-Generator

STEEP HILLSIDE

Searchlight Tower

DETENTION CELLS

LOW SHRUBBERY

SECURITY FENCE
(Chain-Link, topped with electrified wire/razor wire)

DETENTION / EXECUTION COMPOUND

Jabal Ad Farabi, Syria
Plan View

Chapter Sixteen

<u>Spalling</u>

Late January
Jabal ad Farabi, Northwestern Syria

ILL WINNING SAT AGAINST HIS CELL WALL in a state of semi-consciousness, near delirium. It was mid-afternoon, a cold, damp January day. Gary Tarr and Bucky Albostini slept.

The only food that Bill and his cellmates had eaten for the last two days had been a single bucket, about half full, of a watery, cold "soup." It had contained sparse chunks of rancid meat floating in globules of grease. The three prisoners had not questioned the quality, nor had they worried about what kind of creature had donated its flesh for their meal. They had gulped it down in a mere instant, each fighting a tendency to want to take the whole bucket for his own. It had been only by an extraordinary act of selflessness on the part of each of the three men that each had received a fair portion. They also had received a half-bucket of water, placed in the cell the day before. The prisoners had learned to ration it wisely.

The stench of the cell was overwhelming. There were no windows, so only the narrow space between the tops of the walls and the eaves of the roof enabled any sort of air circulation. The only latrine to which the men had access was the pitiful bucket that they tried to keep pushed to the far end of the cell. The bucket was beginning to attract all sorts of mystery bugs, both flying ones and creeping ones. The diarrhea and nausea brought about by the foulness of the sparse food added to the abject misery that had become these men's life.

The throbbing pain continued in Winning's manacled left wrist and in his wounded ankle. In his delirious state, images and memories continued to pass through his mind. He pictured himself once again on the tour bus on its way to Hazor. He could sense the bouncing road. Once again, he imagined glimpsing that shadowy figure emerging from the bushes along the side of the road, throwing that bomb or grenade, or whatever it was, that had begun this horrible ordeal. He could feel again the cold steel of the terrorists' rifle muzzles; he could feel the sharp pain of the punches to his face; he shivered with the numbing fear of uncertainty that now overwhelmed his existence.

He thought of Mel Gold. "Thank you, Lord!" He muttered as he thought of that last-minute expression of faith made by this child of Abraham, now a child of God.

In his delirium, Bill Winning could feel again the rage that had dominated him when the guards had come to take Mel Gold away for execution. He could feel again that enormous sense of frustration as, in a fit of anger, he had jerked his manacle-chain with all his might, but all in vain. He could see again that pitiful tiny chunk of concrete fall away from the wall-bracket for all the violence of his pull.

Suddenly, Bill Winning's eyes opened wide. He snapped out of his daze and swung around on all fours to look closely at his wall-bracket.

"Yes!" exulted Bill Winning aloud. "This concrete is *spalling*!"

Bill Winning had made a career of providing consulting expertise to nuclear power plants, evaluating the integrity of their concrete reactor containment structures. He knew spalling, the tendency of concrete to chip away in layers under various kinds of stress, when he saw it. And *this* was *spalling*.

"Gary," said Winning, "look at this! Have you ever seen spalling like this before?"

Gary Tarr awoke from his semi-sleep. "What are you talking about?" grumbled Tarr. "I've never heard of 'spalling.'"

"Do you remember the other day," said Bill, "when they took Mel Gold away, I jerked on this chain?" Bill's speech was, for the first time in days, animated, hopeful.

"I only remember that we were all pretty upset," muttered Pastor Gary. "I was just hoping you wouldn't make so much of a fuss that they would come and haul you away, too."

Bill began to make a series of short jerks on the chain. Nothing happened. "Well, when I pulled that chain the other day, a piece of concrete spalled away from the wall." Bill stopped jerking the chain and looked around on the floor next to the wall. He found a flat, semi-circular piece of concrete in the corner. He estimated that it was about seven centimeters long and two centimeters wide, by about one-half centimeter in thickness. "This is *it*!" Winning exulted.

Gary Tarr crawled over to look closely at the wall bracket.

"Look Bill," Pastor Gary said after a few moments of studying the concrete around the wall bracket. "I don't want to dampen your enthusiasm, but you are going to have to yank on this chain pretty hard for an awful long time to pull it out of this wall. Don't waste your energy. You're going to need all your strength just to survive."

Bill's eyes were aflame in thought. A smile curled his lips. He put the small chip of concrete in his mouth, and tasted it. He nodded his head.

"Alkaline Concrete Fatigue Spalling...*A.C.F.S.*!" Bill nearly yelled in his excitement.

Bucky Albostini awoke. He rubbed his eyes wearily and mumbled something about the need to maintain silence.

"Bill, get a grip on yourself!" Gary Tarr spoke sternly, as a pastor to his flock. "The last thing we need now is for you to trip off the deep end!" said the Reverend Mr. Tarr. "Now stop dreaming and sit back down."

"No, Gary," persisted Bill Winning. "I'm not dreaming. Listen, one of the things I know best is what can happen to reinforced concrete structures like this. One of the things they pay me for back home is to inspect reactor containment structures. They are just huge concrete buildings that keep nuclear reactors safe inside."

"What does that have to do with us?" asked the pastor. "This is no nuclear reactor, Bill." Gary Tarr was trying to keep his friend in touch with reality.

"Well," said Bill, "I'll tell you. The Skipjack Cove Nuclear Plant site, on the Eastern Shore of Maryland, was having trouble with loose equipment mounting brackets. I went down to investigate. The problem was what they called 'spalling,' or chipping away, of the concrete, immediately adjacent to the brackets. I took some of the spalled chunks back to our labs in Boston, and compared them to samples of concrete that were taken from areas where the problem didn't occur."

Bill Winning did not sound at all delirious. Gary Tarr and Bucky Albostini both sat up and listened carefully.

"What I found out was that the bad concrete, when wet down, was at an extremely high pH...very, very alkaline. The pH was much higher than that of the 'normal' samples. I also noticed that the spalling was occurring in areas where the concrete was subjected to frequent wetting-down and drying cycles. It turns out that the combination of lots of wet-then-dry-then-wet cycles in a highly alkaline concrete tends to cause easy spalling. We called it Alkaline Concrete Fatigue Spalling, or 'A.C.F.S.' We fixed the A.C.F.S. problem on the nuclear plants. But, praise the Lord, it looks as though these guys have got A.C.F.S. problems in their torture chambers!"

"What does it mean?" Gary Tarr was starting to catch on.

"It means God is answering our prayers, Gary," said the suddenly confident Bill Winning.

Four days had elapsed since the inception of Bill Winning's plan to exploit what he called A.C.F.S. Gary Tarr still did not understand it, but Winning's enthusiasm was contagious. The mood in the little cell had changed completely. Earlier, the men had felt almost excruciatingly alone and despondent, only their prayers penetrating the pain and the cold, stinking, gray hopelessness of their existence. But now, as Bill had said, their prayers were being answered.

Even though Bucky Albostini continued to express reservations about the wisdom of their plan, at least now they had a plan. And, for Bill Winning and Gary Tarr, having a plan injected new energy into all their activity.

For all his pessimism, Bucky Albostini did have one particularly valuable asset: he had a keen ear for sounds, and for changes in sounds, in the outside world. He had a knack for picking up the noise of vehicles coming down the main road early enough so that Bill Winning could quickly clamber up on Gary Tarr's shoulders to look out and note arrivals and passers-by.

Such breaks in the routine were rare. An occasional supply truck would visit the compound and then depart, having completed delivering its cargo. On one occasion, a bus, containing what were probably relief troops, visited the compound. About a dozen soldiers carrying bags full of gear dismounted from the bus and entered the barracks compound across from Bill's vantage point. Shortly thereafter, eight soldiers, some of whom Bill had recognized from earlier observations, got on the bus, which soon departed back in the direction from which it had come.

Bill had seen only one passer-by during his scouting observations: a rusty old Ford Bronco that seemed to appear about the same time each Thursday morning, at about four hours after dawn. The Bronco returned, each Friday, at about noon. Only once had Bill been able to observe the driver. The first time he had seen the Bronco, three weeks earlier, Syrian guards had stopped it at a checkpoint along the main road. They had forced the driver out of the vehicle at gunpoint, had placed his hands on the roof of the Bronco, and had spread his feet prior to roughly searching him. They had seemed to find nothing on him, and had sent him on his way. It was hard to see details at such a distance, but the man looked to be a westerner. He was rather large, had light-colored hair, and dressed in western-style khaki work clothes. From the treatment he received, it was obvious to Bill that this Ford Bronco-driver was no friend of the Syrians.

Gary Tarr and Bill Winning took turns applying small amounts of water to the concrete area surrounding Bill's wall bracket. Bucky Albostini's chain did not stretch far enough for him to reach Winning's wall. It was just as well: Albostini had little enthusiasm for the plan.

Water was scarce. There was barely enough to meet the three men's drinking needs. It had been decided early in the planning to limit the application of the wet-dry process to the single bracket, the one connected to Bill's wrist. Bill had determined that adequate drying usually occurred after about 45 minutes following the application of water. None of the men had watches, but they measured the drying time by counting to three thousand at a steady pace. So, approximately every hour, they were able to complete one wet-dry cycle.

After each cycle, Bill or Gary would apply a series of sharp tugs on Bill's chain to attempt to jar loose a spalling piece of concrete. Finally, after having conducted this process night and day for two days, a second small piece of concrete had jarred loose, greatly encouraging Bill Winning. It was, to him, a vindication of his theory.

Bucky Albostini did not share in the exuberance over the small chunks of spalled concrete that Bill and Gary were managing to chip loose. He held little hope for Bill's A.C.F.S. project.

"Suppose you do break this loose," groused Albostini. "What then? Suppose you get over the fence somehow, where will you go? This is crazy, Bill. You're going to get us all shot."

"Bucky," responded Bill Winning, "I don't have answers to your questions right now. All I know is that if we continue to grovel on the floor in this filth as we have been, we will rot, or get eaten by these things," he flicked a multi-legged wormlike creature from his ankle, "if we don't get shot first. If we can break this chain, at least we'll be a little better off than we were before. We *will* find a way to escape, by the grace of God." Bill Winning had learned to be more tolerant of Bucky Albostini and his attitudes, but he was not about to be talked down from his enthusiasm for escape. The work continued.

Early the next morning, before any light had crept in to the cell through the rafter opening, Gary Tarr shook Bill Winning, awakening him.

"Look, Bill," Gary Tarr's voice was excited, impatient. "Look at this!"

"What is it?" Bill asked. He sat up quickly.

"Look at this piece of spall that I just pulled out of the wall!" Gary Tarr held up a large chunk of concrete. It was too dark to see, but Winning could tell by its feel that a major event had occurred. This piece of concrete had the same characteristic semi-circular shape of previous chunks, but this particular piece was a giant by comparison. It was nearly as large as Winning's hand, and about four millimeters thick at its broadest point.

Gary pulled on the chain again and another, smaller piece spalled away from the wall. Only about half the size of the giant piece, it was still an order of magnitude larger than any of the chunks that had been pulled away from the wall up to this time. Tarr continued to pull on the chain but no more chips fell.

"Gary, it's working!" exclaimed Winning. He felt around the

bracket, scratching at the spalled-away portions of the concrete with his fingernail. It was too dark to see, but Bill could sense that his plan was working.

"Go on back to sleep, Bill," said Gary Tarr. "I'll put another couple of cycles on the wall and then wake you for your turn."

———————

The light of the new day showed the extent of the success the two men had accomplished the night before. The two large chunks of concrete that had fallen away revealed some of the wire mesh reinforcing material that had been used in the construction of the concrete cell walls. It was Bill's assumption that the bracket had been welded or wired to some of this reinforcing wire prior to the pouring of concrete. He would have to find a way to disconnect the bracket from the wire, but he would cross that bridge when he came to it.

Bucky Albostini raised a good point: "What happens when one of the guards comes in to inspect our cell?"

"They've never done that before. They just grab the old bucket and leave a new one. They don't come in to inspect anything," Gary Tarr observed.

"I know, but what if they did?" asked Bucky. "Don't you think at least you ought to patch up the wall so it wouldn't be obvious what you're doing?" Albostini's point made sense.

Gary and Bill set about to collect the small and large pieces of concrete that had spalled away from the wall. They ground some of the chips to powder, using their steel chains against the concrete floor as their mortar and pestle. They mixed the powder with a small amount of water and used it as a loose grout to hold in place the larger pieces. The repair would not have withstood close inspection, but neither did the area tend to attract undue attention from a casual glance.

"This'll do in a pinch," Bill Winning announced cheerfully.

Albostini shook his head and settled back down in his spot on the floor.

Gary Tarr and Bill Winning continued their work of applying small amounts of water to the wall, allowing it to dry, and then pulling briskly against the bracket, tugging on Bill Winning's manacle chain. Occasionally, more small pieces of spalled concrete would fall to the floor.

It was Thursday, according to Bill Winning's reckoning, their fifth week in captivity. The Thursday-morning passage by the Ford Bronco had taken place earlier. Later, in the afternoon, Bucky Albostini's ears perked up. A vehicle coming!

"It sounds like the Jeep," said Bucky, "Colonel Boots's Jeep." Albostini took no comfort from the sound. His voice betrayed his dread.

Tarr and Winning went through the drill, now well-rehearsed, of placing Bill on Pastor Gary's shoulders so that Winning could see out through the opening near the rafters.

"It's Bootsie's Jeep, all right," announced Winning. "I wonder what he has in store for us this time." Bill continued to watch as the Jeep made its way down the main road, nearing the guard house that marked the turnoff to the compound.

"Hey!" exclaimed Winning. "There's Ol' Pal again. How did he get in here?" Bill saw the mangy yellow dog rummaging through a trash bin near the utility shed off to his right. As Winning watched, one of the soldiers emerged from the shed, shouting at the dog. Pal raced away from the utility shed over toward the troop barracks to his left. The soldier chased after him, stooped to pick up a stone and threw it with all his might at the retreating cur. The stone narrowly missed hitting the dog, and Pal veered farther off to the left, disappearing into the bushes near the fence and out of Bill's sight.

Bill Winning entertained his cellmates with a play-by-play description of the action: man against dog. But when the dog disappeared into the bushes near the fence, Bill turned his attention again to the Jeep. It had crossed the gully and was heading toward the prison compound.

"Jeep turning into the parking lot next to the utility truck," announced Winning. "Yep, it's Colonel Boots! There's a guard with him. They've got another prisoner. Tall guy, thin. I don't recognize him. They're going through the gates. Now they're going into the barracks office."

Winning watched for a short time after the colonel and his little entourage had gone into the barracks building. He watched as one of the other soldiers removed a box of supplies and a message bag from the rear of the CJ-5.

Some movement at a distance, off to his left and beyond the perimeter fence of the prison compound caught Winning's attention. It was Ol' Pal. Bill wondered how the dog had managed to get out of the compound.

"There's Ol' Pal again, guys," said Winning. "He may be mangy but he's free."

Bill watched for a few more minutes, then quietly called down to his pastor-friend, whose big shoulders were beginning to ache, "Gary, I think you'd better let me down. Looks as though Boots and his buddies may be headed our way."

Bill climbed down off Gary Tarr's shoulders and the two of them quickly scrambled to put a temporary patch over the area around the bracket. The men's work was going well: the wall near the bracket was pockmarked deeply by Alkaline Concrete Fatigue Spalling.

About ten minutes later came the familiar, dreaded sound of keys turning at the outer door of the cell. This was followed by the grand entry of a prison guard and another solider, this one pushing ahead of him the new prisoner. Last to enter was Colonel Boots.

One of the guards pulled the new prisoner roughly over to the place along the wall that had been occupied by Mel Gold. The guard picked up Gold's old manacle and clamped it on the new prisoner's wrist. The prisoner was securely chained to the concrete wall; now the guard was able to remove the handcuffs. The guard returned to the door.

Colonel Boots looked around the cell. He looked at Bill Winning, who was seated, glum, back against the wall, carefully covering his wall bracket. Bill leaned his head back, mouth ajar, appearing to the Colonel to be the very essence of defeat and exhaustion.

"You must try harder to look your best," ordered the Colonel in his heavy accent. "Soon we have more pictures, yes?" Boots looked around at his prisoners.

He pointed at the new prisoner, now sitting beside Bucky Albostini. "Not him," said the Colonel. "No pictures for him. But for you three Americans. We take more pictures soon. It will not be good for you if you do not cooperate." Colonel Boots nodded to the lead guard who held the cell door as his colleagues filed out of the cell.

The four men were silent until they heard the outer door locked and bolted. The bucket containing the previous day's ration of water lay, nearly empty, in the corner near Bill Winning. Winning took the bucket, handed it to Gary Tarr, who slid it with his foot across to the newcomer.

"Welcome," Bill flashed a smile. "I'm Bill Winning. I'm the Activities Director here at Camp Latrine."

The newcomer looked up, gritted his teeth, braced against the wall in what was obvious pain, and forced a response. He did not smile. "I speak only little English," grunted the poor soul. "I am Russian." His thick accent made that statement almost unnecessary. "I study little English. My name is called Viktor Rypkin."

Chapter Seventeen

Escape

Late January
Jabal ad Farabi, Syria

"WHAT LANDED YOU HERE?" Bill Winning asked the newcomer.

Viktor Rypkin shook his head, confused. "I do not understand your words, please."

Winning spoke more slowly. "Why are you here ?" Bill shook his chains for emphasis.

"I ask too much questions." Rypkin struggled with the words. "In Russia we have saying: 'curious is killing the cat.' I am too much a curious cat for them. They kill me here." Rypkin's attitude seemed more angry than depressed.

"Does your country know that you are here?" asked Winning. "Is there any one in your country who knows, anyone who might help you?" Bill remembered to speak slowly.

Rypkin sadly shook his head. "No," he said. "My country is not admitting I am here. My country is making deal with Syria. Is big secret. Is big secret, and, I think, big trouble."

The men continued to talk at the halting pace dictated by the language gap. Viktor took another gulp of the water, leaving only a small amount at the bottom of the bucket.

"What is the 'big trouble' you are afraid of, Viktor?" Bill Winning asked, trying to express his concern, to encourage the newcomer. "Can you tell me?"

"I am guessing. I am not knowing certain." A rueful smile crossed Viktor's face. "Maybe I am guessing too good."

Viktor Rypkin began to explain, laboring in his broken English, the astounding circumstances into which he had stumbled during the previous two weeks. He threw all caution to the winds. All his life, Viktor had been taught the importance of secrecy. He had been indoctrinated from his youth about the dangers of discussing sensitive issues with strangers. And now, here he was, talking with a roomful of Americans about the most crucial secrets he had ever imagined! But, his own country had let him down. Worse yet, he reasoned, Jadeel Dovni had betrayed him. What else was there about which to care?

Rypkin began to describe Project Power Pack as it, presumably, was being conducted in Latakia. He described how he came to suspect that Russian support for the government of Hazael Zabadi was actually taking on much more frightening aspects than a mere power plant project. Rypkin told of Mustafa Mutanabbi, of the weapons system panels in the training area, and of his discovery of the radioactive containers being brought to the huge warehouse at Damsarkhu.

"How I know for sure it is big problem," said Viktor Rypkin, "is when I see Mutanabbi on top-secret Russian trawler. It is then that I guess what is true story." Viktor Rypkin was silent for a moment. He looked around the little cell, glancing at Bucky Albostini and at Gary Tarr and, finally, at Bill Winning.

"Bill Winning," said Rypkin, "you are American. All my life I have studied and worked to kill you. I have worked to build weapons to kill you. Now I am knowing too much, and my own country gives me to Syrians to kill me. And my only hope is in Americans." Viktor smiled at the irony. The smile turned to a grimace of pain as the tightly adjusted manacle cut in to his wrist.

"Bill Winning," continued Rypkin, "you must get message to Americans that Russia soon is giving big new submarine to Syria." Viktor went on to explain what he was now certain was transpiring. He described the secret of Antyey *III* and of the Khokskya Pens. He described the Katapaltes weapons system, and his own brainchild, the Yodel Echo sonar submarine navigation system. "And this is what the Russians are giving to Syria. This is why they place transducers near Israel. This will be nuclear war."

Bill Winning was stunned. There was no question about the authenticity of Viktor Rypkin's statements. "How much time Viktor," asked Winning, "before the submarine is complete, ready to launch?"

"Submarine *now* is being complete," answered Rypkin. "Is launching very soon."

"Viktor, you said that this Katapaltes system is not for nuclear bombs." Winning had another question. "But now you say you believe there is danger of nuclear war. Why do you say this?"

"I am seeing in Damsarkhu not just little radioactive material," said Rypkin, "but *much*. Is carefully guarded, but I know is much. Here is where I am getting caught by guards. Here is where I am knowing too much. Bill Winning, I am not nuclear engineer, but I am very good electronics engineer. I work many years on nuclear weapons. It is certain Syrians are planning nuclear war. You must tell Americans! Bill Winning, I am being killed, but you must tell Americans!"

Bill looked at Gary Tarr and Bucky Albostini. "Do you realize what Viktor's telling us? Do you realize what's going on out there? Listen, we've got to get out of here, and now!"

Bucky Albostini raised his voice, "This is crazy!" he cried. "We're chained up in this stinking cell behind bolted doors and barbed wire fence in the middle of nowhere! And you are talking about saving the world! There is no way...*no way*!...that we can get out of here. Bill, you and your crazy ideas are going to get us all killed."

"Bucky," said Bill Winning, "I'm going to tell you something that I heard, not long ago, from a very wise man. When the enemy is all around us and there seems to be no hope at all, you just remember what the Bible says: 'those that are with us are greater than those that are with them.'

"What do you mean?" asked Albostini. He had an are-you-crazy look in his eye, and a disgusted tone in his voice.

"I mean that 'I can do all things through Christ which strengthens me!' said Bill Winning, quoting one of his favorite verses from the book of Philippians. "I mean that we're getting out of here...*tonight*!"

Winning turned to Viktor Rypkin. Bill spoke slowly, enabling the Russian to understand his words. "Sorry, Viktor. We had to get a few things straight. Mr. Albostini and I had to understand each other better. I will explain this to you sometime. Now, listen carefully." Winning lowered his voice and spoke very slowly, carefully. "*We are getting out of here tonight*. Let me show you something."

Bill went back over to his wall bracket. He peeled away the

chips that had been temporarily plastered in place. He revealed an area that had been spalled away from the concrete wall, approximately ten centimeters in radius around the center of the wall bracket. The wire mesh reinforcing that had been used in the construction of the cell wall was visible in several places. At one point, a corner of the wall bracket base had been laid bare, revealing that it was attached to the reinforcing grid only by a single strand of wire, rat-tail-spliced to the grid.

Winning began to apply a small amount of moisture, to the pit, near the bracket. "We'll have the rest of this concrete away from the bracket before the end of tonight," said Bill Winning. He gave a couple of short tugs on the chain. "I should be free of this thing before dawn tomorrow."

"Is good beginning," said Viktor. He was fascinated and encouraged by what he could see in the fading twilight. But he was not blind to the peril of their predicament. "What is doing next? After you break from wall?"

Bill explained the plan that was, only then, beginning to take full shape in his mind. Until he had heard Viktor's story, he had been content to put off details of such planning for the unspecified future. But now he knew he had no choice but to act, and to act quickly.

"Tomorrow is Friday," said Winning. "So far, early every Friday we get a new bucket of water. A guard comes in, it's still dark outside. He flicks on that light up there, then he opens that little peep hole in the door, then he slips the water bucket in the door. All we have to do is find a way to get him all the way in here. I can surprise him, get his keys and his rifle. Now, we've noticed also that every Friday at around noon, there is a Ford Bronco, an American vehicle, that comes down the main road headed north. We saw the driver stopped and searched once by the Syrians. He's a big guy. Looks like a westerner, has blond hair, dresses like a westerner. I figure that if we can get out of here early in the morning and stay hidden until noon, then we've got a chance to flag down our friend in the Bronco, and hope he really is our friend! I know it's not much, but we don't have a lot of options."

"You're insane, Winning!" exclaimed Bucky Albostini. "What are you going to do, blast your way out of here?" Albostini's voice rose in pitch as he expressed his dismay over Winning's plan.

Gary Tarr, who had been sitting, quietly pondering the astounding things that he had just heard, spoke up. "Bill," said Tarr, "you've forgotten the most important thing."

"What's that?" asked Winning. Bill's tone was abrupt, impatient.

"You mind if we have a word of prayer, Bill?" asked the calm Gary Tarr.

Bill and Gary had shared many moments of prayer during their long ordeal. But now, at the crucial moment of decision, it was time for prayer if there ever was one.

After Winning and Tarr had prayed for a few moments, Gary Tarr offered his thoughts. "We have no choice," he said. "We have to get Viktor safely out of here. If what he says is true, and I don't doubt it, it is unthinkable what might happen. We have to give it every effort. But Bill, Bucky has a point. How do we get out of the fence? You're the only one who's seen it since we've been here."

"Gary," said Bill Winning, "we are just going to have to play it by ear. If the first step works, I'll have us all unlocked, and we can get out of this building. And we'll have an AK-47 rifle. We'll just have to see what comes."

"Well, if that's the best plan you can come up with, let me try an idea on you." Gary Tarr did not say much, but when he spoke, it generally was worth hearing. "Bill," said Pastor Tarr, "do you remember the other day when you saw that dog in the compound?"

"You mean Ol' Pal?" responded Winning. "Sure, I remember that." The light clicked on in Bill's head. "*Of course*! I saw him a few minutes later running down the hillside! He had to get out of the fence somehow. He ran over to our left and into the bushes. Gary, we've got to give it a try!"

The men talked on for some time, now calm and deliberate rather than rash and excited. Gary Tarr brought up another possible alternative: commandeer one of the Jeeps or trucks kept in the parking lot outside the fence.

Bill thought for a moment, but shook his head vigorously. "No, Gary," said Winning. "It would not work. We might make it out to the main road. We might even make it over the top of the mountain out there. But we don't even know where we are! And you can bet there are Syrian choppers and Jeeps and soldiers crawling all over around here. It would be suicide. We must depend on an ally. I just pray that Mr. Bronco turns out to be an ally!"

Bucky Albostini continued to argue heatedly against the plan. He still felt that Bill was being totally irrational. "Religious nut" was a phrase he frequently used to describe his cellmate. Albostini felt that the only sensible thing to do was to wait for the diplomats to secure their release.

Bill Winning had never liked that option, especially since the arbitrary and cruel treatment that had befallen Mel Gold. He did not suppose that any of the four hostages would be spared for an instant the moment there was slightest provocation for their elimination. But the deciding factor was Viktor Rypkin and his extraordinary tale of terror. As Gary Tarr had put it, "At least one of us has to get out of here. There is a whole lot more at stake here than just our survival."

There is nothing quite so stressful as the calm before the storm. Knowing the pain, brutality and deprivation of the past, but not knowing what horrors lay before them, each man handled the anxiety in his own way. The four hostages lay on the floor of the cell, alone for a moment with their own thoughts, their own fears and, for some, their own prayers. All conversation, all planning, and all debate had ended. It was soon to be time for action.

Gary Tarr and Bill Winning had taken less than three hours, earlier that evening, to finish their task. They had exposed the entire base of Bill's wall bracket, and had been able to unfasten it easily from the wire reinforcing that had been buried inside the concrete wall. Bill was free at last!

Tarr and Winning had talked through every detail of the first step, and had laid the trap. The objective was to get the guard far enough into the cell so that Bill could surprise and overwhelm him. Gary Tarr had stretched his chain to a point directly under the cell's ceiling-mounted light bulb. Bill, now free of his wall bracket, had climbed up on Tarr's shoulders, reached up, and unscrewed the light bulb so that it was disconnected from the circuit. According to the plan, this would prompt the guard at least to poke his head into the cell to check on its inhabitants. Better yet, he might enter to inspect the light bulb. Bill and Gary hoped it did not prompt him to call for reinforcements. They put this matter on their prayer list.

As the men waited in the darkness, the only sounds to be heard were the persistent, grinding hum of the diesel generator, and the skittering of insects in and near the latrine-bucket.

Bill Winning thought through every contingency he could imagine of things that might occur over the next few moments. It all depended on the guard's actions.

Bill had not eaten a decent meal, nor had he been given adequate water or exercise for weeks. He was physically depleted, but he had to focus every ounce of what little energy he had left on this one attempt - admittedly, one desperate attempt - at escape. There would be no second chance. And, as Gary Tarr had said, much more was at stake than his freedom.

The minutes crept by slowly, slowly. The only light that broke the complete darkness was a slight reflection off the rafters coming from a spotlight that illuminated the gate of the compound. The four inmates could not see each other at all, but they could hear the fitful breathing, an occasional sigh and the clanking of manacles and chains as they changed position nervously in the darkness.

There was, obviously, no way to determine the exact time. The men had sharpened their time-judgement skills during their long captivity, and they knew that the hour was near that the guard would be approaching with their Friday morning ration of water. The intensity of the situation, however, made the time seem to go much more slowly that it should. And the wait was becoming a nearly unbearable burden to carry.

But there it was! The sound of the screen door in the barracks slamming shut. All four of the men heard it. All adjusted their positions to look normally asleep.

"Remember, Bill," whispered Gary Tarr, "...'those that are with us are greater than those that are with them'..."

"Thanks, Pastor. Keep praying for us," Bill whispered his response.

Now the men lay perfectly still as they heard the guard's steps approaching. Bill Winning curled into a "sleeping" position, a position more closely resembling a cobra about to strike. His eyes focused on the door just above his head to the left.

The sounds they heard were familiar: the footsteps, the setting down of the bucket and the jingling of keys as the guard unbolted and unlocked the outer door of the cell building. They heard the guard approach their inner cell door and set the bucket down, again. They heard the sound of the light switch being pushed: no light. The guard pushed the switch back and forth several times: still no light. The small inspection port of the inner-door was opened: nothing could be seen. The cell was dark. The guard fumbled to feel for the correct key, straining his eyes to see in the dim light that came through the open outer door. The men heard every click as the inner door was unbolted and unlocked and they heard it creak on its hinges as it was cracked and slowly opened.

"Just one little step..." thought Bill Winning as he observed the faint figure of the Syrian guard cautiously look in the cracked-open door.

A slight beam of light came through the doorway from out in the compound yard, enough to make the four inmates barely visible as the guard leaned in. Seeing nothing unusual, the guard took a step inside the door, opening it slightly wider.

That step was, for the Syrian, a major mistake.

The guard's step brought him just above the head of the "sleeping" Bill Winning. At the same moment that the guard's foot stepped down, Bill exploded out of his coiled position, his chain wrapped around his left forearm like a huge brass knuckle. He delivered a tremendous left cross with all the energy he could muster, square into the right temple area of the guard's head. The guard staggered back against the door frame. His rifle flew out of his hands and clattered to the ground near Winning's feet. The ring of keys that he had held in his right hand dropped into the corner to Bill's left. Winning slid the rifle across the floor over to a waiting Gary Tarr, and quickly grabbed the keys, tossing them to Viktor Rypkin.

The guard staggered against the door frame and then sank, unconscious, to the floor. Bill grabbed him under his armpits, and dragged him over to near Gary Tarr where he could keep him in full sight, covering him with the rifle.

"Make sure you find the safety latch on that thing, Gary." Winning pointed to the rifle and whispered excitedly to his companion. "You want to make sure it goes off if you have to pull the trigger."

"I got it," said Gary Tarr.

Meanwhile, Viktor Rypkin was fumbling through the keys in the dim light. He had not found a key that worked. There were well over two dozen keys on the ring.

"Let me see them, Viktor," whispered Winning. "The ones we're looking for are small, smaller than that." Bill took the ring and groped through several keys, coming to a section where some smaller keys lay, six in a row. "I think these are the ones."

Bill picked out one of the six keys and worked it into Viktor's manacle lock. It looked to be about the right size, but it did not open the manacle. He tried another key. It did not work. He tried a third. Viktor Rypkin's manacle fell open. Viktor shook off the chain, stood and lifted his left fist high in the air. "Free!" he exulted silently, in Russian.

Bill selected another of the keys and, after only one miss, freed Gary Tarr.

"Praise the Lord." The big pastor mumbled.

"Here, Gary," said Bill Winning, "take your manacle and put it on the guard."

Bill selected another of the keys and unlocked his own manacle, then unwrapped and discarded the chain. He then reached up with his right hand, grabbed a ragged hole in his own left shirtsleeve, and ripped a long, narrow piece of cloth from his shirt.

"Here, Viktor," directed Winning. "Put this strip of cloth around the guard's mouth." Bill demonstrated briefly what he had in mind, until he was sure the Russian understood. "Tie it tight. Make sure it gags him. We don't want him hollering until we're out of here! I'll release Bucky, over here." Bill turned to the terrified Bucky Albostini who cowered in his corner.

"No way!" cried Bucky. "I'm not having anything to do with this insanity!" Bucky's high-pitched voice shook with fright.

"Keep your voice down," commanded Winning. "Listen, Bucky, this is our only chance. They shot Mel. They'll shoot us, too, as soon as we have been used for all they want. Unless we starve first. *Listen to me*! Now is the time! Lord willing, we'll make it!"

"You're...you're...insane...Winning!" Albostini stammered. "I'm...I'm not going. I'm not going." Albostini sat back and wept.

"Here Bucky," whispered Bill Winning, "let me at least release your manacle." Bill reached down to Albostini's left wrist to unlock the manacle. Albostini jerked his wrist away from Winning and shook his head vigorously. He wanted no part of it.

"Bucky," said Winning, "you're making a huge mistake. But I can't drag you out of here." Bill got up, and turned to Viktor and Gary, who were standing beside the door. The guard was securely bound and gagged.

Winning stooped to pick up the guard's black beret that lay on the floor near the door. He put it on his head.

"Come on, gentlemen," said Winning, signaling for his companions to follow him through the door. "Now the real fun begins." Winning picked up the bucket of water that lay just outside the cell's inner-door.

"Gary, let me hold the rifle for a moment," said Winning. "I'll poke my head outside the outer door to see if anyone's watching. I'll try to look as much like a guard as I can."

The three men assembled at the cell building's outer door. Bill poked his head, covered with the guard's black beret, out of the open door. He glanced quickly in the direction of the guard house at the gate. There was no indication of any special attention being paid to the cell building. Winning stepped out of the door, carrying the rifle and the bucket. He took a longer look. A single guard was visible, seated in the guard house, but his back was turned to the cell area.

"Let's go over there, to the left." Bill whispered just loud enough for his two companions to hear, and pointed. Bill put the bucket back inside the cell, and the three men scurried along the edge of the cell building, quickly rounding the corner and out of sight from the guard at the gate.

The three of them waited for a moment, pressed along the side of the building. Hearing no sounds, at Winning's signal they dashed for the low bushes that lay along the side of the fence off to their left. All three dove into the bushes at about the same time.

The three men lay in the low bushes, panting, out of breath. For Gary Tarr and Bill Winning, it was the most exercise they had

had in weeks. Viktor was only in slightly better shape.

"It's down here somewhere. There must be an opening." Bill Winning panted as he spoke, out of breath. "Gary, this is where Ol' Pal ran when that guard was throwing rocks at him. He must have got out over here, somewhere along the fence."

The men crawled forward toward the fence on their bellies, protected by the bushes. Bill, in the lead, came to a slight depression in the soil. It was a very small wadi, formed as the soil had eroded during the many heavy rains experienced at the site since its construction the previous autumn.

Bill followed the wadi, crawling down to the fence line, and found what he was seeking. Here the small depression went under the chain link fence. Ol' Pal had evidently discovered the little gap, and had expanded it further, leaving a pit about twenty-five centimeters deep by about thirty centimeters wide. It was the dog's secret way of gaining access to the feast available in the garbage cans of the compound. The hole was too small for any of the men to fit through, but the soil around the dog's excavation was relatively loose.

"This is it!" Bill took the muzzle of the guard's rifle and thrust it hard into the rocky, sandy ground. The earth broke away in chunks and he dug at the chunks, sweeping them out of the way using the butt end of the rifle as a spade. He worked quickly, alternately ripping away bits of soil and sweeping them away with the butt of the rifle.

"Here, Viktor," whispered Winning, "see if you can get through this." Bill motioned to Rypkin.

Rypkin crawled up to the hole, and squirmed headfirst under the fence. It was tight. His shirt ripped and his left shoulder was cut slightly as squirmed through, but he made it!

"You and I are going to need some more room, Gary." Bill panted as he hurriedly dug out more rocks and sand to make the hole larger. "There! Give it a shot, Gary."

Big Gary Tarr slid under the fence. He was much larger, and not nearly so agile as the thin, young Russian engineer, but he made it. Bill handed the rifle and the key ring under the fence to Gary Tarr. Then Bill squirmed under the fence. They were on the outside! They were just about fifty meters from the compound's parking lot.

Just as a wave of exhilaration had begun to sweep over Winning, Rypkin and Tarr, their hearts stopped at the sound that came from behind them, back at their old cell building.

"GUARD! GUARD! ESCAPE!" It was the frantic, high-pitched voice of Bucky Albostini.

"Bucky, no!" whispered Bill Winning. The three fugitives, suddenly overcome by terror, fell to the earth and began to crawl along the fence toward the parking lot.

Chapter Eighteen

The Launch of *Hazael*

Late January
Khokskya, Russia

VLADIMIR DREDNEV HAD NEVER BEEN SO FAR NORTH during the winter season. The Russian minister of defense had heard many stories about *Veter Khokskya*; he dreaded the necessity of experiencing it. Drednev regarded this trip as an unpleasant, but essential chore. The army had issued him his own set of Arctic survival clothing, and had thoroughly briefed him in its proper use. But these measures were inadequate to prepare Minister Drednev for the moment when he stepped from his aircraft down to the pavement at the Khokskya air strip.

Before Drednev reached the ground, the wind nearly ripped him from the ladder. A burly soldier, acting as plane attendant, stabilized him until he could get both feet firmly planted. Drednev had the brief sensation that, had the soldier not been there, he would have been swept away by this wind like a piece of rubbish paper.

Minister Drednev had failed to heed the instructions to don his protective goggles. They were uncomfortable, so he had pushed them up on his forehead while waiting to exit the aircraft. When he felt the incredibly brutal wind tear at his face, Drednev clawed frantically at the goggles to push them back down over his eyes. The soldier-escort screamed, motioning vigorously to Drednev, his hands waving over his eyes.

Drednev could make out little of what the soldier said over the mighty sound of the wind: "...eyeballs!...frozen solid! ...wind!" yelled the soldier.

Drednev nodded his head. He understood fully. The soldier pulled Drednev firmly along in the direction of a metal-sided building that was fifty meters beyond them, across the landing strip. The wind was blowing perpendicular to their intended path. It seemed to Minister Drednev that they had to aim their direction of travel at an angle of about 45 degrees into the wind in order to have any chance of arriving at the door of the building.

It took less than two minutes for the men to reach their destination. Even in such a short time, Minister Drednev could begin to feel the chill reaching through the Arctic survival clothing to his body. He burst into the door, exhausted, breathless. He turned and watched with some amusement as his personal bodyguard and his two staff assistants, who were following him across the runway, stumbled through the door. Drednev could well imagine the spectacle he and his fellow Muscovites made for the entertainment of the hardened Khokskya veterans who looked on, barely containing their laughter.

Last to enter the doorway was Admiral Sergei Glutsin, his short, stout figure made to seem all the more ursine by the heavy Arctic survival clothing. Glutsin did not labor to breathe, nor did he require an escort to make the trip. Sergei Glutsin was at home in such an environment.

"You like our little welcoming reception, Alexi?" Glutsin laughed, addressing Drednev's chief of staff, Alexi Borshnoi. The obese Borshnoi leaned over, hands on his knees, gasping for air.

"You should have been here last month, Alexi," Glutsin continued to prod the unfortunate Muscovite. "Then you could have experienced the real *Veter Khokskya*. Then you would know what 'Our Own Wind' is really like."

"I...am satisfied...Admiral..." Alexi Borshnoi spoke in gulps as he attempted to catch his breath, "that your... precious... submarine pens...have little to fear...from ground assault troops!"

Glutsin introduced the visiting party to the director of Project Titus, Dr. Andrei Khalinko. Khalinko led the dignitaries to a bus, waiting near them. The bus would ferry them through the wind to the entrance of the Khokskya Pens, some fifteen kilometers to the east. The bus was far from luxurious, but it was warm. Heat was about all the luxury any of the men wanted at this point.

The bus pulled out of the garage building, and headed east along a narrow, paved road. Drednev noticed a second, identical bus following behind them. It was empty, except for a driver.

Drednev turned to Glutsin, who sat next to him, and motioned toward the other bus. "Were you expecting more company, Sergei?"

"No, Sir," Glutsin responded, "that's just our backup, in case of a breakdown. We would not last out here for more than an hour if we were to have a breakdown. Storms blow up very quickly out of the Kolymskiy mountains, and it is sometimes impossible to get out here with help on short notice. So, we have standing instructions during the winter months to accompany all trips to and from the airstrip with a breakdown-backup vehicle. It is prudent practice in this region."

Drednev checked his wrist watch. He had set it for the local time zone before their aircraft had left Magadan earlier that morning. It was nearly 11:00 a.m., yet there was only a bare hint of sunlight in the southeast. The sky was that of very early dawn.

In the dim light, Drednev observed that the airstrip occupied what was the only flat land in the region. The road wound through rugged hills then suddenly angled sharply down, twisting around several hairpin turns. The buses shifted into their lowest gear to safely negotiate the decline. At the base of the hairpin descent, the road leveled out to a narrow plateau and headed due east. A small village was visible less than a kilometer away.

Glutsin pointed forward into the dimly lit landscape, and announced, "That is the village of Khokskya, Mr. Minister. Beyond that you can see, out there beyond the cliff in the far distance, the Shelikhova Gulf."

Drednev was astounded at the dwellings in the forlorn little village. In most cases, the snow had drifted completely over the rooflines, leaving only occasional spots where the log, sod and cinderblock structures were visible. Except for smoke that trailed out of the chimneys, and lights that shone through some of the windows, there was very little sign of life.

Only one structure in the village rose above one story, above the snow line. It was a government building, erected in the 1950's by the Soviet government: a two story concrete office of the Bureau of Fisheries. A light was visible behind a window in front of the building. Someone had shoveled a narrow access path to its entrance. But, in the entire village, Drednev could see not a single living creature.

To Vladimir Drednev, this was not his country. This was a panorama from a different planet. How disgusted he was to observe this primitive, stone-age scene. He much preferred Moscow, even with its turmoil. In truth, Drednev preferred, even more, Philadelphia or, best of all, Los Angeles or Beverly Hills.

Seated next to Drednev, Admiral Sergei Glutsin had other thoughts. To Glutsin, what he saw outside the windows of the bus was what made the *Rodina*, the "Motherland," great. These people, huddled around their ancient stoves behind these solid log walls, were the indomitable Russians. No matter which mad Czar, or which power-drunk commissar, or which ambitious bureaucrat ruled in Moscow, these people survived. They caught their fish in summer, prepared them in autumn, and feasted off them in winter. In spring, they waited for the thaw, preparing their fishing vessels and their nets to begin the cycle again. For centuries beyond memory, it had been so.

The road led through the village of Khokskya and then turned sharply south toward the pens. A large, low building was visible about one kilometer in the distance, along the cliff that overlooked the gulf. The two buses rolled to a stop in front of a large garage door at one end of the building. The buses pulled into the garage; the occupants disembarked.

Armed security guards began the long entry inspection process. They examined identification passes and searched every briefcase, satchel, and document brought into the garage. Minister of Defense Drednev, Admiral Glutsin, and Project Director Khalinko, the three men at the very pinnacle of the Project Titus organization, were searched every bit as thoroughly as if they had been rank unknowns. The search and identification procedure took nearly thirty minutes.

Director Khalinko then led the party through a door keyed by his own private access-code followed by another access-code inserted by the chief security guard. The door led to a large elevator, with ample room for the entire party. Ears popped as the elevator raced down through the granite cliff toward Center Pen and the next step in executing the sale of *Antyey III*.

The emptiness would not go away. Tatyana Patinova did not regard herself as a woman who was inclined to sentimentality or to melancholy, but lately it seemed impossible to fight back the loneliness. Viktor Rypkin had meant more to her than she realized, certainly more than Viktor realized.

To make matters worse, the rumors about the impending demise of Project Titus continued to circulate around the pens. No one knew for certain when the giant submarine would officially be commissioned. *Antyey III* had, on several occasions, been released from her moorings at North Pen. She had submerged, and slipped out, under the ice, into the Shelikhova Gulf for a series of sea trials. All indications from the Russian Navy personnel indicated the trials had been successful.

One other indisputable fact: a large number of the technicians and specialists had left Khokskya and had not been replaced. In several cases, the technicians had completed previously-agreed terms of assignment. In other cases, as with Viktor Rypkin, the technicians had received other assignments. But in virtually every case, those who stayed noticed that no replacements were being brought in. The population of the Khokskya Pens was diminishing rapidly.

Not long before, Tatyana had teased Viktor because of his anxiety over the impending cancellation of projects at Khokskya. Now she began to feel the same apprehensions.

The latest rumor was that Admiral Glutsin was returning to the Pens.

"So soon?" Tatyana spoke to her friend, Sonja Hankova. "He was last here only six weeks ago. That time he took away Viktor. This time, who will it be?" The two women sat on a bench outside their workstation in North Pen, sharing their lunch break.

Sonja shook her head. "I do not know," she lamented. "My husband wrote last week that he is still unable to find work in Moscow." Sonja's husband was a civil engineer, a highway design specialist. He had been out of work for over eighteen months. He lived off the little money that Sonja could send him, plus the proceeds from the sale of furniture from their small Moscow apartment. "Tatyana," continued Sonja, "if they shut down Project Titus, we will have to give up the apartment; we will lose everything. I do not know where we will go."

Just then, Igor Guzhavnyi drew near. "Good afternoon, ladies. May I join you?" Guzhavnyi was a young electrical engineer who, like Sonja and Tatyana, worked on the navigation systems of Project Titus.

"Did you hear the latest?" Igor opened the paper bag that contained his lunch. "It is not just Glutsin who is visiting Khokskya. It is also the minister of defense, Drednev, himself!"

"Vladimir Drednev! What would he be doing in Khokskya?" Tatyana asked. "Where did you hear such a thing, Igor?"

Igor had stuffed his mouth with a large piece of bread, but spoke anyway. "A friend of mine is a computer technician in Center Pen," mumbled the young engineer. "He was working on one of the computers in the headquarters complex when he saw the visitors' party arrive. He knew it must be somebody big when he saw all the security attention. He had seen Admiral Glutsin when the admiral was here before, and he recognized the man who was with him from pictures in the paper. It was Vladimir Drednev all right! He said he did not realize how tall Drednev was until he saw him up close like that."

"Well, maybe Drednev's here to see what a fine job we have done, and to announce a new project," said Tatyana. "That's it! He's here to announce the start of *Antyey IV*!" Tatyana, even in her deepening state of emptiness, was ever an optimist.

"Sure, 'Yana," snickered Igor Guzhavnyi, "I'm sure that's why they just furloughed the entire Radiation Physics Department down in South Pen." Igor continued to munch on his bread.

"What?" Tatyana exclaimed. "Was it a temporary furlough?"

"They called it 'indefinite,'" answered Igor. "I guess that means permanent." Igor took another bite. "It won't be long now ... for all of us!"

"*Oh...!*" Sonja had been sitting quietly, listening to the rumors. She could stand no more. She got up and, in tears, hurried away.

"What did I say?" asked Igor. He stared blankly at Tatyana, dumbfounded.

"Igor...!" Tatyana started to scold, but merely gave her head a disgusted shake. She got up to hurry after her friend Sonja, to console her.

Later that afternoon an announcement echoed around the Khokskya Pens over the general announcing circuit. All Project Titus personnel were to attend a meeting the following morning in the central auditorium. Attendance was mandatory for all except those involved in security or essential operations functions. Conjecture, rumors, and apprehension spread like wildfire throughout the Pens.

The auditorium was filled to capacity early the next morning. Many sat in the aisles, or stood along the sides, or crowded across the back of the seating section. This was an exceptional assembly of brilliant minds, skilled hands, and troubled hearts. Every individual in the room had heard the rumors. Each had a cause for anxiety. If the rumors were true, it could mean, for many, the end of a hard-earned career and the beginning of poverty, vagrancy, even starvation.

Five men walked onto the stage in front of the auditorium. The assembly gave forth an audible gasp. It was true! The rumors were true! Following the familiar figure of Project Titus Director Khalinko was Admiral Glutsin and, yes, there he was, Minister Vladimir Drednev, himself! Two other men joined them on stage, presumably staff or security agents.

For many in the audience, the anxiety they felt about the fate of the Khokskya Pens was mixed with excitement at seeing this celebrity of the New Russia. The tanned, dapper features of Vladimir Drednev had graced the covers of many magazines, not only in Russia but throughout Europe and America as well. He had a star quality that had not been seen in Russia since...well it was best not to think back too far in Russian history.

Legends had grown up around the story of Vladimir Drednev and his relationships with Boris Yeltsin and Vladimir Putin. Yeltsin's and Putin's stars had long since faded and died, but Drednev's was only beginning to shine. It was rumored that even President Starazhnikoff feared this man. And here he was, live, in person, and on stage at Khokskya!

Director Khalinko called the assembly to order. He made a few brief announcements, and made a short speech about how privileged he felt to work with such a distinguished team as those on Project Titus. Everyone in the audience noted carefully his choice of verb tenses: "...it *is* a privilege to *be working* with you...," not, "...it *has been* a privilege to *have worked* with you..." Some took heart from this observation, most considered it mere politics.

Then it was time for the main event. It was time for Director Khalinko to introduce Minister Drednev.

Tatyana sat, with Igor and Sonja, near the back row in the center of the auditorium. Tatyana was certainly interested in seeing these famous people, and in hearing their words, but she did not seem to share the excitement that she sensed had overwhelmed many in the audience. Her thoughts drifted to thoughts of Viktor Rypkin. Viktor had been so excited when he met Admiral Glutsin. Would he not be enthralled to see Vladimir Drednev himself?

Tatyana glanced at her friend Sonja who sat, grim and unsmiling, next to her. She, too, was apparently unmoved by the show of stars. By contrast, Igor, seated on her other side, was eagerly drinking in every word spoken by the tall, tan, minister of defense. Igor nodded at every point, laughed at every joke. He was spellbound by the celebrity event.

"...And so I tell you, people of Project Titus," Minster Drednev seemed to be nearing a conclusion to his speech, "you are the vanguard of the New Russia. Here in Khokskya we have in mind products ranging from power plant components to commercial shipping vessels, and *you* are the ones that will make these dreams a reality. It is your knowledge and your skill and your determination that will show the *entire world* that there is no higher quality than the quality of a Russian product."

A spontaneous roar of applause erupted in the auditorium. Relief, from the anxiety that had gripped so many minds, and adulation, for the superstar Drednev, combined to generate a thunderous ovation. Drednev stepped back from the podium, smiling broadly as the ovation continued. He turned to utter a few amused words to Director Khalinko and Admiral Glutsin. As the ovation began to die down, Drednev returned to the podium and gave a signal to the crowd, one he had seen used by cheerleaders at American football games: two thumbs up, pumped vigorously in the air. The crowd erupted again in ecstatic applause.

Tatyana stood during the ovation with everyone else in the crowd, but she could not, somehow, manage the wild excitement that was displayed by Igor, and now by Sonja as well. She worried about herself. It was unlike her to be so unenthusiastic.

After a few moments, just before the noise began to subside

again, Drednev raised his hand to quiet the audience. He knew how to handle a crowd. He knew when to quit. His next words were a simple introduction of Admiral Glutsin.

The Americans have a term: "A tough act to follow." Sergei Glutsin had never heard the term, but he certainly would have understood, at that moment, what it meant. He felt roughly the equivalent of a janitor, sent to clean up after the party for Drednev. And, his subject was uninspiring: security. Glutsin spoke at length about the necessity to maintain absolute, zero-tolerance security on all matters related to Project Titus, the *Antyey III* submarine, and even of the existence of the Khokskya Pens. Though he well knew that everyone in this audience was a seasoned professional in the matter of high-security programs, he was very explicit about the need for the highest levels of precautions regarding this facility and its projects.

Sergei Glutsin did have a plum in his pie, however. After having railed at length about security, he made an announcement. "In view of the magnificent work you have all accomplished here," said the admiral, "and recognizing the work that lies ahead, we have decided to reward you all with a furlough...a *paid* furlough...to commence immediately and to last for three weeks..."

Again the audience erupted in applause. Not the wild ovation accorded to Drednev, but still it was warm and appreciative.

"I will remind you one more time," Glutsin could not resist a final marching order, "while you are on furlough, if *any* word of our project, or of Khokskya, leaks out to *anyone*, the entire program will be terminated, and there will be severe consequences." The admiral was satisfied that the audience got the point.

———————

Two days later, the Khokskya Pens resembled a ghost town. Except for the station security staff and a contingent of Russian naval officers and technicians, everyone had gone home. All the engineers, all the scientists, even the shopkeepers and clerical staff had been granted leave. Air transportation to Moscow had been arranged for everyone. From there, all were free to make their own plans to enjoy the precious sabbatical.

For Vladimir Drednev, Sergei Glutsin, and the hand-picked Russian submarine crew, the hard work still lay ahead.

Drednev and Glutsin, accompanied by staff assistants, waited for their Syrian guests in the heated hangar building at the Khokskya airstrip. Drednev sat in a lounge chair, smoking a cigarette, reading a copy of *Newsweek*. He noted, with more than detached amusement, that the Americans continued to express outrage at the inaction of the government of Israel to help in apprehending the extremists who had evidently murdered the tourists at Hazor and taken the now-famous Hazor Hostages.

The Israeli-Syrian war was, at present, a stalemate. Bloody battles had been fought at the Golan Heights and at the Yarmuk River. So far, both sides had limited their air attacks to tactical support of ground troops, but every day there was intensified threat of stepped-up strategic strikes that could easily reach Damascus, Jerusalem or Tel Aviv. The secretary general of the United Nations had made frantic attempts to bring the two sides to a negotiating table. Without the threat of intervention by the Americans, however, there was no reason at all for Hazael Zabadi to negotiate, and he showed no inclination to do so. But neither did Zabadi seem to have the will to engage the Israelis in all-out war. At least, not yet.

Many observers, including the pundits who wrote for *Newsweek*, were surprised that Zabadi, for all his belligerent talk, seemed content to mobilize troops along the border, engaging the Israelis only in skirmishes. Granted, the Israelis had somewhat superior air power. But Zabadi, backed by the finances and by the manpower of his Islamic brothers, had managed to minimize the airpower differential, and Syria had a considerable numerical advantage on the ground. Especially now that the American president was so reluctant to take any action whatever on behalf of Israel, and was even less likely to do so with the current flap over the Hazor Hostages, it was not clear why Zabadi waited.

But it was clear to Drednev. Soon the equation of the Israel-Syrian War would change, dramatically. Soon, with *Antyey III*, Zabadi would have an overwhelming military advantage. And soon he, Vladimir Drednev, would be a wealthy man.

Drednev's meditations were interrupted by Admiral Glutsin. "They're here, Mr. Minister," announced the admiral. Glutsin, followed by a staff assistant and an armed guard, hurried out the door of the hangar to a point near where the arriving aircraft would taxi to a stop. Vladimir Drednev stood, took a last drag on his cigarette, snubbed it out, and went to the window to watch.

It was cold, very cold, and it was pitch dark at 3:30 p.m. But the wind had dropped to a mere breeze, barely noticeable to the Russians as they waited for the Syrians to disembark. Sergei Glutsin was disappointed that there was no wind. He had hoped to be able to show his Syrian clients what their infernal deserts lacked: character. Glutsin thought especially of Walid El Zophar. He wondered how long a snake could survive in Siberia.

The door of the plane opened, and the first to emerge was a Russian crew member, dressed in Arctic survival clothing. The Russian checked to assure that the exit ladder was properly attached to the door of the plane. He then dropped down to the pavement to assist the Arabs as they entered this strange new world of the Siberian winter.

Two armed Syrian security agents left the plane first, jumping quickly to the ground. Glutsin laughed to himself, realizing that if they had to shoot their weapons, they could not get their thickly-gloved fingers into the trigger guards of their rifles. Good thing they were among friends.

The next to emerge was Mustafa Mutanabbi. Even in his heavy Arctic survival clothing and goggles, Glutsin knew him. It was obvious from his swagger and from the attention paid him by the others in the group. He assumed that the larger man helping him down the ladder was Walid El Zophar. At the base of the ladder, Mutanabbi shook off the protective clutch of El Zophar and hurried over to greet Glutsin. The two men embraced warmly, the ritual cheek-kissing somewhat ludicrous through all the heavy parkas and goggles. The men made their way quickly from the aircraft to the warmth of the hangar.

Vladimir Drednev greeted Mustafa Mutanabbi at the door of the hanger as though he were a long lost brother. Mutanabbi introduced Drednev to two Syrian officials, personal representatives of President Zabadi, who had joined him on the trip. One of these was Zabadi's personal accountant, the other a security advisor. The three top-level Syrians joined Drednev, retreating to a far corner of the garage to chat privately, while the rest of the Syrian crew arrived.

Meanwhile, Sergei Glutsin conferred with Walid El Zophar, and greeted the Syrian officers. Glutsin had met many of them during previous visits to Damascus and Latakia. He knew they were grossly inexperienced, but in conducting the training program at Latakia for the last several weeks, he had been impressed with their fierce determination to master the basics of operation of the submarine. Glutsin also respected the intense dedication they had to their leader, the young Mutanabbi. He was glad he was not their enemy.

Glutsin was introduced to several other key members of the Syrian crew whom he had not met before. One of these was a young man introduced as the head of the contingent of interpreters that would be assigned to the ship. The man's name was given as Omar Fassad. Glutsin remembered his name from accounts of the Viktor Rypkin matter. The admiral was pleased to note that Fassad spoke perfect, unaccented Russian. Good interpreters, Glutsin knew, were invaluable assets in a technology transfer operation like this one.

The Syrian crew members filed into two of the waiting buses. Mutanabbi and El Zophar, Drednev and Glutsin, accompanied by their chief officials, boarded the third bus. Three backup buses brought up the rear of the caravan.

Three hours later the parties had cleared security at the Khokskya Pens and had been led into the auditorium in Center Pen to be introduced to the Russian crew that would soon be taking the Syrian client for his first test drive. Drednev and Mutanabbi disappeared, along with Zabadi's accountant, to a private office. It was time, so Glutsin surmised, for them to talk business.

The plan was that Admiral Glutsin, himself, would go to sea with the Syrians on their initial shakedown cruise. He would be the senior Russian official aboard, although Captain First Rank Yuri Yevshenko would be the ship's commanding officer. If everything went well on the shakedown cruise, the actual transfer would take place as the ship returned to Khokskya. At that point, the commanding officer of the ship, to be renamed *Hazael*, would be Admiral-Doctor Mustafa Mutanabbi.

"At that point," Sergei Glutsin had mused to himself, "may

God have mercy on us all." For Sergei Glutsin, who had been an admiral in a godless nation's service, to think of God on this occasion was a novel thought for him, indeed.

The ship would not stay at Khokskya long after the shakedown cruise. Following the departure of Admiral Glutsin, and some of the shipyard specialists who were aboard for the shakedown, the ship would be loaded with provisions for transit, and *Hazael* would put to sea, submerged and bound for the new pier and protective shed at Damsarkhu, Syria. Yevshenko would remain aboard, in command of the small Russian support crew, but by then this would be a Syrian ship.

Vladimir Drednev, Mustafa Mutanabbi, and the accountant returned from their conference after about thirty minutes. All three wore the countenance of satisfaction. Mutanabbi could barely restrain his enthusiasm to see his new ship for the first time.

"Let us waste no more time," Mutanabbi said, speaking in Russian, "let us make way to board *Hazael*."

Captain Yevshenko led the way to the connecting corridor that led to North Pen. The group divided into smaller companies, each consisting of a cadre of Russian support crew members, their Syrian counterparts, and an interpreter. Walid El Zophar acted as interpreter for the upper management cadre: Drednev, Mutanabbi, Glutsin, plus their staff assistants and Zabadi's representatives.

Captain Yevshenko and his Syrian counterpart, Captain Tamsar Talon, were served by Chief Interpreter Fassad.

As the groups came out of the connecting tunnel into North Pen, a stunning sight greeted them: *Antyey III*, lying dark and menacing, her bulk nearly filling the enormous cavern.

North Pen itself was a monumental structure. When, during the early years of World War II, the Khokskya Pens were first dug, North Pen was added as an afterthought. Joseph Stalin had seen to it that more than enough slave labor would be available for the project. The idea of the hidden, bomb-proof shelters was attractive, and the thought dawned on Soviet planners that perhaps the Khokskya Pens need not be limited to submarines. So, with the undeniable logic that bigger is better, they set out to build an annex that could accommodate much larger ships. North Pen became a colossal cavern. At the time of its construction, it was, by far, the largest-volume excavation ever made in solid granite.

No records were kept as to the lives lost in the frigid Shelikhova Gulf waters during the construction of North Pen, but tens of thousands of laborers were brought to Khokskya in 1940 and 1941. Little memory exists of any of them leaving.

As immense as were the dimensions of North Pen, it seemed barely able to contain the monster, *Antyey III*. Upon first seeing the submarine at her mooring, it was hard to imagine that she was a ship at all. *Antyey III* more closely resembled a bloated leviathan; her fairwater sail appearing as a sinister head perched on hideous, fat shoulders. The line of tiny plexiglas windows at the top of the sail gave the impression of eyes, sneering out toward the opening of the cavern, as if the beast were enjoying the thought of the cruel mission she was built to perform.

Vladimir Drednev led the party of Syrians to the gangplank that crossed over from the narrow concrete walkway to the rounded side of the ship. He motioned for Mustafa Mutanabbi to be the first to board. The Syrian did so, remembering to observe the time-honored custom of saluting the ensign, the small Russian flag visible, far off, at the stern of the ship. Mutanabbi then turned to the Russian officer manning the quarterdeck at the shipboard side of the gangplank.

"Request permission to come aboard, Sir," Mutanabbi knew his line well, and spoke in Russian.

"Permission granted. Come aboard, Sir." The Russian officer was also prepared. He gave his response in well-rehearsed Arabic.

There were no formal piping-aboard ceremonies, no bands playing, no side-boys. But boarding this incredible ship for the first time was a moment that seemed to touch Mustafa Mutanabbi deeply. The stocky young Syrian took a deep breath and held it as he went aboard. He stood for a long moment, gazing aft. He had envisioned this moment many times in his dreams, but his dreams had failed to anticipate the shock he felt at beholding the sheer size of this submarine.

Mutanabbi glanced up to the top of the sail, noticing the profusion of antennae, scopes, and masts. These reminded him that this ship was not merely immense, she was a technologically advanced marvel. He let his breath out, and headed forward, ushered by the Russian quarterdeck watch officer.

The officer led Mutanabbi to an open hatch that led below, through a long tube, to the interior of the ship. Drednev followed the Syrian aboard, and each of the Syrian-Russian cadres boarded in turn, according to rank.

Once below, the men assembled in the control room. The first thing that all the newcomers noticed was that, for all its astounding bulk as seen from the outside, *Antyey III* was narrow and crowded within. Much of the apparent bulk was taken up in the annulus between the outer- and inner-hulls. It was this annulus that housed the Katapaltes launch tubes, and associated equipment. The inner space, where the men now stood, was filled with an appalling, congested mass of piping, valves, cables, and instruments. There was little similarity, in the Syrians' minds, to their plush simulator in Latakia. Some of the gages and instrument panels they recognized, but it dawned on many of Mutanabbi's new crew that the first problem would be to merely find those familiar panels, let alone remember how to operate them.

Captain Yevshenko waited until all the Syrians were aboard. He then made a few comments of welcome, and directed his department heads to escort their Syrian counterparts on an indoctrination tour of the ship. Engineering and Katapaltes department personnel headed aft; communications, sonar, torpedo and navigation department personnel headed forward. Russian Captain Yevshenko and Syrian Captain Talon stayed in the control room along with Drednev, Mutanabbi, Glutsin, and the rest of the top brass.

Yevshenko began a well-rehearsed presentation of all the major features of the control room. His performance would have drawn applause from a convention of used car salesmen. With barely suppressed pride, he pointed to each valve manifold, to each hydraulic control station, and to each instrument panel that crowded the tiny area, briefly describing the function of each. He paused to give special attention to features that had been developed especially for *Antyey III* and for the new Katapaltes system.

Vladimir Drednev, as the perceptive sales manager, knew that Yevshenko's pitch was finding its mark. Mutanabbi, especially, was full of excited questions. It was evident that he itched to get behind the wheel.

The plan was to spend the rest of this day in tours and indoctrination sessions. The next morning, they would slip away from Khokskya, and Mutanabbi would have his test drive under the icy waters of the Shelikhova Gulf.

Vladimir Drednev, accompanied by Walid El Zophar, several security agents, and the two representatives of President Zabadi, had disembarked and stood at dockside at North Pen to watch the launch procedure. Admiral Sergei Glutsin and Admiral-Doctor Mustafa Mutanabbi were to be the official senior representatives of seller and buyer embarked for the transition cruise. This cruise would mark the change of *Antyey III* to *Hazael*.

From where they stood on the concrete dock near the bow of *Antyey III*, Drednev and his entourage could barely make out the form of Captain Yevshenko high above them, at the top of the towering fairwater sail. Yevshenko wore the bright red woven-wool cap that had become the unofficial trademark of skippers of the giant Typhoon and Oscar submarines in the old Soviet navy. The bright red caps were treasured by their owners as a true mark of distinction. Only the very best of the Soviet naval officers had been entrusted with these fearsome weapons.

The distinctive red cap also served a practical purpose: getting underway can be a hectic and noisy evolution. It can help to know that, when the man in the red cap speaks on his bullhorn, his voice takes precedence over all else.

Yevshenko directed his bullhorn to the forward part of the ship, "Cast off all bow lines."

Members of the forward deck crew scurried to comply with the order. The deck hands released the giant hawsers from their figure-eight grip on the retractable cleats located high up on the rounded deck of *Antyey III's* bow. A sailor positioned on the starboard side at the dock took in the heavy line, laying it down in a neat coil to be ready when the ship returned.

Meanwhile, the sailor aboard the ship used a heavy rubber-headed mallet to force the retractable cleat to pivot 180 degrees into its stowed position. The sailor then reached into a bag held by his assistant and removed a thick, rubberized plate, an anechoic tile that he placed over the opening left by the stowed-away cleat. He snapped the tile in place, and secured it with several blows from his mallet. Most of the outer hull of *Antyey III* was covered with this sound-energy-absorbing material that added to the stealth of the submarine. A team of sailors on the port side duplicated the action.

After Yevshenko had ordered stern lines cast off, and after he received the signal that cleats were properly stowed and tiles in place, he gave the order for all hands to go below. At this point, *Antyey III* was held into its position only by four cables that ran from the ship through a series of pulleys to dockside cranes. This was the special launch system that had been developed to stabilize the submarines as they submerged at dockside, and then to give them a gentle nudge out to sea.

"Stand by to submerge. Stand by to submerge." The loudspeakers at North Pen blasted out the message.

Ten seconds later, the ear-splitting sound of the old-fashioned klaxon horn reverberated through the cavern, "OOGA! OOGA! Dive! Dive!"

The popping sound of pneumatic valves opening now filled North Pen. Drednev and his observation party had been provided with earplugs. Up to this point no one had wanted to be the first to succumb to the noise. Now, as the screech of air rushing to escape the open vents reached their ears, even the crustiest of the observers quickly reached for the small foam rubber ear protection devices and inserted them promptly.

The water in North Pen, just a moment ago calm, stagnant, and iridescent with oil-stains, was now a foaming cauldron. In some places along the massive, rounded top of *Antyey III's* hull, spouts of water rose like geysers. At regular intervals along both sides of the pier, immense whirlpools formed, drawing the seething foam down into the Pen along with the slowly disappearing *Antyey III*.

It seemed at first that it would take forever for the colossal beast, nearly two football fields in length, to disappear beneath the water. As Drednev watched, he could observe the water line creeping up to a particular line of anechoic tiles, then slowly on to the next, in barely perceptible stages. But as the water began to lap up against the sail structure, the ship went down more rapidly. Three vast whirlpools formed where the monster-hull had once been. One of the whirlpools was directly in front of Drednev. A shudder of fright, near-panic, to be so near the brink of this maelstrom, raced down Drednev's spine. It surprised him. It terrified him.

Soon the ugly fairwater sail and its leering plexiglas windows were covered by the oily, black water. Only the forest of antennae and scopes remained above the surface. Before long, these were gone too. The beast had disappeared, replaced by a giant pond that shimmered in the sickly yellow-green floodlights. Large globules of oil and larger islands of brown foam grouped at the edges of the pen. Debris that had collected, inaccessible, during the two weeks since *Antyey III* had returned from earlier sea trials, now floated free.

For a moment, there was a strange silence. Drednev removed his earplugs and shook his head. He was struck by the sudden quiet, broken only by the tranquil sound of water lapping at the sides of the pen. Now, only minutes after it had all begun, this gigantic cavern, once filled with an ugly black beast of destruction, was hollow, empty, almost peaceful.

A harsh buzzer shattered the peace. "Initiate submerged launch sequence. Stand clear of crane tracks. Stand clear of crane tracks," rasped the North Pen speakers.

Drednev and his group were more than three meters from the nearest crane tracks, but they hurried back toward the cavern wall, anyway.

High-pitched bells began to sound from each of the four cranes. They began to move slowly forward, in the direction of the cavern opening. After a few seconds, the two forward cranes stopped, their bells stopping at the same time. Two muffled "thumps" could be heard coming from below the water's surface. Drednev had been told that the cables were released from the ship's hull by a small explosive charge. He surmised, correctly, that what he had heard was the release of the forward cables.

The bells coming from behind were still ringing, and the two aft cranes were still moving steadily forward. As the cranes came nearer, the drums on which the cables were reeled began to turn. They turned slowly at first, but began to turn more rapidly as the cranes approached the forward limit of their travel. Soon the observers heard two more muffled explosions, and *Antyey III* had been launched like a stone from a giant slingshot, below the ice that covered the Shelikhova Gulf.

Suddenly, the bells stopped ringing, and quiet reigned again in the massive cavern. The men watched for a moment, then turned their attention to the control tower located just above them. The control operator was speaking into his headset, and then broke into a huge grin and flashed a thumbs-up signal to the waiting dignitaries.

The announcement came over the public address speakers: "*Antyey III* reports successful launch. *Antyey III* reports successful launch." Vladimir Drednev patted Walid El Zophar on the back as he led the way to the communications tunnel door. *Antyey III* would be gone for ten days. During that time he, Drednev, would travel to Damascus with El Zophar and with Zabadi's other representatives. He had papers to sign, and a payment to receive. His nation would receive the first installment of desperately needed funds. Glutsin would have what he needed to maintain his programs here at Khokskya and at other shipyards. And he, Vladimir Drednev, would have a healthy commission, for services rendered, waiting in a Swiss bank at his beckoning. As the Americans would say, a "Win-Win Proposition."

When the submarine returned, the flag she flew would carry the red, white and black flag of Syria. She would no longer be *Antyey III*, but *Hazael*. And the red woolen cap of command would be worn by Admiral-Doctor Mustafa Mutanabbi.

SCALE ILLUSTRATION
(Approximate)

100 YARDS

ANTYEY III / HAZAEL

Russian / Syrian Missile Submarine
"Oscar" Class SSGN
Displacement: 13,900 tons (surfaced)
18,300 tons (submerged)
Length: 505.2 ft.
Beam: 59.7 ft.

Chapter Nineteen

<u>Sacrifice</u>

Late January
Jabal ad Farabi, Syria

"GUARD! GUARD! *ESCAPE! ESCAPE!*" Albostini repeated his shouted alarm. Each cry grew shriller, louder

Several sets of lights came on around the compound. Tarr, Winning, and Rypkin, just outside the fence and beyond the direct beams of the searchlights, dove to their bellies in the dust when they first heard the terrifying sounds of Albostini's shouted alarm. They could see half-dressed guards scurrying out of the barracks, readying their weapons and running toward the cell building. The three fugitives crawled rapidly along the fence line toward the parking lot, barely fifty meters beyond them. The parked vehicles were the only objects within sight that might provide some temporary cover.

Soon, more lights came on in the compound, and a siren began to wail. More armed guards rushed from the barracks building, appearing as silhouettes in the glaring emergency lights that now filled the compound's yard. Tarr, Winning and Rypkin, still undetected by the guards, reached the nearest of the two old Soviet ZIL-131 trucks that were parked in the lot, and crawled under it. There they lay, hidden momentarily from the frenzy that was occurring on the other side of the fence.

"Listen Bill," panted Gary Tarr, "There's only one thing to do. Let's grab that Jeep, and hope one of these keys fits it. I'll leave you and Viktor off over the hill. You two can hide there and wait there for the Bronco. I'll lead these guys on a wild goose chase."

"Gary! *No!*" Bill Winning was adamant. "We talked about this before. It's *suicide!* These guys have helicopters. They'll catch up with you. You would never make it. It'll never work. We've all got to hide out and wait for the Bronco!"

More excited noises came from the compound. Soldiers were

fanning out with flashlights, shouting at each other, looking for the runaways.

The high-pitched scream of Bucky Albostini was audible again, rising above the siren and the excited babble of the soldiers.

"*NO! NO! Not me! I....*" Albostini's cry was cut short by a burst of fire from one of the guards' automatic rifles. At least one of the prisoners would not escape this night.

"Bill, there's no choice." Tarr remained calm. "They know we're out. If we stay here, or try to make a run for it on foot, we'll all get wiped out. You've got to get Viktor back to safety and into the right hands back home. Think about what's at stake here!" Pastor Gary Tarr was not about to debate the point further. He started to squirm out from under the truck. "Follow me."

Tarr crawled quickly to the next vehicle in the lot, the Egyptian-built Jeep CJ-5. It was unlocked. The three men crept quietly into the Jeep, Gary Tarr settling low into the driver's seat. Rypkin tumbled into the back seat, and Winning crawled into the passenger seat in the front. They all kept their heads low to avoid detection by any soldier who might look their way.

A group of soldiers was now approaching the rear of the compound fence, not far from the bushes where the three men had made their escape.

Tarr had been fumbling with the keys since the three men were under the Russian truck. He had found one that had looked promisingly like a Jeep-key. He tried it. It fit!

"Hang on!" ordered Tarr as he turned the ignition switch. The starter turned over but the engine did not start. Tarr quickly stepped twice on the accelerator pedal and then turned the switch again. No good. He tried once more, this time pushing the accelerator pedal down firmly while turning the starter switch again. To the three men crouched low in the Jeep, it seemed like an eternity as the starter motor ground around and around. And the noise! It would be only a matter of seconds before the guards heard it and began firing. If the engine didn't start on this next revolution of the starter, it was all over. Bill Winning sucked in his breath.

The engine kicked on and began to growl.

Tarr let out on the clutch. The Jeep bolted forward. They raced out of the parking lot, gravel flying. The Jeep careened down the sharp slope toward the bridge that crossed the gully. They were over the gully and skidding on to the main road before the first shots rang out. Bursts of automatic weapon fire emerged from the guard shack behind them. Mounds of dirt kicked up along both sides of the Jeep. The vehicle tore frantically up the road. Tarr ripped the wheel left, then right. The Jeep zigzagged back and forth across the road. Sparks flew as several shots rang off the right-rear fender and bumper. Other shots skittered off large boulders at the right-hand side of the road.

Suddenly the passenger side window shattered, with a ferocious noise, and the entire right side of the windshield was blown away as several bullets found their mark. But Bill Winning had dropped to the floorboards as the Jeep had begun to move. Except for having to shake off bits of shattered glass, he was not hurt. Gary Tarr, unfazed by the gunshots and by the rush of wind through the blown out half-windshield, somehow managed to shove the Jeep forward at a frightening pace, and they were soon beyond the range of the guards' small arms fire.

Tarr downshifted and accelerated up the steep incline. The road turned slightly off to the east, providing at least temporary screening from larger-caliber fire that now could be heard from back at the prison compound. The wind gushed in through the shattered right-side windshield; more chunks of windshield collapsed into the front seat of the Jeep and down over the cringing Bill Winning.

Although they were now out of weapon range from the prison compound, Tarr knew that the guards would soon climb aboard the two ZIL-131 trucks and be in hot pursuit. Helicopters and additional chase vehicles would be only a radio call away. The chase was likely to be a futile one for the fugitives, but the chase was on. As the Jeep reached the top of the first hill and started heading back down the other side, Gary Tarr suddenly jammed on the brakes and skidded to a stop along the right side of the road.

"OUT!" Tarr shouted. "Get out *NOW!"*

Bill Winning, covered with pieces of shattered glass, emerged from the front right floorboards of the Jeep and sat up, straight. He threw open the side door, but then turned to Tarr and yelled, "Gary, we can't leave the Jeep! We've got to keep going! Albostini blew our plan. Now we've got no choice but to make a run for it!"

"We've been over this before, Bill." Gary Tarr's voice was calm, deliberate. "There's no chance for us if we try to make a run for it. Our only hope now is to hook up with the Bronco and hope he will help us. Now get out! *Move!*"

Winning tumbled out of the Jeep, followed by Viktor Rypkin. Gary Tarr stayed in the driver's seat.

"I'll lead these people on a chase they'll never, ever forget!" Tarr reached over and pulled the passenger door shut. He yelled at Winning, standing beside the road. "Get up in those rocks and hide, quick! They'll be along any second now!" Tarr stepped hard on the accelerator and peeled away, along the rugged road leading down the mountain toward the north.

Just then, Winning heard another sound. It was faint at first, but then it got stronger as it approached the top of the mountain behind him. It was the unmistakable grunting of the ZIL-131's, making their way up the hillside in pursuit of the fugitive Jeep. Winning grabbed the arm of Viktor Rypkin and tugged him away from the road. Bill and Viktor scurried under a thicket of shrubs, hidden from the road by a low rise of ground along the road's edge.

Just as they covered themselves behind the bushes, the two Russian trucks made their appearance at the crest of the hill, their headlight beams bouncing crazily as the heavy trucks pounded through the ruts in the road. Both trucks' drivers shifted gears frantically, trying to maintain control as they sped after the smaller, more agile Jeep. But the Syrians knew that time was on their side: reinforcements were on the way.

Bill and Viktor watched as the trucks rumbled by. Viktor started to speak, but Bill hushed him. The two men could see the headlights of Tarr's Jeep. It had crossed the shallow valley to the north and was heading up the far hillside. The Jeep's headlights disappeared over the crest of the hill. Gary had increased his lead over the two trailing trucks, which now were visible just starting to climb up the mountain following him.

"God bless you, Gary Tarr." There were tears in Bill's eyes, a near-sob in his voice.

"What is Gary Tarr doing?" Rypkin whispered. "Syrians will catch him! It is no escaping in Syrian desert!"

"What he's doing, Viktor, is saving our lives." Winning pointed to a spot above them on the mountainside. "Come on! Let's get up to those rocks before the sun comes up. We need to find a place where they can't see us, but where we can see the Bronco when it comes."

Gary Tarr knew how to handle a Jeep. He did some deft heel-and-toe driving, negotiating the sharp turns up and down the mountains. The inclines were getting steeper, and the roads much more rugged as he headed north.

His mind was racing even faster than the four wheels that drove his Jeep along the road. He had no idea where in Syria he was. "But," his mind reasoned, "this road will likely lead me to another Syrian town, or check point, where there will be soldiers. The only chance is if I am able to stay out here long enough, away from soldiers, for Bill and Viktor to get to safety. As long as the Syrians think we three are still together, they will not mount a search for the other two."

Tarr downshifted to low gear and wheeled the Jeep off the main road to his right, on to a small sheep trail that led away to the east. It was the only exit from the main road he had seen for the past several miles. He glanced down at the fuel gage. He still had about three-quarters of a tank of fuel.

"God help me," he said aloud, as he left the main road, slowing just enough to allow him to negotiate the narrow path he now followed. If he could not escape, he could at least delay the inevitable. Perhaps it would be enough.

Tarr crept cautiously forward in the Jeep, up and down the hills. Over an hour had passed. As he reached the base of a shallow valley, he had to apply all his skill to keep the Jeep moving forward through a wet, swampy wadi. He deftly maneuvered the vehicle beyond the soft spot and proceeded up toward what appeared to be a gap between two rocky peaks. As he headed up the hill, he leaned out of his window and looked behind him.

"No!" he muttered as he saw the two sets of headlights, bouncing down the mountain on the far side of the valley, about seven kilometers away. But at least he had gained some precious distance from the last time he had seen the trucks. And he knew that distance equaled time, and that time was what he needed, more than anything, to preserve Bill, Viktor, and their message.

———————

Viktor and Bill had hurried away from the road and had groped their way in the darkness up the rocky hillside. Having climbed about three-quarters of the way up the slope, they rested on a rocky ledge. Their perch was hidden from view from the road directly below them, but gave them a vista to the south that enabled them to see the compound from which they had escaped. They could also see beyond, well to the south, to the road along which, so Bill prayed, the Bronco Rescuer would come.

The prison compound, about three kilometers away, was lively with activity. Two vehicles had arrived from the south. The smaller of the two had remained at the prison compound, but the larger had proceeded up the road in the direction of the runaways. The vehicle, bristling with antennae and armed with a large automatic cannon mounted in the rear, sped through the darkness, its occupants unaware that it passed less than a hundred meters from two of the fugitives whom they sought. The armed vehicle disappeared out of sight over the mountain to the north.

As dawn began to spread over the barren landscape, Bill and Viktor waited, exhausted, still barely able to speak. A misty, chilling rain began to fall, driven by a breeze.

"Viktor," panted Bill Winning, "you go down under those rocks and keep warm for a bit. I'll stay on watch. You can come relieve me in a few minutes."

Viktor nodded, "Bill, you rest first, I watch."

Bill quickly agreed to the offer. He handed the weapon over to Viktor, and slid down from the rocky promontory to a spot under a jutting rock, protected from rain and wind.

About fifteen minutes later, Bill came back up to the ledge, where Viktor sat, shivering, wet. "My turn. Go down and take a break."

Bill and Viktor continued this routine for the next hour and a half, when both the wind and the rain began to subside. The morning sun began to burn away the haze, and the men found they could see the road several miles farther to the south, as it rounded a mountainside. They watched for hopeful signs of the Bronco.

The two men waited for another forty-five minutes with no sound nor motion nor evidence of any living creature beyond the bustle that continued within the distant prison compound. But then, the stillness was broken by a distressing sound: a helicopter. It was too far away to determine the type, but it moved rapidly from left to right across their view, from the southwest toward the northeast. Bill's thoughts turned to Gary Tarr.

Tarr was thankful to see the rain as he negotiated his Jeep across yet another shallow valley and up the side of another mountain. The rain would tend to reduce his dust cloud, and it might keep those awkward Russian trucks stuck in the muddy valleys. But as he neared the top of the next hill, he could see a truck stubbornly emerging over the crest of the hill behind him.

"Bad news," mumbled Tarr. "These people are getting smart. They have probably siphoned the gas out of one tank, so that this guy is operating with a full load." Tarr spoke to himself as he looked at his own gas gage. He had less than one-quarter tank remaining. As he approached the bottom of the next valley, he saw an encouraging sight: a relatively deep, muddy wadi, traversed only by a flimsy, wooden cart-bridge. He knew that his Jeep just might make it, but there was no way the big Russian truck would get over this bridge.

Far in the distance to the east he saw smoke rising from a shepherd's camp. He could see the black specs of the animals but he saw no evidence of people. "Just as well," mumbled Tarr.

Tarr eased the Jeep onto the bridge, which creaked with the strain. He kept the pace steady and kept the front wheels carefully aligned on the two boards that formed the cart track. He could see the deflection of the bridge as the Jeep's weight was fully supported, but his quickly muttered prayer was answered, and Gary Tarr's Jeep made it across.

As he climbed over the crest of the next hill, Gary Tarr had another idea. The trail ran on to the east, but Gary saw that in the relatively gentler terrain, he would be able to maneuver the Jeep off the trail. He turned sharply to the right, to the south. He was encouraged by the speed he was able to make, and that he was raising very little dust, and leaving no discernable trail. He planned to stay below the ridge that formed the crest of the hill and to proceed in this direction as long as he could, until he might be able to find some cover with which to conceal the Jeep.

Viktor saw it first. A glimmer of sunshine reflecting off the windshield. It must be the Bronco! He was right on time, heading north, still about six kilometers from their lookout point. He called to Bill Winning. It was time to put their plans into action.

Viktor, armed with the AK-47, slid down the hillside to the edge of the road and proceeded north about fifty meters, where he crouched beside a small bush that hid him from the view of the road. Bill stayed in position on the promontory as he watched the Bronco head past the prison compound.

The Bronco approached the compound, and two Syrian soldiers stopped the vehicle, forcing its occupant out. As Bill had seen earlier, the Bronco-driver was searched at gunpoint. The second guard searched the Bronco. After what was about a five-minute stop, the Bronco-driver was allowed to get back in his vehicle and proceed. At that point, Bill slid quickly down the hill. He hid in a shallow ditch along the side of the road.

It was prayer time again. "Lord, let your will be done." Bill waited, holding his breath.

He could hear the Bronco's engine laboring up the hill, then arriving at the crest, then starting down. And then he saw it, perhaps sixty meters from him, now forty meters, *NOW*!

Bill leaped from the side of the road waving his arms in front of the Bronco, which was moving slowly toward him. The Bronco stopped suddenly, skidding to a halt about three paces from where Winning stood.

Bill Winning waved both arms, and pleaded, "Help, help! Can you help me?"

The driver rolled down his window and looked out.

"For heaven's sake man, get down!" shouted the Bronco driver.

He quickly set the emergency brake on his vehicle and reached across to open the passenger-side door. "Get down on the floor! They may have someone following me!"

The driver released the emergency break and shifted into low gear, beginning to pull away. "Get in, *quickly*, will you?"

"Wait! Wait! There's another one! I've got to get him!" Bill held the door open, but did not get in. The driver again jammed on his brakes.

"Hurry up, man!" said Professor Archibald Pender-Cudlipp. "These people could be right on my bloody tail!"

Bill Winning slipped away from the Bronco and signaled to Viktor Rypkin, who scurried out from behind his hiding-bush, carrying his rifle. Viktor jumped down to the road, and hurried to the Bronco. He and Bill tumbled in, Winning in front, Rypkin in back.

"What in God's name are you doing here?" Pender-Cudlipp spoke as he eased back out onto the road. "You're American, aren't you?"

"I'm American," said Winning. "He's Russian." Bill nodded toward his companion.

"Well, whoever you are, you've managed to stir things up a bit back there at the 'resort.' What happened?" Pender-Cudlipp looked down at Winning and flashed a quick smile. "Did you leave without paying the bill?"

Bill blurted out briefly what had taken place. Breathlessly, in quick, excited bursts, he tried to describe the capture of his bus, the murder of Mel Gold, and the arrival of Viktor Rypkin. He told how they had managed to escape, and about Gary Tarr's valor in distracting the pursuers attention to the north.

"He'll never make it, poor bloke," said the professor, referring to Tarr. "There is a guard station about twenty kilometers north along this road, and a whole fortress near the Turkish border. I'm surprised they haven't got him by now, and that they haven't sent more troops back here to look for you." Pender-Cudlipp grimaced and stepped harder on the accelerator.

Gary Tarr steered the Jeep southward along the side of the hill, near the summit. A rocky ridge rose above him to the right protecting him from the view of any possible pursuers to his north. The hillside sloped gently down to a shallow valley to his left. There was sparse vegetation, but what there was shimmered emerald-green in the late morning sun. The rain had stopped, much of the haze had burned off, and Gary Tarr knew that if Bill Winning's plan was to work at all, it would have worked by now. God had been gracious: Gary Tarr had accomplished his mission. Now, the longer he could keep the location of Bill and Viktor a mystery to their pursuers, the greater would be the chances of their escape.

His gas gage was now riding just above the empty mark: he figured he could travel no more than twelve to fifteen kilometers more.

Before him, the hillside curved around to his right, toward the west. As he rounded the curve he saw, below him another promising sign. There, possibly five kilometers distant in the valley, the wadi widened into a small pool. There was some brush-like foliage near the pool, even a few nondescript trees. There was enough vegetation that perhaps Gary would be able to fashion at least partial camouflage for his Jeep and hide out for a bit longer. Who knows..?

Even as the hopeful thought entered his mind, a piercing sound shattered the idyllic scene: the shriek of a helicopter's turbine engine and the rapid flutter-flutter-flutter of its rotors whipping the air. The chopper skimmed near the top of the rock ledge to Tarr's right and passed just in front of him, about thirty meters overhead.

Startled beyond expression, Tarr's reaction was to press the Jeep's accelerator down to the floorboard. The Jeep lurched forward and raced through the thin green scrub brush down toward the valley.

In the helicopter, the pilot and the Syrian soldiers riding with him were no less startled to come upon their prey so suddenly. The chopper wheeled around in a steep bank and bore down on Tarr's careening Jeep. Shots rang out from the helicopter, but came nowhere near Gary Tarr, who maintained course for the wadi, now less than two kilometers distant.

The chopper turned sharply again, this time to its left and raced ahead to a position just in front of the pool at the wadi, directly in the path of Tarr's oncoming Jeep. The helicopter hovered for a moment as it turned perpendicular to the Jeep's path, giving the chopper's gunner a clean field of fire, directly at the Jeep. The chopper gently sat down on the ground, stabilizing the platform for the gunner.

"Our orders," the chopper pilot screamed at the top of his voice to be heard by the gunner at the side entrance of the helicopter, "are to take them alive if possible!" Try to fire in front of them to stop them!"

The gunner laid several rows of lead in front of the oncoming Jeep, but the vehicle did not slow in the slightest.

Gary Tarr knew that he could not be taken alive. He knew that there must be no way that the whereabouts of his two companions, and the terrible secret they carried, could be traced.

The Jeep raced closer, undaunted by the machine gunner's warning shots.

"Go for his tires!" shouted the pilot, and then, beginning to realize the intent of the Jeep's driver, the pilot screamed, *NO! IT'S TOO LATE! KILL THEM! KILL THEM! KILL..."*

The gunner had fired directly into the driver's windshield, but on came the Jeep. It hit the helicopter just aft of the gunner's door, both Jeep and chopper bursting into flames almost immediately.

A Syrian combat-command vehicle, bristling with guns and antennae, appeared along the trail some distance back, at the point where the trail crossed over the ridge. The vehicle was drawn to a pillar of smoke rising several kilometers to the south. The occupants of the vehicle were confronted, as they rounded the hillside and gazed down into the emerald green valley below them, by a conflagration of twisted metal, fire, and smoke.

Chapter Twenty

Fugitives

Wadi El-Jari, Syria
Late January

PROFESSOR ARCHIBALD PENDER-CUDLIPP LISTENED, amazed, at the story that was unfolding from this extraordinary American and his mostly silent, but well-armed, Russian companion. As he listened, the professor kept his Ford Bronco on a steady pace, headed north along the dirt road. The Englishman frequently checked his rear view mirror, and anxiously glanced around the horizon for signs of Syrian pursuers. At length he turned off the main road, and on to a rugged trail that lay along the valley to the north of the Jabal ad Farabi. Here, the Wadi El-Jari and its tiny tributaries formed ugly, jagged scars across the face of the barren landscape.

Pender-Cudlipp drove westward, along the southern edge of the mini-canyon formed by the El-Jari. Crude wood-plank bridges enabled the Bronco to pass across some of the small wadis that fed into the El-Jari. On other occasions, there was no bridge at all and the professor had to steer the Bronco well upstream, to the south, in order to find a suitable spot to cross.

Though it was the middle of the rainy season in the region, none of these streams, including the Wadi El-Jari, contained any more than a trickle of water. During the furious storms that sometimes struck at this time of year, however, these little wadis could become raging torrents in a matter of minutes. Flash floods presented a common and fearsome hazard in the deserts of Syria.

As Bill Winning related the tale of escape to Pender-Cudlipp, he was reluctant at first to share Viktor Rypkin's whole, terrifying theory of nuclear submarines and massive missile launches to this stranger. It was enough to seek refuge from the Englishman. He didn't want to press his credibility too far.

From his perspective, Archibald had heard enough in Bill's narrative to eliminate any doubts he may have had regarding the two hitchhikers. Pender-Cudlipp had heard the news about the hostages, and the story fit. Plus, Professor Archie knew, only too well, this brutal Syrian whom Bill Winning called "Colonel Boots." It was, most certainly, that same demon that Archibald knew as Colonel Adib Bildad.

"Bill," said Professor Archie, "I assure you I have no love for Hazael Zabadi's thugs. My relationship with the Syrian government was always difficult, but since Zabadi has taken over the country, it has become nearly impossible. My wife, Shari, was…was Syrian." There was a crack in his voice, and his chin quivered slightly. "Her family had some connections in the previous regime. Not at a high level, but at least they helped me operate my archaeological dig with little interference. Now, Shari is gone," Pender-Cudlipp looked across at Winning, gritted his teeth, and shook his head, "and so is the old regime, and so are any contacts I have in Syria. I want to help you, believe me. But the most I can offer you now is to try to keep you hidden from Zabadi's bloody henchmen."

The men were silent for a moment as Pender-Cudlipp negotiated a two-plank bridge over a small wadi.

At length, Bill Winning spoke up, "Archie, there's one more thing you ought to know. I haven't told you why Viktor, here, was sent to the extermination camp. You'd better tighten your seat belt when you hear this."

Winning went on to briefly describe Rypkin's theory about the Russian submarine and the nuclear-tipped missiles that Rypkin believed were being assembled at Damsarkhu. Viktor Rypkin had been silent, listening to the conversation between the Englishman and the American. He understood only bits and pieces. But he had understood a couple of words that troubled him.

"Is not 'theory!'" Rypkin protested. "Is not 'maybe!' Is *true* what I say! Is certain these Syrians planning to use nuclear Katapaltes. Submarine is ready now. Is not time for wasting, we must be telling Americans!"

Pender-Cudlipp puffed his cheeks with air and exhaled slowly. "I don't doubt your story, Viktor," said the Englishman. "This is like a bloody nightmare, but it fits everything I have feared about Hazael Zabadi. The problem is, I don't know how we can get the word out, much less get you two out of here. Once they find out you were not with the bloke who drove away in the Jeep, every little road and sheep-trail from the Orontes to the Med will be covered with Syrian Army checkpoints."

"Do you have any communications equipment at your camp?" Bill Winning asked.

"You must be joking." The Englishman's eyes twinkled as he smiled at Bill's question. "My friend, we have no telephones, no running water, and our pitiful little diesel generator...well, we have to operate it only two hours a day to conserve fuel." Archibald shook his head. "This is strictly a low-budget operation, Winning. Now, I do have a short-wave-radio. It enables me to keep track of the news. But, to send messages out, I have to travel to Q'adi, about thirty-five kilometers south of here. The mail service is dreadfully unreliable, and the censors cut everything to bits, anyway. My only reliable means of communication is the Message Center in Q'adi."

"Any chance you could get a message out for us at Q'adi?" Bill asked.

Pender-Cudlipp shook his head. "Not likely. No, it's not possible at all. A government bureau runs the Message Center, of course. Since Zabadi's government took over, they've been censoring every message I send out, and every message I receive through them. Now, with the war and all, the censors have been especially wary. No, frankly, I don't see any way we could get a message to your authorities past the noses of the government agents at the Message Center in Q'adi." The Englishman tapped on the steering wheel with his fingertips, thinking. After a moment, he shook his head, as if rejecting an idea.

"Listen, gentlemen," said Pender-Cudlipp, "before we even begin to think about ways to get you out of here, we've got to find a safe place to put you up. We have about two more kilometers to go before we get to the camp. Now, I can't bring you directly into the camp. There are four Syrian nationals in my crew at the dig, and there are some whom I would not trust to keep our little secret."

Pender-Cudlipp slowed the Bronco as he rounded a small hill to the left. "I have an idea," he said, "that will keep you hidden, at least until we think of something better."

Coming into sight around the bend was a small camper-trailer. Its two tires were hopelessly flat. Its aluminum sides were badly dented and scarred. Its only window was covered with plywood.

Archibald explained, "This was our first headquarters when we opened the dig six years ago." The professor turned off the trail and drove the Bronco slowly toward the camper. "We had started to dig at this site, until we found more promising artifacts just west of here. I only use the trailer now for storage. I still hope one day to come back and open this location as a new dig site, but who knows..."

Pender-Cudlipp stopped near the trailer. He got out and walked toward the rear of the Bronco. Winning and Rypkin disembarked the Bronco and followed. Bill limped on his left ankle: it was being exercised again for the first time since he had been taken captive. Viktor carried the Syrian guard's AK-47 rifle at the ready, his eyes anxiously darting from side to side.

"Let me leave you some provisions for your stay," suggested Pender-Cudlipp. "It doesn't appear that the Syrians fed you very graciously. You both look bloody awful!" Pender-Cudlipp began to fill a box with cans of food, some fresh fruit and bread that he had obtained on his latest trip to Q'adi. He handed the box to Winning, and pointed the way to the door of the camper.

"You don't know how good this looks!" Winning took the box of food. "You are truly an answer to prayer, Professor."

Pender-Cudlipp lifted a five-gallon container of water out of the rear of the vehicle. Viktor Rypkin set the safety latch on his weapon and held it in one hand. With the other hand, he helped the professor carry the water container to the trailer.

Professor Archie opened the padlock on the trailer door and carefully opened it. One of the hinges of the door was damaged; it took several tugs to get the stubborn door to open wide enough for entry. Inside, the trailer was crowded with engine parts, tools, and boxes of papers.

"You'll have to move this stuff over to make room," said the professor. "It's jolly well no palace, I am afraid. I'm sorry, gentlemen, that I can't accommodate you better for the time being."

Bill Winning extended his hand to the Englishman and shook it vigorously. "Hey! Compared to where we've been, this *is* a palace! Thanks, Archie."

Winning and Rypkin scurried inside the trailer and cleared out a space. They began immediately to feast on the fresh fruits and to crack open a few cans of vegetables with a can opener provided by the professor.

Pender-Cudlipp continued on his way to his camp, to make preparations for the camp's Friday Night Return-From-Q'adi Feast. Pender-Cudlipp did his best to pretend that nothing was out of the ordinary.

The professor knew, however, that no matter how the drama unfolded, his days were numbered at this place, as they were for the occupants of the little village of Jaris two millennia before.

Archibald Pender-Cudlipp had conducted his routine that evening as he had every Friday night. He seldom had trouble sleeping, but on this night, as a strong wind whistled outside, he tossed and turned restlessly, contemplating the remarkable story he had heard from the American and the Russian. Was it possible to get a message out? Was there any way to get these men to safety? The stakes in this card game were incredibly high. He, Professor Archibald Pender-Cudlipp, had been dealt a hand. Now it was his play.

But this was no game, and the reality of it promptly got more frightening. Pender-Cudlipp's thoughts were interrupted by the unmistakable flap-flap-flapping sound of a helicopter in the distance. The sound was getting louder, clearly distinguishable from the blustery wind.

"Here they come," the professor mumbled to himself as he sprang out of bed, pulling on his trousers and a jacket. "I've got to warn Bill and Viktor!" But then he stopped abruptly. No, any attempt that he might make now would simply alert the oncoming Syrians to the fugitives' location. It was too late. He would have to try a bluff.

A gusty, early-morning wind had blown in from the south, bringing with it the certainty of a major downpour.

The helicopter's pilot skillfully negotiated the wind gusts and settled the machine down at a flat area near the center of Pender-Cudlipp's camp. Bright lights shining from the helicopter's nose illuminated the landing zone. Dust, from the chopper's props and from the swirling breeze, filled the lights' beams.

The professor pulled his hat resolutely onto his head and strode out into the darkness to meet the Syrians, just now emerging from the helicopter. The chopper's searchlights projected garish shadows from the figures approaching Pender-Cudlipp. The professor shielded his eyes from the brightly shining lights, and from the dusty blast of wind. He was able to make out a familiar face: it was Colonel Adib Bildad.

Pender-Cudlipp greeted the Colonel in his impeccable Arabic, "Good morning, Colonel!" yelled Archie over the sound of wind and machine. "To what do I owe the pleasure of seeing you so early this morning?" Archibald checked his watch: it was 4:49 a.m.

"My dear professor," responded Colonel Bildad, "it is my delight indeed to see you up and about." Bildad had a way, even in cordial conversation, of inducing a note of terror in those to whom he spoke. "I suspect you know why we are here."

The two men turned to walk toward Pender-Cudlipp's headquarters dwelling. The helicopter pilot shut down the engines. Three armed soldiers emerged from the searchlight beams to join Bildad and Pender-Cudlipp.

"I have no idea why you are here, Colonel." Pender-Cudlipp's mind raced. Somehow he had to divert the attention of Colonel Bildad from the fugitives' trailer. "Ah!" the professor exclaimed. "But wait! You have been talking with Butros! I cannot believe he would call in the army over that incident in the bazaar! That took place over four months ago."

"Butros?" asked the perplexed colonel. "Who is Butros? You mean that bumbling sergeant who works in the prefect's office in Q'adi?" Bildad was confused.

"Of course," said the professor. "Now, Colonel, I know Butros is not happy with me. He took exception to the way I retrieved my boots and my glasses when they were stolen a few months ago by some Das-Q'adi swine. But, to tell you the truth, I was not very happy with him, either. He did nothing to apprehend the scum. They tried to slit my throat! In any event, I hardly see why this is a matter to call in the Syrian army, let alone send you out at this hour of the morning!"

"Listen, professor," said the colonel. "This has nothing to do with that fool, Butros, or with Q'adi. I am here on quite another matter, and if you are playing games with me, I promise you it will be your most serious mistake." All pretense at cordiality had disappeared from the colonel's speech. That, somehow, was nearly a relief to Pender-Cudlipp.

"What is it, Colonel?" asked the Englishman, working as hard as he could to feign innocence. "What brings you here?"

Flashes of lightning were coming closer, from the direction of the Jabal ad Farabi. The sky, illuminated by the lightning, revealed huge, dark clouds rolling toward them. Drops of rain were already beginning to fall. This promised to be a genuine deluge, of the type common for this time of year in northern Syria.

"We are searching for two fugitives." Bildad explained what Pender-Cudlipp knew, only too well. "Two men who have escaped from Syrian justice."

There's an oxymoron, if there ever was one! thought Pender-Cudlipp to himself.

"Two men," continued Bildad. "Both foreigners. We have reason to believe they are in this area." Colonel Bildad signaled his men to enter Pender-Cudlipp's headquarters. Armed with flashlights and semi-automatic weapons, they began to rummage through the wood-pole and canvas structure. Bildad and Professor Archie stepped inside also, to avoid the rain that was beginning to fall in earnest.

"You think they may be here?" Professor Pender-Cudlipp asked, lightly. His voice was unruffled, but his thoughts were greatly troubled. Had they captured Winning's third companion, the one who had hijacked the Syrian Jeep? Had he somehow confessed to knowing of their plan to seek assistance from the Bronco? Did Bildad know something?

"We only know that these two are in the region of the Jabal ad-Farabi," pronounced Colonel Bildad, solemnly. "You were the only person, other than my troops, who passed this way during the last twenty-four hours. You must have seen something!"

For all the threat in Bildad's voice, Pender-Cudlipp took great comfort in the colonel's response. He knows nothing for sure! He's guessing! thought the professor.

Professor Archie was emboldened to continue his story. "Yes, I did come back from Q'adi yesterday morning as I usually do. Your guards stopped me – as usual - on the other side of Jabal ad-Farabi, near that camp you have recently built there...camp or whatever it is." Archie paused. "Two foreigners?" Pender-Cudlipp shrugged his shoulders, "I am a foreigner. I am certain I would know one if I saw one."

"This is not a game we play, Pender-Cudlipp!" The tone of each slowly spoken word in Bildad's response was dark with threat. "We will search for ourselves. You will do well," Bildad lowered his voice, adding to its chill, "to remember to tell us anything that you have seen. Anything at all that might interest us."

Pender-Cudlipp responded cheerfully, "Proceed with your search Colonel! I would certainly be unhappy to have unwanted foreigners in our midst."

Archie turned to walk away, toward the door. He had to try to find a way to warn the fugitives. It would be risky, but they must be alerted, if at all possible! Before Archie could take a half-dozen paces, he was stopped by one of the Colonel's armed guards. The guard nudged Pender-Cudlipp back in the direction of the Colonel.

"I will have you stay with me, Professor," said Bildad. "Perhaps you will be able to help us think of clever hiding places for fugitives."

Pender-Cudlipp watched with Colonel Bildad as the soldiers searched in every corner, behind every door, and in every box, cabinet, and shelf for evidence of the foreigners. After vainly searching for about thirty minutes, they proceeded to inspect the rest of the archaeological camp. Sleepy camp workers, awakened by the noise of the helicopter, watched curiously as the soldiers poked through the workers' meager belongings, leaving no corner uninspected. The soldiers spoke to each of the camp workers, asking about any unusual events they might have observed. It was in vain.

"What other facilities would you recommend we consider, Professor Pender-Cudlipp?" The Colonel was not yet satisfied with his search.

"Well, there is the pump house and the engine room," the professor suggested, "and there are the trenches of our archaeological excavations. But, Colonel, I would respectfully request that you ask your men to be careful in the trenches. It is the history of your own country that lies buried there. I would hope that your men would treat it with respect."

"My dear Professor," replied the colonel. "We always treat you with respect, as much as you earn it. You must remember, your interest is in ancient history; ours is in modern history. What we seek here, Professor, is as significant to the history of Syria as anything you might dig up from thousands of years ago." Colonel Bildad did not exaggerate.

Two more hours passed as Bildad's soldiers continued their vain search. Dawn had revealed the continuing fury of the rainstorm. Colonel Bildad, who had been inspecting one of the archaeological excavations, approached Pender-Cudlipp.

"One of your people tells me," said Bildad, yelling over the noise of the pouring rain and frequent bursts of thunder, "that there is a place we should be looking that you have not revealed to us."

"Indeed," responded Archibald Pender-Cudlipp, "there may be many such places. This is a large camp. I have told you the places that would seem to me to be the most likely hiding places." Pender-Cudlipp tried to disguise the tightness he felt in his belly. "What place is it that was suggested?"

"Evidently, Professor," yelled the colonel, "you have a small trailer not far from here. We must go and inspect it now."

"Oh, yes, of course!" The Professor smiled at the Colonel. "The old trailer was my first headquarters. We have not used that trailer for over two years. It is only used for storage now. But, of course, you are welcome to inspect it, if you feel you have time. It is about two kilometers to the east, along the wadi. You may certainly help yourself, Colonel. I am sure you will allow me to stay here and tend to my business, and stay dry." Pender-Cudlipp's mind reeled. He had to shake free from Bildad and get word to...

"No, Professor," growled Bildad. "You will come with me. I will leave one of my men here to assure that business is properly attended." The colonel sensed tension in the voice of the Englishman.

The Professor slowly donned his raincoat, stalling. But he could think of nothing more to do. He led off toward the east, followed by Colonel Bildad and two armed soldiers. The soldiers had put away their flashlights, no longer needed as the morning sun drew higher in the dark, boiling sky. The rain continued to fall in irregular, torrential spasms.

Archibald Pender-Cudlipp had stalled as long as he could. As hard as he had tried to appear calm, Archie's heart pounded incessantly as the men slogged down the muddy trail toward the fugitives' hiding place. Now, Archie's only hope was that the American and the Russian had heard the chopper arrive early that morning and had found another place to hide. Would they also have had the presence of mind to remove all evidence from the trailer?

Fortunately, the rain would have erased all footprints and the marks of his Bronco tires near the trailer. That would have required some more explanation. How much more of his "explaining" would Colonel Bildad tolerate?

Archibald Pender-Cudlipp was not one to shrink from difficult odds. As a youth in the British army, he had been among the first in his unit to volunteer for duty in Northern Ireland. Later, after establishing a record as a top student at the University of London, he had forsaken lucrative teaching and research positions for a life in the field, a life that rarely saw a day pass without some challenge to him or to those about him for whom he cared. Archibald Pender-Cudlipp thrived on overcoming challenges.

And so, his thoughts were not of cowering in terror, but rather of plans for action, depending on what was found in the trailer. He remembered that the Russian carried an AK-47. That might enable the fugitives to deal with the immediate problem, but it would certainly make it more difficult to accomplish their ultimate objective: escape.

The rain began to pour in sheets, rather than drops, a vicious deluge.

This rain is good, thought Archibald. Not only would this take care of any problem with tracks left by the Bronco and by the fugitives, it also might make the Colonel a little less inclined to spend hours searching. The quartet continued to trudge toward the trailer, struggling against the stiff wind and the soaking rain.

There was no evidence of any life around the trailer as they approached. The colonel ordered his men to carefully approach and search inside. These were trained soldiers and their method for accomplishing their mission was textbook-efficient. As they burst open the trailer door, Archibald Pender-Cudlipp drew a deep breath through his nostrils. His body coiled, ready for action. He noticed that Colonel Bildad had reached to his holster and unlatched the cover to his sidearm. The colonel's hand caressed the handgrip of the weapon.

But there was no motion, not a sound from within the trailer. Archibald let the air out of his lungs, slowly, through his mouth, hoping to hide his tension from the Syrians. He fought the tendency to look around to see if he could catch a glimpse of the fugitives. The rain continued to fall in sheets.

"Check it out quickly, men, and let's move on!" Colonel Bildad screamed over the roar of the rainstorm. The soldiers, glad for an opportunity to get out of the rain, climbed inside the trailer. They glanced around quickly, seeing only boxes of papers, a few tools and some old engine parts stacked along one side of the trailer. They saw nothing else. One of the soldiers leaned out and called to his colonel.

"Nothing here sir," yelled the soldier. "Do you want to stay here, or move on?" Bildad indicated with his hand for them to follow him back to the main camp where the helicopter awaited them.

The rain let up briefly, but soon resumed, in full force. Such precipitation might have been welcomed in some parts of the world. But here in the shallow, rocky terrain of the Jari region of Syria, instead of settling gently into the soil to enable the growth of trees and crops, the rain merely dashed against the ground, bounced, grabbed sandy earth, and rushed toward the thirsty wadis.

The little streams merged together to make larger torrents, all eating away at what little loose soil existed. Some of these small tributaries fed into the Wadi El-Jari. Now the El-Jari stream that, only hours before had been a mere trickle at the base of a deep wadi-canyon, had risen in the downpour to a raging, muddy flood of almost three meters depth, already half-filling the canyon.

Moments before, as the two Syrian soldiers briefly inspected the old trailer, Viktor Rypkin and Bill Winning stood on a ledge of the wadi-canyon, backs pressed against the rocky wall, about one hundred meters away. The rising stream had come up around their legs, and Viktor and Bill both wondered how long they could stand in the angry torrent. Viktor held the AK-47 at high-port, ready for action if it became necessary. His arms ached from the effort.

The previous evening, after Pender-Cudlipp had left the two fugitives off at the trailer, they had gorged themselves on the provisions supplied by their English rescuer. Never had canned beans, a fresh loaf of bread, and fresh fruit tasted so delicious to Bill Winning. For weeks he had eaten nothing but the occasional foul gruel served up by his captors. And fresh water! It was as sweet as anything he had ever tasted.

Bill Winning and Viktor Rypkin had established their watch routine. One would stand watch, alert for any sign of trouble outside, while the other slept or ate. They had carefully stowed all cans, wrappers, cores and other trash to be quickly disposed of if necessary.

It was Viktor who had been on watch in the morning when the sounds of the helicopter were first audible. He quickly awoke Bill. The men had immediately surmised what had occurred, and had hurried to clean the trailer of evidence. They realized that the trailer would be one obvious hiding place that would prompt a search, so they crawled cautiously outside to find a safer refuge.

They had found what they thought would be a particularly good hiding place. It was a spot in the wadi, where the walls of the little canyon were steepest. There was a ledge, about three meters below the top of the wadi, on which they could stand, even could sit, while hidden from view from the terrain near the trailer. It was near enough to the trailer for them to have a good chance of keeping an eye on what was happening, but far enough away to avoid easy detection. The AK-47 provided their contingency plan.

They had not counted on the storm; even less on the flash flood. The muddy water was now flowing rapidly at nearly waist level of the two fugitives. They had heard the soldiers at the trailer, but it seemed that the noise had abated.

Bill Winning whispered to his Russian companion, "Time for a peek, Viktor! I hope those guys disappear before this water reaches our earlobes."

"I do not understand!" Rypkin whispered his worried reply.

"I am going to take a look," Bill whispered. He found a small root extending from a bush growing overhead, and used it to turn his body around, toward the rocky wall. The root was too flimsy to support his entire weight, but it enabled Winning to maintain balance as he put his foot on a jutting rock, which looked to be firmly embedded. He eased his head up above the rim of the wadi. The rain was still pouring steadily, but not with its previous violence. Bill could see the four men retreating down the road toward the main campsite, jogging to get out of the storm, about a half-kilometer away.

"They're going!" Bill Winning called down to Viktor, "It's clear! Let's get out of here before we drown!" He reached up and grabbed another bush, steadying his weight on the jutting rock and pulling himself up, almost over the rim.

But this time, Winning had miscalculated. The rain had loosened the soil around the rock on which he put his weight, and although the rock held firm for a moment, it suddenly broke loose. Winning lost his balance. He began to slide back down the wall, toward the torrent below. He clawed frantically at exposed rocks and roots. One of the roots held tight and he was able to stop his fall, but Winning barged heavily into Viktor Rypkin, who had been watching helplessly just below.

As he was bumped, it was Rypkin who now lost his balance. Still clutching the heavy rifle in one hand, he grasped madly toward Bill Winning with his free hand. Bill reached for him, but they failed to connect.

Viktor Rypkin fell further backward toward the churning flood. In desperation, just as he completely lost his footing, Rypkin swung the barrel of the AK-47 toward Winning: a last, frantic lifeline as Rypkin's head disappeared below the swirling brown rush of water.

The terror and frenzy of the moment left no time for thought. No time for Bill to wonder if Rypkin had set the safety on the weapon. No time for Bill to be certain that his own stability on the ledge was set. Bill Winning reached out with both hands for the rifle barrel. He caught it, just as Viktor Rypkin was being swept away with the flood. Bill Winning nearly lost his balance again, but he held the rifle barrel with his left hand and grabbed again with his right hand, in one last, mighty surge at the root that had saved him a moment before. He was able to grab the exposed root and regain his stability.

Viktor Rypkin, now holding his end of the rifle with both hands, pulled himself up to the surface, and sputtered for a gulp of air as he struggled toward Winning. Viktor's feet found the same small ledge on which Bill Winning was planted. Gasping and spewing, he clamored for a grip on the same life-saving root to which Winning clung.

Both men held on to that root, and to each other, for several minutes, catching their breath. They were both exhausted. Less than fifteen seconds had elapsed for the entire incident, but Bill Winning and Viktor Rypkin had exerted every last erg in their weary, beaten bodies to survive.

At length, Rypkin panted, "We...must...be trying...again. Water...still rising!"

"More...careful...this time!" Winning panted back.

Slowly, slowly they maneuvered back up the wadi wall. Cautiously they tested each root, each stone before they trusted it with their weight. And with each move upward, they carefully helped balance each other, ready for a snapped root or loose stone.

At length they finally rolled over the top of the wadi edge, thoroughly exhausted, thoroughly soaked. They quickly made their way over to their trailer. As they closed the door behind them, they settled back into the dry comfort of their now-precious safe haven.

Neither man spoke for a long time. They heard the sound of the Syrian helicopter taking off, fading into the distance.

Viktor Rypkin spoke: "Too close!" He shook his head, and shrugged his shoulders. He was baffled at the astounding events that had engulfed him. "Bill Winning, I ask you, what is happening?"

"What's happening, Viktor, is that somebody is praying for us, and God is listening."

Viktor shrugged again and shook his head. But for a time, both men felt an almost giddy sense of relief settle over them. Still alive! And free. Still free!

Chapter Twenty-One

The Quitting Bell

February
Manassas, Virginia

TRACE DAWSON SLIPPED OUT OF BED silently. He glanced at the clock radio on the lampstand beside the bed. It was 3:47 a.m. His stomach churned. He knew it would be futile to try to get back to sleep. He crept quietly across his bedroom floor. There was no need to disturb his wife.

Dawson could not determine whether he had been awakened by his upset stomach, or by the nightmare. No matter, he had planned to get up at 4:30 anyway. He had an early-morning meeting scheduled with some of the brass at the Pentagon; he might as well take advantage of this earlier start.

Navy Captain Trace Dawson was terrified by the nightmare. There was no need for a psychiatrist to interpret: Dawson knew exactly what prompted it. Captain Dawson recently had been selected for admiral and had been named director of naval special warfare. He was now head of the Navy's Sea-Air-Land Special Combat Forces, the SEALs. The higher he got in the Navy's command structure, the further away he got from the mud and blood and guts of his chosen profession. The further away he got from the real work of the SEALs, the more he got embroiled in the politics, and the more he tended to suffer from stomach problems and sleepless nights.

The worst part of the nightmare was that Dawson knew it was not too much of a stretch of reality, that it conceivably could come true at any time. In his dream, Captain Dawson saw the lifeless body of a young man pulled from a pit of slime and mud. Even the foul smell of the muck in the pit seemed to be part of his dream. The young man's body, covered from head to foot with the slime, was placed in an inflated rubber raft, and the raft was hoisted to the heads of the five SEAL trainees that survived him.

All five of the surviving SEAL trainees were thoroughly caked in the filthy mud. These men were as finely conditioned as any human beings that walked the earth. Their physical training regimen would put to shame even the most fanatic professional athlete. But they were exhausted; they could barely lift the raft and their departed comrade above their heads.

In Trace Dawson's nightmare, he scanned the faces of the young trainees. The fatigue of four straight days without sleep drew their mouths tight, their eyes nearly shut.

The voice of their SEAL instructor pierced the dream, "move out, SEALs!"

The dream-unit moved out of the slime pit and up a tall sand dune. The instructor moved rapidly up the dune at a trot, exhorting his charges. "When I say move, I mean *move!*" The pitiful squad tried to break into a trot up the dune. For every one-meter step they took in the sand, they slid back three-quarters of a meter. But they did not stop.

The squad broke into a chant: "He should'a' rung the Quittin' Bell!...He should'a' rung the Quittin' Bell!...He should'a' rung the Quittin' Bell!..." The SEALs forced their legs to move in time with the cadence.

It was as the dream-SEAL trainees broke over the top of the dune that Captain Dawson awoke and felt a wave of relief that this dead young SEAL was only a hideous dream.

As Dawson slipped quietly out his bedroom door, he let out a quiet, deep sigh. Now he only had to face his searing gut-ache, and a day of bickering with Pentagon budget-makers.

Dawson visited the downstairs bathroom so as not to bother his wife. He then went into the kitchen to prepare some coffee. His thoughts were absorbed by the dream he had just experienced. He remembered his own Basic Underwater Demolition/SEAL ("BUD/S") training, over thirty years before. He had heard all the stories: BUD/S training was reputed to be the toughest formal endurance training program in the world. As a hotshot young ensign and top athlete, Dawson had laughed at the rumors, and signed up for the SEAL-dare.

It was everything they said it would be, times ten. On more than one occasion, young Trace Dawson, buffeted by the instructors' ceaseless pressure, had partly revived from his near-zombie trance to consider ringing the "Quitting Bell."

During all four phases of the BUD/S training program, the instructors kept a brass bell within easy access of the trainees. If, at any time during the program, a trainee's limit was reached by the deprivation of sleep, food, or water, or due to the extraordinary mental stress placed on them, he could gain immediate relief by ringing the Quitting Bell three times in quick succession. Upon ringing the bell, he would be swept immediately out of the training unit, away from the training center at Coronado, into clean sheets, and hot and cold running water. He would be out of the SEALs.

But, Dawson did not ring the bell. More than anything else, it was his devotion to the others in his squad that would not let him ring the bell. He had made it through Coronado, and it was the crowning achievement of his life. Trace Dawson had gone on to Viet Nam, had earned a Silver Star for gallantry and two Purple Hearts. He had risen rapidly to become one of the youngest SEAL team leaders in the proud history of Navy UDT/SEALs, and now he was a Rear Admiral-select, the new Boss SEAL. But nothing he had ever done had challenged him as had those twenty-six weeks at BUD/S training.

And they were still doing it.

"Where do these kids come from?" Dawson mumbled to himself as he poured skim milk over his raisin bran. There were long waiting lists of bright, capable kids who wanted to test themselves against the fabled SEAL training program. But, even with diligent screening, and the most rigorous entry specifications, only about five percent of an entering SEAL class graduates, on time, with their class. Many are allowed to continue, following injury or other setback, with a following class. But even considering this, well under half of an entering SEAL class will ever graduate. One class, Class Number Seventy-Eight, graduated no one at all!

Trace Dawson loved these kids that signed up for his program. He knew what made them tick. The ones he picked for the program were not Rambos. "Rambo wouldn't make it in this outfit." Dawson was fond of telling new recruits. "We don't want any loners here. We want people who are as smart as they are fast and strong. Most of all, we want people who know how to work as a team. I don't care how good you are, if you can't play team ball you won't last long around here."

It was true. Teamwork problems were usually prime factors in the ringing of the Quitting Bell. In other programs, an individual could cheat. For example, unless the coach is watching, the football player can relax on a few of his assigned push-ups. For SEAL push-ups, however, the instructor places a telephone pole on the SEAL trainee and his squad-mates. If anyone in the squad slacks, the telephone pole doesn't go up, and the entire squad suffers.

It is said that many good athletes could stand one day of SEAL training. But twenty-six weeks, 182 days, of this carefully designed torture was too much for most.

The thing that troubled Dawson, what was stirring his stomach to rebel, was the feeling that he was letting down his men. In the few short months since he had taken over as director of SEAL operations, his budget had been cut another fifteen percent. He was going to have to cut some people from the program. How could he tell some kid that had given every ounce of effort to get through the program that it wasn't important enough to his country's leaders to keep him on?

Dawson finished his bowl of cereal, gulped down a glass of cranberry juice, and headed back upstairs to shave and shower. He had to get to his office at the Pentagon early. He had to find some allies in his budget battle to keep his program healthy. Dawson would rather, much rather, have slopped through a slime pit at the SEAL training center than to have to fight with some of the bureaucrats he faced in the Pentagon and on the Hill.

But his first meeting of the day was with one of the Good Guys: a three-star submariner named Copper. Dawson knew that Bob Copper felt pretty much the same way he did about much of the politics of the job. He was glad that Bob had called him in for an early-morning planning session. Misery loves company.

The Pentagon, Arlington, Virginia

Vice Admiral Bob Copper heard the footsteps coming down the hall. He was waiting at the outer entrance to the conference room when Captain Dawson arrived. Copper extended his hand and warmly greeted the Captain. "Thanks for slipping in early, Daws. Come on in! We found out where they keep the coffee around here and I've got some brewing. Be ready in just a minute. You know Chip DePew, don't you?" He indicated his aide, who stood to greet the Boss SEAL.

"Hello, Daws," said DePew, "good to see you again! Last time was, when? Homecoming, a couple of years ago? Congratulations on your new job."

Trace Dawson shook hands warmly with Chip DePew. "Thanks, Chip, but I may not have a job much longer, if they keep hacking away at my budget."

"Well, Daws," Admiral Copper said, "that's why I wanted to meet with you this morning. I'm getting hacked to pieces, also. It's one thing to economize, I understand that perfectly. But J.O.K. Scrubbs and his buddies up on Capitol Hill have stopped economizing and are just plain eating us alive. The enemy threat has changed, I know that. But these guys on the Hill act as though they have forgotten there is any threat at all! This is how wars get started. We keep getting weaker, someone will think they can challenge us."

"I know, Bob," Dawson agreed. "And then we'll have to send our kids out into the field to fight, without adequate weapons and supplies, and backups. It's those kids who'll pay the price."

Bob Copper nodded, and continued, "Meanwhile, Daws, it's you and I that have to sit down and figure how to best use what we have. And we both know that each of us needs what the other has to make our cases stick. Look, I know that we submariners used to snub the SEALs. Going all the way back to the days of the old *Grayback*, all you SEALs got from us was the dregs." Copper referred to an old, out-of-commission diesel boat that was modified for use by SEALs in the late 1960's.

"That's been changing, Bob," said Trace Dawson, "and we

appreciate what you've done for us since you took over here. Look, I understand what you are saying. Believe me, I agree that unless somebody in the world starts buying Russian submarines, or unless somebody points nuclear ICBMs at us again, about the most important thing you pig-boat people can do is to deliver SEALs."

"And no one can deliver you as quickly and quietly as we can," said the submariner. "Absolute stealth." Copper leaned over to take a notebook from Chip Depew. "But, Daws, we don't have to sell each other on this, we need to sell J.O.K. Scrubbs and his subcommittee."

"I'd rather 'rassle a crocodile," said Trace Dawson. Dawson had the appearance of a man who had wrestled a few crocodiles.

"Daws," counseled Admiral Copper, "your crocodile 'rasslin' days are over. The minute you pin those stars on your collar, you stop being a SEAL and become a SEAL-salesman. Know what I mean?"

"Okay, Bob," said Dawson. "Let's see what you've got in the book."

Admiral Copper turned the large three-ring binder notebook around, exposing its cover. Large red-stenciled letters proclaimed, "Top Secret." Smaller letters presented the title: *Meeting the Threat; Improving the Stealth-Delivery of SEAL Teams.*

"Your predecessor, Admiral Ragano, worked pretty closely with us on this," said Copper. "I don't know if you had a chance to talk to him about it before he died."

Admiral Tony Ragano had died suddenly of a heart attack three months earlier. "Rags" had been a legend among his SEALs. Trace Dawson had big shoes to fill, and he had to start without a proper turnover of information.

Captain Dawson thumbed through the briefing notebook. "I knew Rags had been talking to you guys. I heard it had something to do with modifying O*hio* class SSBNs. I think I can guess some of it, but I haven't seen anything official."

Chip DePew took over the briefing. He went through the contents of the notebook, showing the history of development of SEAL insertion by submarine. An entire section was devoted to the old *Grayback*. She had been initially built in the 1950's to transport and fire the giant *Regulus* cruise missiles. Technologies were changing rapidly in the early 60's, and soon the spectacular new nuclear-powered "boomers" replaced the old diesel boats and their awkward air-breathing missiles. *Grayback* was decommissioned in 1964.

About that time, however, a new kind of threat, a new kind of warfare, was bursting into flames in Southeast Asia. The Navy SEALs, little more than footnotes to the massive troop deployments of World War II and the Korean War, were finding themselves in much more prominent roles in Viet Nam. The old *Grayback*, with her giant missile hangars, seemed like a natural for underwater delivery of SEALs. These SEAL teams were augmented by another new development, the Seal Delivery Vehicles, "SDVs". An SDV is a miniature submarine, only about seven meters long, that can carry a team of SEALs rapidly from their big-submarine home base into their target area. It was a great idea, and it worked well. But, the concept of SEAL insertion and extraction was far from being a top concern to submariners. In those Cold War years, submariners were absorbed with the problems of hunting other submarines and of being able to launch ICBMs. The SEALs received very little attention, and very low budget priority.

Chip DePew turned to the next section. It described the current state-of-the-art in submarine/SEAL technology. A couple of the old Sturgeon class nuclear attack submarines had been fitted with a strange-looking "wart" fastened to the after escape hatch. Called the Dry Deck Shelter ("DDS") system, it was capable of carrying a Mark VIII or Mark IX SDV. Their use was primarily regarded as experimental. The same was true of adaptations made in the 1980's to two old fleet ballistic missile submarines the *Sam Houston* and the *John Marshall*. Later, two other ex-boomers, the *Kamehameha* and the *Joshua L. Chamberlain* were converted to accommodate the DDS and to be primarily dedicated to special operations.

"Given the diverse nature of the threat in third-world countries all over the globe," Chip DePew was practicing the sales pitch, "this re-fitting of old equipment on a very limited scale is pathetically inadequate." Chip turned the page to the last section of the notebook. It contained artists' conceptions of adaptations to the *Los Angeles* class SSNs, and the *Ohio* class SSBNs. The men began to discuss details of the system designs, and implications on force deployment, and how they might accommodate this in their budget plans.

Captain Dawson remembered how skeptical he had been early in his career about SDVs. "SEALs don't need these James Bond gimmicks," he had scoffed. "Gimme an inflatable boat and a K-Bar knife," was his attitude, "and I'll take care of things for you." But his Viet Nam experience had taught him the value of technology in his business. The amazing Remington 7188 showed him what high-tech could do to a simple shotgun: it gave SEALs the ability to pump seventy-two .33-caliber OO buckshot pellets into a target in under a second and a half. Night-vision scopes and satellite navigation systems dramatically improved performance in the field. He quickly came to realize that, if these screwball SDVs could get more of his SEALs in quicker, and get them out safer, then he was all for them.

Now, Trace Dawson realized something else. With Bob Copper's budget support, and with the incredible delivery potential of nuclear submarines and SDV's, he could make the SEAL force what it deserved to be: the highest priority fighting unit in the country.

Dawson liked this man Bob Copper. Copper had a quick mind, he had a lot of good ideas, and he seemed to be the kind of person that could be trusted. Not bad, for a nuke.

Capitol Hill

"Oh, yes, Mrs. Winning! Miss Bennett asked me to call her as soon as you arrived." The Rayburn Building security guard picked up the phone and punched in the number. "Miss Bennett? This is Security, down in the lobby. Mrs. Winning has arrived. You asked me to call you." The security guard nodded to Susan. "Miss Bennett will be right down. May I check your purse, please?" Security in the House of Representatives' office buildings had intensified after several recent bomb threats.

"Of course," said Susan Winning.

The guard briefly went through Susan's purse. He then waved her through the security checkpoint and into a large waiting area, and pointed, "You can wait there...Oh, here is Miss Bennett now!"

Jodi Bennett emerged from the stairwell and rushed over to greet Susan Winning. "Thanks for coming early, Susan," said the congressional staffer. "The congressman can see us right now. The elevators are slow and we're only one floor up. Do you mind walking?"

"Let's go." Susan appreciated the energy and drive of this young girl. She wished she could bottle some of it and dispense it to others she had confronted during this bureaucratic ordeal. Susan was still struggling with the State Department. She had appeared again on Gregg Bentley's television show, and had also been interviewed several times for radio and newspaper features. But in each of these, she felt more that she was being held up as a spectacle – people enjoy watching others suffer – than that she was actually accomplishing anything for the hostages. But she purposed to keep trying.

Susan, Jodi and Congressman Hamilton McCall sat around the coffee table in his office. This was McCall's first term in Congress, and he had been assigned this office only four weeks previously. A few favorite pictures hung on the walls, a few books took their place in the large, mostly empty bookcases, but the congressman had been too busy to decorate his office properly. It gave the appearance of temporary quarters. He was a realist, and he was the first of his party to carry his district since before the Great Depression. He had two years to produce, or else he wouldn't be back.

"Mrs. Winning," began Congressman McCall, "I want to thank you for coming in to see me. I haven't been able to get home to Massachusetts since I started this job, and I have wanted to talk to you about this Hazor mess." He consulted a small calendar that he removed from his coat pocket. "As you know, Secretary of State Valencia is in Rome with the President at the summit meeting. I sent him a cable yesterday to request that he push hard on the summit delegates for any information he can get about the hostages." The Rome Summit was an attempt by the major powers to meet with representatives of Syria and Israel to defuse the war simmering between the two.

"But I've got to tell you, Mrs. Winning," continued McCall, "I'm not getting much better response than what Jodi tells me you have had from the State..." Just then, a secretary opened the door, and beckoned to the congressman. He got up from his seat, and went to the door.

Susan could not hear what the secretary said, but the congressman vigorously shook his head, "No, Bonnie, I'm with a constituent. I will be very happy to talk with them when we are finished. I don't know how long that will be. However long we need. Tell them to leave their information and see if you can find out when they will be available again. I'll be glad to talk to them, but not now!"

Congressman McCall came back to his seat and explained, "Lobbyists. Expect me to drop everything when they come around." He quickly returned to the subject of the meeting. "The Secretary of State will not be able to meet with us until he gets back from Rome. Right now, that's not scheduled to be for another week at the earliest. But, I've set up a meeting for tomorrow morning with one of his assistants, Dr. Francis Williams. He's the senior State Department official remaining here in Washington while the Rome Summit is under way. Jodi tells me you will still be here tomorrow, is that right?"

"Yes. I'm staying with my father here in the area until day after tomorrow."

"Good. I hope we can get some better information tomorrow. Mrs. Winning, I must confess I do not understand what I am hearing about this. All my inquiries to the State Department have led me to only one place: they all are holding to a single line: 'it's Israeli extremists.' The National Security Advisor's staff tells me the same thing. Nobody at the Pentagon will tell me a thing, but I heard the Secretary of Defense on C-Span yesterday taking the same line: 'Israeli extremists.' I know there are several in Congress who don't buy that, but I don't believe they have any hard facts to back their opinions." McCall looked through a file handed to him by Jodi Bennett. It contained press clippings, letters, and memoranda related to the Hazor Hostages.

The congressman continued, "What worries me is that it just

doesn't make any sense. There is absolutely no possible gain for the Israelis in this. And, except for that stupid demand that America 'declare immediate all-out war against Syria,' there has been no further demand made. No communication at all. If this were the work of a single mad terrorist, I could understand such irrational behavior. But this was a well-organized and well-planned attack on that bus. This was a sophisticated military operation. These were not 'mad terrorists.' It just does not figure that there would be such a weak link to Israeli terrorists."

Susan nodded, "I agree Congressman McCall..."

"Please call me Ham."

"I agree, Ham," Susan Winning continued. "I don't have any way of knowing who is behind this, but it seems to me that someone has decided that it's Israelis, and no one is willing to consider any alternative possibilities. Frankly...frankly..." Susan had tried hard to keep her composure throughout the whole ordeal, but sometimes, unexpectedly, she would lose it. This was one of those times, and tears began to pour.

Jodi Bennett handed Susan a tissue and patted her on the shoulder.

"I'm sorry." Susan was regaining control. "I'm sorry, but frankly, I'm not so worried about who's behind this as I am that we have somebody on our side who's trying to find my husband and the others and get them out. Maybe they know something at the State Department that we don't, but if so, they should at least give us a little tip to let us know that someone is on the ball here."

"Yes, that's my feeling, too," said Hamilton McCall. "You know what I think? I think that the President is just plain scared to get involved in this problem between Israel and Syria. Now, he has no pressure at all, of course, to side with the Syrians, but the Israel lobby is on him big-time. If he can keep blaming Israelis for the Hazor Hostages thing, he's got all he needs to keep the Israel-supporters at bay." Turning to his staff assistant, the congressman continued, "Jodi, show Mrs. Winning..."

"Susan."

"Show Susan the list of contacts that we want to try to hit today and tomorrow, while she's in town."

Jodi Bennett produced a sheet from the file: times and locations for several meetings with various congressmen, defense department officials, and the scheduled meeting on the following day with Assistant Secretary Williams.

Susan, Jodi, and Ham spent the next half-hour discussing the meetings and what to expect from each. Jodi Bennett would accompany Susan to all the meetings.

"Susan, didn't I understand you to say that your father lives here in the D.C. area?" McCall asked.

"Yes. He is a professor at the Washington Bible College in Lanham. He lives in Bowie."

"Good," said the congressman. "I will try to set some more meetings for next week. If he'd like to, I can give him a call to attend with Jodi and me, even if you can't make it down from Massachusetts."

Jodi Bennett interjected, "Susan, we have a meeting in fifteen minutes over at Congressman Schlegel's office." Jodi referred to the congressman from Pennsylvania who represented the Albostinis' and the Golds' district. "We had better get moving to make that appointment. But, I'll warn you, he's like the President: he doesn't want to get involved."

"Well," Susan got up to go. "That's why we need to talk to him. None of us wants to be involved in this. Least of all my husband, or Pastor Tarr, or Mel Gold, or Bucky Albostini."

Chapter Twenty-Two

The Message

February
Wadi El-Jari, Northeast Syria

VIKTOR RYPKIN AND BILL WINNING had spent much of the day sitting in the old trailer, drying out, munching the food provided by the professor, and discussing their plight. Of only one thing were they certain: after the morning's narrow escape they knew they would need help - lots of it. They had to get a message out, somehow.

Their conversation was cut short as the men heard a vehicle approaching. Winning hobbled over and peeked through a crack in the old trailer's plywood window cover. He was relieved to see that it was Professor Archie's Ford Bronco, but he continued to watch cautiously as it pulled near and stopped. Professor Archibald Pender-Cudlipp stepped out of the Bronco and approached slowly. He stood in the headlights of his Bronco so that he might show himself in the deepening twilight to any occupant who might be in the trailer. The Professor did not want to be mistaken for a Syrian soldier by anyone with an AK-47.

"I'm alone," called Pender-Cudlipp, in a stage-whisper. "If you're in there, I'm alone. I've brought more food."

Bill Winning reached over, nudged the door of the trailer open, and cautiously looked out, his weapon at the ready. Satisfied that the professor was, indeed, alone, Bill handed the firearm to Viktor. He smiled, waved at the Englishman, and jumped down from the trailer, gingerly as he favored his aching ankle. The rain had stopped hours before, but the ground was still covered with muddy pools of water left over from the morning's storm.

"I stalled them as long as I could this morning," said the professor. "I was jolly glad to see that empty trailer when they opened the door."

The men went to the rear of the Bronco. They removed another box of food, another jug of water.

"Listen," said the Englishman, "I've been thinking about our situation." To Archibald Pender-Cudlipp, the American, the Russian, and their message had become *his* problem, not just *a* problem. "I believe I can get a message out for us, but it's going to take some thought. I have with me a few examples of some of my recent outgoing messages. I send them out every week to my sponsoring agencies. One of my benefactors is in America. Maybe we could get a message through them to people in your country. I don't know what they could do to help us, but..."

Bill noticed Pender-Cudlipp's use of the words "we" and "us."

"God bless you, Archie," said Winning. "Look, I know you're risking everything. Your life, your project...you're risking everything to help us."

"Winning," said Pender-Cudlipp, "I don't care what it takes, we've got to get you out of here. If what Rypkin says about that Russian sub is correct, we don't have much time to spare. I'm in this whole thing with you already. No point in looking back now!"

"Well," said Bill Winning, "Viktor and I have been talking about this all afternoon. We've got some ideas, but, as you say, we need to get some messages out, somehow. We need help. And we need one other thing: we need to know where we are." Bill gave his shoulders an exaggerated shrug. "Where are we? I mean, let's start with this: what hemisphere are we in?"

Pender-Cudlipp chuckled and began to sketch a map in the dust and sand on the floor of the trailer. "Well," said Archie, "last time I looked, we were in Syria. Northern Syria, about ten kilometers south of the Turkish border. It is very rugged country between here and the border. Only dirt-path roads, and heavily patrolled. Especially heavily patrolled now that you have managed to ruin Bildad's whole day." Pender-Cudlipp looked up with a grin at the two fugitives.

"O.K." Bill pointed his flashlight beam to the dot on the map that represented their location. He noticed something interesting about the map Pender-Cudlipp had drawn. "How far are we from the Mediterranean?"

"Well," answered the professor, "it's only about fifteen kilometers to the west, but it is a rough go. No roads at all."

"Not as heavily patrolled?"

"Not patrolled much at all," Pender-Cudlipp responded. "But, Winning, if you're thinking of hiking to the sea, suppose we made it. What do we do when we get to the beach? Swim to Cyprus?" Professor Archie shook his head.

"And, listen," continued the professor, "I don't want to spoil your planning, but even if we could get a message to the States, they're not likely to bring anyone in to get us. Perhaps you haven't heard, but Syria and Israel are at war with each other. Your president has made a big show of removing all American forces completely away from the region. Hey, your government thinks you hostages were taken by the bloomin' Israelis!"

"What! ..." Bill Winning was incredulous.

"I'm telling you, Winning," said the professor, "this thing is getting out of hand."

Bill Winning shook his head, as if to clear it. "All right, look," he said. "There's nothing we can do about that unless we can at least get some sort of message out of here. What about your idea?"

Pender-Cudlipp described the procedure he normally followed to send messages to various sponsors of his project. He sorted through a folder of messages.

"Here are two that I sent just last week," said Pender-Cudlipp. He handed Winning a pair of rumpled sheets taken from the folder.

Bill read the first:

TO: DR. J.W.L. MCQUAID
 PROFESSOR, DEPARTMENT OF MIDDLE
  EASTERN ARCHAEOLOGY
 UNIVERSITY OF LONDON
 LONDON 75, ENGLAND, U.K.

 BD 80 TO 85 STILL UN-PRODUCTIVE. ONLY
 SPURIOUS POTSHERDS, NO GRAVES. STILL
 MUCH IN NEED OF SUPPORT-PAID
 VOLUNTEERS TO WORK THE NEW SITES.
 TOSHIBA LAPTOP FINE, BUT NEED MORE
 DISKS. GROVER SUGGESTS MOVE SEARCH
 FOR CYRENIAN ARTIFACTS PER ACTS 11:20
 TO NORTH AND WEST OF CURRENT TEST

PITS. I AGREE.

> DR. A.A. PENDER-CUDLIPP
> Q'ADI, AL-JUMHURIA AL-ARABIA AL-SURIA
>   655JAS/841QAF 02440X:0705

The second was similar:

> TO: DR. SAMUEL G. GROVER
>   DIRECTOR OF FIELD OPERATIONS
>   SMITHSONIAN INSTITUTION
>   900 JEFFERSON DRIVE
>   WASHINGTON, D.C., U.S.A. 20560

> STILL NO SUCCESS IN BD 80 TO 85. I AM
> MOVING SEARCH FOR GRAVE SITES WEST TO
> ALPHA ROWS AND TO NORTH AS YOU
> RECOMMENDED. LOOKING FOR CYRENIAN
> ARTIFACTS PER ACTS 11:20. WILL
> APPRECIATE ANY VOLUNTEERS YOU CAN
> SEND US. STAFFING PROBLEMS MAKING IT
> DIFFICULT TO CONTINUE SEARCH.

> DR. A.A. PENDER-CUDLIPP
> Q'ADI, AL-JUMHURIA AL-ARABIA AL-SURIA
>   655JAS/841QAF 02239X:0710

"What are these letters and numbers, 'BD 80 to 85'?" asked Bill Winning. He pointed to the message. "Is this a grid numbering system or something?"

"Exactly," responded the professor. "The site is a square, divided into ten thousand smaller grid units. We have a grid system with one hundred measures across the top, running from west to east, and one hundred measures running down, from north to south. The grid sectors are labeled from AA00 to CV99 so that our discoveries can be labeled accurately and traced by the different agencies that are sponsoring us. We also have a third dimension in the labeling system, to record the depth of the finds."

"I see." Bill continued to study the messages. "So if we could construct another message that appeared like these, we might be able to slip it past the censor at the message center."

"There's a chance." Pender-Cudlipp nodded, extracting a pencil and small notepad from his jacket pocket.

The two men sat, sharing ideas, constructing a message. They considered where to send it, how to word it, what help to request in it.

Viktor Rypkin understood only parts of the conversation. His entire life had, in just the last two days, been caught up in a maddening swirl of manacles and chains, bullets and Broncos, flooding wadis, and crazy plans. His life would never be the same, if it lasted much longer at all. But Viktor had concluded one thing: if he had to place his life in the hands of another man, that man would be Bill Winning. There seemed to be something that was worth following in this American who kept talking to some invisible God. It bothered Rypkin to hear Winning when he talked about God, but he had to admit there was something admirable about him, even so.

From what Rypkin could understand of the conversation between the American and the Englishman, Bill Winning had a relative, apparently a professor at a college in the Washington, D.C. area. The plan was to address a message to this relative, to this Dr. Steve Whitney.

Rypkin also understood that Bill had in mind another old friend who was evidently a high official in the American navy, a man named Admiral Copper. The hope was that this man Copper might be able to organize some kind of rescue effort by people called "seals." This was totally confusing to the Russian engineer, but he maintained silence about his doubts. Rypkin did hear them discussing one thing he understood: submarines. He gathered that this Admiral Copper person might be able to somehow enlist American submarines to help in a rescue attempt. That was one thing that made sense to the Russian.

The men talked for several hours, making additions and deletions to the message, seeking to cram as much information as was possible without making it the object of suspicion to the Syrian censor in Q'adi.

The men understood it would not be until the following Friday that Pender-Cudlipp could return again to Q'adi to send the message. They would remain hidden until that time. There was nothing to do now but to wait. Wait and pray.

Lanham, Maryland
Washington Bible College

The Reverend Dr. Steve Whitney had just finished teaching his morning class. It was his favorite class, "Old Testament Survey." It was a freshman-level course, and he loved the wide-eyed enthusiasm of these students. Steve Whitney had never forgotten the thrill he felt as a freshman in Bible college a half-century earlier, when it first dawned on him that the entire Old Testament, every book, pointed to the coming Messiah.

Steve Whitney sat at his desk and glanced outside the window. A light dusting of snow covered the grounds, just enough to dampen the harsh noises of the city and to make the scene crisp and clean. Steve began to pray. He prayed first for his students, each one, by name. He then prayed that he, himself, might never lose the feeling of awe that he had when he first contemplated the supernatural continuity of the Bible. He prayed that he would be able to pass on to a new generation that stunning feeling of coming to the recognition that - of all things - it was *true*!

Dr. Whitney then began to pray for his son-in-law. He prayed also for his daughter, and for his grandchildren. He prayed for the others involved in the Hazor tragedy as well. Steve Whitney had dropped to his knees, his head placed in his folded hands on the seat of his chair as he prayed.

Suddenly his secretary burst into the room, without knocking.

"Oh, excuse me, Doctor Whitney! I didn't know...I just got this telegram...I thought you'd want to see it immediately...Oh, I am so sorry!"

"That's quite all right, Dottie." Steve got up from his knees and smiled at his secretary. "I was just having a talk with the Father. What is this? A telegram?"

"Yes," explained Dottie. "At first I thought it must have been sent to the wrong place. It says, 'To: Dr. Steven Whitney, Professor of Religious History...' that's not your correct title, and it's sent to 'Washington College,' not 'Washington *Bible* College.' I thought at first it was sent in error." Dottie handed the telegram to Steve Whitney. "But look at this, Doctor Whitney! Look...here! It says, 'Winning A.W....!'"

"Yes!" Steve grabbed the telegram, adjusted his glasses, and studied it closely.

TO: DR. STEVEN WHITNEY
   PROFESSOR OF RELIGIOUS HISTORY
   WASHINGTON COLLEGE
   PRINCESS GARDEN PARKWAY
   LANHAM, MARYLAND, USA, 20728

   WINNING A.W. 75. REPEAT SUCCESS IN
   SECTOR A.W. 75. NEED MORE
   RESOURCES IMMEDIATELY. CONTACT
   DR. COPPER IN ARLINGTON. GRAVE
   SITUATION AS IN 2 KINGS 6:17. SUGGEST
   COPPER SEND HIS BEST MODEL SIERRA
   SIERRA NOVEMBER EQUIPMENT.
   REQUEST SEND VOLUNTEERS WITH DR.
   SEALS FOR URGENT ASSISTANCE. CALL
   UNIVERSITY OF LONDON, PROFESSOR
   MCQUAID FOR EXACT LOCATION.

   DR. A.A. PENDER-CUDLIPP
   Q'ADI, AL-JUMHURIA AL-ARABIA AL-SURIA
          655JAS/841QAF 02239X:0712

"Look at this, Dottie!" exclaimed Steve Whitney. "This is unquestionably about Bill Winning! Angus William, 'A.W.,' Winning! Look! It was sent from...what is this? '*Al-Jumhuria Al-Arabia Al-Suria*.' Dottie! That's Arabic for 'Syrian Arab Republic.' Syria! He's in Syria, Dottie! This is it! Praise the Lord, this is what we have been praying for!"

Steve sat down at his desk, and took out a pad of paper. He

jotted down a name and address. "Dottie, will you please do me a favor? Will you call this number and try to get a message to my daughter? Have her call me immediately. She had a meeting this morning with Congressman McCall in downtown Washington. She may still be there, I don't know. Please see if you can catch up with her. Just tell her we may have some important news and she needs to get in touch with me right away. Thanks."

Dottie took the note and hurried out of the office to make the call from her desk.

Steve Whitney got back down on his knees and continued his prayer.

Wadi El-Jari, Syria

By contrast with the stench, chains, starvation, and horror at the extermination camp, to the American and his new Russian companion, the trailer was luxury. There was plenty of food supplied by Pender-Cudlipp, who visited nearly every day, and there were no steel manacles to chafe the wrists. Viktor Rypkin and Bill Winning caught up on their sleep, although they never both slept at the same time. One always stood guard while the other rested.

At night, they enjoyed the freedom to slip out of their hiding place to visit their makeshift privy, to carefully explore the immediate surroundings, and to limber up their aching joints and muscles. For the most part, during the day, they stayed concealed in the battered little trailer. It gave them much time to talk, to plan, and to learn each other well.

They talked of many things. Viktor Rypkin was fascinated to learn more from Bill about Gary Tarr. Viktor had known the big man only briefly, but this Pastor Gary Tarr had been willing to sacrifice himself to give freedom to Rypkin and Winning. Viktor had never personally experienced anything like this idea of sacrifice, and it astounded him.

Meanwhile, Bill learned more about Viktor Rypkin. Mostly, he heard about a girl named Jadeel Dovni, and about the depth of Viktor's passion for her. It seemed to Bill that Viktor was almost totally dominated by his despair over her treachery. Viktor found it difficult to believe in anyone, in anything, after having been jolted so hard by this Russian-Syrian woman.

Viktor and Bill began to develop a strong relationship, a brotherhood of shared trial. But the relationship had its limits, and there were some topics that Bill learned were out of bounds for conversation with his moody Russian comrade.

Archibald Pender-Cudlipp welcomed the intrusion of these two newcomers, though he knew it brought great hazard. Life without Shari had become hopelessly empty. The professor had little in common with his other associates at the dig. Old Khalil Hinnawi was loyal, to be sure, but his understanding was limited. The other veteran crewman, Fadl Rafat, was very bright, very clever...perhaps too clever. Professor Archie felt, whenever speaking to Rafat, that he should keep one hand on his wallet, and never turn his back. The others were transients. Usually they stayed around only long enough to make some quick money, and then they were gone.

The professor found that he looked forward to those mornings when he could stroll out to the trailer, before dawn and well before the workers arose, to slip in for conversation with Viktor and Bill. What remarkable men these were: the brilliant young Russian electronics engineer, and the stalwart American tourist. Let come what may, these were two fine men, and Archie was glad to have a hand, if he could, in helping them escape Hazael Zabadi's tyranny and Colonel Bildad's brutality. As they awaited some response to their message, the conversation alone was, to Professor Archie, a treasure worth the risks he was taking.

"It sounds to me, Archie, that you have been driven hard by a passion for finding some significance in the land here...buried significance." Winning, Rypkin, and Pender-Cudlipp often found themselves talking about their chosen professions. Bill Winning, seated on a wooden crate and leaning back against the trailer's wall, continued, "Was Shari like that, too – looking for meaning in the digs?"

"Oh, yes!" The professor was most animated when talking about Shari. Losing her still carried an unbearable sting. "Shari was even more driven than I am about Project Jaris. To me, sometimes, it has been more like an interesting hobby. But to her, proving the significance – yes, that's the right word – the significance of this land was what really drove her. It was her life. In the end, it is what killed her..." Archie's voice trailed off dimly. There was a silent moment. Then, he collected himself, and resumed the conversation. "But tell me, Bill, about Susan, your wife. I take it from what you've said that she, too, is a woman with great drive. What is it that motivates her?"

Bill nodded pensively, and smiled. "Well...the kids...her mom and dad...me, I hope." Bill paused and thought again, as he had thought countless times since the ordeal had begun, about what Susan must be going through right now. Then, he straightened and gently slapped both knees. "But, I'll tell you, Archie, what really motivates Susan is the word of God. The Bible. Reading it. Trying to obey it. Telling other people about it. And, to go even deeper, what motivates her is the God who is revealed in the Bible. Her relationship with Him. That's what I'd say motivates her." He paused. "Archie, tell me more about you and Shari. How about your church upbringing?"

"Well...certainly," said the professor, haltingly. "I...used to go to the chapel...at the university. My father was a fixture there. Board of Vestrymen or some such. When I was a child, he insisted we go to chapel every week. I went through confirmation class, and I took communion there. We used to go every year to hear Handel's *Messiah*. Beautiful. So, I guess you could say I'm a Christian. Both my father and my mother had their funerals in that chapel. Shari and I were married there. Shari never was seriously into Islam, didn't have any problem converting...I guess that's the word...to Christianity. But, I guess there are many roads to heaven, Muslim or Christian, or whatever, as long as you're sincere about it." Pender-Cudlipp spoke calmly, thoughtfully. "You know, if it gives comfort, then it must be worthwhile, it seems to me. I'm glad Susan is able to take comfort from her beliefs. You do, too, I take it?"

Viktor Rypkin, sitting on the floor in one corner of the trailer, got up and went to a crate that contained some apples. The Russian picked out an apple and bit into it with a loud crunch. He walked over to the plywood window-cover and peered out, munching on the apple.

Bill Winning answered Pender-Cudlipp. "Yes, I do. And

Archie, I'll tell you up front, frankly I don't agree with you that 'there are many roads to heaven,' or that all it takes is 'sincerity'." Bill had a way of disagreeing and staying pleasant at the same time. "To tell you the truth, though, that's exactly what I did think –you know, 'many roads to the top' - when I was younger. To the extent I thought about it at all, which wasn't much. Actually, Archie, I've got a notion that your parents gave you a lot stronger start at things of the church than I had. I rarely went to church…mostly scoffed at those who did. Maybe I'd go to a funeral, or a wedding, but I never heard anything there that impressed me very much.

"You know, it's sad. A lot of churches seem to do a pretty poor job of explaining what the church is all about. They get so caught up in the trappings of 'religion' that they forget that the whole thing is not at all about the 'brand' of church where you go. It's not about what flowery language the minister uses, or how many times you can repeat a memorized prayer. It's about who God is and how we can have a relationship with Him. A lot of churches miss the point, it seems to me. And, as a result, a lot of people miss the point, too. It's more than sad: it's tragic. People are missing out on eternal life."

Archie scratched his head absently and diverted his gaze from Bill Winning. He stared down at the scuffed linoleum floor of the trailer. "Mmmm," he grunted.

"Hey, Archie," said Bill, "May I ask you another question?"

"Fine. Go ahead, ask." The Englishman responded warily.

Just then, Viktor Rypkin held up a hand. "Shhh!" he cautioned. "Listen!" The faint sound of a helicopter's chop-chop-chop could be heard in the distance, to the south.

Winning hobbled to the door of the trailer and cracked it, to peer out. Nothing to be seen in the sky to the south, and the chopper's noise continued to fade away in that direction.

"Just an army scout," said Pender-Cudlipp. "He's probably headed to Damascus. Not a problem to us – at least not yet. I guess I'd better get back to camp pretty soon. But, Bill, go ahead and ask your question."

"All right," said Bill. "Listen: have you come to the place in your spiritual life where you know for certain that if you were to die today you would go to heaven, or is that something you would say you're still working on?"[1]

The professor considered it for a moment, then answered, "Bill, I don't think this is something that anyone can know for certain. Heaven is out there, I suppose. Must be. This earth can't be all there is. But nobody can know if he's going there. I figure the best we can do is to wonder about it. To hope so. Where do you get the idea that you can know for sure?"

"Glad you asked." Bill slapped his knees again. "In the Bible it says, *These things have I written unto you...that ye may know that ye have eternal life!* It says the reason the Bible was written is that you may *know*! You don't have to go through life merely wondering, or hoping, maybe." He took a slip of paper from his pocket and scribbled on it, *I John 5:13*.

Bill Winning continued, "May I share with you how I came to know – for certain – that I have eternal life?"

"Sure."

"Before I do, let me ask you another question, O.K.?"

"O.K."

"Now, Archie, suppose you were to die today, and stand before God, and he were to say to you, 'Why should I let you in to my heaven?' What would you say?"

Archie bristled, and smiled a wry smile. "Where did you get these questions?"

Bill smiled back. "Actually, these are a couple of questions that a friend asked me several years ago that got me to running deep with my thoughts. It got me to thinking about who is God, and who am I, and where am I headed. He was in an outfit called *Evangelism Explosion* that helps churches focus on what's important about church...what we were talking about earlier. Now, quit stalling, Archie. Answer the question!"

"Mmmm." Pender-Cudlipp grunted again. "Well, as I said, I've

---

[1]   *Note to the reader*: the dialogue in this section of the novel is based on real presentations, under real-life circumstances, of the gospel of Jesus Christ. The presentation draws on material provided in a booklet, *Do You Know?* Published by Evangelism Explosion International, Ft. Lauderdale, FL. , and on "E.E." training developed by that organization. If you are interested in more details of this presentation, or if you would like to understand from the Bible how YOU can know for sure that you have eternal life, please write the author c/o Anchorhouse Publishing Company, P.O. Box 3361, Crofton, MD 21114.

been confirmed. I've taken communion. Plus, I really have always tried to do my best. Never hurt anyone...that I know of...who didn't jolly well deserve it. Listen, I picked you fellows up off a mountain when you had Bildad's goons all over looking for you, didn't I? That ought to get me a few points, I'd say!"

"Makes points with me, that's for sure, Archie!" laughed Bill Winning. Then, with a dead-serious look, he eyed Pender-Cudlipp. "Is that what you'd say to God?"

"Well," said Archie, "it seems to me that if my good deeds outweigh my bad ones, then I should make it in."

"So, you'd tell God that you were confirmed, and went to chapel with your parents, and that your good deeds outweigh your bad ones. Is that right?

"Yes," nodded the professor. "I don't know, maybe that's a little weak, but that's what I'd say. I hope he would let me in. I don't know."

"Well, Archie," Bill brightened, "when you answered that first question, I thought I had some good news for you. But, after hearing your answer to this second question, I know that I have the *greatest news you have ever heard!*"

"And that is...?" asked Pender-Cudlipp.

Viktor Rypkin turned from the window and interrupted again. "Bill, I think it is best to let Professor Archie to be getting back to his camp. Choppers are gone, but who knows what is coming next?"

Bill nodded, "Yeah, Viktor, you're probably right." Then, turning to Pender-Cudlipp, "Archie, do you have a Bible back at your camp?"

"Yes."

"O.K. Get it out and look up these verses." Bill took the slip of paper from Archie and wrote some additional Bible verses on it. "Tell me what you think about what they say."

The Professor, delighted to have been given his first homework assignment in years, responded with glee. "O.K., Reverend Bill! I'll go you one better. I'll bring the Bible out here and you can show me!"

"It's a deal," said the American, "if you agree you'll also teach me more about what you are doing here at the Jaris Site."

Winning observed that much of the conversation had escaped

the comprehension of the Russian, Viktor Rypkin. Bill and Archie spoke too quickly, with too many words Viktor did not understand. Winning slowed his speech and summarized the conversation for Viktor's benefit.

"Archie will bring us a copy of the Bible, Viktor!" Bill concluded his summary. "Then I can show you these things I have been telling you!"

"I am very happy," said Viktor, "that you are being so much loving with this...this book, my friend." When Viktor was upset, he struggled with his English, and he spoke haltingly. "I respect you, Bill Winning. And I am pleased that you are taking such...such comfort... from your faith." Viktor had been eating an apple; he flung the core into the trash box with a sudden flourish of anger bordering on disgust. "But please do not expect me to become so excited as you are about your...your religious book. We have more important things to be discussing and to be studying than...*your religious myths!*"

There were times, in the many lengthy conversations between Bill Winning and Viktor Rypkin, that the Russian would slip into a deep, stubborn melancholy. His anger and fright would show through in his demeanor. These excursions into despair often seemed to follow Bill's attempts to explain his faith.

Bill Winning looked for a moment into the eyes of his Russian friend. What he saw, behind the anger and fear was something he had felt, himself, many years before. Winning understood. It was self-pride.

"Viktor," said Winning at length, "I will speak no more of this now. But I will offer this one last observation: There are those who are so intelligent, and so accomplished in their own field, or so troubled by the world, that they never take time to run deep with the truly important things of life. You have told me of your accomplishments and ambitions as an engineer. You have told me many times about the girl, Jadeel, who betrayed you. We both know how desperate our situation is. But, if you never allow your thoughts to run deeper than these circumstances, you will miss the greatest blessing of all: eternal life. Until you run deep with your thoughts, Viktor, beyond electronics, beyond the Syrians, beyond this girl, you will seek answers, and only find more questions."

There was silence in the trailer for a moment. Viktor Rypkin set his jaw tightly, shook his head, and stared into a dark corner of the trailer.

The silence was broken by the cheerful voice of Professor Pender-Cudlipp. "I say, Winning! Don't you Americans have a term, 'Cabin Fever?' I must find a way to get you two out of this bloomin' trailer before you strangle each other! I hope that message we sent will find its mark! Soon!"

Pender-Cudlipp left the trailer. He returned later that evening, bringing his Bible, and several other books, scholarly works that dealt with the history of Jaris and the surrounding area.

Bill, Viktor and Archie spent the next half-hour, using flashlights in the gathering darkness, looking through some of the professor's books, including one written by none other than Dr. Archibald Pender-Cudlipp.

The professor described more of the details of some of the important finds he and Shari had made at the digs. But the professor had a question for Bill, something that had been gnawing at him since the conversation earlier that day: "O.K., Bill, what's this 'great news' you promised. You've got my attention."

"The great news, Archie, is that heaven is a *free gift* of God. It can not be earned or deserved. A great many people get confused over this, and think they have to work their way into heaven. But the Bible says that's not true at all. Here, I'll show you. Let's look up those verses I jotted down this afternoon."

Archie handed his big, leather-bound Bible to Bill Winning. Its gilded-edge pages had obviously been spared the burden of over-use. "I'm afraid I haven't cracked it open for awhile," muttered the professor. "Well, I do know parts of the Book of Acts...you know, the parts that talk about the Christians at Antioch. They're the ones that came down here to Jaris. That's what we're digging up around here. But I'm not...I never...maybe you could help me find these verses?"

"Sure." Bill opened to the New Testament book of *Romans*, turning to chapter six; the verse numbered 6:23.

"Look," he directed the flashlight beam at a spot on the page. "Here it says, ...*the gift of God is eternal life...*" Then flipping over a few pages, to the book of *Ephesians*, he found verses in chapter 2, numbered 2:8 and :9. "Here it says, *For by grace are ye saved through faith; and that not of yourselves: it is the gift of God: Not of works, lest any man should boast.* See, heaven is a free gift! It is not, can not be, earned or deserved."

"Come on, Bill," said Archie. That's only one small part of a very fat book. Don't go taking these sayings out of context, now." The professor repeated a caution he had remembered from his youth.

"Good point, Archie." The battle was on.

Viktor Rypkin brusquely stood and excused himself from the conversation. "I will be going for walk-around outside," he said. He slipped quietly out of the trailer into the dark of the evening.

Bill and Archie spent the next hour going through Bible verses, considering their import, relating them to the matter of knowing God, of having eternal life, and of knowing it.

They discussed mankind: are we really all sinners, destined for hell? Can a man earn his way into heaven? Who is God? How can he be both merciful *(God is love...)* and exhibit perfect justice *(The wages of sin is death...)* at the same time? How did God solve this dilemma? Who is Jesus Christ? What was it that he did at the cross?

Sixty minutes. An hour that embraced the questions of the ages. Two men under extraordinary circumstances, to be sure, but they wrestled with questions that have perplexed all of humankind, men and women, ordinary and extraordinary, for millennia.

"Let's go back to the Old Testament, Archie." Bill was on to a point. "Look, here in the book of *Isaiah.* Chapter 53, verse 6: *All we like sheep have gone astray,"* Bill read, *"we have turned every one to his own way...* see, the Bible keeps on pointing out how all of us – no exceptions – are unqualified for God's heaven. You talk about keeping it in context! It's all throughout the Bible. Old *and* New Testaments." Bill picked up a book that was on the crate next to him, a heavy volume.

"It's like this: suppose God has written down in this book all the sins I've committed. Big things and little things. Thoughts as well as deeds. And not just the things I've done that are wrong, but also the things I *should have done*, but didn't. Thousands of entries on the list. Enough to fill this book." He placed the heavy book on his outstretched left hand. "Now this is me." He indicated his left hand, supporting the book. "And say this hand is God," he indicated his right hand, hovering over his left hand, but unable to clasp it because of the bulky book that separated them.

"Now, go back and look at what the prophet Isaiah said: *All we like sheep have gone astray; we have turned every one to his own way…*" Bill's two hands stayed apart, separated by the "sin-book." "But now, Archie, look at the rest of that passage: *…and the LORD hath laid on Him the iniquity of us all!*" Bill took the big "sin-book" and flopped it loudly from his left hand (representing himself) over into his right hand (representing God) as he quoted the last part of the passage. "See," said Bill, "that was what Jesus was doing on the cross! He was fulfilling Isaiah's prophecy! Jesus had the sins of all of us laid on him as he died. So now our sins are off us, and on him. He was tortured to death to pay the penalty that we deserved to pay. He died. He was buried, and our sins were buried with him." Here Bill put his right hand, now carrying the big "sin-book" down on the floor beside him to indicate the burial.

"But then…" Bill paused for a moment, and looked into the eyes of Archibald Pender-Cudlipp. Archie was listening. "…then he rose up from the tomb! Resurrection! And he left my sins down there." Bill raised his right hand back up, leaving the "sin-book" on the floor. He clasped his two hands firmly together. "And now I can have fellowship with God! Now…and into eternity. He paid the price for eternal life, and gave it to me as a free gift."

"Mmmm!" Archie repeated his favorite comment. But this time it carried a tone of hope.

The two men continued their dialogue into the next hour. They discussed what is meant by "saving faith," and the difference between this and mere "head-knowledge." Professor Pender-Cudlipp felt his spirit growing beyond contentment in his own meager head-knowledge toward a hunger to go beyond knowledge.

About twenty minutes later, Viktor Rypkin returned from his walk-around. As the Russian approached the trailer, he found a scene of laughter and joyful talk.

"Hush!" scolded Rypkin, as he cracked open the trailer door. "You will give us away to all of Syria! You must be quiet in here! You must be still!"

Bill Winning extended his arm to Viktor and helped him up

into the trailer. "Viktor, Viktor. How can we keep silent at such a time as this? Our friend, Archie, has prayed to receive Christ as his Savior. Archie has been born again; he is now a child of the King! The Bible says that the angels in heaven rejoice over this. How can we keep silent?"

"Humph," grumbled the dour Russian. He went to his corner and sat, arms folded. He closed his eyes to try to find rest.

Chapter Twenty-Three

Dr. Copper and Dr. Seals

February
Lanham, Maryland

"WHAT DO YOU THINK IT MEANS, DAD?" Susan Winning did not know whether to laugh or cry. This mysterious message, couched in such strange terms, was clearly from, or at least about, her husband. "Is this for real," asked Susan, "or is this somebody's idea of a joke?"

"I don't think it's a joke, Suze," said the Reverend Dr. Steve Whitney. "Look! It says 'Winning A.W. seventy-five...' I don't understand the second sentence but, look! The 'A' and the 'W' are his initials, and the 'seventy-five' is more than a coincidence. Does that number mean anything to you?" Steve looked quizzically at his daughter.

"Well, yes," admitted Susan. "Bill is a graduate of the Naval Academy, class of '75. When he's writing to a classmate, he often signs his notes 'A.W. Winning, '75.'"

"Yep," said Steve. "And if he wanted to get a message to us that had a verification, wouldn't that be something he might use?"

"Yes, Dad," acknowledged Susan, "but it could be just a coincidence. Listen, I don't want to throw cold water on this, but I can't handle a hoax, or a coincidence, or a false lead. That's the last thing we need at this time."

"I know, Honey," Steve comforted his daughter, "but, look at this! The Bible reference in this note. Second Kings 6:17. Do you know what that is?"

"No."

"It's the Old Testament story of Elisha and the 'Chariots of Fire,'" continued Steve. "Susan, the night before you and Bill left for your trip to Israel, Bill and I sat upstairs and told the kids a bedtime Bible story. It was from this very passage! Right from Second Kings Chapter Six. One coincidence, maybe I could swallow. But not two. And, look at this." Dr. Whitney pointed to another word in the message.

"Don't you and Bill know someone named Copper?" asked Steve. "I don't think he's a doctor, but isn't he a big brass in the Navy, or something?"

"Oh, Daddy, you're right!" exclaimed Susan. "This is it! This really *is* from Bill!" Susan hugged her father. Tears pouring from her eyes, she fought back the sobs.

Steve Whitney hugged his daughter close to him, and was silent for a long moment. He brushed her golden hair back off her forehead, as he had done so often when she was but a small child. He knew that she needed nothing more, nor less, at this moment than the quiet reassurance of her father. He knew the feeling well, having rested countless times in the loving kindness of his own Heavenly Father. "Be still," the Bible said, "and know that I am God."

At length, Susan wiped the tears from her eyes with a brusque flip of her hand, and said, "Okay. We've got a lot to do. Let's get him back! Let me see that message." Susan studied the message for a few seconds.

"The guy from the State Department said we should contact him if we heard anything," said Susan. "He wants to be the focal point for whatever plans or responses have to be made. I guess we have to follow up on that, but first, it seems that we should do what Bill asks us to do, here, in his message."

"Call Doctor Copper?" suggested Steve Whitney.

"Exactly."

The Pentagon, Arlington, Virginia

Three-Star-Admiral Robert Copper was not happy. Not even a little bit. "Admiral," Copper addressed his remarks to his boss, Four-Star-Admiral Edward Hrupak, the Chief of Naval Operations ("CNO"), "cutbacks are one thing, but what they're doing now is lethal. Not just to submarines, not just to the Navy, but to our entire defense posture."

Copper shut his briefing book with a loud "pop" and pushed it away from him. He glanced down momentarily at the polished mahogany table in the CNO's conference room. This table was a relic. It briefly crossed Copper's mind that this grand old table was a reminder of days, now long past, when his country sought the very best for those who served in her armed forces. It was no longer the case. It seemed now that the only priority that the military had in the thinking of the current government leaders on the Hill and in parts of the Administration was as the top-priority victim of budget cuts.

"Sir," continued Vice Admiral Copper, "do you remember back in nuclear power school when they taught us about critical mass?" Ed Hrupak, like Bob Copper, had gone through the nuclear power training program in the early 1970's. "Put enough fissionable material together in a single mass, and it will give you a sustained chain reaction. You start to take away from that mass, you get to a point where you no longer have a sustainable chain reaction, and you shut down. You lose the critical mass. Sir, that's what we're doing to the Navy. And I'm not talking about neutrons; I'm talking about men. We are already making up for personnel shortfalls by keeping these kids at sea far beyond reasonable limits, and pushing them to double-duty. And we're way behind the curve on providing adequate housing for their families. I'll speak at least for the nuclear Navy, we can't recruit any more, and we're losing our very best people."

Hrupak was quick with his response. "Bob, you'd do better to save your speeches for Congressman Scrubbs. And I'd advise you not to use your 'nuclear critical mass' analogy with him. He's as anti-nuke as he is anti-Navy." Ed Hrupak was a powerfully built man with close-cropped white hair and a tough, square jaw. Hrupak had a reputation for integrity and for a steel-trap mind. "I never forget a name, and I never forget a number," was, for him, less a boast than a statement of fact. Here, surrounded by his two-dozen top admirals, he was trying to lead the way out of the Navy's greatest crisis since Pearl Harbor. The threat this time was not Japanese dive-bombers, but bureaucratic budget-axe wielders.

"While I'm at it, Bob," continued Admiral Hrupak, "you and I have to talk about your problem with J.O.K. Scrubbs. You have managed to rile him up something fierce."

"Admiral," said Copper, "you know as well as I do what

Scrubbs is trying to do. He wants to be a hero to all his special-interest-group supporters, and he's using his control of the military budget to get what they want. Sir, we've backed off too far on this, already."

"I know Bob." Hrupak looked around at the other officers that surrounded the table. "I know how you all feel about this. And you know that I agree with you. But, Bob," he looked back at Copper, "it does no good at all to pick little fights with Scrubbs and his staff. We have to find more effective ways to deal with..."

Just then, Captain Chip DePew entered the room, preceded by a loud knock on the door. He came quickly to the side of Admiral Copper. DePew leaned down to whisper an urgent message. "Admiral Copper, you have a call, waiting outside. It is very urgent. I think you might want to take it. It's from Bill Winning's wife."

Bob Copper stood abruptly and addressed the CNO, "Admiral Hrupak, I have an urgent call. Chip tells me I had better take it right away. I'll be back in as soon as I can."

"It's not Scrubbs, is it, Chip? If it is, tell your boss not to make any more speeches to him." Hrupak grinned at Captain DePew.

"No sir, it's not Scrubbs," Depew reassured the CNO.

"Okay, Bob," said Hrupak. "Let me know if there's anything I can do to help."

As soon as the two officers left the CNO's conference room, Chip DePew escorted his boss to a phone in a small, empty office nearby.

Before Copper picked up the receiver, his aide explained, "I'm sorry to bother you in such an important meeting with the CNO, Admiral, but I know you have been concerned over this thing with your old shipmate, Bill Winning. I figured you'd want to talk with Mrs. Winning. It sounds to me as though she may have heard something important."

"You did the right thing, Chip. If Susan has heard something from Bill, I want to know about it, no matter what. Thanks." Copper picked up the telephone and punched the appropriate button to connect him with the waiting call.

"Hello, Susan? This is Bob Copper. Chip tells me you might have something!" Copper listened for a moment as Susan began to explain the message.

"Wait, wait, Susan," said Copper. "It's probably best not to read this over the phone. Where are you?... O.K., you stay put. I'll be right out!" Copper placed the telephone back in its place, and turned to Captain DePew, "Chip get us a driver as quickly as you can. We need to get out to Lanham right away! I'll meet you down at the car pool lot."

Captain DePew left quickly to get a car and driver. Bob Copper went back to Admiral Hrupak's conference room.

"Excuse me, Admiral," interrupted Copper, "may I have a quick word with you?"

"Sure, Bob." The CNO got up from his place at the end of the mahogany table and came over near the door where Copper stood.

"Sir," explained Copper, quietly, "I just got a call from Susan Winning. You know Bill Winning, one of the Hazor Hostages? This is his wife. She may have some information that could help find him. I'd like to go out and talk to her. This could be important."

"Wait," responded the CNO, "this is State Department business, maybe the C.I.A. The last thing we need is for *you* to get involved in this mess!"

"Admiral, I've known Bill and Susan Winning for a long time." Bob Copper was adamant. "Bill saved my life once. Mine and about two hundred others. You know the *Muskellunge* story. If there's a way I can help him now, I want to do it. But there's more: Susan has a message she thinks is from Bill. I don't know the details, but it does mention me, by name, and it sounds legit. I didn't want her to read it over the phone on an unsecured line. Admiral, I need to get over to Lanham to see it, myself."

"Okay. Do you need anyone from Security to go with you? You want me to call Langley?"

"No, thank you, Sir. Not right now. I want to look at this thing myself, first."

"Check with me when you get back," said the Chief of Naval Operations. "I'll be here late tonight."

"Aye-Aye, Sir."

The clock on the wall was an old "Regulator" pendulum clock

that had belonged to Admiral Hrupak's grandfather. The clock struck its chimes on the hour. Even the sound was antique. It was eleven o'clock p.m.

Three men sat around a small table in the office of the Chief of Naval Operations: Ed Hrupak, Bob Copper, and Rear Admiral-Select Trace Dawson, the head of Navy SEALs. A knock on the door announced the arrival of a fourth man, Mike Schaeffer, from the C.I.A. Hrupak had called Schaeffer earlier in the evening on his secure line to Langley. Ed had worked with him before, and respected his advice. He knew that Mike Schaeffer could be trusted.

Schaeffer sat beside Trace Dawson at the table. Bob Copper handed him a copy of Bill Winning's message.

Schaeffer took several minutes to study the message. "If this isn't legitimate, Sir, someone has gone to a lot of trouble to plant a hoax. Look at this." Schaeffer pointed at the coded letters at the bottom of the message. "This is the code for the sending station. I don't recognize this particular station, but it is definitely a code for a station in Syria. I can check back at Langley to find out which station.

"The reference to Bill Winning is obvious." Schaeffer continued, "but why the second sentence? 'REPEAT SUCCESS IN SECTOR A.W. 75.' This looks clearly to be masked to get it by a censor. The Syrians have been censoring all transmissions out of their message centers ever since Zabadi took over – even before the war. Now, who is this 'Dr. A.A. Pender-Cudlipp?' Has anyone called this 'Dr. McQuaid' at the University of London?"

"No, Mike. I wanted to talk to you, first." Admiral Hrupak spoke. "I want to be real careful about how many people get their hands on this thing."

"You're right, Admiral." Schaeffer continued, "What about this Bible reference: '2 Kings 6:17.' Anybody check it out?"

Bob Copper responded, "Mike, that Bible reference cinches it. This message is no hoax. It was sent to Dr. Steve Whitney. He is a professor at Washington Bible College out in Lanham. He is Bill Winning's father-in-law. I met with him and with Susan Winning all afternoon. This Bible reference is very special." Admiral Copper took a copy of the Bible that was among the stack of documents piled before him on the desk. A bookmark guided him to the correct passage.

"Look at this." Copper opened the Bible to the sixth chapter of the Second Book of Kings, and set it in front of the C.I.A. man. "This is a story about war between the Syrians and the Israelis. In the story, the Syrians are about to wipe out an Israeli prophet, but God sends his 'Chariots of Fire' and saves him. Now, Mike, this is what absolutely convinces me this is not a hoax: Dr. Whitney tells me that on the very night before Susan and Bill Winning left for their vacation to the Holy Land, they tucked their kids into bed with this bedtime story. There's not a doubt in my mind that this is Bill Winning verifying a message to us."

"O.K., Bob, I agree," Schaeffer continued to study the message, "but I think there's more to it than that. Look at the way he's worded this: 'Grave situation as in 2 Kings 6:17.' What is the 'grave situation' in 2 Kings 6:17?" Schaeffer picked up Bob Copper's Bible. He read for a moment in silence.

"He may be trying to tell us something else, too. What is the 'grave situation' here? The Syrians have surrounded the Israelis with an overwhelming force. Only God's Chariots of Fire could intervene to protect them. And then, Bob, the very next thing he asks for is your 'Sierra Sierra November equipment.' SSNs! He's calling for nuclear fast attack submarines!"

"He also wants Dawson's SEALs in on this," Copper said. "I agree, gentlemen. This looks pretty clear. As clear as you can get in a jury-rigged, censored, coded message. Now, the big question: what should we do about it?"

Bob Copper continued, "First thing, we need to call this guy McQuaid in London." Copper pointed to the message. "'Call the University of London, Professor McQuaid for location.' It sounds as though 'Professor McQuaid' might know where the message originated. Maybe he could tell us who is this 'Professor A.A. Pender-Cudlipp.' Then, when we know where Bill is, I send in a couple of submarines rigged with SDV's, and Daws, here, can send in some of his SEALs to get Bill out. Can you handle that, Daws?"

"That's what they pay us for, Bob." Trace Dawson smiled. "You tell us where he is, we'll get him back."

"Sounds great, people, but you're forgetting something." The CNO, Ed Hrupak, unfurled his wet blanket. "There's a war going on over there. The President himself has directly ordered me not to place any unit of any kind within two hundred fifty kilometers of that combat zone. I've got the Chairman of the Joint Chiefs of Staff checking with me twice a day to be sure that I properly understand that order. I can't allow you people to go charging into Syria like John Wayne and the Cavalry."

"Sir," said Vice Admiral Copper, "if we find out where Bill Winning is, I plan to go get him myself, even if I have to turn in my badge. Bill Winning is a citizen of the United States of America. So are the other people those thugs took off the bus and shot in cold blood. I know very well that we have to walk carefully as a country in this world, but it's high time we stood up for our own citizens when they are kidnapped and murdered like this."

"O.K., O.K., Bob," Hrupak held up his hand, "you can simmer down for a moment. Here's what we can do. First, I agree, let's call this Professor McQuaid in London. Mike, can you take care of that?"

"Sure," Mike Schaeffer responded.

"Bob," continued the CNO, "I want you and Admiral Dawson to work up an operating plan for this rescue. Daws, this is obviously SEAL Team Six business."

The CNO referred to the super-elite SEAL force that was so secret even its existence had never been officially recognized by the American government. With headquarters at Dam Neck, Virginia, away from other SEAL organizations, SEAL Team Six was specially trained and equipped to perform counter-terrorism and rescue operations. This Hazor Hostages job was right up their alley. One hitch: SEAL Team Six received orders only from the Secretary of Defense, or the President of the United States, directly.

Admiral Hrupak continued, "I will call the Chairman of the Joint Chiefs of Staff right now." We need to get the National Security Advisor, the Secretary of Defense, and the President in on this right away."

"How about State?" interjected Mike Schaeffer.

"Oh, sure, why not?" Admiral Hrupak scowled at his friend from C.I.A. "Thanks a lot, Mike. I'll let General Tippett handle that." General Vernon Tippett was the Chairman of the Joint Chiefs of Staff.

———————

Admiral Bob Copper slept fitfully on the couch in his temporary Pentagon office. He had been awake all night, working with Chip DePew, Trace Dawson and several of their top staff assistants to prepare a detailed operations plan for the rescue of Bill Winning and the other Hazor Hostages. The next step was to get the thumbs-up from Admiral Hrupak.

Earlier, at about three o'clock a.m., Mike Schaeffer had called with good news. He had been able to contact Professor Allen McQuaid in London. McQuaid knew this Pender-Cudlipp. Dr. Archibald Pender-Cudlipp was a respected archaeologist working on a dig in northern Syria. Without revealing the nature of the situation, Schaeffer had been able to get the precise location of Pender-Cudlipp's archaeology site. It was not far from the message center indicated by the coded figures at the bottom of the message. Schaeffer had traced the code to a little village called Q'adi, in northwest Syria. This information fit well the tone of the message; it enabled Copper and Dawson to put the finishing touch on the details of their operations plan.

At about seven a.m., Bob Copper called Lanham. He informed Steve and Susan that they had been in touch with McQuaid in London, and that "appropriate steps were being taken to find a ride" for Susan's husband. Copper promised to contact them later in the day with more details.

Before he reclined for his nap, Admiral Copper had left word with Captain DePew to wake him if Admiral Hrupak called, or if there was any more news.

Bob Copper's nap was a short one. At about ten fifteen a.m., Chip DePew knocked on the door and entered the darkened office. "Excuse me, Admiral Copper! Admiral Hrupak just called."

Bob Copper sat up immediately and began to straighten his tie. "What did he say, Chip? Is it a go?"

"He didn't say," answered Captain DePew. "He wants to get together with you and the others at ten thirty in his office."

It took Bob Copper about ten minutes to shave and splash his face with cold water and after-shave. He arrived at the CNO's office at exactly ten thirty a.m., just as Mike Schaeffer was entering from another stairwell. Trace Dawson was already at his place at Hrupak's conference table, as was Preston Sullivan, from the State Department. Copper and Schaeffer took their seats.

A moment later, Ed Hrupak entered the room, accompanied by the Chairman of the Joint Chiefs of Staff, General Vernon Tippett. They were not smiling. Not a good sign, thought Bob Copper.

Admiral Hrupak opened the meeting. "I don't know if what I'm about to say is good news or not, gentlemen. The President has been personally briefed on this message, and our request for action. I will tell you, he was initially dead-set against our taking any action, at all. He wants no potential for interference in the Syria-Israel War. The President was against our request, the Secretary of Defense was against it, and the Secretary of State was against it. Well, I took a page out of your book, Bob Copper. I gave them the *These are American Citizens...I'll Turn in My Badge* speech. It's a speech you can only use about once in a career, but I figured this was the time to use it. Then, what do you know? General Tippett offers to turn in his badge, too." Admiral Hrupak looked over at the Chairman of the Joint Chiefs of Staff.

"You should have heard your boss, Bob." General Tippett pointed his thumb at Hrupak. He sounded like Travis at the Alamo. 'We've got to draw the line, Mr. President. I don't care who's at war with whom; we cannot allow American citizens to be treated like this. Anywhere. Anytime.' Fortunately, Stan Summ was at the meeting." Tippett referred to the powerful North Carolina senator who headed the Senate Armed Services Committee. "Senator Summ took our point, and at least got us a partial victory."

"That's the good news." Ed Hrupak leaned forward at the table as he grumbled, "Here's the bad news: Only one submarine. Only one SEAL team. No torpedoes."

Bob Copper broke the brief silence that had enveloped the room. "One submarine, I understand, Admiral. One SEAL team I understand. But why specify 'no torpedoes'? We always have to get Presidential release on any torpedo firing unless it is in direct response to an enemy attack."

"I'm not just talking about not being released to shoot your torpedoes, Bob. I mean *no torpedoes at all*. You won't be authorized to carry torpedoes on this mission."

"Admiral...!"

"Bob," Hrupak cut Copper short, "this is an order from the President, himself. This is the President's idea; it is his condition for this mission. This is to be strictly a SEAL team operation. The sub is to be merely a SEAL delivery platform. Whatever you can accomplish with one SEAL Team and no torpedoes is fair game, but nothing more. Even Stan Summ backed down on this one, Bob. If you think we can't do it, let me know now, and I'll tell the President that the mission is off."

Copper paused for a moment. Then he said, "Sir, let me talk to Will Garrett over in Naples. I'll get him right now on a secure line. It's his boat I want to use. The old *Joshua L. Chamberlain*. But I'm not going to send him in to a war zone unarmed unless he knows what it's all about, and agrees to it. Will you excuse me while I make a phone call?"

"Sure, Bob."

Navy Lieutenant Eric Lindahl was a farm boy. He had grown up in near poverty on a small farm in southeastern Kansas. The flinty soil struggled to provide enough crops to keep the Lindahl family solvent. To young Eric, the prospect of following his forefathers and his older brothers into the farming business was unthinkable. His impression of farming was that of a constant stream of battles with drought, floods, mortgage bankers, and government agents. Eric was a battler, he had been a state champion high school wrestler, but he wanted better odds in the fight than what he got as a farmer.

Lindahl was a quiet, serious young man. He was an excellent student, and a determined athlete, so it surprised few people when he was offered an appointment to the Naval Academy at Annapolis. What did surprise the folks back in Wilson County Kansas, however, was that, upon graduation, Eric Lindahl had chosen to become a Navy SEAL.

Eric knew the legend and the numbers: No more than one new trainee in twenty graduated with their entering class at BUD/SEAL training. But, to Eric Lindahl, those were much better odds than his family of farmers faced back in Kansas.

Everyone struggles through the SEAL training program. That certainly included Ensign Eric Lindahl. But, not once during the entire twenty-six weeks did it cross Eric's mind that he might not make it. Not once did he contemplate ringing the "Quitting Bell." Lindahl did well, very well. His reputation and his calm, quiet demeanor came to the attention of Commander Dave Carry, who commanded SEAL Team Six. Carry resolved to keep an eye on the career of the farm boy from the Flint Hills of Kansas.

---

1 March
Dam Neck, Virginia

Commander Carry was an excellent judge of SEAL-potential. By now a lieutenant, Eric Lindahl had proved to be an exceptional leader of SEALs. He was placed in command of a special unit called the "Gold Squad" of SEAL Team Six that was prepared especially for assignment, as necessary, in the Middle East. Lieutenant Lindahl was "boss," the only officer on the squad. The second in command was Chief Hospital Corpsman (HMC) Brett Nelson, a seasoned veteran of the SEALs, whose special areas of expertise included near-fluency in the Arabic language and extensive para-medical training. Radioman First Class (RM1) John Scott had been a SEAL for eight years. He was the communicator and the navigator of the squad. Scott was a computer and electronics wizard, whether on duty or at home with his beloved personal computer and ham radio gear. Rob Petrocelli, a machinist first class (MM1), rounded out the elite unit. Rob had that mechanic's knack of being able to fix anything that was broken: weapons, trucks, boats, anything. Machines were his element. All four men were proficient with virtually every field weapon available to the SEALs. Among them, they had racked up many impressive titles at shooting tournaments around the country.

John Scott poked his head into Lieutenant Lindahl's office trailer. "'Scuse me, sir. Commander Carry wants to see you right away over at headquarters."

"Okay, John, thanks," said Lindahl. "What's up? Did he say?"

"No, Sir," responded Scott, "but he was on the secure line to the Pentagon talking to Admiral Dawson just a little earlier."

"The Pentagon?" groused Lindahl. "They probably want to cut some more out of our budget. You don't really need a radio, do you, John?"

"Nahh! We can use smoke signals, boss."

Lindahl pulled on his windbreaker, and headed across the yard to the headquarters building.

"Good morning, Dave." Eric Lindahl addressed Commander Carry. "John said you wanted to see me."

"Yes, Eric. We've got a big one." Dave Carry took a folder from the desk in front of him. "It looks like the real thing. You know those hostages that were taken two months ago at Hazor in Israel? You've been keeping tabs on this in your Current Situations File, right?"

"Yes, sir!" Eric replied. "I figured we might get involved in it somehow, sooner or later."

"Good," said Carry. "You are going to get involved, all right. The President has authorized Team Six to go in to Syria and get the hostages out. I want to use your Gold Squad."

"Syria?" Eric was surprised. "Everything in our file says they are probably in Israel. Did we get a tip? What do we know?"

Commander Carry spent the next forty-five minutes briefing Eric Lindahl on the situation. "That's all we know for now, Eric," concluded Commander Carry. "Get your squad together. We will board the chopper at fourteen thirty; you'll be on your way to Naples in an hour."

"Aye-Aye Sir." Eric Lindahl did not have to tell his boss that he was ready. Commander Carry knew it.

---

2 March
U.S. Naval Base, Naples, Italy

USS Joshua L. Chamberlain sat low and dark next to the huge gray submarine tender. A casual observer, passing by the wharf at the Naval Base in Naples very likely would have missed seeing the submarine at all. Her fairwater sail looked like a flattened black barrel, sitting on end in the water, with absurd fin-like appurtenances sticking out each side. These were *Chamberlain* 's fairwater planes. Two sailors stood, one on each of the two fairwater planes, tied down with safety harnesses. Each wore his blue patrol coveralls, an orange life vest, and a set of sound-powered phones. Just above them, three officers crowded into the small opening at the top of the sail, just forward of the periscopes. Lieutenant Wayne Bryant, the OOD, shouted orders down to the line-handlers, on the deck below them.

"Cast off all lines!"

Every step was watched closely by *Chamberlain*'s Commanding Officer, Commander Will Garrett, and by one of the US submarine force's top brass, Vice Admiral Robert Copper. The officers were also dressed in blue coveralls and baseball caps.

Bryant ordered the use of *Chamberlain*'s "SPM," the Secondary Propulsion Motor. The SPM was lowered through the outer hull in a special compartment near the ship's longitudinal centerline. Rotated ninety degrees, the SPM enabled the ship to move slowly away from her berth alongside the tender. Once safely free of the tender, and with lines safely cast off the submarine, Bryant gave orders to the lookout that stood on the fairwater plane at his port side, "House the SPM".

The port lookout repeated the order, "House the SPM, Aye." Then, speaking into his sound-powered phone mouthpiece, the lookout relayed the order below. "House the SPM."

After a few seconds' wait, the port lookout reported back to the OOD, "SPM reports housed, Sir."

"Very well. Ahead one-third. Steer course one-six-zero."

"Ahead one-third, steer course one-six-zero, aye." Into the sound-powered phones, "Ahead one-third, steer course one-six-zero."

Chamberlain was underway. People who have spent time around the water, who are familiar with boats, are often surprised watching a nuclear submarine go to sea. Getting underway is, traditionally, a noisy business. Every fisherman knows the sound: yank on the outboard engine motor, rev 'er up to max RPM, peel away in a turmoil of smoke and noise, frighten every fish in the pond. Nuclear ships are not like that. Following the order to apply power from the main engines to the propeller shaft, not a sound could be heard. The noisy, high-pitched SPM had been tucked away, and now the silent, powerful main engines went to work. The only evidence of the enormous power under Lieutenant Bryant's control was the churning of the water of Naples harbor into a muddy gray soup.

The old submarine had been built back in the sixties as a *Polaris* missile-firing Fleet Ballistic Missile "boomer." Like all her *Benjamin Franklin* class sister-ships, she had been named after great American patriots. *Joshua Lawrence Chamberlain* was named to honor the great Hero of Little Round Top from the Civil War Battle of Gettysburg. The ship's name had also been a thank-you to the congressional delegation from Chamberlain's home state of Maine for their support of the Navy's budget requests for the expensive boomers.

As *Chamberlain* twisted her way out of the harbor, observers would note that she was uglier than the ordinary submarine. Unlike many of her sister-boomers, *Chamberlain* had been spared the indignity of being decommissioned and cut up for scrap. She had been converted to a special-purpose attack submarine. A cluster of black-painted tanks was stuck to *Chamberlain*'s hull just aft of her sail, giving the appearance of giant parasites. The cluster consisted of two large horizontal cylinders. These were known as the Dry Deck Shelters ("DDSs"). These are the "storage barns" that hold the Swimmer Delivery Vehicles ("SDVs"), the mini-subs that SEALs use to sneak into their mission zones.

For the mission at hand, Eric Lindahl and his Gold Squad would be using an old Mark VIII SDV. It was just what the doctor ordered.

H ⟋⟋⟋⟋⟋⟋⟋⟋⟋⟋⟋⟋ H

|←————100 YARDS————→|

SCALE ILLUSTRATION
(Approximate)

USS *JOSHUA L. CHAMBERLAIN*

American Nuclear Attack Submarine
SSN (ex-SSBN)
Converted from
Benjamin Franklin Class Fleet Ballistic Missile
Submarine
Displacement: 7,330 tons (surfaced)
8,250 tons (submerged)
Length: 425 ft.
Beam: 33 ft.

Chapter Twenty-Four

Angels

3 March
Eastern Mediterranean

L IEUTENANT ERIC LINDAHL WAS IN CHARGE of the SEAL aspects of "Operation Angel." His squad had practiced the exit maneuver countless times, in mock-up facilities at Dam Neck and at sea aboard DDS-modified submarines. There was little need for Lindahl to give verbal orders; each man knew what he was to do and how he was to do it.

Six SEALs and one submariner waited in the SEAL Launch/Recovery Area of *USS Joshua L. Chamberlain*. This was in the space that had been, back in *Chamberlain*'s boomer-days, the Missile Compartment, affectionately known then by the crew as the "Rocket Room." It was the largest compartment on the ship, but was now known as the "Game Room" or the "Arcade" because of all the SEAL-support physical fitness equipment, special weapons, ammunition, and other gear carried there. Eric Lindahl stood just under the DDS access hatch. He would supervise the opening of the hatch, along with the submariner, *Chamberlain*'s Engineering Watch Supervisor, Master Chief Electrician Dennis Brunnert. Standing just aft of Lindahl, the two SEAL SDV mini-sub operators would be the first to enter the first-stage access trunk. Chief Machinist (MMC) John Logan would be the SDV pilot. Logan was known throughout the SEAL community as "Poco," for no apparent reason. He was not small, as the Spanish word would suggest. The name just seemed to fit. Quartermaster First Class (QM1) Paul Crandall would be the SDV navigator. Crandall was known as "Fogie," and everyone knew why: his disdain for popular music and modern culture of any type firmly established him as an "Old Fogie." Both Logan and Crandall were experienced SEALs, specially trained in operation and maintenance of the SDV mini-subs that would deliver Lindahl's angel team part way to its destination.

The angel team waited patiently in a line just aft of the SDV operators. HMC Brett Nelson was first. In addition to his old eight-shot Ithaca 37 pump shotgun, he carried a special pack of medical equipment and supplies. Chief Nelson had assembled the pack especially for this mission, anticipating the particular needs that the hostages might have.

RM1 John Scott waited next. He carried, in addition to his Hechler & Koch submachine gun, a Special Operations Communications rig, including satellite navigation and voice communications gear.

Last in the line was MM1 Rob Petrocelli. He carried an M-16 rifle with an M203 40-mm grenade launcher that was designed to be mounted under the barrel of the rifle. He also carried a Special Weapons Pack, with explosives, silencers and other devices selected for this mission.

Eric Lindahl and his team had spent hours since they left Dam Neck, pouring over maps and intelligence reports. They had gone over every scenario that they could imagine for this operation. Information gleaned from Professor McQuaid at the University of London described the area of the site mentioned by Pender-Cudlipp in the message. Their "M.L.S.," Most Likely Scenario, involved action at a remote site on the far side of the mountain called Jabal ad Farabi, in the desert region of Wadi el-Jari. But the SEALs were also ready for action, if necessary, in the mountains, along the seashore, or even in the villages of northwestern Syria.

USS Joshua L. Chamberlain had arrived at the specified drop point, 8.5 kilometers off the coast of Syria, about twenty kilometers northwest of the Syrian port city of Latakia. *Chamberlain* had crept slowly into the war zone, her skipper cognizant of orders, directly from the American Commander-in-Chief, to remain undetected. Now, at the drop point, she prepared to hover.

Hovering was a relatively simple task for the newer classes of American submarines. These were equipped with specially designed hovering ballast tanks that allowed water to be moved quietly as needed to maintain proper trim, by computer-operated valves and pumps. But, on the old *Chamberlain*, her antique hovering system was perpetually inoperable, a victim of budget cuts that curtailed maintenance and upgrades. So, the delicate hovering procedure had to be accomplished by the sheer skill of the ship's diving officer, using the submarine's ordinary trim tanks. The normal first three priorities of submarine depth control are ruled out when hovering: use of planes, angle and speed. The planes and the ship's angle have absolutely no effect on depth control with the speed at zero, and hovering can be a tricky maneuver. But *Chamberlain*'s battle stations diving officer was Lieutenant Chuck Staggs, a veteran of two tours of duty aboard the old ex-boomer. That experience was about to pay off.

Staggs had made fine-tuning adjustments to the ship's trim as she crept in at very low speed to the drop point. He not only had to assure that the ship had just enough water in her ballast tanks to achieve, precisely, neutral buoyancy, he had also to assure that exactly the right amount of water was pumped from forward trim tanks to aft trim tanks to maintain exact fore-and-aft balance. It was a delicate maneuver, accomplished as much by experience and "feel" as by calculation.

Little things could make a big difference: a ship at exact neutral buoyancy moving into a layer of relatively warmer water might sink like a rock because of the increased density of the water in her tanks compared to that of the surrounding ocean. Or, if a large number of the ship's crew emerged from the crew's mess after a movie, and proceeded as a group to the bow compartment for a card game, the fore and aft trim could be affected: the ship would tend to tip down.

With all this in mind, Lieutenant Staggs watched the digital readout of the ship's speed indicator. He watched it count down, slowly, to zero point zero-zero knots. He also watched the ship's depth indicator approach 150 feet.

The ship's angle held steady at two degrees down bubble.

Staggs waited, calmly glancing at his wrist watch. One minute had passed since the speed had indicated dead stop. The ship's digital depth indicator had been fluttering between 150.5 and 149.0 feet. Soon, the fluttering stopped, and the depth settled at exactly 150.0 feet. The ship's angle stayed constant. Another minute passed. At the three minute mark, Staggs made a fist and silently cheered, "Yes!" He turned to *Chamberlain*'s captain, Commander Garrett, and reported, "Ship is hovering at 150 feet, Sir. Diving station ready to commence SDV launch sequence, Sir."

"Very well." Will Garrett took the 1-MC general announcing circuit mike off its hook and spoke. "Now, this is the captain. Commence SDV launch sequence. Commence SDV launch sequence." The skipper put the 1-MC mike back on its hook and turned to his diving officer. "Good job, Chuck. Now we get a chance to see how good your compensation calcs are after they launch that thing."

"No problem, Skipper," responded Lieutenant Staggs. "I revised the density factor since last time. We'll be right on the money. No more circles this time."

During their last practice run, Lieutenant Staggs had over-compensated for the weight of the launched SDV plus its SEALs. He had flooded too much water in to the ballast tanks, and the ship began to sink too quickly for him to correct by pumping. He had to ask for speed in order to bring the ship back up to ordered depth. *Chamberlain* had sunk to 235 feet and had to circle around at one-third speed before Staggs could get the depth back under control, hovering again at the practice drop point at 150 feet. But now, Staggs was confident that his revised formula for figuring compensation would avoid that problem.

Back aft, Lieutenant Lindahl, his SDV drivers, and his angel team welcomed the order that came over the 1-MC. Now it was time for action. Chief Brunnert relayed messages to Control by way of a sailor who operated the sound powered phones.

"Chief, Control reports conditions dry in after escape trunk. Straight board," reported the phone operator. "Permission granted to crack lower trunk hatch."

"Crack lower trunk hatch, Aye." Brunnert took three steps up the ladder leading up to the trunk. He grabbed the stainless steel hand wheel and firmly hammered it open. The hatch cracked slightly, accompanied by a rush of air, equalizing the pressure between the escape hatch and the submarine.

"Lower escape trunk hatch cracked, escape trunk dry, permission to go up?" requested Chief Brunnert.

The phone operator repeated the request, seeking permission from the captain up in the control room. After a moment, he reported, "Control acknowledges lower hatch open, Chief.

Permission granted to go up into the trunk."

Chief Brunnert scurried up into the access trunk. He turned on the battle lantern, triggered the 27-MC speaker-phone and conducted a phone check with it. He inspected other vital features of the trunk, and found conditions to be normal. Brunnert would now supervise the rest of the DDS entry procedure, getting the SDV-drivers, Logan and Crandall, in the barn first.

Illuminated by four emergency battle lanterns, the pudgy SDV rested in its hangar, resembling an Olympic-type bobsled, stuck in a large sewer pipe. This Mark VIII SDV was 6.35 meters long, 1.3 meters wide, and 1.3 meters high. Her gray-black fiberglass hull had two hinged ports, one on each side near the bow, for the pilot and navigator, and four ports near the stern, two on each side for the angel team.

Logan and Crandall finished their pre-launch checks. Crandall triggered the 27-MC speaker in the hangar chamber. "Control, Hangar. Pre-launch checks complete. You can send up the angels."

Poco Logan took his place in the left-hand pilot's station. Fogie Crandall sat beside him, in the navigator's position.

Back inside the submarine, Chief Brunnert ushered the angel team into the access trunk, and on in to the hangar chambers. Arriving at the SDV, each man placed his weapons and cargo in special cells in the vehicle, then took his seat.

John Scott and Rob Petrocelli sat side-by-side in the two middle positions. Brett Nelson and Eric Lindahl sat in the aft section. All six SEALs locked their safety harnesses in place and connected the Mark XV underwater breathing apparatus "UBA." This connected them to the SDV's on-board computer controlled, mixed gas breathing system. Its full-face mask was also fitted with connections to the on-board communications circuit. While the SDV remained aboard *Chamberlain*, they could also communicate with the submarine's control room on the ship's 27-MC circuit.

Poco Logan was now in tactical control of the launch sequence. "Angel check, over." Logan spoke into the Mark XV system.

"Angel three, locked in, ready," Rob Petrocelli reported.

"Angel two locked in, ready." John Scott.

"Angel one locked in, ready." Brett Nelson.

"Angel boss locked in, ready. Let's go, Poco." Eric Lindahl.

Switching to the ship's 27-MC circuit, Chief Logan continued the procedure. "Control, this is Pilot. Ready to proceed with launch sequence. Ready to launch. Flood hangar."

"Flood hangar, Aye." It was the voice of Chief Quartermaster Lee MacWaters, *Chamberlain*'s Chief of the Watch, located in the control room. It was his job to communicate on the 27-MC circuit to the SDV Pilot, and to manipulate the switches that controlled the pneumatic and hydraulic systems that would, in turn, flood the DDS. He also had to operate the ballast control panel, maintaining hover trim as ordered by the diving officer, Lieutenant Staggs. Chief MacWaters was a busy man.

The process of keeping pressure equalized across the eardrums while the chamber was being pressurized was second nature to the SEALs. This came as easy to them as breathing and swallowing. The noise and discomfort of the flooding and pressurizing of the launch chamber was just another day at work. The process, by design, was slow. They waited, and equalized as the water in the chamber crept up over their shoulders and over their heads. The men breathed easily through their Mark XV system and rehearsed one more time, in their minds, the procedures they would follow.

"Pilot, Control. Hangar indicates flooded. Pressure indicates equalized."

"Control, Pilot. Roger. Request you open outer door. Stand by for launch."

"Pilot, Control. Open outer door, Aye." Soon, the SEALs could hear the muffled "pop" of the pilot valves controlling the hydraulic rams that would un-dog the outer door and push it open.

There were no windows on the SDV. When Chief Logan triggered the lever to activate his battery-powered five bladed propeller, he would be piloting blind. He would depend on his sidekick, the navigator, Fogie Crandall, to give him the correct course to steer and depth to maintain.

Nelson had at his disposal some very effective hi-tech aids, including a computerized Doppler Navigation System ("DNS"). This gave the SEALs some idea of where they were, and where they were headed, until they could emerge on land and John Scott could use his satellite navigation equipment to get a more accurate fix.

Fogie Crandall also operated a special Obstacle Avoidance System. The "OAS" was a sophisticated sonar system that could give early warning of obstacles that might confront the mini-sub as she made her 4.5 knots toward the beach.

"Pilot, Control." It was Chief MacWaters again. "Outer door indicates open, you are free to launch. Repeat you are free to launch. Bring 'em back safe, Angels."

"That's a Roger, Control. Commencing launch. Shifting to Gertrude." Poco Logan reached for the power control handle. He depressed the button in the top of the handle and eased it forward, to about one third of its limit of travel. He then turned his communications switch from "27-MC" to "Gertrude." As the SDV moved out of its launch tube, it would be severed from the ship's 27-MC circuit. Angel Chariot would now communicate with *Chamberlain* by means of the old sonar-energy ship-to-ship communications system known as "Gertrude."

The SEALs felt a gentle nudge as the SDV began to exit its hangar. The sound was that of a child playing in a bathtub, dragging a metal toy across the bottom of the tub. The SDV slid along its launch rail, nosing down slightly as it exited the hangar. Poco Logan manipulated the trim switch, adjusting the moveable lead weight that ran along the bottom of the vessel, to adjust their fore-and-aft trim. The SDV leveled out, and all was quiet, except for the steady hum of the battery-operated motor. Logan nudged the stick forward, and the pitch of the motor's hum increased slightly.

"We're free of *Chamberlain*," Fogie Nelson spoke into his Mark XV headset. "Increase to full speed and steer course zero-eight-five."

"Increase to full speed, steer course zero-eight-five, Aye. Maintaining depth at 150 feet," said Logan. He nudged the stick all the way forward. He turned his steering control wheel to the right, and watched the course indicator steady on 085 degrees. They were headed east, toward the coast of Syria.

Logan depressed the Gertrude button, and addressed *Chamberlain*'s call sign. "Maine Yankee, Maine Yankee...this is Angel Chariot, Angel Chariot...We're free. Launch complete, over."

"Angel Chariot, this is Maine Yankee. Launch complete, Aye. God Bless, Angels."

"Poco! The bottom's coming up too fast! Recommend you come up to depth five-zero feet!" QM1 Fogie Crandall pointed his light on a plastic-coated navigation chart and kept an eye on the depth sounder. "The water here is a lot shallower than it shows on the charts," reported Crandall, a note of concern in his voice.

"Five-zero feet, Aye." MMC Poco Logan adjusted the lead trim-weight aft to give the SDV a slight up angle. He went to "full rise" on the bow planes of their mini-sub.

The depth indicator began to click down from 150 feet to 148 feet, then, slowly to 145 feet. Logan settled out the SDV for a time at each fifteen feet of ascent, according to standard procedure.

"Depth sounding here is coming up rapidly, Poco! " said Crandall. "255 feet and decreasing. Recommend you slow to one-third."

"Slow to one-third, Aye," responded Logan. "Passing seven-two feet coming to six-zero feet. Fogie, I don't remember seeing any sea mounts indicated anywhere near us from studying the charts, do you? I thought this was supposed to be pretty flat country."

"There are a few little hills to the north of our track, but nothing like this!" answered Crandall. "Depth sounding now 175 feet and decreasing. According to our charts and the DNS we should be in depths of over 400 feet here. We are about 4.5 kilometers from the shore line...Wait! Poco, I've got a signal on the OAS. Dead ahead. It's faint, but it's there. Recommend dead-slow."

"Dead-slow, Aye." Logan moved the control stick almost all the way back to its stop position. "Let's move up to 45 feet. Do you hear anything else in the area?"

"Negative. Not a thing." Crandall checked the scope on his sonar set. "Nobody out here tonight but us."

"O.K., I'm going to ease to the south for a while to see if we can clear the OAS." Logan turned his wheel to the right.

Angel Chariot made her way slowly around the southern edge of the uncharted underwater hillock. Seated in the right rear position, Lieutenant Eric Lindahl listened intently to the communications between his pilot and his navigator. He was thankful that this little craft was equipped with such effective high-tech gear. He also hoped that there would be no additional surprises on this trip. There were enough uncertainties in this mission without having to worry about inaccurate navigational charts.

About ninety minutes later, a full twenty minutes behind their original schedule, Angel Chariot arrived at the selected rendezvous, "Romeo point." Here, the sandy bottom was fifteen feet deep, and the tide was negligible. Eric Lindahl's angel team would have an easy 500 meter swim to what was expected to be a narrow, uninhabited beach. Thick, jungle-like forest spread out for miles to the north and to the south along the shore line. A small fishing village lay about five kilometers north, and an old resort hotel sat on the beach about fifteen kilometers to the south, but this particular point was selected because it was known rarely to be used by anyone.

Although Lindahl's team was late, there was still plenty of darkness left. It was 4:12 a.m., local time. As he first emerged from the SDV to the surface, Lindahl noticed with satisfaction that low, dark clouds hid, at least for the moment, the full moon that could have yielded dangerous bright moonlight.

The plan was for each member of the angel team to proceed directly to the beach with their equipment packs and weapons. The angels would then move rapidly into the forest to reassemble, check their gear, and take final instructions prior to moving out to the area of the Jabal ad Farabi.

Meanwhile, Logan and Crandall would stay near the Romeo point to keep an eye on Angel Chariot and wait for the angels' return. They would anchor the SDV at the sandy bottom of the Romeo point, and then paddle in with two rubber rafts, establishing a base camp at a spot to be indicated by the angel team, which the angels would mark with an electronic beeper. When the angels returned, they hoped to be bringing rescued hostages with them. From what Lindahl could gather, there would be no more than four hostages, but, regardless of how many there were, the SEALs intended to ferry them back to the safety of *Chamberlain*.

Eric Lindahl arrived at the beach first, and he scurried with his pack into the forest. The beach was only about fifteen meters wide at this point, just as the intelligence had indicated. There was no evidence of any human activity in the area. Brett Nelson followed closely on the lieutenant's heels, and hustled into the cover of the woods. John Scott arrived next. He looked around briefly for his team, and caught a glimpse of Lindahl's pen light signal, flashing from the edge of the forest, just to his south. Rob Petrocelli, struggling with the heaviest of the equipment packs, arrived about one minute later. He quickly caught sight of Lindahl's pen light and joined his team.

The SEALs all donned their night-vision glasses. They stepped slowly, quietly through the thick underbrush. Month after month of training in the thicker brush around Dam Neck in the Virginia Tidewater area had made Lindahl and his team experts in moving swiftly and silently in such conditions. They moved inland about one hundred fifty meters to a spot where a fallen tree made for good natural cover. Lindahl and his team set their gear down near the tree and rested.

"This spot looks as though it has the makings of a decent base camp," observed Lindahl. Thick vegetation grew on three sides. Behind them, a six-meter embankment rose to provide shelter as well as good possible vantage points for viewing the area. "Brett, you and Rob go scan the area for the next ten minutes and let me know if you see a better spot," directed the lieutenant.

"Aye, aye, Sir." The two SEALs crept off to the north.

"John, let me see the map for a minute," the angel boss spoke to his navigation-communicator.

"Aye, Sir." John Scott removed a plastic-covered map from a pocket in his equipment pack. Lindahl cupped his hand over the tiny beam of his pen-light, and studied the map.

"O.K., John," said the lieutenant. "Looks as though we've hit the beach just north of target. We're off maybe 750 meters. I'm glad the chart is better here than it was back there in the Med." The two men studied the map for several minutes.

"Sir, I didn't see any evidence of any people, north or south of us," said RM1 Scott. "Looks to me that we'll be able to take the primary route that we had laid out to Jabal ad Farabi."

"I hope so," replied Lindahl as he studied the map. "Let's wait to see what Brett and Rob report when they come back. Will you hand me the chart of the Wadi el-Jari region?"

Scott went back to his equipment pack and brought out another map. The two men unfolded it and scanned it for a moment. A cricket's chirp could be heard, nearby, toward the southern base of the hill that rose just behind them. Lindahl looked up quickly, flicking the pen-light off. He then repeated the chirp.

Brett Nelson stepped from behind a tree, followed by Rob Petrocelli. Without making a sound, they joined Lindahl and Scott.

"Looks like a good spot, Sir," reported Nelson. "Rob climbed a tree near the top of that hill. He says it gives a good view, 360 degrees, for about 1500 meters."

"I looked around," Rob Petrocelli whispered. "Saw a few birds. That's all. This is a good spot for our base camp. Also looks as though we can probably use our primary trail to the Wadi, wouldn't you say, boss?"

"Looks like it, Rob," agreed Eric Lindahl. "O.K., gentlemen, assemble your gear and saddle up. John, are you ready to set the beeper?"

"It's all set, Sir."

"O.K.," said the angel boss, "let's head 'em up and move 'em out."

Chapter Twenty-Five

Discoveries

3 March
Wadi el Jari, Syria

PROFESSOR ARCHIBALD PENDER-CUDLIPP awoke just after midnight. It had been almost two days since he had last been able to slip out to the trailer to visit Bill Winning and Viktor Rypkin. It was time to replenish their supplies, and it was time to talk about plans. Archie pulled on his trousers, a light jacket, and his favorite straw hat. He went to his supply cabinet, and pulled out a box full of carefully selected items. Water was always at a premium; he had placed two gallons in another box. There were cans of beans and two packages of hard rolls. He also included a full bag of fresh oranges. It was no feast, but it was about the best he could do until he made another trip to Q'adi, later that morning.

Pender-Cudlipp took the boxes quietly out of his quarters, and placed them in the back of the Ford Bronco. He tried to be quiet, to place the doors barely on their latch, so that he would not arouse the suspicion of any of his workers. Not that many workers remained. Since the death of his wife, three more of the locals had quit. That left Professor Archie with only three others to work the dig. Of those, only Khalil Hinnawi and Fadl Rafat had any experience and Rafat was a difficult man, one he had to discipline often.

To make matters worse for the future of his project, the professor had received a message from London that indicated there was little hope of receiving any additional help during the upcoming season. For six long years, Archibald Pender-Cudlipp had fought every sort of battle to keep this project alive. He had suffered hunger, had been subjected to the harsh whims of Syrian officials, had cravenly begged for money, and had buried his wife, all to keep Project Jaris alive. But, with the receipt of London's message, it was obvious: it was over.

Now, he had stumbled across a story every bit as remarkable as the story that lay buried beneath the sands at Jaris. The American and the Russian were not fools and they were not insane. They were fugitives in a chase that had unimaginably high stakes. And now, Archibald was a vital part of it. While he may have been disappointed in his failing to fully uncover ancient history of great significance, he recognized that he might very well be involved in affecting current history in an even more profound way.

Professor Archie drove slowly away from the campsite, and crept the two kilometers around the hill to where the old trailer stood, along the bank of the wadi. Swift-moving dark clouds momentarily covered a bright, full moon. Archie stopped just in front of the trailer door. Glancing to his right and left and seeing no one, he knocked twice and then three times on the trailer door.

Professor Pender-Cudlipp had seen no one, but someone had seen him. Fadl Rafat had been suffering a sleepless night, worried about a variety of personal difficulties. He had heard the professor milling about his vehicle. It had struck Rafat as odd that the professor would be placing provisions in the back of his Bronco so early in the morning. So, Rafat, silently, secretly, had followed on foot behind the professor. As Pender-Cudlipp emerged from his vehicle and made his way to the trailer door, Fadl Rafat simply watched from a distance in curiosity.

"Hello, Archie," greeted Bill Winning. Winning had the sentry duty as Rypkin slept at the far end of the trailer. "It's great to see you this morning! We've been wondering what's up!" Winning extended a hand to help the professor into the trailer.

"I have a couple of boxes of goodies for you out in the Bronco," said Professor Archie. "I'll get them, in a minute. I wanted to let you two know what my plan for the day is."

"It's Thursday, isn't it? You're planning your Q'adi trip, right?" Bill asked.

"Yes," said the professor. "And, unless we have some kind of response to our message that I sent last week, I think I should send it again. It is, really, our only hope. Security has tightened all over. Soldiers are running all around Q'adi. I'm told they have beefed up the security checkpoints at all the border crossings. These people are at war, and it is getting very difficult to even breathe around here. Of course, I don't need to tell you two about that!"

"So you think it would be best to send the message, again?"

asked Winning.

"I think so, Bill," answered Pender-Cudlipp. "First of all, the censor did not seem to suspect anything when he read the message. He asked a few questions about the troubles we're having here at the dig, but I think the message seemed to slip by him just fine. My only concern is that either the message did not get through, or else your father-in-law had difficulty interpreting it. Maybe he thought it was a hoax. But, if we send it again, maybe he will have an easier time getting help. I don't know, but it is jolly well worth a try."

"Well, Archie, I agree with that," said Bill Winning. "Listen, you are putting your life on the line for us. I can't ask you to do any more. Maybe if Viktor and I just try to make a run for it to the west..."

"No more of that talk!" Pender-Cudlipp scolded Winning. "We have already covered that! I am in this all the way with you. We will, all of us, find a way out of here. Now, come and help me unload these provisions, before the moon comes out from behind those clouds and someone observes us."

Fadl Rafat, viewing the scene from a hillside about seventy meters away, was startled to see a man, a westerner, emerge from the old trailer, limping slightly, to join Pender-Cudlipp at the rear of the Bronco. He then saw another man, tall and thin, carrying a military rifle at his side. This third man jumped down from the trailer door and assisted in bringing provisions back into the trailer.

A thought developed in Fadl Rafat's mind. Had he not heard the story in Q'adi? Were there not two men fitting this description that were being sought by the Syrian army? Might there not be, in his observations, a partial solution to his own, pressing personal difficulties?

Fadl Rafat hurried away from his perch on the hillside back to his hut, two kilometers away at the campsite. He scurried back into his bed, without waking Khalil Hinnawi or the other Syrian who shared the hut. Rafat's mind raced as he considered the value that this new knowledge could bring him. He tingled with excitement at the thought of dashing Pender-Cudlipp's little secret. That pompous Englishman! Fadl Rafat relished the imagination of seeing Pender-Cudlipp, or any Englishman, grovel in the dust before a Syrian army inquisitor.

Rafat heard the sounds of Pender-Cudlipp's returning Bronco. He heard the professor go back in to his headquarters-house. A plan began to develop in Rafat's mind. Today was Thursday. Pender-Cudlipp would, no doubt, be making his weekly visit to Q'adi. He would, of course, have to travel past the new army installation on the other side of Jabal ad Farabi...

———

Professor Pender-Cudlipp had placed his papers and his suitcase in the back seat of the Bronco; he was nearly ready to depart for Q'adi. He went back into his kitchen to get a fresh cup of tea to sustain him for the first part of his trip. As he came back out to the vehicle, he noticed the Syrian, Fadl Rafat, standing nearby.

"Professor," said Rafat, in his meekly subservient tone, "you are preparing to depart for Q'adi, is this not so, Sir?"

"Yes, Rafat. You know that I ordinarily travel to Q'adi on Thursday. I expect to return tomorrow, as usual." Pender-Cudlipp thought this to be most unusual. Fadl Rafat rarely was up and about this early. Rafat was not a reliable worker. He had been caught, about a year before, pilfering small tools, which he evidently intended to resell at the market at Q'adi. That incident was behind them, now, but he never felt that he could trust Fadl Rafat.

"Professor, Sir," said Rafat. "I have noticed how difficult it has been to conduct our work at the excavation site since we have lost so many workers. I have an idea, Professor, Sir, that may be of interest to you."

"We are, certainly, short of workers, Rafat," acknowledged Pender-Cudlipp. "What is your idea?"

"My sister lives in Q'adi," explained Fadl Rafat. "Her husband has a large family in that village. I am certain there may be some among them who would be willing to partake of the joy of archaeology. Let me accompany you to Q'adi, Sir. I will speak to my sister about this matter."

This was an interesting twist. Pender-Cudlipp had frequently asked his Syrian crew if they had friends or relatives who might be interested in joining the work at the digs. The pay was pitifully small, but it included room and board and, for the intellectually curious, it offered considerable satisfaction. This latter was not a factor that had ever seemed to have impressed Fadl Rafat, but Pender-Cudlipp was appealed by the suggestion, anyway.

Pender-Cudlipp had all but given up plans for continuing at the dig. But, who knows? Perhaps it would be useful to know someone else in Q'adi who might help him find additional manpower if needed in the future. Besides, it might be helpful to have a Syrian national along with him when he tried to get through the increasingly belligerent Syrian army checkpoints.

"Rafat," said the professor, "you are welcome to accompany me on the trip. I plan to stay overnight, however. I will not be able to pay for your accommodations."

"It is not a problem, Professor, Sir," Fadl protested meekly. "I will stay with my sister's husband's family."

"Well, then, get your things and hop in. I want to try to be in Q'adi before the shops close." Pender-Cudlipp was thinking especially of the message center, which closed at three o'clock p.m.

As the two men drove from the campsite, no more words were spoken. Fadl Rafat watched the Professor closely as they passed the old trailer around the hill by the wadi. He noted that Pender-Cudlipp carefully avoided looking at the trailer. Rather, he pretended to look off into the hills in the other direction as they drove past.

Rafat did not know exactly what to expect at the Syrian army checkpoint. He only had a rough idea as to how to carry out the next step of his plan. But he would think of something.

The day was gray, overcast. As the trail wound up and over the Jabal ad Farabi, a light rain speckled the windshield, and occasional muddy spots in the road slowed their progress. Heavy fog hung low in the valley on the other side of the mountains. Both men, for very different reasons, squinted through the fog to attempt to see what kind of situation would exist at the army checkpoint, normally visible in the distance from this spot on the mountainside.

At length, the Bronco reached the bottom of the valley, and began to travel along the narrow wadi. They soon drew near the mysterious new army installation. The guardhouse suddenly appeared through the fog. It was as Pender-Cudlipp feared and Fadl Rafat hoped: two army vehicles were parked near the guard station, and a sentry stood in the middle of the road, signaling for the vehicle to stop. Pender-Cudlipp recognized the soldier; the professor had met him before at this same checkpoint. Archie did not know the guard's name, but he remembered that this one, a corporal, was particularly picky, and brutal in conducting his searches.

Pender-Cudlipp pulled the Bronco to the side of the road, as indicated by the guard, and stopped.

"Rafat," said the professor to his traveling companion, "this could be somewhat unpleasant. They will want to search us, and they will want to search the vehicle. It is important that we do whatever they say. I hope this will not delay us too long. But, we have nothing to hide, nothing to fear."

Nothing to hide? thought Fadl Rafat. Is that so, Englishman? We shall see how much you have to hide! Fadl Rafat nearly laughed out loud, but controlled himself. He calmly got out of the vehicle and placed his hands on the roof, as did Pender-Cudlipp, on the other side of the Bronco.

The corporal signaled to another guard, a private, who was huddled in the sentry shack, shielded from the misty rain. To Pender-Cudlipp's relief, the corporal went around the vehicle to search Fadl Rafat. The Professor did not recognize the private, but he hoped for somewhat less painful treatment from him than he could expect from his colleague, the corporal. The pat-search was, indeed, relatively painless this time. Pender-Cudlipp heard talking on the other side of the vehicle. He could not see what was happening, but he had a moment of sympathy for Fadl Rafat. That particular corporal of the Syrian army seemed to take delight in inflicting pain as part of his search procedures.

The next sight that came to Pender-Cudlipp's eyes struck terror, down to the very depth of his being. The Syrian corporal leaped around the front of the Bronco, his service pistol drawn, held in both hands, and pointed directly at Pender-Cudlipp's forehead. A cruel smile twisted the corporal's features, his eyes expressing sheer delight in having the opportunity to draw his weapon like this, in dead earnest.

"You will drop to the ground, Englishman!" ordered the corporal. "Immediately!"

Pender-Cudlipp collapsed to the ground, belly first. His hands were still raised high above his head.

"Hands behind your back!" the corporal commanded. "Quickly!"

The Professor complied. "What is the meaning..." A swift kick in the ribs silenced the professor.

"I think it is time *we* asked the questions, here, Professor," said the guard.

What followed was a flurry of pain and terror. Kicks to the ribs, slaps to the face, blows to the mid-section. Questions. No answers. Pender-Cudlipp was dragged up the hill to the military compound headquarters. More blows to the face, more excruciating tugs at his now-manacled arms. Professor Archibald Pender-Cudlipp passed into unconsciousness.

The professor awoke as searing pain shot through his arms and shoulders. He was lying on his back on a concrete floor. Both arms were drawn tightly behind him, his wrists cuffed tightly by steel manacles. The slightest motion caused his arms to ache; it felt as though his arms were being pulled out at the shoulder joints. It was the pain that awakened him from his unconsciousness.

Pender-Cudlipp had no idea how much time had elapsed since that frightful moment at the sentry shack. He had but hazy recollections of what had happened, but it was obvious that Fadl Rafat had discovered Pender-Cudlipp's secret. The implications of this, he knew, were worse than any potential danger he, himself, might be in. Winning and Rypkin were now in dire peril, as was the terrifying information they held: giant nuclear submarines prepared to launch huge volumes of radioactive waste-tipped warheads! The world, Pender-Cudlipp knew, was already a fragile, fragile place. This could well be more than it could bear.

Pender-Cudlipp lapsed again, briefly, into unconsciousness. He awoke again as he heard voices outside his cell. He could only catch portions of what was being said: "Bildad on his way... Englishman still unconscious..." The conversation drifted lower in volume; Pender-Cudlipp could not hear. He glanced around his cell, as much as was possible without painfully moving his head. It seemed to be a small, cubical room. In the dim light, he could see nothing at all in the room. Nothing. No bed, no light, no window. Only a single door with a small viewing port broke the completely plain cubic interior.

The professor vomited and faded back into unconsciousness.

He was aroused again, this time by two Syrian soldiers who gripped him under the armpits and hoisted him to his feet. The pain in his shoulders was excruciating. The professor felt a wave of nausea pour over him as he dangled, barely standing, between the two Syrians. He opened his eyes. A familiar figure stood before him: Colonel Adib Bildad.

"It seems we have trusted you too much, Professor," said the Colonel. Bildad was not a happy man. "You have managed to make a very, very serious mistake. You probably do not even yet know how serious is your mistake. Let us now give you an opportunity to correct your mistake." Colonel Bildad turned on the heels of his polished boots and left the tiny cell. The two soldiers hoisted Pender-Cudlipp out of the cell, and carried the professor away, following behind Bildad.

Three vehicles made their way along the road to the north over the Jabal ad Farabi. Bildad, one of his lieutenants, and the informant, Fadl Rafat rode in the lead in a Syrian army Jeep. Pender-Cudlipp's Bronco followed, driven by a security guard. The Bronco carried another guard, heavily armed, and Professor Archibald Pender-Cudlipp, his arms still painfully bound behind his back. Every bump in the rugged road sent jabbing pain through his body. The last vehicle in the caravan was a Russian ZIL-131 truck, carrying a security squad of six soldiers. Bildad had brought this specially-trained squad with him from Latakia when he got the call earlier that day from Captain al-Atasi at the Farabi compound. Bildad could not afford to take any chances this time.

It was nearly twilight when the caravan turned off the main road to the trail that led to the west along Wadi el-Jari. According to their plan, the caravan drove to within two kilometers of the trailer, then stopped. The six soldiers emerged from the ZIL-131 and proceeded swiftly and quietly along the bank of the wadi toward the trailer. Bildad's lieutenant stopped the Jeep behind the truck. The lieutenant, the colonel, and the informant all left the Jeep, came back to Pender-Cudlipp's Bronco, and got in. The guard, a Syrian army sergeant, drove the Bronco slowly forward down the trail.

Pender-Cudlipp had been quiet during the entire trip. He remained silent as the three men crowded into his vehicle. But Bildad was taking no chances. He turned around from his position in the front seat and ordered one of the guards to tie a gag over the professor's mouth.

"I do not want you to make any noise, Professor," said Bildad, "unless it is to answer our questions. If these two westerners are not in the trailer where Rafat tells us they are hidden, I want you to be certain that you tell us where we can find them. You have experienced no pain to compare to what you will feel if you try to play more games with us. Please be thinking about that, Professor."

"Bill! It's Professor Archie!" Viktor Rypkin peeked out of the gap in the plywood board that covered the trailer window.

Winning clicked off his flashlight, put down the paper and pencil with which he had been working, and came over to the window. "He's back early!" exclaimed Winning. "He was not planning to return until tomorrow morning. I wonder what happened."

The Bronco proceeded past the trailer, and around the corner out of sight beyond the hill. The two men watched the Bronco's headlights move slowly along the road and watched its taillights disappear. It was too dark to see anyone in the vehicle.

"I wonder if he got a response to our message! I'm sure he will come and tell us, as soon as he is able," said Bill Winning. Winning went back to his corner of the trailer and picked up his flashlight and the maps he had been studying. He and Viktor Rypkin had spent many of the countless hours waiting in the trailer memorizing every detail of the maps that the professor had provided. If they had to make a run for it, at least they wanted to know where to run.

Bill handed the maps to Rypkin, and went back to his paper and pencil. He was making notes to himself, describing alternative escape routes, should they become necessary.

There was no warning. Absolutely none. No sound of a twig breaking underfoot, no sound of breathing or whispering. Nothing.

Before Winning could drop his pencil and paper, before Rypkin could put his map down and reach for the AK-47, the flimsy door to the old trailer was pounded completely off its hinges, the door fell flat, and two soldiers wearing black berets stormed into the little trailer. The barrel of a rifle was pressed against the forehead of each of the two fugitives.

Two more soldiers stormed into the trailer. In a matter of seconds, Bill and Viktor were on the floor, hands cuffed behind them. Just as quickly, rough, insistent hands dragged them to their feet, and thrust them out of the trailer door into the darkness.

As he stumbled from the doorway, Winning landed on his already-injured left ankle. He rolled over in agonizing pain in the damp, sandy earth. A bright flashlight glared at him off to his left. Bill could see four soldiers crouched behind the flashlight, automatic weapons pointed directly at him. Just to their left, he could see two Syrian officers. Another group of soldiers crouched to the right.

A shudder of terrifying recognition raced through Winning's mind: one of the officers was "Colonel Boots," Adib Bildad.

Just behind Bildad and off to his left, Winning could make out, in the darkness, the forms of two more individuals. One was a short, raggedly-dressed Syrian. The Syrian pushed the other man to the ground, out in front of the flashlight beam. This other wretched man was Professor Archibald Pender-Cudlipp, who now writhed in the sand about three meters away from Winning.

"Bill," Professor Archie moaned the words, the gag having worked loose from his mouth, "I am so sorry! One of my workers saw...! The scraggly-looking Syrian planted a kick directly in Pender-Cudlipp's face, silencing him.

"Quiet! You will be quiet!" The Syrian's voice sounded like the growl of a maddened animal.

"Step back, Rafat!" Bildad ordered the Syrian away from Pender-Cudlipp. "We will deal with this."

Bill Winning closed his eyes momentarily, cringing in stunned terror. In that instant, a remarkable thought crossed his mind, a verse he had memorized along with his wife: "Fear thou not, for I am with thee..." They were words of God, recorded in Isaiah 41:10.

Bill opened his eyes and shouted to Pender-Cudlipp, "Don't

fear, Archie, God is with us..." It was Bill Winning's turn to feel the silencing boot, this time from a Syrian soldier.

"Shall I have them loaded into the vehicle, Colonel," Bildad's lieutenant asked. "Shall we take them back now to the extermination camp?"

"No!" Bildad responded. "We will dispose of them right here and right now. I merely wanted to be certain we had the right men." Bildad unsnapped the holster of his SIG-Sauer P-220 pistol.

"Let me have the Englishman, Colonel" begged the Syrian, Rafat. "He is mine!"

"Very well, Rafat." Turning to one of the soldiers, Bildad indicated that the soldier should let Rafat use his weapon on Pender-Cudlipp.

Another soldier aimed his rifle at Viktor Rypkin. Bildad drew his pistol and walked slowly over to Bill Winning. He held the pistol to Winning's head.

Two loud, sharp sounds: *Clack!   Clack!* occurred almost simultaneously, followed in a fraction of a second by a third: *Clack!*

Bill Winning felt an enormous dead weight press down upon him. Warm fluid rushed out over his left shoulder, in a pulsating flow. Bill's instinct caused him to roll out from under the weight, and stagger to his knees.

More sounds rang out, this time a different noise, resembling an incredibly loud, low roll of a drum, followed by an ear-splitting roar that seemed to last for seconds. Flashes of fire and smoke emerged from the woods near the base of the hill across the road, and from the edge of the wadi, behind him and to his left. The flashlight held by the Syrian soldiers was dashed to pieces. In an instant, all was darkness except for the flashes of light that accompanied the ferocious noises that came from the tree line and from the wadi. Bill wobbled to his feet and began to run back toward the trailer, limping badly because of his injured ankle.

"*Get down, Mr. Winning! Please get down until we can secure the area!*" Bill heard a strange voice coming from across the road. The voice was speaking English! It was an American voice!

Bill immediately dove down to the ground. "Oh! My God! I praise Your Name!"

There were no more sounds of weapons fire, but Bill could

hear footsteps: men rushing across the road toward him.

"Mr. Winning? Sir, I am Eric Lindahl, Lieutenant, United States Navy. I am the leader of a Navy SEAL team. We are here to take you home."

Chapter Twenty-Six

Playing Hurt

3 March
Wadi el Jari, Syria

THE SEALS MOVED QUICKLY to clear the area and to tend to the erstwhile hostages. John Scott crouched on one knee, his M-16 at the ready, his night vision goggles in place to scan the area for possible enemy reinforcements. Eric Lindahl, Brett Nelson, and Rob Petrocelli rapidly - roughly - moved the three fugitives to a spot they had selected along the side of a rocky hill that would provide effective cover if they confronted additional enemy action. Rescue operations behind enemy lines is no place for niceties.

"Lieutenant," panted Bill Winning, still stunned from the ordeal, stumbling, vainly trying to maintain balance despite his gimpy ankle and his cuffed wrists, "this is Viktor Rypkin. He's a Russian...an engineer. Listen! Before you do anything else, you must listen to him..."

Lindahl cut him off sharply. "Sir, you're going to have to shut up." It was about as polite as he could be at the moment. "We've got to clear the area. Then we can talk. Just *move!*"

When they were at least temporarily safe in their cover zone, Petrocelli began to wield his mechanic's tools, setting about to remove the shackles from the hostages' wrists. Chief Medic Nelson, using the special tools of his own trade, rapidly checked each of the men to determine the appropriate priority of treatment.

"OK, Mr. Winning, who are these people?" Lindahl needed rapid answers.

Winning, by now exhausted, and wincing from the pain of Petrocelli's cuff-release techniques, began again to pour out the incredible story. "Syrians..." he gasped, "...going to fire nuclear-tipped missiles...from a Russian nuke submarine! You've got to talk to this man...Viktor Rypkin!"

Lindahl's first reaction to this revelation was to suspect that the American was suffering from delirium. It would not be the first time a rescued hostage had experienced hysteria induced by the stress of having a gun pointed at his head.

"I'll talk to your friend, Mr. Winning," said Lindahl, mustering as much calmness in his voice as he could. The last thing he needed was for Winning to turn hysterical. "Just as soon as Chief Nelson has had a chance to look him over and make sure he's O.K. Your other buddy looks to be in pretty bad shape." Eric led Bill Winning's attention over to where Nelson was tending to Archie.

"This is Doctor Archibald Pender-Cudlipp," Winning explained. "...Englishman...archeologist...lives here. Listen....this guy saved our lives!"

Bill crawled over, near to where the big Englishman was being tended by Chief Medical Corpsman Brett Nelson. "How're you doing, Archie?"

Pender-Cudlipp opened his eyes, then winced at the bright flashlight wielded by Chief Nelson. Bill could see the ugly, puffy bruises around both of Archie's eyes, and the blood that was caked and still seeping around his nose and mouth.

"Doin' quite well, under the circumstances," the Englishman grunted. "Glad to see you American blokes. You showed up none too soon!"

"Shut up and drink this!" ordered Brett Nelson. The chief medic gently raised Pender-Cudlipp's head and offered a container of fluid to the Professor.

"You'll have to excuse Doc's bedside manner, Doctor Pender-Cudlipp," Eric Lindahl apologized, "but I have learned that when he tells you to take your medicine, you'd better do it!" Turning to Nelson, he asked, "How's he doing, Brett?"

"I think he's going to be O.K., Sir, but he's been beaten badly," said the chief medical corpsman. "He may have a concussion, and, as you can see, he has plenty of contusions. I think the nose is broken - maybe a cheekbone, too. Maybe his ribs, too. They did a job on him. He's dehydrated, he has a dislocated shoulder, and he has some bad cuts on his wrist from the cuffs. He could sure use some rest. I'm getting an I-V going on him. I need to check him out some more, but I think he'll be O.K."

Turning to Bill, Brett Nelson continued, "Mr. Winning, you have a badly sprained ankle. I don't think it's broken. I'll break out an ice pack here in a second to try to get the swelling down."

Brett finished administering the medicine to Pender-Cudlipp and turned to the other two men for their first aid.

"Listen, Lieutenant!" Bill Winning was back on his point. "We've got to get the word out about the Russian nuke that the Syrians are about to put to sea! We can't waste any time!"

"O.K., Mr. Winning." Eric replied. "Just hold on! Rob and John will set up our perimeter defense. Nobody wants out of here fast more than I do. Our rendezvous point is about fifteen kilometers west of here. It's pretty rugged traveling. That's the bad news. The good news is we didn't see any unfriendlies on the way over here, and we have a nice, warm submarine waiting back there to take you home."

"Submarine? Outstanding! Did Bob Copper get my message? Of course! He must have. That's why you're here!" For Bill Winning, the shock was wearing off; the trauma of the last few minutes was fading, replaced by grim reality.

"Look, Lieutenant," said Winning, "we need to fill you in on more of the details of this Syrian plan to use a Russian submarine. Viktor believes that this could be happening very soon. We've got to get back quickly to stop this thing."

Bill and Viktor began again to explain the story.

After he had listened for a few moments, Lindahl waved his hand to Brett Nelson, motioning him over. "Brett, we have a situation here. Mr. Rypkin has information about the Syrians acquiring a Russian nuclear submarine. He believes they are about to use it to shoot radioactive-tipped warheads at Israel. He thinks it is imminent." Lindahl sensed that there was more to the hostages' story than hysteria. "We've got to get these guys back right away. How is the Englishman? Can he move?"

"No, Lieutenant, he cannot,"

"Can he survive a move?"

"Only if we carry him. He is unconscious again, and badly dehydrated. The I-V'll get some more fluids in him, but he's out of it right now. Ordinarily, I wouldn't want to move him at all for at least another twenty-four." Brett Nelson paused for an instant, then continued. The plan was obvious. "It'll slow us down, but, hey, this'll be like old times at BUD/SEAL training in Coronado! We need the exercise!"

Nelson turned to Bill Winning. "We're also going to have a problem with your ankle, Sir. It's badly sprained. I've only got one litter..."

Bill Winning sprang to his feet, "Hey!" said Bill, "This ankle's been gimpy for the past couple of months, and I've learned to move with it. Sometimes you gotta play hurt in the Bigs."

"Yes, Sir. Let's just be sure we win the game." Bill winced as Chief Nelson injected the painkiller into his ankle.

John Scott and Rob Petrocelli returned from their chores and conferred with their boss.

"Let's saddle up and move out," ordered Eric Lindahl. "I want to make it back before dawn."

Morning, 4 March
Near the Mediterranean Coast, Northeastern Syria

Fogie Crandall was nearing the end of his two-hour stint on sentry duty. His partner, Poco Logan, slept soundly, curled in his poncho at Crandall's feet. Fogie had to nudge Logan every once in a while when he started to snore.

It had been over twenty-four hours since the angel team had left the Romeo point. According to Crandall's conjecture, it would probably not be until the following morning, at the earliest, that they could reasonably expect the return of the SEALs. He knew that, unless there was some kind of emergency, Lieutenant Lindahl much preferred to move only in darkness. Crandall glanced at his watch. 5:47 a.m. In only about a quarter hour, he would wake his partner, and he could settle in, himself, for a brief nap prior to establishing the daytime routine.

The SEAL cocked his ear to the east. What was that? A barely perceptible sound had reached his ear. A cough? Just the wind? He raised his M-16 to a ready position, and kicked Poco Logan twice sharply in the shoulder. Without a sound, Poco awoke, collected the M-16 that lay beside him and rolled quietly away to Crandall's left.

Both men waited, weapons at the ready.

Then it came, loud and clear: a cricket chirp. Crandall had never heard a real-life critter make a noise like this, but it sounded so much like background biological noise that an untrained ear would never notice it. Two distinct chirps followed by a pause, a single chirp, then two more chirps. Fogie Crandall returned the signal.

John Scott emerged from behind a group of large rocks to the south of Crandall and Logan. At the same time, Rob Petrocelli appeared from a thicket of shrubs to the north. John came over to join the two waiting SDV-drivers. Rob made a hand signal, and disappeared back into the woods.

In about five minutes, Rob Petrocelli returned, exchanging cricket signals with Crandall. He appeared out of the thicket, leading the way for Eric Lindahl and Brett Nelson, who were carrying a litter, complete with the medic's I-V rig stuck into a large man who now resembled an old boxer who had lost a fifteen-round slugfest.

Following the litter were two strangers, one of whom Crandall recognized from pictures as the hostage, A.W. Winning. Winning was limping badly, but making his way with a makeshift wooden cane. The other man, younger, leaner, looked to be in fairly decent condition, but Crandall did not recognize him from any of the pictures he had studied.

"You don't waste time, Lieutenant." Fogie Crandall spoke to his boss. "We didn't expect you until tomorrow morning, at the earliest."

"We have to move quickly, Fogie!" Eric Lindahl was in no mood for small talk. "We need to get these people back aboard *Chamberlain* as quickly as possible. Poco, you and Fogie go rev up Angel Chariot while we take this scuba gear and give our three friends a crash course in using it."

Logan and Crandall hurried to collect their equipment packs and move out toward the beach. Brett Nelson, an experienced diving instructor, took over the lessons for the three civilians. Pender-Cudlipp, with his injuries, would present a special problem, but Brett had handled this kind of thing before.

The plan was for Nelson to lead Winning, Rypkin, and Pender-

Cudlipp down to board the Angel Chariot for the return trip to *Joshua L. Chamberlain.* The trip would be made at shallow depth, and, when in range, they would contact *Chamberlain* by Gertrude to come shallow, enabling the newcomers to come aboard with a minimum of danger. Crandall and Logan would quickly take on a fresh battery, and return to the beach to collect Lindahl, Scott, and Petrocelli.

At that point, the rescue would be complete. But not the battle.

Aboard *USS Joshua L. Chamberlain*

Admiral Robert Copper and Commander Will Garrett sat at the wardroom table, sharing conversation and coffee. As they waited for word of the angel team, they discussed recent developments in submarine-SEAL technology with Commander Dave Carry, the SEAL Team Six Commanding Officer who had accompanied the SEALs on the mission.

"That's a good idea, Will," said Admiral Copper as he sorted through some sketches that had been prepared by Will Garrett. "When we get back, I want you to meet with Trace Dawson to go over this concept. I don't know how we can cram it into our budget for this year, but..." The conversation was cut short by the scratchy voice of the 1-MC speaker.

"Captain to Control. Captain to Control. Sonar reports Angel Chariot in-coming." It was the voice of Wayne Bryant, the officer-of-the-deck.

Commander Garrett placed the coffee cup back in its saucer, and triggered the 21-MC speaker-phone just above his right shoulder. "Conn, wardroom, this is the captain. I'm on my way." Copper, Garrett, and Carry left the wardroom and headed rapidly to Control. As they arrived, they heard the message coming in on the Gertrude receiver.

"Maine Yankee, Maine Yankee. This is Angel Chariot, Angel Chariot. How do you read me, over?"

"Angel Chariot, this is Maine Yankee." Lieutenant Bryant spoke slowly into the Gertrude handset. "Read you loud and clear, over."

"Maine Yankee, we have three orphans aboard," reported Angel Chariot. "One infirm. Condition green. Request you come to five-zero feet for recovery procedure, over."

"Roger, Angel Chariot. Commence normal docking sequence. Coming to five-zero feet. Stand by to receive my signal. Out."

Lieutenant Bryant replaced the Gertrude handset on its hook and picked up the 1-MC mike. He pressed the trigger on the 1-MC: "Man SEAL recovery stations. Man SEAL recovery stations."

In less than two minutes, the SEAL recovery stations watch had been set throughout the ship. Lieutenant Chuck Staggs arrived in Control to lend his expert hand as diving officer for the procedure.

This would be a tricky one. Staggs would try to time it just right: pumping just enough water out of *Chamberlain*'s ballast tanks to create a small amount of positive buoyancy. Then, with experience as his only guide, he would judge when to begin flooding again to bring her to a stop at 50 feet without sinking back down too far. They had practiced this many times, and, even though Staggs was the best in the business at this operation, he occasionally had to ask for some speed to maintain depth control. Now, with real "orphans" out there, they did not want to have to go through the circling routine. The pressure was again on Staggs.

Aboard SDV "Angel Chariot"

Poco Logan circled Angel Chariot just below the surface at dead slow speed. He waited for the signal from *Chamberlain*.

Soon, it came. "Angel Chariot, Angel Chariot, this is Maine Yankee, Maine Yankee. Do you read me? Over." The Gertrude squawked at Logan and Crandall, seated in the front section of the Mark VIII SDV.

"Maine Yankee, this is Angel Chariot. Read you loud and clear, over."

"Roger, Angel Chariot. We are at five-zero feet. Speed zero. The barn's outer door is open. Continue docking sequence. Over."

"Roger, Maine Yankee. Understand you are at five-zero feet, speed zero, outer door open. Continuing docking sequence. Angel Chariot, out."

Poco Logan now spoke on the SDV's interior communications circuit, "Orphans, this is Poco. We have established contact with *Chamberlain*. We are going ahead with the docking sequence. Please stand by. Fogie, let's look for home."

Logan bumped the speed up a bit to give Angel Chariot better depth and direction control. He steered the SDV around to an easterly course and nosed her down to about ten degrees down bubble. If *Chamberlain* was precisely at the correct Romeo point, this should get Fogie a clear sight of the host submarine.

"O.K., Fogie," said MMC Logan, "we should be in range. Now you can unhook and get out to man the headlights."

"Unhook, get out, man headlights, aye." Fogie Crandall quickly changed his breathing-supply mouthpiece to his self-contained tanks, disconnecting from the SDV's breathing system. He then unbuckled his safety harness, and cracked the hatch above his seat. He slowly maneuvered to swim free of the SDV. Angel Chariot continued to pitch forward, at just under one knot, toward the presumed location of the host submarine.

As the SDV moved slowly forward and down, it was Crandall's job to rig the headlights. There were two: one mounted on each side of the SDV's stubby bow. Crandall rigged the starboard headlight first, opening its hatch-fairing, disengaging its lock-pin, and extending its bracket to full length. He then re-engaged the lock-pin and the lamp was ready to operate. It was a powerful searchlight that allowed its operator to see, in clear water, up to 100 meters. Crandall set about to rig the portside light.

Having completed his task, he swam over to the pilot's hatch. He rapped two times on the hatch with his deck wrench. Poco Logan returned the signal from below with his own deck wrench. Fogie Crandall stayed on the port side, turning the light on to high beam.

Angel Chariot slowly made her way deeper. Though Crandall had performed this operation many times in training, it always thrilled him to see the sight of the submarine looming under him. His first glimpse of *Chamberlain* revealed the forest of scopes and antennae that protruded from the top of the sail.

Soon *Chamberlain*'s entire sail came clearly into view in the headlights' beams. Crandall rapped three more times on the pilot's hatch. This was the signal for Logan to stop power to the SDV's drive motor, and for the pilot to transfer to his own self-contained breathing system. Then Logan would exit Angel Chariot. He would attach the SDV's remote control cable, and steer the SDV toward the hangar from the outside. He would be assisted by Fogie Crandall, who would physically wrangle Angel Chariot into place at the hangar's outer door. It was a tricky, dangerous maneuver that required an extraordinary combination of experience, good judgment, and physical strength.

The two swimmers manhandled the ungainly Angel Chariot down the back edge of *Chamberlain*'s sail and along the top of the submarine's hull toward the long, cylindrical hangar chamber.

Logan operated the remote control panel. He occasionally boosted the SDV along with a brief surge to the propeller motor, but for the most part, the two SEALs guided her and dragged her along by hand. After about ten minutes, Angel Chariot was properly lined up to enter the chamber, stern first.

As he observed Crandall's thumbs up, Logan turned the control switch, slowly rotating the SDV's propeller in reverse. He kept the power on for about ten seconds, then switched it off. The Angel Chariot moved, slowly backing into her cylindrical barn.

Once inside the hangar, Crandall busied himself, engaging the tie-down clamps, while Logan attached the connector to the ship's 27-MC circuit. He then returned to his pilot's seat, and re-connected himself to the SDV's breathing and communications systems.

"Control, Angel Chariot Pilot. We are secured in the hangar. Close outer door." Logan spoke on the 27-MC circuit.

"Pilot, Control. You are secure, aye. Welcome home, Poco! Close outer hangar door, aye." The muffled pneumatic and hydraulic noises sounded their own "welcome home," as the huge outer door of the DDS hangar-chamber slowly swung shut.

"Pilot, Control. Stand-by to blow down hangar chamber."

"Control, Pilot. Standing by for blow-down." Back in the aft section of Angel Chariot, Bill Winning had struggled to avoid sleep during the long journey. The excitement and pure novelty of this underwater sleigh ride had rapidly worn off, and the fatigue of his ordeal had overtaken him. He had quickly learned the knack of regulating his breathing, and had settled back to trust in the skill of his SEAL-hosts.

Winning had come fully awake when the SDV had angled down to make its rendezvous with the submarine, and he had listened attentively to the 27-MC communications. Now, however, he was blasted nearly out of his seat by the sound of the high pressure air blowing the hangar chamber dry. After a few seconds of the noise, he felt the water level dropping around his head, down his shoulders and on down to his feet. He felt a great sense of relief to be, once again, relatively dry.

Bill heard a loud rapping on the top of his hatch, and looked up to see Brett Nelson, smiling at him as he opened the hatch and helped him remove his breathing mask. Winning unbuckled his safety harness and stood up, shifting weight off his injured ankle. Bill struggled out of the SDV. The air inside the chamber was stale; it had a strange, rubbery odor. But it was air! How wonderful to be safe inside this tube!

Bill Winning looked across the SDV to see Viktor Rypkin standing, stretching, appreciating his latest safe-haven.

Behind him, Brett Nelson tended to Archibald Pender-Cudlipp. Archie's hatch was open, and Bill peeked in to see how his English friend had fared. The professor looked up, and managed a big smile, despite his nearly swollen-shut eyes and bleeding nose. Archie gave Bill Winning a vigorous thumbs-up signal. The relief they felt seemed unreal, like a dream, the flip side of the bizarre nightmare they had just endured.

"We'll move into the decompression chamber as soon as we can," said Brett Nelson. "Then we will equalize pressure very slowly. No need to take chances here." Chief Nelson was an expert in the problems of compression and decompression. His specialty was how to avoid those problems.

At length they stood at the hatch that led to the inside of the *Chamberlain*. Bill Winning and Viktor Rypkin supported the weight of their friend, Archie Pender-Cudlipp. They waited patiently for the men in the trunk to carry out the long entry procedure in communication with the men below, in the submarine.

The remarkable achievement of this moment, to be back in friendly hands, was not lost on Bill Winning. As they waited for Chief Brunnert to crack the lower hatch from below, he said to Chief Nelson, "Brett, you have no idea how good this feels. I sure do appreciate what you and your buddies have done..."

Just then, the lower hatch cracked open and a rush of fresher air poured into the tiny access trunk. Brunnert pointed first at Bill Winning. "You first, Sir. Please come this way." Bill looked up at Brett Nelson with a "what other way is there?" smile. He stepped gingerly down the ladder, avoiding putting weight on his left ankle.

At the base of the ladder Winning stood, momentarily dazed by the familiarity of the scene. *Joshua L. Chamberlain* was about the same age as Winning's old boat, the attack submarine *Muskellunge*, built in the same New London shipyard. With all the modifications over the years, and despite the differences in mission, she still looked much the same inside. Still felt the same. Most of all, she still smelled the same. All submarines of that era smell like this. There's something about that smell. Tough to duplicate the smell of years of artificial, self-manufactured, cooped-up atmosphere. Anyway, who would want to duplicate such an aberration? Only an old bubblehead like Bill Winning – or any man who had served on those boats that did so much to help win the Cold War. It certainly smelled like home to Bill Winning.

A familiar old face appeared, and the admiral came forward to embrace his former shipmate. "Welcome home, Bill!"

"Bob Copper! You don't know how great it is to see you! This is answered prayer!"

Chapter Twenty-Seven

Searching for Yodel Echo

4 March
Eastern Mediterranean

FOR BILL WINNING, the reunion was sweet. To be, of all places, back aboard a ship not unlike, in essence, his old *Muskellunge*, and to be in the sovereign domain of his old friend Bob Copper, was of enormous comfort to him. Less than a day earlier, Bill and his companions had been on the very brink of execution. Now they rested secure in the belly of a great steel fish called the *USS Joshua L. Chamberlain*. Yet there was an awful storm cloud still hanging over the heads of these men: knowledge of the terrible Syrian weapon about to be unleashed on the Holy Land.

Admiral Copper's original plan had been to make a hasty exit from the Syrian war zone immediately following safe return of the hostages, and following Angel Chariot's return to the beach to collect the remaining SEALs. But Bill Winning prevailed on him to wait at least long enough to hear Rypkin's story.

"What do you think, Bill? Do you realize what this means?" Admiral Copper turned to his old shipmate.

"Bob, since the day I first heard this from Viktor I have been able to think of little else. It's why we busted out of that prison camp when we did. It's why Gary Tarr made the sacrifice he did. We had to get the word out. This thing has got to be stopped!"

Copper turned back to Viktor Rypkin. "Viktor, explain to me again why you think this is so imminent. Why do you think the Syrians will use this submarine to attack so soon? Don't you think they might feel they need to do more training? Don't you think they might try threatening with it first, before they use it?"

Bill Winning interrupted, rephrasing Copper's question, speaking more slowly so that his Russian companion could understand.

Rypkin responded, "Yes, is possible they delay. Is always possible I am wrong. But I do not think so. Is great fastness - how do you say it Bill Winning?"

"Hurry."

"Yes - hurry! Is hurry when we set Yodel Echo System. Great hurry!"

"I think he's right, Bob." Bill Winning continued the argument. "The whole thing is based on surprise. The longer they wait, the more chance there is for their plot to be discovered. Especially, now that we have escaped. We've got to whistle in help, fast."

Copper shook his head. "It's not going to be that easy. First of all, I'm not authorized to go active on any communication until after we leave the war zone. Even if I could, there is no way the President is going to authorize any more submarine action in this area. I had to practically offer my head on a platter to get permission to come and get you. The CNO, even the JCS Chairman did the same thing. There is no way they are going to authorize any help for us short of a six-month congressional hearing."

"No good, Bob," said Bill Winning. "We have to stop them."

"Bill, we had to come in here unarmed. I mean totally unarmed. I mean we are carrying zero torpedoes. And I can't even communicate with home until I get out of here. I don't doubt your story, Viktor. I believe you. I also agree it's likely they'll strike soon. I just don't have the assets to deal with it."

"I have an idea," Bill Winning was not ready to give in. "There might not be much we can do about that Russian submarine, but maybe we can wipe out the navigation hydrophones that Viktor has described." Winning turned to his Russian comrade. "Viktor, you said you spent a long time studying the bottom contour charts to place those hydrophones. Do you think you could get us close?"

"Yes, I get you close," responded Viktor. "Maybe close enough to get return echo, if you have correct sonar equipment."

Winning looked over at Lieutenant Eric Lindahl, who sat at the far end of the wardroom table, sipping coffee, listening to the conversation. "Eric, if we could find those hydrophones, do you have anything in your bag of tricks that could blow them up? I mean, you guys still do get involved in underwater demolition, don't you?"

"We sure do, Sir," answered the SEAL. "We brought a normal supply of explosive charges with us on this trip. Actually, we brought a double load. We didn't know what we might expect. It's kept in a special storage bin on the SDV.

Commander Will Garrett, the captain of *Chamberlain*, now spoke up. "Admiral, this does make sense. We could drop down to where Viktor believes these hydrophones are, and get some information on them. That would help give us a lot more evidence for that congressional hearing you were talking about! Possibly we could even take them out of operation.

Admiral Copper nodded, thoughtfully. "Big problem is finding them," said Copper, after a long pause. "Viktor, you might be able to get us close, but it's a big ocean. Tell me more about those hydrophones. Maybe we need to think about how we might be able to get an echo, ourselves."

Viktor Rypkin attempted a description of his brainchild, the Yodel Echo Sonar Navigation System. His English was too limited to make the conversation easy, but in the weeks that he and Bill had shared at such close quarters, they had learned to communicate very well. Bill was able to clarify Rypkin's ragged descriptions for the other men. As the conversation proceeded, Commander Garrett invited his own sonar expert, Lieutenant "Monk" Laughton, to join them in the wardroom. Senior Chief Sonarman Reid Smith accompanied Laughton. Eric Lindahl called Rob Petrocelli up to the wardroom, also. Petrocelli had some experience with submarine sonar systems, and it began to look as though they might need his mechanic's expertise, as well.

The men spent the next forty-five minutes brainstorming around the wardroom table. Rypkin felt he could get the ship close enough to get a signal from the Yodel Echo hydrophones, if they could adapt the *Chamberlain* sonar system to give the proper trigger pulse signal and to hear the echo as it returned. He gave a detailed description of the frequencies of operation, and the physical characteristics of the hydrophones.

Chief Smith sketched some schematics on a piece of graph paper, and offered his opinion: "We can get that frequency from the AN\BQS 14A." The chief referred to the Raytheon high-frequency sonar system that had been developed primarily for under-ice submarine operations and adapted for mine detection and avoidance. "We'll have to tweak the frequency response here...and here." He jabbed his pencil at two of the boxes on his schematic. "But we can do it." The chief scratched his bald head, and looked at Lieutenant Laughton. "Hard part, boss, will be to trigger the pulse down at Rypkin's hydrophones. We need a very intense directional signal. We don't have any horns like that on this boat."

"Can we make some?" Lieutenant Laughton pushed his chief. "I mean, you can get the signal to the output hydrophone by making those adjustments on the system. Now all you need is the right horn to project the sound into the water, right?"

"Right. I remember doing some work several years ago up in Puget Sound. We were trying to do some things with directional sonar signals. We were using horns that looked a little like what Rypkin has sketched. Maybe if I had a chat with Chief Corderman..." Chief Smith referred to Chief Machinist Larry Corderman who had a compact, but remarkably well-supplied, little machine shop in the lower level auxiliary room of the submarine.

The ideas soon jelled into a provisional action plan. Lieutenant Laughton went below, with the chief sonarman, and with Viktor Rypkin's sketches and specifications.. They would begin to tweak the AN\BQS 14A Sonar System and work with Chief Corderman to try to fabricate workable trigger-pulse hydrophone "horns." Rob Petrocelli accompanied them. It would be his job, when the time came, to put the horns in place, outside the ship.

Viktor Rypkin went with Commander Garrett. They headed to the ship's control center, where Rypkin would be introduced to Lieutenant Commander Patrick "Tex" Barker, the navigator. They would study the charts of the area, and determine the appropriate course to make way to the Yodel Echo drop point.

Chamberlain crept along at one third speed. She was rigged for quiet: all unnecessary equipment was secured. The only asset she had in this war zone was her stealth. Remaining undetected was her only defense. The control room was rigged for red. Above, on the surface, it was dark; it was nearly midnight, local time.

Winning had spent most of the evening with his friend, Archibald Pender-Cudlipp, who was recuperating in a special berth prepared for him by Chief Nelson up in the bow compartment. Winning had crawled into his own bunk in his small stateroom at about 11:00 pm, but soon had been awakened and summoned to Control.

As Bill Winning arrived in the control room, he saw that Admiral Copper and Commander Garrett were already there, crouched over the chart table with the chief quartermaster and with the navigator. Viktor Rypkin was there, too, trying to communicate with Lieutenant Commander Barker.

Ever since the disastrous collision between the submarine *Greenville* and a Japanese fishing vessel off the coast of Hawaii, there were strict rules about non-watch personnel in a submarine's control room. But the Navigator needed Rypkin's knowledge of the underground contours in the area, and he needed Winning to try to help understand the Russian.

"Bill!" Rypkin gestured to his friend, "is good you are here. Is trouble to understanding Navigator." Lieutenant Commander Tex Barker hailed from Nacogdoches. Viktor Rypkin was not the first person to feel he needed an interpreter to decode Barker's East Texas twang.

Studying the chart for a moment, Winning could see that they were rapidly approaching "Station Hotel" the plot marked on the chart by Rypkin as the estimated drop point for the Yodel-Echo hydrophones. Winning noted that Station Hotel lay only a few kilometers off the Mediterranean coast of Israel.

The men continued to ply over the charts, discussing ways to approach the hydrophones, looking at water temperature profiles, and considering operational options, when they were interrupted by a call on the 27-MC.

"Conn, Sonar. I have a new contact bearing one-three-zero. Range in excess of thirty thousand meters. Label this contact Sierra Niner."

"Sonar, Conn, aye." Lieutenant Commander Barker responded. Battle Stations had been set and Barker was now the OOD. Lieutenant Staggs was also at his battle station: diving officer. The *Chamberlain* team was getting a good workout.

Chief Hospital Corpsman Brett Nelson stepped into the control room from the forward hatch. "Good evening Mr. Winning, Mr.

Rypkin. I just checked out your buddy, the professor. He's doing great. He's even getting cranky. Didn't like it when I told him he had to stay in his bunk. I told him I'd bust his nose again if he got up."

"Does he have a concussion?" Bill Winning asked.

"Oh, yeah!" answered Nelson. "And he's got some damage in his shoulders. Both of them. Plus those shiners on his eyes. And his nose is broken. But he'll be okay. He needs rest. Willis will keep a close eye on him. He'll make sure he doesn't try to get up." Nelson referred to the ship's corpsman, a second class petty officer. "Listen, gents, I've got to run. Lieutenant Lindahl has called me back aft. We're going to saddle up the SDV to go out and put those sonar phones on."

Brett Nelson gave a wave to Bill and Viktor and headed aft.

Winning went back to the chart table. He watched the dead-reckoning cursor walk its slow, computer-generated way toward Station Hotel. It was now about thirty kilometers away to the southwest.

"Conn, Sonar. Contact Sierra Niner still closing. Still bearing one-three-zero. Zero bearing rate. Can't get good range, but estimate greater than twenty-five thousand meters. Sounds like maybe there's two of them. They sound like destroyer-types, Sir. Let's designate them Sierra Niner and Sierra Ten."

"Sonar, Conn, aye." Lieutenant Commander Barker turned to Commander Garrett. "Captain, I would like to slow down and get below the layer."

"I agree, Tex. In fact, let's get well below. Let's go down to eight hundred feet."

"Aye." The Officer of the deck gave the orders, and the crew went to work. The submarine took a slight down-bubble, and she began her transient to get down to depths where the water temperature "layers" would bend sound waves away from listening sonar-ears on Sierra Niner and Ten.

"Chuck, after you get me on depth, I intend to slow to two knots." Tex Barker gave a heads-up to his diving officer, Chuck Staggs.

"Okay, Tex, thanks." The OOD would maintain speed at one third until they settled out at the new depth; it made Staggs's depth control job easier.

As they approached ordered depth, Lieutenant Commander Barker triggered the 27-MC again, "Sonar, Conn, report contacts Sierra Niner and Sierra Ten"

"Conn, Sonar, Sierra Niner and Sierra Ten are still out there at bearing one-three-zero. Still zero bearing rate, closing. I estimate them at greater than twenty thousand meters. I'll have better identification on them shortly, Sir."

"Sonar, Conn, aye. We are almost at eight hundred feet, I'll be slowing to two knots when we get there."

"Conn, Sonar, aye. Thank you, Sir." There would have been very little chance that two destroyers at such long range could have heard *Chamberlain* as she moved slowly, at one third speed, at her previous cruising depth. Now, as she rode well below the thermal layer, the submarine would be nearly impossible to detect. But, this would also make it more difficult for *Chamberlain* to hear Sierra Niner and Sierra Ten. Slowing to two knots would give *Chamberlain's* sonarmen better conditions, less background noise.

Meanwhile, Lieutenant Eric Lindahl once again assembled his SEAL Team in the Arcade. The plan was for Poco Logan and Fogie Crandall to launch the SDV, with John Scott and Rob Petrocelli aboard. They would carry with them the new hydrophone horns manufactured by Chief Corderman to Viktor Rypkin's specifications.

After launching the vehicle, the SDV drivers were to steer it around to the bow of the hovering submarine. They would then operate the SDV's headlights as Petrocelli and Scott put the new hydrophone horns in place.

They would then, all four of them, stand clear as *Chamberlain's* sonarmen attempted to make contact with the Yodel Echo hydrophones. Armed with the location information obtained by the sonarmen, Eric Lindahl and Brett Nelson would then swim out to join the other SEALs as they took on the task of placing explosives on the Yodel Echo grid.

After completion of the mission, the SEALs planned to return with their SDV to the hangar, reenter the submarine, and *Chamberlain* would then beat a hasty, silent retreat. She would be far clear of the area before the explosion occurred that would eliminate the Russian Oscar submarine's navigational capability to fire her weapons. Such, at least, was the plan.

Back up in Control, however, *Chamberlain*'s brain trust was trying to avoid a glitch in the plan.

"Conn, Sonar. Sierra Niner and Sierra Ten. are still at one-three-zero degrees, true. Zero bearing rate. They are closing, but I can't get a good range on them. Request you change course to give me a bearing rate so I can get a range."

"Sonar, Conn, aye. We'll come left to zero-four-five. See if that helps."

"Conn, Sonar, aye. Thank you, Sir."

Tex Barker gave the orders, and the ship turned to a northeasterly course. She stayed at 800 feet and maintained her two-knot speed. Admiral Copper left his position on the periscope stand and went into the nearby sonar shack. Several minutes later the report came back to control.

"Conn, Sonar. Sierra Niner and Sierra Ten bearing one-three-five degrees, drawing right. Estimate range twelve thousand five hundred meters. They sound like destroyers, Sir, twin screws. They're moving abreast about fifteen hundred meters apart. Doing about fourteen knots. They sound like they may be a couple of those new Israeli Lahav class corvettes. I'll keep checking 'till I'm sure."

"Sonar, Conn, aye. We'll stay on this course until they pass to the west of our track. Then we'll come back around to head for Station Hotel."

"Conn, Sonar, aye."

Lieutenant Commander Barker passed the word back to Eric Lindahl in the engine room that there would be a delay in getting to Station Hotel. Lindahl took the news in stride; he and his men could use additional review of the procedures they would use to connect the hydrophone horns.

Station Hotel

The Israeli destroyers had long since made their way southward, far beyond sonar range, without noticing the American submarine lurking below.

Chamberlain had resumed her quiet trek to the spot identified by Viktor Rypkin as the drop point for the Yodel Echo Grid. Here she hovered, at one hundred feet.

Poco Logan used the remote control cable to guide the SDV along the long, narrow hull of *Chamberlain* toward the bow. The particular section they sought was at a point on the bow, along the centerline of the ship, identifiable by measuring around the hull from a bench mark located precisely at the tip of *Chamberlain*'s rounded bow. The task at hand involved cutting through a portion of the fiberglass outer hull bow faring. This would expose the four sonar hydrophones that were to be replaced. It was a delicate operation. Rob Petrocelli and John Scott had practiced it several times, down in Chief Corderman's machine shop. They estimated that it would take about two hours to complete the cut, to remove the old hydrophones, to install the new horns, and to replace the fiberglass fairing.

There was little difficulty in finding the forward benchmark. Fogie Crandall pointed the spotlight directly into the work zone, giving John and Rob plenty of light in which to work. The tools they required had been carefully laid out in advance and placed in their compartments in the SDV. Rob Petrocelli performed the operation, supervised by John Scott, who also served as his gopher, providing the necessary tools and materials.

Part of the procedure was to make saw-cuts in short ten-second bursts, followed by twenty-second pauses. This would give the sonar operators back aboard *Chamberlain* opportunity to listen for possible contacts in the area. If a contact were encountered, three low-level pulses would be sent out on the Gertrude. This would be the signal to cease operations until a two-pulse "all clear" signal sounded. Four pulses followed by one pulse followed by four more pulses would indicate an emergency return to the ship was required.

Back aboard *Chamberlain*, it was 3:45 am; it was time for Sonarman Second Class Clarence Shelp to take over the watch up in the sonar shack. Shelp forced his exhausted body through the hatch that led forward from the crew's mess into the control room. For practical purposes, his mind was still asleep. His only conscious thought was to try to avoid spilling his coffee as he stepped through the watertight door. During the past thirty-six hours, Shelp had slept for only three. Budget cutbacks in the Navy had reduced manning levels to the point where those who stayed in were required to nearly double their already demanding workload. Shelp had stood his normal four-hour watch the evening before in the sonar shack, then had spent what normally would have been his sleep time conducting maintenance on the ship's sonar gear. After a fitful three-hour snooze, it was time, once again, to relieve the watch for another four hours.

"What you got, Kirkwood?" Shelp mumbled as he slouched into the sonar shack. He flopped heavily on a spare stool in front of one of the sonar control panels.

"Good to see you, Shelp," said Sonarman First Class Ron Kirkwood. "Eyelids are gettin' heavy. We're hovering at one hundred feet. We've got two SEALs in the water working on the BQS 14A. You know about that modification they're making to the fourteen alpha?"

Shelp grunted, nodding his head as he took a sip of coffee. "Yeah, I read the procedure they want to use."

"Well, they'll be starting to cut any time now," Kirkwood continued giving his relief information. "We had a coupl'a contacts early in the watch." Kirkwood picked up the contact log and showed them to Shelp. "Chief identified them as Israeli Lahav-class corvettes. They were designated Sierra Niner and Ten. They drew off the scope at 0135, out at bearing one-seven-four degrees. We've had no contacts since. The latest thermal shows a layer at seventy-five feet. We're sittin' just below it. Anybody on top is going to be hard to hear at any distance. But we ought to be able to pick up anything below the layer pretty well."

Shelp finished another sip from his coffee mug. "BQS 14A being modified by a coupl'a SEALs," he summarized. "Two Israeli corvettes passed by, headed south. Micropuffs still down for repair. Anything else?"

"No, that's it."

"Okay, Kirkwood," said Shelp. "Ship hovering at one hundred feet, twenty-five feet below the layer. Ship's heading: two-seven-zero degrees. No sonar contacts. I relieve you." Shelp took the headphones that are the badge of the duty sonar operator's station.

The headphones are also the submariner's primary sensory link to the outer world. Underwater, a submarine is totally blind. Here, she relies only on her acute sense of hearing. She is dependent on the complex and sophisticated electronics operated from the tiny enclave known as the sonar shack. And, she is dependent on the judgment, expertise, and ears of sonarmen like the twenty-four-year-old Clarence Shelp who had just relieved the watch.

Kirkwood stood and stretched, giving forth a loud, exaggerated yawn. "I stand relieved," he announced. "I am ready for some serious rack time!"

"Lots o'luck, K-Wood!" said Shelp. "Chief says he wants to see you down in the bow compartment. He's still working on the Micropuffs. He told me to send you down there when you get off watch."

Kirkwood protested, "What? Shelp, I haven't been in the rack since..."

"Save it for the chief, K-Wood," said Shelp. "But you can't put it too hard to him. He's been down there since yesterday morning, along with Lieutenant Laughton, trying to fix that thing. I was down there myself, until one-thirty this morning. Listen, K-Wood, Chief knows you're tired. He'll make sure you get some rack time before you have to relieve again."

Kirkwood drowsily shrugged his shoulders and waved at Shelp as he left the sonar shack.

Shelp slipped into the chair behind the main sonar console. He adjusted the headphones to a more comfortable fit. He took another long sip of coffee. He settled back for what he hoped would be a quiet four-hour watch.

Shelp could hear the clanking noises produced by the SEALs outside the bow of the submarine. Shelp knew that, according to the procedure, the SEALs would soon be starting to saw the sonar dome. They were supposed to give him a "start" signal - six taps of a wrench - so that he could turn down the gain on his sonar receiver to protect his ears from the loud sawing process.

Shelp turned the control wheel of his sonar set to conduct a 360-degree scan. He took another draw from his mug of coffee to try to boost himself awake as he slowly turned the wheel. He could still hear the SEALs laboring up forward as he turned the dial to connect with hydrophones located further aft, but their noise faded as he scanned further aft. There were some biologicals off to the south: a mass of clicking noises, probably shrimp, that they had heard off and on for several days. Continuing his sweep, Shelp stopped briefly at a very slight, high-pitched hiss, barely noticeable, to the north. He could also begin to hear the noises of the SEALs at this point in his full-circle sweep. He continued around to the front of the search pattern, where the SEAL-noise dominated his earphones and his scope.

"What is that, up there to the north." Shelp casually thought to himself. It was such a slight noise that his scope showed no deflection whatever. He looked up at the continuous paper printout and studied it carefully. There was no noticeable deflection in the printout, other than a slight streak at about 355 degrees, but hardly anything to notice. Maybe it was just his sleep-deprived mind making things up. Shelp took another sip of coffee, and settled back into his seat. The next sound to hit Shelp's ear was not at all subtle. Three loud wrench-clanks followed by a pause, and three more clanks.

"Saw-time," muttered Shelp, "better turn down the forward gain." He reached forward to make the adjustment. He also turned his control wheel, this time counterclockwise to the north.

Shelp took his earphones off momentarily as the SEALs began to use the saw. Even with the gain turned to its minimum, the scope and the continuous paper printout went berserk as the sawing began. When the ten seconds were up, Shelp made a quick sweep back around the ship. He knew he had only twenty seconds before the sawing began again. He slowed his search down a bit as he passed around the northern quadrant of his scope. Was that just his imagination?

He continued around the dial, hurrying to meet the twenty-second time limit. Nothing else caught his attention. He turned the gain down again. He would spend more time next round on the northern sector. This on-again, off-again procedure would not allow him to use the continuous paper printout or the CRT very effectively; he would have to do this with his ears. He wished Chief Smith were here; Chief was good at this sort of thing. But the chief was busy down in the bow compartment. Chief was also tired and cranky. Shelp did not want to disturb him unless there was very good cause to do so.

During the next twenty-second search interval, Shelp turned back to the north to listen. He decided that there was probably nothing there. It must have been his imagination.

Outside, Rob Petrocelli was making progress in cutting through to the AN/BQS 14A hydrophones. Petrocelli had made his first saw-cut, a seventy-five centimeter cut across the ship's centerline in the forty-millimeter-thick fiberglass.

As Petrocelli began to make his first longitudinal cut, three short "burps" sounded from the Gertrude speaker. John Scott held up his hand and waved it in front of Rob Petrocelli's facemask. This was the signal to cease saw-operations. The sonarmen inside must have heard something!

There was no doubt about it. The continuous paper printout was inconclusive, and the scope on the console showed nothing, but Shelp heard it. He was sure enough that he picked up the phone to call Chief Smith down in the bow compartment.

"You sure, Shelp?" The raspy, exhausted voice of Chief Smith was in no mood for games.

"I'm sure enough to call you about it, Chief," said Shelp.

"That's good enough for me," concluded Chief Smith. "Tell the OOD right away. I'm on my way up."

Shelp activated 27-MC to Control. "Conn, Sonar, I have a possible contact at three-five-five degrees. Possible submerged contact."

"Sonar, Conn, aye." This was the simple response to what was very bad news, news that shattered the relative calm of *Chamberlain*'s control room.

Before the last transmission was complete, Commander Garrett and Admiral Copper were headed for the sonar shack. They had been in the control room along with Commander Carry and Lieutenant Lindahl to monitor the SEAL operations outside.

"What do you have, Shelp?" Commander Garrett asked the burning question.

"High-pitched noises to the north," said the sonarman, frowning in concentration. "I believe it to be engine noises, Captain. Also getting occasional cavitation. Sounds as if there might be two screws." Shelp continued to adjust the control wheel back and forth around the area of interest.

Soon Chief Reid Smith arrived, crowding into the tiny sonar shack.

"Boy, am I glad to see you, Chief!" Shelp got up from his seat, and handed the headphones to his chief. "Sounds like a submerged contact to me. Machinery noise and some cavitation. It almost sounds to me like twin screws."

Chief Smith scowled as he donned the headphones and took the chair. "You take the other set, Shelp, and keep scanning. I'll listen to this." Shelp's interpretation, if correct, would be bad tidings, indeed. The chief centered the hand-wheel at 355 degrees, then rotated to either side about 10 degrees, then came back to 355 degrees. He then made a quick sweep around the dial, coming back again to 355 degrees. He listened for a few more moments and then announced, without looking up, "This is a Russian *Oscar*, Captain. I've never heard this one before, but I'm pretty certain it's an *Oscar*. We're sitting under a layer. He probably is, too. He might be fairly well out there, maybe twenty thousand meters, but we can't get a good range on him until we get a bearing rate. He is operating at a slow speed, but he's closing."

Commander Garrett turned to Admiral Copper, "Rypkin was on the money, Admiral. It sounds as if these guys are serious."

"And we're sitting here with SEALs outside and no torpedoes," acknowledged Bob Copper. There was no panic in his voice; he merely summarized a most difficult situation.

Turning to Lieutenant Lindahl, who stood just outside the sonar shack door, Copper asked, "Eric, how long will it take to get your guys back in here?"

"About forty minutes, Admiral," responded Lindahl. "And it's a noisy operation, as you've noticed." Lindahl paused for a moment, then continued, "Sir, I've been thinking. If this is the *Oscar*, and if he's here to try to launch his missiles, won't he have to slow down and hover when he gets here?"

"That's what Rypkin tells us," Admiral Copper answered.

"O.K., Admiral," said Lindahl, "you may not have any torpedoes, but you've got something better!"

"What's that?"

"SEALs with explosives."

Eric Lindahl briefly described the plan that had been forming in his mind. He and Nelson would go out and join the other SEALs, and carry out the plan. There had never been anything quite like this in the annals of naval warfare, but there was not a trace of doubt in the young lieutenant's mind that he could pull it off.

Bob Copper shook his head and smiled. It had come to this; it would be up to a twenty-six year old Navy lieutenant and a handful of SEALs to prevent nuclear devastation. And it would be done by hand. But the admiral had no other reasonable alternatives. He had no weapons, so he could not intervene using conventional tactics. He could not try to quietly slip away without leaving his SEAL team behind, and he was not about to do that. And he would not sit by and listen as a Russian submarine, acquired by the Syrians well outside the constraints of legally binding international agreements, and firing weapons that were horrifying as well as illegal, rained devastation on countless thousands of people.

Admiral Hrupak's guidelines rang in Copper's ears: "*Whatever you can accomplish with one SEAL team and no torpedoes is fair game, but nothing more.*"

Lindahl's was the only option that made sense.

"Okay, Eric, suit up," said Bob Copper. He had made his decision. "I'll meet you back at the escape hatch. I want to write up my orders to you. When we get back, there are likely to be a few questions about why we're doing this. I want my orders, and the reasons for them, to be very clear."

"Aye, aye, Sir."

Chapter Twenty-Eight

<u>The Battle</u>

5 March
Eastern Mediterranean

Aboard *Hazael*

THE ENTIRE ENTERPRISE WAS TURNING decidedly unpleasant to Captain First Rank Yuri Yevshenko. It was not prudent to be entering this war zone with such a poorly-trained crew. It had been only five weeks since the *Antyey III*, rechristened *Hazael*, had slipped free for the last time from the caves at Khokskya and had set out for her new home.

During the short transit cruise, the hybrid Russian-Syrian crew had managed to perform only the most elementary of emergency drills. The Russian sailors assigned as the support crew were experienced, but not, of course, on this particular ship. The Syrians, though eager learners, were still dangerously sluggish and uncertain, except when it came to the missile-firing systems. Yevshenko's new Syrian boss, the young Mustafa Mutanabbi, seemingly had been interested only in performing full-scale drills on weapons launch sequences. They had practiced working with the Yodel Echo grids in the sea of Okhotsk, and those drills, at least, had gone reasonably well.

Yevshenko looked around the control room. *Hazael* was, indeed, a masterpiece. Glutsin had assembled at Khokskya a truly exceptional work force. This was the most finely crafted submarine that Yevshenko had ever taken to sea. He could not suppress a feeling of pride and of professional respect for his shipyard colleagues who had produced such a fine example of the shipbuilder's art. But his pride was mixed with a growing sense of anxiety – even shame – over having to sell out this, his beautiful baby. The mission toward which she now pointed held little interest to Yevshenko. War was war. But placing this extraordinary ship in the foul hands of such an amateurish crew was, to Yevshenko's mind, almost immoral.

Admiral Glutsin's instructions had been very explicit: Yevshenko was to obey every command of Mustafa Mutanabbi as though it were from Glutsin, himself. After all, it was Mutanabbi's ship. Yevshenko was, in fact, merely a hired hand. His term of service was, by contract, six months. True, after those six months, Yevshenko would be handsomely rewarded. His fee for his services would total more than he would have earned in an entire career in the old Soviet Navy. This certainly helped ease the pain for Yuri Yevshenko. It kept his anxieties and his shame at bay.

The ship had settled secretly into its security shed at the long pier at Damsarkhu five days previously. At Mutanabbi's insistence, Yevshenko, his entire Russian crew and many of his Syrian "clients" had been bussed to Latakia. They were to conduct training at the simulators in the Ministry of Power Production building. Mutanabbi, meanwhile, had remained behind in Damsarkhu to supervise Syrian stevedores in the process of loading weapons aboard *Hazael*. Having none of the Russians present while weapons were being loaded was another of the points that displeased Yevshenko, but he had his orders. An even higher authority than Admiral Glutsin had made it clear. Vladimir Drednev, the minister of defense, himself, had given Yevshenko a personal order, in the form of an American proverb: "the customer is always right."

Mustafa Mutanabbi emerged from the door that led into the control room from the weapons compartment. Following behind him were Captain Talon and the interpreter, Omar Fassad.

"Good morning, Captain Yevshenko." Mutanabbi spoke in flawless Russian. "Conditions appear to be well established in the missile compartment. Do we continue to make appropriate progress toward our destination point?"

"Yes, Admiral. Come and look." Yevshenko led the entourage over to a red-lit chart table. "We are proceeding at four knots on a course of one-seven-five degrees. This should put us at the Yodel Echo grid at 0415 this morning."

Omar Fassad translated the Russian captain's words for the Syrian captain Talon.

"Four knots!" Mutanabbi made an impatient gesture with his

hands. "I thought I ordered you to increase our speed!"

"Admiral," explained Yevshenko, "I have considered an increase in speed, but at this depth if we exceed four knots, our propellers will cavitate."

"Cavitate? What is it to 'cavitate?'" asked Mutanabbi.

Mutanabbi's ignorance of the fundamentals of submarining was revolting to Captain Yevshenko. But he had his orders (not to mention his promise of remuneration). He explained to Mutanabbi, in a patient, teacher's voice, "When the propeller turns, it 'bites' into the water, to provide thrust. If too much power is applied, the propeller spins too fast, and small bubbles appear along the edges of the propeller. These bubbles then collapse, making a noise as they collapse, like tiny balloons bursting. This noise can be picked up by enemy sonar. We do not know of any enemy in our area, but it is never good submarining practice to cavitate. If we could run deep, we could go faster, but you have wanted to make your weapons settings, and we must, therefore, run at launch depth, 150 feet." Yevshenko looked at his watch "It is now 0345. We should be at launch position within one half hour."

"Very well, Captain," said Mutanabbi. "Thank you for the lesson. Please instruct your crew to operate at the limit of this cavitation. Increase speed to just under what will cause cavitation."

"Yes, Admiral." Drednev had said it: "the customer is always right." Yevshenko went over to the Russian helmsman and his Syrian counterpart to give instructions to increase speed until they detected cavitation, then to cut back to just under that speed. Yevshenko knew from experience that, for all this, they would be able to make no more than one or two additional propeller revolutions-per-minute. But it was easier, and safer, to add a couple of "turns" than to question Mutanabbi further.

Mutanabbi was in no mood for patience. To him, prudence in this exercise was not to move more slowly, but to move more rapidly. Mutanabbi had but one mission in mind: to launch his missiles at Israel. Every question had to be resolved in the context of how it affected the chances of success for this mission. It might be that, by cavitating, the principles of "good submarining practice" might be violated, but it was more important to Mutanabbi to launch quickly. He fully realized that the chances of this huge, complex enterprise remaining a secret diminished with every passing moment.

Mutanabbi's impatience on this subject had grown when he had heard the news about the escape of the Russian Jew, Rypkin, from the compound at Jabal ad-Farabi. It was hearing this news, three weeks before, that had prompted Mutanabbi to speed up his calendar for launch. He had decided at that point to forego much of the training that initially had been planned.

Mutanabbi's alarm had abated somewhat as, two days previously, *Hazael* was about to depart from the pier at Damsarkhu. Bildad had reported the news that an informant had identified the fugitives. Mutanabbi was comforted that Bildad, himself, was planning to go to apprehend them, and to execute swift justice. But this news did not diminish Mutanabbi's determination to push ahead with his plan at the accelerated pace.

The idea to confuse the Americans with the hostage-taking had worked wonderfully well so far: the Americans were nowhere in the area. As long as the Americans stayed away, who else could stop *Hazael*? Certainly not the Israelis with their pathetic old diesel submarines or their noisy corvettes. But time could well be the enemy. Mutanabbi was certain of it. Moving quickly was the prudent action.

The plan was simple: Hazael would approach the Yodel Echo grid from the north, coming to dead-slow at the computer-generated location, until she could establish lock-on with the Yodel Echo system. At that point, she would hover at all stop while the navigational corrections were inserted into the missile fire-control system computers. If they failed to come close enough on the first pass over the presumed launch point, they would have to make spiraling circles until they could hit the grid. In all their trial runs in the Sea of Okhotsk, they had never had to make more than one search circle. Mutanabbi desperately hoped that they would be as successful this time.

The clock read 0400: only fifteen minutes to D-Hour, the expected time of *Hazael*'s arrival at the destination point. Missile launch stations were manned, and Captain Yevshenko and Captain Talon shared the conn, but no one doubted who was in charge. Admiral-Doctor Mustafa Mutanabbi stood at the stainless steel rail that surrounded the periscope station. This was his submarine. This was his moment. Mutanabbi's mind raced with excitement. He had dreamed for years of dealing a blow of vengeance at those who had tortured his father to death, at those who had tortured the pride of his nation for so long.

Mutanabbi was aware that the Holy Scriptures quoted God, "*To Me belongeth vengeance, and recompense...*" To Mutanabbi, only fools believed that. As he stood in the red-lit shadows of *Hazael*'s control room, Mutanabbi muttered to himself, "No! It is to *me* that vengeance belongeth. And it is *I* that will repay!"

Yevshenko looked up from the navigation chart toward Mutanabbi. "Admiral, we are now 3,000 meters from the destination point. Recommend we decrease speed to dead-slow."

"Make it so, Yevshenko."

Yevshenko spoke calmly to the Russian serving as helmsman, "All stop."

"All stop, yes, Captain."

"Come right to one-eight-zero degrees," ordered Yevshenko.

"Coming right to one-eight-zero degrees, Captain. Engine room answers all stop."

"Very well." Captain Yevshenko picked up the communications microphone. "Sonar Commander, this is the Captain. Stand by to engage Yodel Echo trigger pulse."

———

Outside *Chamberlain*

Lieutenant Eric Lindahl waited with his SEAL Team, seated in their positions in Angel Chariot. In this way, they could breathe off the SDV's breathing system, and conserve their own, individual air packs. Poco Logan sat in the pilot's seat, maintaining depth at 50 feet, 100 feet above the expected arrival depth of the intruder submarine. Fogie Crandall stayed outside Angel Chariot, to operate the headlights, sweeping them slowly back and forth, scanning the gloomy darkness below him. The water at this location in the eastern Mediterranean is relatively clear. Only an occasional jellyfish or school of tiny sardines crossed the path of Crandall's searching lights. Lindahl pointed his flashlight at his diver's watch: 4:15 a.m.

Three taps rang out in quick succession on the front of Angel Chariot. It was Crandall's signal. He had visual contact!

As thoroughly as the SEALs had reviewed all the information they could gather about this Russian submarine, none of them were prepared for what they saw. Below them, and about 50 meters to the right of the SDV, the little windows in *Hazael's* sail resembled the eyes of a grotesque sea monster, leering at them from the depths. Below the sail and extending out of range of the searchlights' beams was the massive outer hull of the submarine. At this close a range, it was hard to perceive that the hull was, in fact, a cylinder of finite dimensions. It more closely resembled a giant, flat sheet, extending infinitely in all directions in the dark water.

SEALs are a tough, hardened lot. They are not easily struck with awe. But, to a man, each of them was momentarily stunned as they viewed this apparition from the deep. It was easy for Eric Lindahl to imagine that this was not a submarine, at all. It had the appearance of a giant, ghostly aircraft carrier gliding slowly through the depths.

It was time for action. Each man had his job to do, and the equipment and material with which to do it. Off they swam, in pursuit of the barely-moving sea monster.

The SEALs performed their tasks swiftly. Nelson, Scott, and Petrocelli each had been assigned a section of the sonar-dome area near the bow of *Hazael*. Working in the light of Angel Chariot's headlights, they placed charges of plastic explosives completely around the bulbous bow. Brett Nelson, having studied Rypkin's sketches of where to find the Yodel Echo hydrophones, at a point aft of the bow sonar array, along the bottom centerline of the ship, headed for that area, and rigged an explosive charge at what he recognized was just the right spot.

Lieutenant Lindahl had taken on what was the most difficult, and dangerous, of the chores: the propellers and rudder assembly located at the extreme aft end of the giant submarine. Working with only the light of his submersible flashlight, he swam along the flat deck that extended 154 meters aft from *Hazael's* bow, and immediately went to work placing coils of plastic explosives completely around the outboard shaft-seals of both of the propeller shafts. Each of the giant brass propeller blades extended five meters radially out from the shaft, dwarfing the two-meter tall Navy SEAL. If *Hazael's* commander had chosen that moment to move his ship by rotating the propellers, Eric Lindahl might have been doomed, mangled by the enormous blades.

But the blades remained still, and Lindahl completed his work on the two propeller shafts, then used his flashlight to follow the superstructure around to find the rudder joints and the rudder-operating ram. He quickly placed explosives at what he considered vulnerable points, and rapidly swam back toward the bow, to meet with his SEAL Team at Angel Chariot. The headlights of Angel Chariot came into sight off to his left as Lindahl rounded the corner of *Hazael's* massive sail. Nelson, Scott and Petrocelli clung to the sides of Angel Chariot, still on their own individual breathing systems.

Poco Logan, seated in the pilot's position inside Angel Chariot, adjusted trim to maintain his angle and depth. He began to silently, slowly nudge the SDV backward, away from the giant submarine, and the mini-explosions that were about to occur. About three minutes remained on the detonation timers. The timers were crude mechanical devices that were not precise, but the explosions would occur nearly simultaneously.

Aboard Hazael

"Good!" Mutanabbi smiled grimly as he received the report from Yevshenko that a locator signal had been received back from a Yodel Echo transceiver on the very first trigger pulse. It was now necessary to allow the ship to drift slightly to the south, and get a final round of Yodel Echo position-verifications. This would then be sufficient to insert into the missiles' internal guidance systems. Then the launch sequence could begin.

In the sonar room of *Hazael*, located in a small compartment forward of the ship's control center, the Russian operator had turned the earphones over to his Syrian counterpart about an hour earlier, before the missile firing watch stations had been set. It was part of the duty of the Russian Support Crew to transfer responsibility to the Syrians as quickly as the Syrians were able to accommodate it. The young Syrian assigned to the sonar shack was very bright, indeed, and showed considerable promise as a sonar operator. He lacked only experience.

The Syrian sonar-operator-apprentice, Muhammad Buhairi, had thought he had heard a metallic sound in the area of the destination point a few minutes earlier. But there had been no repeat of the sound, and the Syrian had not been able to describe it well, anyway.

"You must learn, Muhammad," said the Russian mentor through their interpreter, "that imagination will play tricks on you, especially when you are going to launch stations."

Muhammad Buhairi thought he heard it again. This time two clear metallic sounds. But, the Russian was an experienced operator. If he said it was nothing to worry about, perhaps he was right. Possibly it was, simply, his imagination, or maybe it was something adrift on deck of *Hazael*. But...wait! Here was a loud "Thump!" This was accompanied by a "whirrr" sound, similar to a small electric motor. This was not his imagination!

"There is a noise here, Yevgeny!" said Buhairi. The interpreter began to relay the message, but Yevgeny had seen the bright blip on the sonar scope.

Yevgeny reached quickly for the headphones. "Let me see what this is all about." He moved Muhammad out of the operator's chair. He heard no unusual sounds on the headphones. The shrimp beds made their familiar cracking sounds well to the south, but no other unusual noise was evident to the Russian. "I saw the blip, too, Muhammad. Must be a dolphin, or something."

"Thump, thump!" Two more loud noises filled the sonar screen with bright blips, close aboard.

Yevgeny picked up the communications microphone. "Control, Sonar Commander. I have..."

Yevgeny was lifted nearly out of his chair by the noise of the explosion. His ears rang, in pain. All the sonar receivers in the sonar control room blinked bright and then went completely dark. Suddenly a number of explosions could be heard, close aboard. After a pause, a low rumble appeared to come from well aft, from another explosion in the vicinity of the engineering spaces.

Mustafa Mutanabbi, standing at the rail at the control station, was completely dazed by the noise of the explosions, and by the immediate cascade of red lights and tiny alarm buzzers that began to blare from the control panels surrounding him.

"What? What have you done, Yevshenko? What is..." Mutanabbi stammered, first speaking in Arabic, then shifting to Russian.

Yevshenko pushed past Mutanabbi toward the front of the control station. "Sound the collision alarm! Sound the collision alarm! Shut all water tight doors!" Yevshenko shouted the command to the ship's control panel operator, a senior Russian sailor named Larichev.

In an instant, the warbling shriek of *Hazael*'s collision alarm sounded throughout the ship, followed by the command, in Russian, "Shut all water tight doors. Shut all water tight doors."

Yevshenko picked up the ship's announcing circuit microphone, and calmly spoke into it. "We have suffered explosions. We do not know their origin. All compartments report conditions to Control. All compartments report conditions to Control."

Yevshenko now turned to Mutanabbi. The Syrian stood, his hands tightly gripping the stainless steel rail before him, his eyes wide, his face black with rage. He was staring in the direction of the flashing lights on the submarine control panel, but his vision was not focused: he seemed to be staring well beyond the lights.

Mutanabbi muttered, in guttural tones between clenched teeth, "Yevshenko, if you have sabotaged this mission, you will die like a dog."

Another sound crackled through the tiny control room, "Control, this is the engine room. We have had a major explosion outside, along our shaft seals. We are getting heavy leakage in both shaft seals. These were explosions outside the ship, Sir. There is no smoke or fire in the engine room. We still have the reactors critical, operating at self-sustaining power."

Another report came in from the bow compartment, reporting outside explosions, complete destruction of all bow-mounted sonar systems, but no flooding.

Yevshenko spoke to the maddened Mutanabbi. "Admiral, these explosions are all from the outside. We have no indication of any enemy ships in the area, and we heard no evidence of any torpedoes or other weapons. I cannot explain to you what has happened, but if there is any sabotage here, it is not by my men. I would look to your own crew, Mutanabbi!" Yevshenko raised his voice, "Who was tending the ship last week in Damsarkhu while we were all carried off to your training building in Latakia?"

Another report screeched into the control room. "Control, this is the engine room. We have serious leakage in both shaft seals!" The report could barely be heard above the background noise. "Sir, we have tightened down on the shaft seal packing to its maximum, but we have not been able to slow the leakage! Both shafts are badly bent, sir! I do not recommend we attempt to turn either shaft. It would completely wipe out the seals and we would be flooded in a moment!"

"Mutanabbi, we must surface this vessel immediately!" Yevshenko nearly yelled the words to his client. Turning to the ship's control panel operator, he began to give the order.

"You will not touch those switches!" Mutanabbi screamed the words, in clear Russian. Yevshenko turned to protest, but was confronted with the barrel of Mutanabbi's pistol. Mutanabbi pointed it first at Larichev, the SCP operator, then back to Yevshenko. "We will not come to the surface. We will fire the Katapaltes system now!" Mutanabbi spoke loudly, slowly, firmly.

"We cannot launch the missiles, Admiral!" protested Yevshenko. "We do not have the corrections from the Yodel Echo system. The explosions have wiped out all the sensors. You would not come within miles of your targets."

"I have only one target, Yevshenko." Mutanabbi kept his pistol pointed at the Russian captain. "That target is Israel. It will serve my purposes well enough to put each of these warheads anywhere into the belly of that wicked land! It matters less to me that the missiles hit their exact targets, as long as they hit Israeli territory! Now let us proceed to the launch, without delay."

"No, Mutanabbi! This is madness! You will be hitting villages and cities as well as..."

Before Yevshenko could finish, a loud shot rang out from Mutanabbi's pistol. The Russian captain doubled over; he was thrust backward against the periscope stand by the force of Mutanabbi's bullet. Yevshenko immediately collapsed in a heap.

"I intend to launch the missiles, immediately." Mutanabbi lowered the volume of his speech, but he continued to speak forcefully and slowly. He gripped the pistol in both hands and pointed it directly at the head of Larichev, the ship control panel operator. "You will *not* surface this ship," Mutanabbi said, in Russian. "You will now give the order to commence the Katapaltes launch sequence."

Larichev picked up the microphone for the ship's announcing circuit. "Commence Katapaltes launch sequence. Commence Katapaltes launch sequence." Larichev's voice quavered, nearly choked in fright.

Mutanabbi kept the gun pointed at Larichev's head. He turned briefly to his aide, Omar Fassad, and yelled, "Fassad! You cover these people in control. No matter what you have to do, we *must launch these missiles*! Do you hear? Whatever you have to do, we must launch! You will be rewarded! I must go aft to supervise the launch. Talon, I am placing Fassad in command here. He speaks the Russians' language, and he will see to it that the Russians cooperate in executing the launch. You are to obey his orders."

"Yes, Admiral."

Fassad drew his weapon, and brandished it at the Russians who stood in utter terror before the two Syrians. "I have control here, Sir," said Fassad. "I will see to it that the launch sequence is properly conducted."

Outside *Hazael*

Fogie Crandall kept the Angel Chariot headlights pointed in the direction of *Hazael*. The submarine was no longer visible. The explosions had surrounded the giant ship in billions of tiny bubbles and pieces of debris, the debris primarily composed of shattered pieces of anechoic tile. Crandall and the four other SEALs clung to the sides of Angel Chariot, watching in fascination at the results of their handiwork. Poco Logan, seated in his pilot's seat, maintained slow headway, just enough to maintain positive control of the SDV's depth and trim.

The SEALs reached inside the SDV to connect to the vehicle's Mark XV breathing system, conserving their own individual air supplies. This also allowed them to talk on Angel Chariot's interior communications circuit. They knew that their small explosive charges would not come close to damaging the submarine's pressure hull, but they hoped they had been able to deafen and cripple the giant ship to the point that she would have to abandon her deadly mission and come, helplessly, to the surface.

These SEALs had trained for years for operations just like this one. They were, each of them, in superior physical condition. Even so, their muscles ached from the effort of lugging the heavy packages of explosives through the water, placing them properly, and swimming rapidly away. They breathed heavily into their Mark XV system facemasks, relieved at the opportunity to rest for a moment.

The SEALs' rest terminated abruptly. The halo of bubbles and debris soon dissolved away, bringing in to view again the terrifying sight of the enormous Russian-Syrian submarine. A new sound shook the surrounding waters, jarring the SEALs from their momentary lull.

"CHUNK!...CHUNK!...CHUNK!...CHUNK!...   "   The frightening sound of twelve massive missile hatches opening, six on either side of *Hazael*'s outer hull.

Eric Lindahl watched, incredulous. It was impossible! They could not be launching missiles! There is no way they could have received their Yodel Echo navigational launch-fix! But there was no denying what he saw. Crippled or not, deafened or not, *the Syrians were proceeding to launch their missiles*!

Lindahl panted into the communications circuit, "More work to do, SEALs! Poco, you take Angel Chariot along with Rob and John and start on the missile tubes at the stern. Fogie, bring the portable lantern. You, Brett and I will take the forward tubes and work our way aft. We'll try to meet in the middle. Use single-unit charges; set fuses for thirty-second delay. It won't take much to shut them down, but we've got to move quickly! Let's move out!"

Lindahl grabbed his tow-basket, loaded with explosive charges and detonating devices, and swam down into the darkness, illuminated by the high-intensity portable spotlight wielded by Fogie Crandall, to attack the wounded leviathan that lay in the depths before him. Brett Nelson swam just behind him, carrying his tow-basket and his flashlight. Hand-to-hand combat with a high-tech sea monster.

Angel Chariot turned off toward the stern of the giant submarine, John Scott and Rob Petrocelli trailing from it as pilot fish from a shark. They would attack the monster's rear.

Aboard *Hazael*

Omar Fassad, standing by Syrian Captain Talon, watched as the twelve missile hatch lights on the ship's control panel blinked from green to red. The two Syrians had trained sufficiently on the mock-up panel at Latakia to know that this meant the outer doors of the missile tubes were open and ready for firing. Talon gave the next order; Fassad translated it from Arabic to Russian.

"Missile tube doors indicate open. Activate trim control system."

Larichev, nearly overcome by the terror of having Fassad's pistol pointed at his head, shook as he hurried to comply with the order.

Omar Fassad pressed the speaker button to communicate with Mustafa Mutanabbi, who waited with the launch trigger in his hand back in the missile compartment. "Admiral, we have indication that the missile hatches are open. We have begun the activation of the trim control system."

"This is good!" exclaimed Mutanabbi. "The first missile salvo indicates 'ready!' We now have only to wait for the reload system and for the trim system to give us the ready signal." Mutanabbi's voice, although distorted by the communication circuit's crude electronics, clearly betrayed the intense excitement he felt at this moment. Mutanabbi could not begin to explain what had caused the explosions in the sonar hydrophones or around the two propeller shafts, but he was not about to be stopped by anyone! It was nearly time!

The next explosion was a muffled "PHOOM!" heard in the forward portside missile tube. It was soon followed by a similar explosion in the forward starboard tube, then by two more explosions in the next two tubes. Soon, similar explosions were heard from the aft tubes.

Mutanabbi, standing before the missile control panel, held in his hand the Katapaltes trigger-baton. He depressed the activation switch frantically, repeatedly, at the sound of the first explosion. It could not be possible that he would again be frustrated in his mission! He pulled the trigger activation switch again and again. There was no response!

Electrical interlocks were built into the system that prevented the trigger from initiating the launch if the ship's trim control system was not properly engaged. Even without the interlock, the missile standing ready in Tube One had been hopelessly disabled by the explosive charge dropped outside by Lieutenant Eric Lindahl. Soon, the missiles in all twelve launch tubes were immobilized.

Back in *Hazael*'s control compartment, the scene was bedlam. The explosions, and new, frantic reports of flooding from the engine room and then from the missile compartment sent everyone in the compartment into a frenzy. Talon screamed in Arabic at the top of his voice, trying to maintain order. But there was too much noise, too much confusion, and Talon was too inexperienced on this vessel, and too poorly trained to know what to do. Besides, it was the young interpreter, Fassad, who had been put in command, and Fassad was totally bewildered.

A torrent of red flashing lights and insistent alarm buzzers and sirens sounded from the ship's control panel, increasing the feeling of panic.

"We're sinking!" shouted Fassad "We're sinking! Larichev, blow us to the surface!" He screamed, maintaining enough composure to scream in Russian. Fassad also remembered something else: there was an eight-man inflatable life raft in the escape tower that led from the sail of *Hazael*.

"What is happening? What are you doing?" Captain Talon was now completely confounded by the explosions, the profusion of alarm lights, and the orders flying about in the Russian language.

"Admiral Mutanabbi will want us to preserve his ship!" Fassad yelled in Arabic at Talon over the noise of the ballast tanks, now being blown by high pressure air as Larichev activated the "surfacing" switches. "Talon! You must stay here with the ship! Mutanabbi has placed me in charge here, and he will hold you accountable to do as I say! I will take the emergency vehicle ashore and find a way to get a message to Latakia to come with help! You! Nizzar! Come with me. As soon as we break the surface, we will go topside and go for assistance!" Nizzar was a young Syrian sailor who had been recruited for the mission. He was a strong lad; he might be helpful in making an escape from this steel tube of death.

Outside *Hazael*

The SEALs had made short work of depositing explosive charges in each of the open missile hatches. They met just above the deck of *Hazael*, amidships. They grabbed the sides of Angel Chariot, exhausted, as Poco Logan pushed his power control lever full-forward, leading the SEALs away from *Hazael*. Muffled explosions thundered behind them. Logan pointed Angel Chariot toward *Chamberlain*, toward home.

The SEALs were about five hundred meters from *Chamberlain* when they heard the unmistakable sound of ballast tanks being blown behind them. The giant submarine was surfacing.

"Let's take Angel Chariot to the top, Poco, and see what the sub's doing." Lieutenant Lindahl spoke to Angel Chariot's pilot.

"Aye, aye, Sir."

Angel Chariot gently nudged upward, toward the surface.

To Eric Lindahl, the exhilaration he felt whenever he came to the surface after an extended time below was identical to the feeling of wonder he felt whenever he first dived into the water. The thrill was in the transition, from one world to another. As Eric poked his head above the surface, the faint glow of dawn established a clear horizon to the east. In the dim light, he could see, about seven hundred meters away, the ugly, bulbous bow of *Hazael*, sticking crazily out of the water, like a water-logged tree stump. The top of *Hazael*'s sail was visible, just barely above the surface, about fifty meters farther aft.

There was something more! As the SEALs drew nearer to the limping behemoth, Lindahl could make out the forms of two men. Lindahl could see that the men were attempting to get down from the sail to an inflatable life raft that one of them held in place with a line. The other man had a flashlight. There seemed to be only two of them! Perhaps they would appreciate some company. A surprise party.

Chapter Twenty-Nine

Recognition – Running Deep

5 March
Aboard *USS Joshua L. Chamberlain*

VIKTOR RYPKIN, AS EXHAUSTED AS HE WAS from his ordeal, had a difficult time sleeping. During the past two months he had suffered such extremes of emotion that his mind seemed to refuse to take comfort in any assumption that he might now, at last, be safe within this American submarine. Twice during the past month he had been shaken to the roots of his soul by the imminence of death at the hands of the Syrians.

Escape from the extermination camp at the Jabal ad-Farabi had brought only temporary relief. A shudder surged throughout Rypkin's body as his mind recalled the utter terror he felt when Bildad had apprehended them at the Wadi. That last-moment rescue had now brought him to this, his latest haven. Rypkin's life had taken so many turns since those secure, comfortable days in the caves below Khokskya, that Rypkin wondered if he could ever again find a feeling of security, of peace.

Rypkin rolled out of his bunk, intending to slip into the wardroom for a cup of coffee. He tried to be quiet, taking care not to disturb Bill Winning, who slept in the bunk just below him.

Rypkin stole around the corner to the wardroom. It was empty and it was dark, except for a light that glowed dimly in the passageway outside. Viktor took a mug from a dispenser near the small stainless steel sink, and filled it with coffee from the urn that sat on the counter nearby. He pulled out the captain's chair at the head of the table, near him, and sat down heavily. He needed to clear his thoughts. Perhaps then he could go back to his bunk and sleep.

As a professional builder of submarines, Viktor Rypkin was much impressed with what he saw of this *Joshua L. Chamberlain*. She was an old ship; Rypkin would have been a mere child when her keel was laid in New London back in the late sixties. She was old, but *Chamberlain* glistened from the fastidious care that had been afforded her.

Impressed as he was by the machine, it was the men of *Chamberlain* who impressed Viktor Rypkin more. He had not had the opportunity to meet many of them; he had been asked to refrain from entering security-controlled areas such as the engineering spaces, radio room, and sonar shack. But those whom he had met were, every one, exceptional submariners. He had worked closely with Lieutenant Laughton, Chief Smith, and Chief Corderman to modify *Chamberlain*'s under-ice sonar system to accommodate the Yodel Echo system. Rypkin had the impression that, if he could work with these men for a week or so, they could have manufactured a system that would have put the old Yodel Echo system into obsolescence. They were that good!

This captain, Will Garrett, was solid. He had a knack for knowing what his men could do, and letting them do it. And then there were the SEALs! From his youth, the Soviet propaganda machine had taught Rypkin that Americans were soft, gluttonous consumers. This is not what Rypkin saw in the SEALs. He was glad he did not have to fight against such as these.

Just then Lieutenant Monk Laughton slouched into the wardroom. His eyes were bloodshot and his hair disheveled. He had obviously been involved in an all-night vigil. " 'Lo, Vik. What are you doing up so early? I thought we put you to bed a couple of hours ago."

"I am not sleeping," Viktor responded, "I have too much thinking. How is working the Yodel Echo hydrophone? You promised you would wake me if it is not working."

"Well, Vik," said Laughton, "we never got a chance to use it. Before we could get it lined up, we had company. Your *Oscar* buddies.

"Oscar?" asked Rypkin. "You mean *Antyey III? Antyey III* is here, now?" Viktor Rypkin had been telling everyone that he thought the Syrians would act soon, but he was still astounded by the news.

"That's right," said Laughton. "We've been hovering here at 100 feet, listening to the whole thing. Eric Lindahl took his SEALs down to get her. Sounded as if they did a pretty good job. We just made Gertrude contact with Angel Chariot, and they're headed back in with a couple of prisoners, of all things." Laughton shook his head. What could the SEALs do to top this?

"Listen, Vik," Laughton continued. "I just came down here to use the head and get a dish of ice cream. I've got to get back to the sonar shack. I'll let you know when Eric and the boys get back. If any of the prisoners are Russian, maybe we can use an interpreter." Monk Laughton trundled into the wardroom pantry to scavenge a dish of ice cream.

Viktor rose and followed the American lieutenant into the pantry. "Do you think your captain will allow me to come up to your sonar room and listen to this?"

"Vik, we can't do that." Laughton said, politely cheerful. "You are not cleared for security. But I'll talk to the skipper and see if you can come up to control when we bring the prisoners aboard. You stay here, I'll call you when it's time." Monk Laughton finished filling his bowl with ice cream. "Say, you want some ice cream? I've got my own secret little container of chocolate chip mint. Want some?"

"Is *green* ice cream! I have not seen such a thing!" Rypkin stared suspiciously at the bowl Laughton had prepared.

"Rypkin," boasted the American lieutenant, "you're in for the treat of your life."

After Laughton had departed to go back to his duty station in the sonar shack, Rypkin sampled the bowl of ice cream that Monk had prepared for him. He could see why the American would want to sequester away his own private stock of the green stuff! Russia had much to learn from these American capitalists.

Viktor Rypkin felt enormous relief that he had got the message out in time to stop the *Antyey III* from fulfilling Mutanabbi's horrible plan. But the magnitude of his accomplishment had not yet dawned on him. He was exhausted.

Rypkin had just consumed the ice cream when Bill Winning poked his head into the wardroom, and took a seat at the table. "Good morning, Viktor. I thought I heard your voice in here. What's the latest news?"

Viktor began relating the report he had heard from Lieutenant

Laughton.

"What are you saying? The *Oscar*…I mean the *Antyey*… is out there right now?"

"Yes! Is what Monk Laughton says. He says I am to wait here…"

"Viktor, I'll be right back," Winning rose to his feet and started to make his way out of the wardroom. "I've got to see what's going on."

"Is amazing, Bill," said Rypkin. "We have arrived in time."

"It's amazing, all right," said Bill Winning. "I told you, Viktor, the Bible says 'all things work together for good.'"

Viktor Rypkin frowned at his friend, shook his head, and then buried it in his hands on the table. All he felt was a swarm of confusion. He looked up to say more, but Bill had already exited the wardroom on his way aft to Control.

Some time later, the 21-MC communications circuit speaker broke into Viktor's thoughts. "Wardroom, Conn. Mr. Rypkin, you there? This is Monk Laughton. Captain says it's okay if you want to come on up to Control."

Viktor carefully placed his dishes in the galley sink, rinsed them, and then headed slowly toward Control. His mind still reeled. *What is it that I have done? Who, in truth, are my friends? Whom can I, in truth, trust? What is truth?*

———

Modern nuclear submarines are normally kind to those who suffer from seasickness. Operating deep, they ordinarily avoid much of the repeated pitching and rolling motion so dreaded by landlubbers. But *Chamberlain* was coming to periscope depth at dead-slow speed, and she bobbed like a cork in the moderately heavy seas. Up in the submarine's control room, Viktor Rypkin and Bill Winning braced themselves by gripping a stainless steel rail as they observed the procedure. They both fought back queasiness.

"Bring her up to periscope depth, Mr. Staggs." The Captain had the Conn and he ordered the diving officer to bring the ship to a shallow depth that would allow extension of the submarine's periscopes above the surface. If no visual or electronic contacts were confronted, the plan was for *Chamberlain* to come briefly to the surface, take the prisoners aboard, and then dive again. After the SEALs had brought Angel Chariot back into her barn, *Chamberlain* could go deep, run fast and slip out of the war zone. Mission accomplished.

So far, so good: there was no indication of any radar signal in the area. The ship's Electronic Counter Measures (ECM) system would have detected any such dangers.

Commander Garrett danced with the periscope. "Angel Chariot is closing at zero-eight-five degrees, range eight hundred meters." He rotated the periscope slightly clockwise. "I have the *Oscar* here, at zero-nine-five degrees, range three thousand five hundred meters. She's sitting at the surface with her bow out of the water. Looks as if she has about a fifteen degree up bubble. She's in bad shape. I don't see any scopes or antennae raised above her sail. Those SEALs did a pretty thorough job; they must have thrown a charge into the top of the sail to foul up their mast and antenna systems. There's a plume of smoke rising up from the sail. Not much smoke, just a little wisp." The Captain continued to rotate the scope clockwise, coming back again to Angel Chariot at 085 degrees. No other contacts. Okay, Chief Nagele, you can get your boys up in the escape trunk. Chuck, let's prepare to surface."

Chief Torpedoman Max Nagele waited at the lower hatch with two other experienced sailors. They wore orange life jackets, and carried heavy rescue lines. Their job would be to assist the SEALs in bringing the prisoners aboard the submarine. They also carried Navy-issue automatic pistols at their side. Chief Nagele would take official custody of the prisoners before they came below.

Angel Chariot was awkward and slow at the surface. Her little five-bladed propeller beat furiously against the water, and she rolled sluggishly in the heavy swells. It was hard to imagine that she was making any headway at all, except that the ugly form of *Hazael*, glowering behind them, continued to grow smaller and slightly smaller. Poco Logan sat in his pilot's seat beside his navigator, Fogie Crandall.

At the aft end of Angel Chariot, seated on the top of the hull frame, legs dangling through the open hatches were HMC Brett Nelson and MM1 Rob Petrocelli. They resembled politicians riding on the back of a convertible during a Fourth of July Parade. Seated just in front of them, in the cockpit seat positions normally occupied by the SEALs, were two terrified Syrians: Seaman Nizzar and the interpreter Omar Fassad.

Lieutenant Eric Lindahl and RM1 John Scott sat in the two forward passenger seats.

Rob Petrocelli was the first to see it. "Scope!" Petrocelli announced. "Two points off the port bow. Five hundred meters." He pointed off to the left.

Fogie Crandall stood up in his open cockpit and looked quickly in the direction indicated by Petrocelli. "I have it," called Crandall. He sat back down and gave steering instructions to his pilot, Poco Logan.

Chamberlain was making so little headway that the scope barely disturbed the water's rough surface. At normal speeds, a periscope will kick up a characteristic splash, a "rooster tail," but *Chamberlain*'s scope merely sat there. It appeared as a simple bronze-colored metal pipe standing upright, as though it were stuck to the ocean floor.

As the eight men watched from 500 meters away, however, it soon became evident that the metal pipe was attached to something. As they watched, where once there was only a tiny metal pipe, suddenly a large, black, object rose out of the waves.

Soon the giant sail planes emerged, making it evident that this was *Chamberlain*, come to the surface. The ship rolled slowly in the surging swells. Occasionally a wave would break near *Chamberlain*'s bow and the entire deck would be visible briefly in the troughs. Logan steered Angel Chariot toward the submarine, turning to a course nearly parallel with *Chamberlain*'s. He cut back Angel Chariot's speed to match the submarine's.

Soon, three figures could be seen from the top of *Chamberlain*'s sail.

"There's Chief Nagele and his posse." Brett Nelson pointed up to the top of the sail, now looming just over them. Leaning forward to speak in Arabic to his two prisoners, he pointed up to Nagele.

"Those are the guards who will now take custody of you. If you cooperate, you will not be harmed. As we draw close to the submarine, they will throw you a line. Attach it to your life vest, and grab the line with your hands. The guards will pull you safely aboard the ship. Do you understand?"

The two Syrians both nodded their heads enthusiastically, "We understand! We understand!"

Nizzar was pulled aboard first, followed by Omar Fassad, Brett Nelson, and then Eric Lindahl. Rob Petrocelli and John Scott stayed with Angel Chariot to help the two SDV-drivers in the docking operation.

Back down in the submarine's control room, Chief MacWaters kept his eyes on the ship control panel.

"Upper hatch indicates shut, Sir," announced the Chief of the Watch. "Request permission to open the lower hatch."

"Open the lower hatch." Commander Garrett kept his eyes pressed to the eyepiece of the periscope. He looked up briefly to watch as the lower hatch opened. He was as curious as everyone else in Control to see what sort of creatures the SEALs had managed to bring home.

The hatch sprang upward, opening with a heavy metallic clang. A bucketful of water trickled down from the compartment just above, and a leg bedecked in a wetsuit extended down from the hatch onto the ladder. It was one of the SEALs. Commander Garrett pressed his eyes back to the periscope eyepiece.

Brett Nelson was the first one down. With a showman's flourish, he extended both arms to the hatch and said, "Gentlemen, may I present, direct from Damascus..." He turned his head to call up through the hatch, in Arabic "Come down...now!" He turned his head back to the audience at the periscope stand and, with his arms still extended in their "now presenting" gesture, he flashed a huge, exaggerated grin.

Nizzar was the first Syrian down. Shivering, partly from the cold, but mostly from fright, he landed firmly on the deck of the control room, but dropped to his knees, whimpering.

Nelson spoke to him firmly in Arabic, "Come now, it is not our plan to harm you."

Nizzar looked up at Nelson and pleaded, "I am only a seaman! I have no knowledge that can help you!"

Nelson took some towels and a blanket that were offered by one of *Chamberlain's* crewmen and handed them to the shivering Syrian. "Take these. Dry out. We'll talk later."

Soon another figure emerged through the hatch and climbed down the ladder. This one was not whimpering, but he looked furtively around the strange environment of the American submarine's control room. His dark eyes darted back and forth. He appeared to be every bit as frightened as Nizzar, but not overcome by it. Rather he looked cunning, seeking what advantage he could find.

To Fassad's utter amazement, in this most extraordinary circumstance, Omar Fassad saw an advantage! It was unbelievable, but there he was! Yes, it was the Russian, Viktor Rypkin!

Omar Fassad stepped toward Rypkin, who had been momentarily astonished into silence by the totally unexpected appearance of his former Syrian "client associate" from Latakia. Before Fassad could take two steps, however, two American sailors grabbed him roughly. Fassad stopped and the Americans released their grip.

"Viktor Rypkin! Viktor Rypkin!" shouted Fassad. "I can hardly believe my eyes! What good fortune to see you here!"

In his amazement at seeing Fassad, Rypkin at first failed to notice that the Syrian "engineer" spoke in flawless Russian. Rypkin stammered, "Fassad...Omar Fassad! What are you doing here? What were you doing aboard *Antyey III*? Why ... " Then it struck him.

"You speak Russian!" Rypkin screamed at the top of his voice. *"YOU SPEAK RUSSIAN!* You are not just a Syrian engineer...it was *you all the time!"* Rypkin shouted, as he lunged into the Syrian at full force, knocking him back against the ladder. Before anyone could stop them, they careened to the deck. Rypkin grabbed Fassad by the shirt collar and began pushing him hard into the bulkhead. "*You* were the informant! Not Jadeel! Where is she? Where is Jadeel?"

This furious exchange in Russian was understood by no one in the control room, but in an instant, several strong hands pulled Viktor Rypkin away from the horrified Syrian.

"Keep him away!" cried Omar Fassad. "Keep him away! He will kill me!" Fassad screamed, now in Arabic, to Brett Nelson. Suddenly, to Omar Fassad, the massive SEAL appeared less threatening than did the scrawny Russian engineer.

The wheels of the Syrian's mind continued to spin. Turning back to Rypkin, he said, in Russian, "Jadeel Dovni was taken into custody shortly after you were arrested. She has been taken for interrogation. I can tell you where she is! But you must guarantee that these Americans will not harm me. You must guarantee that I will be set free! Only then will I tell you how to find Jadeel Dovni."

The two prisoners had been taken aft to the crew's mess, where Admiral Copper, assisted by Chief Nelson and Commander Carry, attempted to question them. Viktor Rypkin, calmed from his tirade, was ushered back to his stateroom, accompanied by Bill Winning.

Captain Garrett wanted to get some more pictures of the *Oscar*, from closer range, so he ordered the ship to periscope depth and edged slowly closer to the limping Russian-Syrian submarine. Lieutenant Bryant, who served in a collateral duty as ship's photographer, clicked away with his periscope-camera equipment.

"Got some good ones, Captain," said Bryant, handing control of the periscope back over to the skipper. "Maybe if we could come around to the left, I could get some shots of her from a zero degree angle on the bow."

Suddenly, before Commander Garrett could respond to Bryant's request, an irritating "buzz-buzz!" alarm sounded from the periscope instrument assembly. It was the ECM alarm. The Electronic Counter Measures antenna that bristled above the periscope had detected the electro-magnetic rays radiating from a radar installation. If *Chamberlain* were discovered in this war zone, it could be embarrassing, if not fatal.

"Down scope!" ordered Garrett as he snapped the periscope handles in their stowed position. "Make your depth 100 feet! Left full rudder! I want to come all the way around to course two-seven-zero! Make turns for eight knots."

The orders were repeated, and executed. The periscope and its ECM antenna hissed down into their stowed positions as *Chamberlain* slipped back below the layer.

"How are the SEALs doing with Angel Chariot back aft?" Garrett asked the chief of the watch, who was connected by a sound-powered phone to the after escape trunk.

"They have Angel Chariot stowed, Captain," responded the chief. "Two of the SEALs are aboard, in the engine room. We only have two more SEALs to go, the SEAL drivers. They are running Angel Chariot through her post-operational checks and should be back aboard within about ten minutes."

"No good, Chief," said Garrett. "Tell them to come aboard immediately. I want to get out of here, *now*. Tell the SEALs we'll slow down and let them go out to the hangar to complete their checks after we get out of the war zone."

"Aye aye, Captain." The Chief relayed the message back to Lieutenant Lindahl, who was supervising the SEAL operations back in the engine room.

———

Viktor Rypkin lay in his bunk, staring blankly at the metal bottom of the bunk just above him. Bill Winning had assured the two Navy guards that he had everything under control, and he had dismissed them. Winning stared down at the linoleum deck, his hands folded. He said nothing, at least not aloud.

Viktor Rypkin turned to his friend. Viktor had not known Bill long, but he knew him well. "For what is it that you are praying, Bill Winning?"

Bill looked up. He was silent for a moment, and then said, "I am praying for you, Viktor."

"Good," said Viktor. "When you pray for me, pray that I will be able to find Jadeel. Pray that when I find her, they will not have harmed her." Viktor rolled back, staring once again at the bunk above him.

There was a gentle knock on the stateroom door. Admiral Bob Copper entered. he stood near the door cradling a mug of coffee.

"How's it going in here, Bill?" asked the admiral.

"We're okay, thanks," answered Winning. "What's happening topside? I hear we had an ECM contact."

"That's right. It was from an Israeli patrol aircraft. Pretty long range when the ECM alarm sounded. No way they would have seen us. But they sure saw the *Oscar*. Now we're also getting sonar noises of Israeli ships in the area. My guess is they'll probably tow her into Haifa. Ought to make for interesting viewing on the evening news!"

"Ought to," agreed Bill. "Have you talked to the Syrian? The one called Omar Fassad? What has he told you? Anything about Viktor's friend, Jadeel Dovni?"

Hearing this, Viktor Rypkin sat up, straight, intent on hearing the Admiral's response.

Bob Copper directed his answer to Rypkin. "Viktor, first let me tell you this: Omar Fassad is an intelligence agent. He is very clever, so I am not at all certain how much truth is in what he has told us. But I also know that he is very, very frightened. Chief Nelson has managed to convince him that it would be unwise for him to mislead us. Fassad is clever; I hope he is clever enough to play it straight with us." Admiral Copper took a chair next to Bill Winning.

"Fassad told us," continued Copper, "that he was assigned to you when you first came to Latakia in January. Evidently your boss... is it Admiral Sergei Glutsin?"

"Yes," responded Rypkin, "Admiral Glutsin was in charge of the *Antyey III* project. We called it 'Project Titus.'"

"I know of this Glutsin," Copper continued, "he has been around for a long time. He is the one who built up the Typhoons and Oscars in the Soviet Navy. He's a tough cookie. It seems that he was suspicious of you, Viktor. Evidently you ask lots of questions. Also, he found out you were Jewish."

"Jewish! What...?" Rypkin was genuinely puzzled. "My mother was Jewish, but she died when I was little. I barely remember her! Besides, I have never given any thought to this religion business..."

"Hold on, hold on." Bob Copper held up his hand. "I'm just telling you what Fassad has reported. It appears that, so far, he has fed it to us straight. Well, whatever the reasons, Glutsin talked the

Syrian authorities into putting an agent on you. That agent was
Omar Fassad. He speaks fluent Russian, but of course, you did not
know that. He listened into your conversations with your interpreter,
this girl named Jadeel Dovni, and he got the notion that you had
seen too much. He said you observed a radioactive waste shipment
to Damsarkhu that even he, Fassad, didn't know about before. When
you began to share with Jadeel your concern for what was going on,
he blew the whistle on you."

"But what about Jadeel? Why did they arrest her?" asked
Rypkin.

"Viktor, from all I can gather, she was just an innocent
bystander. She just saw too much, and heard too much. These are
brutal, lawless people. They had a big-time secret that they were
trying to protect. Anyone who stood in the way, or who might
potentially stand in the way, was fair game for their brutality. We
can only hope that Jadeel is still alive. Fassad tells us that she *is*
alive, but that they have decided to keep her in prison in Damascus
indefinitely." Copper stood again, preparing to leave the stateroom.
He took a gulp from his coffee mug.

"We have obtained enough information on this mission to stop
Hazael Zabadi dead in his tracks. It was Zabadi's men that murdered
those Americans at Hazor, to blame it on Israelis. He took Bill and
the other hostages, and slaughtered them at will. He bought a
Russian submarine, armed it with nuclear waste-tipped warheads,
and intended to make a radioactive wasteland out of parts of Israel.
In a few moments, we'll be free from the war zone, I'll be free of my
communications restrictions, and the whole world will know about
these things. And the Israelis will have a giant, floating museum as a
testimony to the monstrosity of Zabadi's plans. Now, Viktor, I don't
know for certain that Jadeel is still alive. I believe Fassad is telling
the truth, but I am not certain. If she is alive, and if she is in prison,
we are holding enough cards in our hand that Zabadi will find it
tough not to release her when we push him."

"Thank you, Admiral Copper," Viktor spoke slowly. He had
not understood all of the Admiral's words, but he understood
enough, especially the last part about Jadeel.

"Thank your buddy, here," Copper gestured toward Bill
Winning. "He's the one who's been praying for you." Bob Copper

left the stateroom, headed back up to Control.

There was a lengthy silence in the stateroom. *Joshua L. Chamberlain* ran deep, fast, and quiet; she was soon to slip away from the war zone. The information she carried and the mission she had accomplished would soon put an end to this latest hot conflict between Israel and her ancient foes.

There would, of course, be other conflicts in the future. There would be many questions left to be answered, many issues to be confronted. But, for the present, there would be cause for rejoicing.

Viktor Rypkin broke the silence in the wardroom with his thick Russian accent. "Bill, I am remembering what you told me when we are hiding in trailer at Wadi el Jari. You told me I am too proud of my work and my studies to be 'running deep' with important things of life. I did not understand. I did not agree. Now, I think I am understanding."

Viktor paused for a long time, staring at his hands, folded before him on the table. At length, he looked up at Bill Winning and said, "Now I am seeing. Now I think I am ready to be running deep."

<u>Scheduled for publication in 2003</u>
from Anchorhouse Publishing

Don't miss Book Two of the
Winning the Battle Series

Great Was the Fall of It

Robert Evan Stevens, in Book Two of the *Winning the Battle* Series, continues to trace the unfolding drama emerging from the shattered Soviet Empire. Many, both in Syria and in Russia pay a dear price for the failure of the *Hazael* submarine enterprise. But Vladimir Drednev survives, even flourishes in the wake of the international political disaster. As he sees it, the problem was: he was thinking too small. But Drednev has new plans, and this time he will not be guilty of thinking small...

Viktor Rypkin has only one plan, and that is to find Jadeel Dovni - whatever the expense, wherever it leads him, and whatever the danger to him and to his new-found brothers in Christ, Bill Winning and Archibald Pender-Cudlipp.

And who is the mysterious foreigner rumored to be hidden among the nomads of the Syrian desert?

To reserve your pre-Publication-Date copy of <u>Great Was the Fall of It</u>, simply check off the block in the attached feedback/order forms.

Anchorhouse Publishing
Feedback Form

Our goal at Anchorhouse Publishing is to produce books that run deep, challenge, edify, and proclaim as well as entertain. The most important person in meeting this goal is you, the reader. Please help us by filling out the questionnaire below. We will read your feedback, and use it to help us improve our books.

Meanwhile, if you would like to order additional copies of *Running Deep* (or perhaps to have a copy sent to a friend or relative), you can use the convenient order form on the reverse. You can also reserve an advance copy (pre-Publication-Date) of the sequel, *Great Was the Fall of It*. (Scheduled Publication Date: 2003.)

(Check any blocks that apply, below)

I read *Running Deep* because:

[ ] *I'm interested in submarines.*
[ ] *I'm interested in international politics.*
[ ] *I'm interested in books that deal with Christian precepts.*
[ ] *Someone gave it to me and suggested I read it.*
[ ] *Other:*_____

Overall, how do you rate this book compared with your expectations?

[ ] *Excellent*   [ ] *Good*   [ ] *OK, but...*   [ ] *Poor*

I most appreciated the following about this book:

_____
_____

I would suggest the following to make this book better:

_____
_____

Other comments (include name and address if desired):

_____
_____
_____
_____

MAIL TO: **Anchorhouse Publishing Company**
Department 03
P.O. Box 3361
Crofton, MD 21114

ORDER / RESERVATION FORM ON REVERSE

Anchorhouse Publishing
Order / Reservation Form

Running Deep

Winning the Battle Series – BOOK ONE

☐ **Please send** _____ **copies of** *Running Deep* **to the following address:**

Name:_____

Address:_____

_____

City_____**State**_____**Zip**_____

Price: $19.95 per copy x _____ **copies : $**_____

+ 5% sales tax : **$**_____
     Additional, only for books shipped to Maryland addresses

+Special shipping by air (if desired): **$**_____
     US: $4.00 for the first book plus $2.00 for each additional book
     International: $9.00 for the first book plus $5.00 for each add'l book

Total Payment by enclosed check: **$**_____

ADVANCE RESERVATION

Great Was the Fall of It

Winning the Battle Series – BOOK TWO

☐   **Please send me free information on the sequel** to *Running Deep,* **and on how I can get a pre-Publication-Date copy of** *Great Was the Fall of It* **– Book Two of the** *Winning the Battle* **Series (currently scheduled Publication Date: 2003).**

Name:_____

Address:_____

_____

City_____**State**_____**Zip**_____

Mail this form to: Anchorhouse Publishing Company
                         Department 03
                         P.O. Box 3361
                         Crofton, MD 21114